Future?

LUCY KING
LOUISA HEATON
LOUISA GEORGE

First Published in Great Britain 2017
By Mills & Boon, an imprint of HarperCollins*Publishers*
1 London Bridge Street, London, SE1 9GF

HER EX, HER FUTURE? © 2017 Harlequin Books S. A.

One Night With Her Ex, *Seven Nights With Her Ex* and *Backstage With Her Ex* were first published in Great Britain by Harlequin (UK) Limited.

One Night With Her Ex © 2014 Lucy King
Seven Nights With Her Ex © 2016 Louisa Heaton
Backstage With Her Ex © 2013 Louisa George

ISBN: 978-0-263-92991-1

05-1217

MIX
Paper from
responsible sources
FSC C007454

This book is produced from independently certified FSC™ paper to ensure responsible forest management.

For more information visit: www.harpercollins.co.uk/green

Printed and bound in Spain
by CPI, Barcelona

ONE NIGHT WITH HER EX

BY
LUCY KING

Lucy King spent her formative years lost in the world of Mills & Boon romance when she really ought to have been paying attention to her teachers. Up against sparkling heroines, gorgeous heroes and the magic of falling in love, trigonometry and absolute ablatives didn't stand a chance.

But as she couldn't live in a dream world for ever she eventually acquired a degree in languages and an eclectic collection of jobs. A stroll to the River Thames one Saturday morning led her to her very own hero. The minute she laid eyes on the hunky rower getting out of a boat, clad only in Lycra and carrying a three-metre oar as if it was a toothpick, she knew she'd met the man she was going to marry. Luckily the rower thought the same.

She will always be grateful to whatever it was that made her stop dithering and actually sit down to type 'Chapter One', because dreaming up her own sparkling heroines and gorgeous heroes is pretty much her idea of the perfect job.

Originally a Londoner, Lucy now lives in Spain, where she spends much of her time reading, failing to finish cryptic crosswords, and trying to convince herself that lying on the beach really *is* the best way to work.

Visit her at www.lucykingbooks.com

To the challenging, tough, frustrating,
wonderful, crazy thing that is marriage.

CHAPTER ONE

RIGHT. THAT WAS IT. Enough was enough.

As the last of Big Ben's twelve bongs echoed through the night and the sky began to explode with fireworks, Kit Buchanan knocked back the inch of whisky that was left in his glass and glowered at the dazzling display erupting over the Thames beyond the floor-to-ceiling windows of his penthouse suite.

Forget the work he'd lined up to do this evening; he hadn't touched it anyway. Forget the fact that it was the middle of the night and freezing cold; what with the burning sensation of the alcohol and the relentlessness of the thoughts drumming through his head he felt as if he were on fire.

And forget the fact that he was about to embark on a course of action that probably required a good deal more consideration than the ten minutes he'd just given it.

He needed to sort out the mess he was in. Now.

For five years he'd been suffering. Five long, torturous, frustrating-as-hell years, and he'd finally had it. He was through with the lingering guilt, the excruciating tension and the crippling anxiety, all of which vibrated through him pretty much constantly and all of which he'd had to live with for far too long. He'd had enough of beating himself around the head with more self-recrimination and regret than any man needed to experience in one lifetime.

And he was sick of having no option but to split up with the women he dated.

The last one, Carla, whom he'd been seeing for a month and with whom he'd broken up just a few hours ago, he'd liked more than usual. He wouldn't have minded seeing a bit more of her, seeing where the relationship might head.

But that was pretty impossible given the problem he suffered, wasn't it?

It really couldn't go on.

Kit slammed the glass down on his desk and made a quick call to commandeer one of his hotel's limousines. Then he grabbed his coat and strode towards the lift. He punched the little round button and waited, bristling with impatience as his mind churned with details of the trouble he had with sex.

For the first couple of years following his divorce he hadn't been too bothered by his inability to function in bed. He'd told himself that after what he'd done he'd deserved it, and would willingly take the punishment. He'd assured himself that it wouldn't last for ever, and that as he wasn't a hormone-ridden, sex-obsessed teenager he could live with it.

But depressingly—and worryingly—it *had* lasted, and when matters hadn't improved a year or two later he'd begun to get a bit concerned.

And while pride and the potential for total humiliation had stopped him from doing anything about it initially, eventually he'd gritted his teeth and summoned up the courage to make an appointment with his doctor.

Which hadn't helped in the slightest.

The doctor had told him that there was nothing physically wrong with him and had suggested that perhaps his problem was psychological. He'd recommended a course of therapy, which had been pointless largely because Kit hadn't been able to bring himself to be entirely open and honest with the therapist about his relationship with Lily or the circumstances surrounding their divorce.

After that he'd tried almost every option that was left, astounding himself with the lengths he'd been willing to go to to find a cure. He'd read books, scoured the Internet and acquainted himself with homeopathy. Plumbing the depths of desperation, he'd even given hypnosis a shot.

But he needn't have bothered with any of it because nothing he'd tried had worked, and it had been driving him nuts.

This evening, after he'd said a regret-laden goodbye to Carla, he'd racked his brains for any course of action he might have missed, *anything* that might help, and it had suddenly struck him that there *was* something he hadn't tried.

It wasn't guaranteed to succeed, he thought, his jaw tight and a deep frown etched on his forehead as the lift doors opened with a sibilant swoosh and he strode inside, and God knew it wasn't in the slightest bit appealing, but if the only avenue left open to him was to head straight to what the therapist had suggested might be the source of his problem—namely his ex-wife—and to see if talking might work where everything else had failed, then that was what he'd do, because frankly he couldn't stand this affliction any longer.

'You're engaged?'

Lily leaned against the kitchen counter for support and wondered what more the evening held in store for her in the shock-to-the-system stakes, because if there was anything else waiting in the wings she was off to bed the minute she hung up.

'That's right,' replied her sister, her voice holding a thread of excitement and happiness that should have been infectious but for Lily, who held the institute of marriage in deep mistrust, wasn't.

'Who to?'

'What do you mean, who to?' said Zoe, her laugh of disbelief echoing down the line. 'Dan, of course.'

'But I thought you'd split up.' With the hand that wasn't holding her mobile to her ear, Lily emptied the remains of the champagne bottle into her glass, and took a much-needed gulp.

'We had.'

'Didn't you say you were over for good?'

'I did. And I genuinely thought we were.'

Lily lowered her glass and frowned as she tried to make sense of what her sister was saying. 'So what happened?'

'Tonight happened,' said Zoe with an uncharacteristic dreamy sort of sigh. 'He came to find me.'

'Where are you?' Judging from the thumping music in the background it sounded as if Zoe was out, somewhere busy, which in itself was unusual given she spent practically every evening in cuddling up to her computer.

'I'm at a party.'

'A party?' Lily echoed, faintly reeling all over again because while going out in the first place was rare her socially inept sister had always considered attending parties a fate worse than death.

'I know,' said Zoe, her delight clear in her voice. 'Can you believe it? I can't. But anyway Dan showed up about an hour ago, rescued me from an overenthusiastic dance partner and then basically told me he realised what a jerk he'd been and apologised in the loveliest way imaginable. It was very masterful. Very romantic.'

There was a pause while Zoe presumably drifted off into a blissful memory of the moment before dragging herself back to the conversation. 'Then he proposed,' she added dreamily, 'and I said yes.'

Just like that? A few softly spoken magical words and Zoe had fallen headlong into Dan's arms? That didn't sound like her ever logical sister any more than dreamy romance did, yet there was no denying that it appeared that that was exactly what had happened.

Hmm, thought Lily, an odd ribbon of apprehension rippling through her. Tonight was turning out to be unexpectedly and oddly unsettling. 'But didn't you say over Christmas that you wouldn't take Dan back even if he were the last man on earth and he came crawling on his knees?' she asked.

'Did I?'

'You did.'

'Oh, well, that was then,' said Zoe lightly, as if the fortnight of tears and misery Lily had just mopped up had never happened, as if she hadn't swung between despair and fury like some kind of demented pendulum, as if she hadn't given her surprisingly large repertoire of four-letter words an extensive airing. 'But now it's all fine and we're engaged. Isn't it great?'

Lily took another gulp of champagne and thought that she wasn't so sure it was all that great. She'd been there, done that, and while she might not be the older of the two she was definitely the wiser when it came to marriage. In her brief but turbulent experience it wasn't all it was cracked up to be, as she'd spent the last half an hour only too vividly and infuriatingly remembering. 'But you've only known him, what? A couple of months?'

'Three.'

'Don't you think it's a bit soon?'

'You were married within six,' Zoe pointed out.

'And look what happened there,' said Lily darkly. A mere two years after they'd met and embarked on a whirlwind romance she and Kit had divorced. She'd married in haste and had ended up very much repenting at leisure. Not that she thought much about it these days. Normally.

'Dan isn't Kit,' said Zoe, beginning to sound a little defensive.

'I should hope not.'

'And I'm not you.'

'That's true,' Lily said, suppressing a sigh. 'You're a lot more level-headed and mature than I ever was. And older. But are you sure you know what you're doing?'

'Absolutely,' said Zoe with a quiet, firm certainty that Lily had never heard from her before. 'He's the best thing that's ever happened to me so be happy for me, Lil,' she added. 'Please?'

The plea was so soft, so sincere, so beseeching that Lily felt a sudden and unexpected wave of guilt and remorse sweeping through her. What was she doing? She was ruining what was the happiest night of her sister's life, and why? Because, unsettled by the last half an hour, she was only thinking about herself and *her* experience. What kind of sister was she?

Pinching the bridge of her nose, Lily closed her eyes and took a deep, steadying breath.

Just because she and Kit had made a mess of things didn't mean that Zoe and Dan would. Maybe her sister's would be one of the marriages that lasted. Dan was great, Zoe was great, so maybe they'd be fine. It happened, she'd heard.

And just because her night had nosedived and she'd been unexpectedly hit by a deluge of memories about what had been right about her own marriage and then a double whammy of regret and self-recrimination over what had gone wrong, that didn't give her the right to dampen Zoe's happiness.

Determinedly pushing her cynicism aside Lily pulled herself together. 'I am happy for you,' she said, pasting a smile on her face that she made sure her voice reflected.

'Really?'

'Really,' she said even more firmly. 'I'm sorry I wasn't more enthusiastic earlier. It was unexpected and I was just a bit surprised, that's all. Congratulations. I hope—no, I *know*—you'll both be very happy.'

'Thanks and we will.'

Lily heard the elation and the hope in her sister's voice and felt her heart squeeze. 'I think I might be the teensiest bit jealous,' she said. Because she could remember how Zoe was feeling all too well. The giddy happiness. The permanent grin. The excitement about the future...

'Are you all right, Lil?'

'I'm fine,' she said, to her irritation her voice cracking a little.

Down the line came a sharp intake of breath and the sound of the heel of a hand hitting a forehead. 'Oh, crap. Tonight's your anniversary, isn't it?'

What would have been her seventh. Not that she'd been counting. Until the clock had struck midnight and she'd been reminded of it at the most inconvenient moment imaginable. 'It is, but it doesn't matter.'

'Of course it does,' said Zoe. 'God, I'm sorry. And here's me banging on about Dan and getting engaged and stuff. I really am quite spectacularly insensitive. I should have thought.'

Lily shrugged as if it didn't bother her in the slightest. Which it didn't. Generally. 'Forget it.'

'Want to talk about it?'

'Nope.'

'Sure?'

'Quite.' She didn't want to even think about it, let alone talk about it, although that was proving annoyingly difficult to achieve this evening.

'OK, well, call me if you do. Any time. Really.'

Lily knew she meant it. Zoe had been a rock following

the divorce, and looking back Lily didn't know how she would have got through it without her. 'Thanks. I will.'

'Look, I'd better go. It's late and you have an early flight.'

'It is and I do.' A smile spread across her face at the thought of the week's holiday she'd booked following the week of work she had to do first. It would be the first holiday she'd had in ages and she couldn't wait. 'And shouldn't you be snuggling up to Dan instead of calling me?'

'Plenty of time for that later, I hope. Anyway, he's gone to get our coats and I wanted you to be the first to know.'

Lily's smile deepened. 'Thanks. You do realise that the second I get back I'll be grilling you for details?'

'You might regret saying that.'

'Never. I want to hear every single—'

The ring that reverberated through the silence of the house cut off her sentence and made her jump.

'What's that?' asked Zoe.

'Someone at the door,' she said, her smile fading and her heart sinking a little at the thought of who it might be. 'I should go.'

'Are you sure you ought to be answering it this late?' said Zoe, sounding like the older sister she was. 'I mean, I know there are first-footers and whatnot around, but you are on your own and it is well past midnight.'

'Don't worry, it'll probably be Nick,' said Lily, despondently pushing herself off the counter and heading into the hall. 'He left his scarf.' She'd texted him to say she'd put it in the post, but maybe, despite the disastrous outcome of the evening, he didn't want to have to wait that long and had decided returning to pick it up was a risk worth taking.

'Who's Nick?'

At the interest in Zoe's voice, Lily inwardly cringed because Nick was history, that was what he was. Unfortunately.

Earlier, however, he'd been the guy she'd invited over for

dinner. Nick was an interesting, intelligent, entertaining, good-looking man who made her laugh, and even though they'd only been on three dates she'd been ready to take things to the next level. Had *wanted* to take things to the next level, because from what she knew about him so far he seemed pretty much perfect: in addition to his favourable personality and looks, he didn't want children, he didn't make her pulse race and didn't appear to have any problem with communicating.

In her book those last few qualities especially made him an ideal future partner, hence the invitation to spend New Year's Eve with her.

The early part of the evening had gone swimmingly, and exactly according to plan. Nick had turned up on the dot of nine bearing a bottle of champagne and a warm smile that had turned even warmer when Lily had presented him with a deliberately lavish designed-to-seduce menu of four courses, vintage champagne and handmade chocolates.

Over the table and the next couple of hours they'd chatted easily and flirted outrageously, and things had been looking promising. Then they'd moved to the sofa in her sitting room to have coffee and chocolates in front of the roaring fire and at midnight he'd leaned forwards to kiss her.

And that was when everything had gone wrong.

The clock had been striking twelve and as Nick had drawn closer and closer she'd been suddenly and totally unexpectedly hit by a snapshot of her wedding day.

She hadn't thought about it for years, but around the sixth chime the image of her and Kit wrapped in each other's arms on the dance floor and kissing as they wished each other a happy new year was there flashing in her head as clearly as if it had happened yesterday.

The image had been deeply unwelcome—and not only because it couldn't have come at a more inconvenient moment—and she'd tried to blink it away. So much so that

Nick had eventually pulled back a fraction and asked her if she had something in her eye.

At that she'd stopped blinking, which hadn't been working anyway, and instead had told herself to ignore the memory and keep her focus one hundred per cent on the man next to her, who was leaning in once again for a kiss.

She'd studied his eyes wondering exactly what shade of green they could be described as, run her hands through his fair hair and then lowered her gaze to his mouth, but that hadn't worked either because within seconds she'd found herself imagining she was looking into the dark chocolate-brown eyes of her ex-husband, running her hands through *his* thick dark hair and kissing *his* mouth.

Then a bolt of desire had shot through her, her bones had begun to dissolve and her stomach had started to melt while her heart rate doubled.

Deeply unsettled by her body's behaviour, because first she was pretty sure the desire had nothing to do with Nick and second she'd spent the last five years deliberately avoiding that sort of head-screwing stuff and thus was *not* happy to feel it now, she hadn't been able to help jerking back a moment before Nick's lips touched hers.

Clearly and justifiably surprised, he'd sat back and frowned and asked what was up. She'd been so confused and disturbed by what was going on that Lily hadn't been able to do more than mutter an apology and something about having an early start.

Nick had said that in that case he ought to be making a move, and it was hard to say who was more startled when she jumped to her feet and thrust his coat into his hand practically before he'd finished speaking.

He'd left, sans the scarf, which in her haste to bustle him out had been overlooked, and she hadn't been expecting to see him again. Now it seemed she would, and what a way to round off New Year's Eve *that* was going to be.

'Never mind,' she muttered, because there was no point in Zoe being interested in who Nick was when she'd so well and truly screwed this evening and a potentially perfectly decent relationship up.

Zoe huffed. 'Never mind? That's all I'm getting?'

'Yup.'

'Hmm. Sounds like my engagement isn't the only thing we'll be having a chat about when you get back.'

Lily murmured something non-committal.

'OK,' said Zoe. 'Well, have a good flight and keep me posted about how it goes.'

'I will. I'll call you when I get there. And congratulations again, Zoe. I'm happy for you. I really am.'

'Thank you. Goodnight.'

''Night.'

Lily hung up and with a sigh dropped her phone on the table beside the spot where Nick's scarf lay folded, waiting to be stuffed into an envelope and put in the post. She plucked it off the table and through the frosted glass panels of her front door gloomily eyed the dark shape of a man.

Damn, she'd had such high hopes for him. Why, tonight of all nights, had the memories of Kit and their marriage managed to break through the impenetrable—she'd thought—barriers she'd erected? She'd done a pretty good job over the years of not thinking about her marriage, so why now could she think about little else?

Was it because this was the first year she'd actually spent the anniversary alone with a man instead of flinging herself around a dance floor in the company of dozens? Was it because she was stone-cold sober instead of rip-roaringly drunk?

And why hadn't she been able to suppress the memories and feelings even once Nick had gone? Why had they stormed round her head as if on some interminable flipping loop: images of Kit kissing her at the altar, feeding her wedding cake and holding her close as they danced; memories of the way she'd felt that day, how deliriously happy she'd been in the months that had followed and then how badly everything had imploded.

As a fresh wave of emotion rolled over her, her head swam and her throat closed over and she filled with an ache so strong her knees nearly gave way.

Well, if this was what New Year's Eve on her own or in the company of only one other was like she was never doing it again. Next year it would be hundreds of revellers and margaritas all the way.

Drawing in a shaky breath, Lily told herself to get a grip. All she had to do was open the door and hand over the scarf with, perhaps, an apology and the hint of an explanation.

Then she could take herself off to bed, bury herself under her duvet and hope that unconsciousness would take over until her alarm went off and she could busy herself with getting ready for the flight and work.

Simple.

Bracing herself, she pulled her shoulders back. She undid the latch and wrapped her fingers round the door handle. Then she pasted a smile on her face, turned the handle and opened the door wide.

She looked up.

And froze.

The greeting that hovered on her lips died. The apology she'd planned fled. Her smile vanished and her brain and body went into shock because the man standing on her doorstep, stamping his feet against the cold and blowing on his hands, wasn't Nick. It wasn't a first-footer.

It was Kit.

CHAPTER TWO

FOR A MOMENT Lily couldn't move. Couldn't breathe. Couldn't think.

All she could do was stare at him, her heart thumping too fast, the blood rushing to her feet and her head swimming with the effort of processing the fact that Kit, the man who'd made her happier and more wretched than she'd ever imagined possible, the man with whom she'd had no contact for the last five years but about whom she'd been thinking pretty much non-stop for the last half an hour, was here.

As shocks to the system went this evening this one was definitely the worst.

Half wondering whether her imagination might not have conjured him up what with the unauthorised way it had been behaving this evening, Lily swallowed, then blinked. Hard. Twice. She gave herself a quick shake just for good measure, but he was still there, tall and broad and as jaw-droppingly good-looking as he'd ever been.

More so, actually, she thought, flicking her gaze over him to give her time to gather her scattered wits. He'd changed in the last five years. Physically at least. He seemed bigger, more imposing somehow. He was only, what, thirty-two, but his dark hair was flecked with grey at the temples, and there were faint lines bracketing his mouth and fanning out from the corners of his eyes.

He looked harder, more cynical than she remembered

too. But then perhaps that wasn't surprising since she must have made life pretty tricky for him following the breakdown of their relationship.

Not that either the way he looked or his attitude to life was in the slightest bit relevant to anything any more. No, she'd got over Kit long ago, and she was now totally immune to looks that were overly good and attitudes that were dangerously and possibly attractively edgy, whoever they belonged to.

Still, she could really have done without seeing him this evening. Or ever again, for that matter.

'Happy New Year, Lily,' said Kit, his warm breath making little white clouds in the cold night air while his deep voice rumbled right through her and fired a tiny spark of heat deep inside her.

Which she *really* didn't need.

Damn.

Telling herself to stay cool and focused, and reminding herself that she was immune to voices as well as looks, Lily stamped out the heat and straightened her spine.

'What the hell are *you* doing here?' she asked, too on edge with everything that had happened tonight and too pissed off about the spark to bother about mollifying her words.

His eyebrows lifted at her bordering-on-rude tone. 'Expecting someone else?'

'Obviously.'

'Who?'

'The owner of this.' She lifted the scarf and he glanced down at it, a slight frown creasing his forehead.

'Nice,' he murmured, as well he might seeing as how it was one hundred per cent cashmere and enticingly soft.

'Very.' And she wasn't just talking about the scarf.

'Is he on his way back?'

'I doubt it.' Presumably the return of the scarf by post was fine.

'Then can I come in?'

'Why?'

'Well, for one thing it's absolutely freezing out here,' said Kit, turning the collar of his coat up and tugging it higher, 'and for another I need to talk to you.'

'About what?' As far as she was aware they'd said all they had to say to each other years ago.

'Let me in and I'll tell you.'

'I don't think that's a very good idea.'

'Why not?'

Lily frowned. That was an excellent question indeed. Logically there was no reason not to let Kit in. They'd been divorced for years, and it wasn't as if the experience had been particularly acrimonious or anything. It had been devastating and sad, of course, but in the end they'd both been so numbed by everything that had happened that they hadn't had either the energy or the will to fight it out.

In fact, the overwhelming emotion she could remember was a sort of resigned relief, because by the time they'd signed the papers there'd been nothing left and nowhere else for their relationship to go.

So logically she ought to give him a wide smile, stand back, wave him in and listen to what he wanted to say.

But then there was that damn spark of heat that was stubbornly and infuriatingly refusing to die.

If anything, it was getting stronger the longer she looked into his eyes, and that alone was reason enough to send him on his way because a spark was how this whole thing had started in the first place, and she was *not* falling under Kit's spell all over again.

Therefore he wasn't coming in.

'I'm sorry but I'm busy,' she said firmly.

He shot her a sceptical look. 'At half past midnight on New Year's Day?'

'Yes.'

'Doing what?'

'None of your business. Come back tomorrow.' When she'd be long gone.

'I'd rather get this over with now if you don't mind.'

'I do mind.'

'Can't we at least talk?'

Lily fought the urge to roll her eyes. Oh, the irony. Lack of communication was above all what had led to the breakdown of their marriage, and *now* he wanted to talk?

'When were we ever able to talk?' she asked with more than a hint of sarcasm.

As he contemplated her point, Kit sighed, then gave a brief nod. 'That's fair enough, I suppose. So how about you listening while I talk?'

'I don't remember that working either.'

'Doesn't mean it wouldn't work now.'

Lily folded her arms and lifted her chin. 'Doesn't mean it would.'

Kit noted both, and with a scowl shoved his hands through his hair, clearly deciding now not to bother hiding his exasperation at her intransigence.

'Look, Lily, it's been five years,' he said, sounding as if he was struggling to keep a grip on both his temper and his patience. 'Are you really telling me you don't think we can behave like rational, sensible adults about this?'

Rational and sensible? Hah. Reason and sense had never featured much in their relationship, and the clear implication that she was the one not being rational or sensible here seriously wound her up.

'Oh, I'm sure *I* can,' she said.

'Well, I *know* I can,' he said, his eyes glittering in the dark and taking on an intensity that made her breath go all skittery. 'So why are you so against us having a conversation? Can you really not even manage that? Haven't you changed at all?'

As the questions hit her one after the other, Lily reeled for a moment, stung at the accusation that she wasn't capable of conversation, then had to concede that he might have a point about the whole having changed thing.

She *had* changed. She was nothing like the spontaneous, adventure-loving, but possibly a bit self-absorbed girl who didn't have a clue how to handle what life was suddenly throwing at her she'd been at twenty-four. She was now responsible, successful and focused, and while she still made sure she had fun, the fun wasn't quite as abandoned as it once had been. She was also way more mature than she had been back then, and way more grounded. And she could converse with the best of them.

And if she'd changed, then why wouldn't Kit have changed too? After all, she'd read that he'd achieved his dream of owning a string of luxury hotels, which presumably meant that he'd overcome the very large obstacle she'd put in his way and had then set about putting all that nascent ambition she'd seen in him to good use.

From the other snippets of information she'd gleaned over the years—not that she'd specifically looked out for gossip about him or anything—she'd gathered that he was now regarded as something of a cool, ruthless operator in the business world, a man who was intuitive and decisive and rarely put a foot wrong. Given how keen he was to have this cosy little chat, he might even have learned how to communicate.

And as he said, it *had* been five years.

So maybe she was being a bit obstinate about this, and, dared she say it, childish?

Surely, despite their history, they could behave civilly towards each other? Surely they could talk, catch up even, without things descending into a trip down memory lane littered with bitter accusations, hurtful lashing out and pointless blame-laying?

Maybe she owed it to him to listen to what he wanted to say. In the dark days following their divorce she'd subjected herself to extensive self-analysis and had come to realise, among many other things, that she hadn't listened much during the latter stage of their marriage, and if he was here, now, it must be important.

Besides, if she continued to refuse, Kit might think she was protesting just a bit too much, and there was no way she wanted him thinking she was affected in any way other than being in shock at his appearance on her doorstep.

Plus it *was* Arctic out here.

And then there was her curiosity over what had brought him here. Despite her best efforts to crush it that was just about eating her up alive, so all in all what choice did she have?

'Fine,' she muttered. 'But it's late and I have an early start, so you can have ten minutes and no more.'

'Thanks.'

His expression relaxed and he shot her a quick, devastating grin that made her stomach flip, her heart skip a beat and that damn spark of heat flare up, all of which reminded her that she had to be careful. Very careful indeed.

Starting now, she thought, standing back and watching warily as he moved past her. She pulled back so that no part of him brushed against her, closed the door and tried not to think about the way the hallway she'd always considered rather spacious now felt like the size of a wardrobe and about as claustrophobic.

'Go on through,' she said, her voice annoyingly breathy. 'The sitting room's on your right.'

Following her instructions, Kit strode down the hall and into the sitting room. Lily put Nick's scarf back on the hall table and then followed him, assuring herself with each step that really there was nothing to worry about. She'd got over her marriage and Kit years ago and it was just the shock of seeing him after all this time that was making her react so oddly, that was all.

After taking up a position by the fireplace about as far away from him as possible, she watched him unbutton his coat, shrug it off and drape it over the arm of the sofa. He straightened, thrust his hands in the pockets of his jeans and looked around.

While the fire crackled merrily in the grate, she saw him take in the deep indentations in the cushions of the sofa, the pair of cups on the low coffee table in front of the fire and then, beyond the open doors that divided the space, towards the back of the house, the dining table upon which sat the evidence of what had clearly been a romantic dinner for two.

Surveying the scene through Kit's eyes, Lily knew what it looked like and was suddenly rather glad she hadn't got round to tidying up.

She was especially glad she hadn't done anything about putting out the dozens of flickering candles, turning up the low seductive lighting she'd chosen for this evening or switching off the slow, sexy music that drifted from the speakers embedded in the ceiling in the four corners of the room.

Why she was glad, though, was something she wasn't particularly keen to dwell on.

'You've been entertaining,' Kit said in a tone that suggested he didn't like it, which was tough because he'd given up the right to have an opinion about anything she did the minute he'd chosen to have a one-night stand with someone from the PR department of the hotel where he'd worked while their marriage lay in tatters.

Resisting the temptation to think about that, Lily allowed herself a slow, deliberately wistful smile. 'Yes,' she murmured softly, blissfully, as if dinner had turned into something much, much more.

Kit's jaw tightened gratifyingly. 'The man with the scarf?'

'That's right.'

'Boyfriend?'

Nope. Sadly. 'That,' she said, 'is none of your business.'

Kit tutted. 'Goodness, aren't we defensive?'

'I prefer "private",' she said, deepening her smile as she vaguely wondered what was stopping her from just telling him the truth about Nick.

'So I recall,' he said, and in that instant an image flashed into her head of the two of them in his car, hidden from view, she'd thought, by trees.

They'd been driving back from a party in Kit's convertible, and it had been end-of-the-summer hot. He'd said something that she hadn't caught, and as she'd turned to ask him what he'd said she'd been hit by a bolt of desire so strong that it had wiped her head clean of thought. He'd looked so mouth-wateringly gorgeous, tanned and laughing, with the wind ruffling his hair, so confident and in control, that, totally riddled with lust, she'd ordered him to pull over.

Once he had, in a conveniently secluded spot, she'd practically leapt on him. Kit hadn't complained, and with their mouths meeting and their hands grappling at relevant bits of clothing they'd been too desperate to notice the group of walkers heading along the path in their direction, and then too absorbed in each other to see them hurry straight past.

It was only when Lily lifted her head from the nook where his neck met his shoulder, eased herself off him and turned to face forwards, that she saw the backs of a few stragglers and realised what had just happened. After that mortifying experience, Lily had insisted on sex indoors.

Why Kit had had to bring it up now she had no idea, but

she really wished he hadn't because she could so do without the memory of it. Or the accompanying rush of heat that was sweeping through her.

She could definitely do without the faint knowing amusement with which he was looking at her that suggested he knew exactly what was going through her head.

Hmm. Maybe it wouldn't be such a bad thing for him to believe she had a boyfriend. If her immunity to him wasn't quite as strong as she'd always thought and if he was even *thinking* of continuing with this line of conversation, then a boyfriend seemed like an excellent deterrent/defence.

Lily shrugged away the images. 'Well, it's early days,' she said with a coolness that came from who knew where. 'With Nick and me, I mean. But yes, things are looking good.'

'Great,' he said, sounding as if he thought it anything but.

Snapping his gaze from hers, he glanced down at the glasses that were on the coffee table and frowned. 'Are those ours?'

The crystal champagne flutes had once upon a time indeed been theirs, although now, technically, they were hers. They'd been a wedding present, and until tonight had spent the last five years encased in bubble wrap and stashed in her attic.

Lily wasn't entirely sure why she'd brought them down and unwrapped them this evening, but she had, and that had been a mistake because every time she'd lifted hers to her mouth she'd been hit by a string of bittersweet memories of drinking champagne with Kit.

'I have no idea,' she said with a dismissive shrug because there was no way she was going to confess to any of *that*.

'Looks like they are.'

'Does it matter?'

'It does if you're drinking out of them with another man. I think I might be offended.'

She fought the urge to bristle and channelled her inner calm instead. 'Well, you could have had them, so you should have thought about that when you displayed so little interest in how our things were divided up.'

He nodded and rubbed a hand along his jaw before shooting her a rueful smile. 'I probably should have. Although from what I remember I was too devastated by the realisation that we were over to be worrying about who got what.'

Lily stared at him in astonishment, all pretence of cool detachment gone. 'You were devastated?'

'Of course I was.' He said it as if she should have been able to tell, but by that point he'd been so cold, so distant, so damn unreadable that she hadn't been able to work out what he'd been thinking. 'Weren't you?'

'Oh, well, yes, I was in bits.' Which she'd clearly done a pretty good job of hiding too, if he'd had to ask. 'Although I do remember, above all, an overwhelming sense of relief.'

He nodded. 'Yes, there was that too.'

Silence fell then, and all she could hear as they continued to look at each other was the ticking of the antique mahogany clock on the mantelpiece. And all she could suddenly—and irrationally—think was, had he really been as devastated as she'd been? Had they been too quick to divorce? Should they have tried harder? Should they have given it another shot?

The clock struck a quarter to one and she came to with a jolt.

No. They could have given their marriage a million different shots but it wouldn't have made any difference because before divorce had ever been mentioned, before Kit's one-night stand even, they'd totally lost the ability to communicate and their relationship had gone way beyond the point of no return.

With her throat beginning to ache with regret Lily quickly reined in her thoughts and pulled herself together. She swallowed hard and perched her bottom on the ledge of the built-in cupboard to the left of the fireplace.

Maybe they'd be better off focusing on the present and why Kit was here. And come to think of it…

'How did you know where I lived?' she asked, curious and now a bit suspicious because she'd moved a couple of times before buying this place, and the forwarding address of the flat she'd rented after their divorce had been out of date for years.

He blinked and gave his head a quick shake as if he too had been lost in thought. 'I have for a while.'

'That doesn't answer the question.'

'Doesn't it?'

'Have you been checking up on me?'

'From time to time.'

'Why?'

'I'm not sure.'

Lily didn't know what to make of that. 'Am I supposed to be flattered?'

'Not remotely.'

'Good.' Because she wasn't. Not even a little bit. Truly. 'Then why didn't you just call?' Presumably if he had her address he also had her phone number.

'It's late.'

'Or email?'

'Couldn't wait.'

'Sounds like you were desperate.'

'You have no idea,' he muttered.

'You're right. I don't,' she said loftily, as if she was way above desperation when it came to him.

At her tone, a small smile played at his mouth. 'This is a nice place.'

'Thank you.'

'You've done well.'

She'd done more than well. Following their split she'd jacked in her marketing job and set up her own business, asking her sister—practically the only person she'd been able to trust—to run it with her.

At the time it had saved her. Been something of her own, something that had belonged to her and she to it, and she'd desperately needed it. That the two of them had been so successful had been unexpected, although of course greatly welcome.

'I think so. So have you.'

Kit's smile faded and he tilted his head as he fixed her with a look designed to make her feel uncomfortable. Which it did. 'In spite of your best efforts to sabotage me.'

Lily inwardly cringed. When Kit had broken down and confessed to having a one-night stand she'd cut up his suits and scratched his car and then fired off an email to every one of the institutions he'd been planning to seek financial investment from, telling them in no uncertain terms exactly the sort of man they'd be backing. It must have made things difficult for a while to say the least.

'Are you here for an apology?' she asked, because although it seemed unlikely it wasn't beyond the realms of possibility, she supposed.

'If I were would I get one?'

She bit her lip and nodded. 'You might.'

His eyebrows rose. 'Seriously?'

She gave a nonchalant shrug as if she hadn't been racked with guilt for months afterwards. 'Well, like you said it has been five years and maybe with hindsight I've realised that what I did was unforgivable.'

He held her gaze steadily and to her dismay she felt the

beginnings of a blush. 'I guess you did have some justification,' he said. Then, 'It was what I did that was the truly unforgivable thing.'

For several long moments, there was utter silence and the air began to thicken with a tension that Lily really didn't want to explore.

It would be so easy to slip into a painful post-mortem of their marriage but what good would that do? While time had healed the wounds no amount of talk would wipe out the scars, and picking over the bones of their relationship was the last thing she wanted to do when she was feeling so out of sorts. Or ever, for that matter, because she'd done plenty of it at the time. She certainly wasn't about to launch into a full confessional about how she'd come to acknowledge her role in the breakdown of their marriage.

Besides, presumably Kit was here for a reason, and one that in all likelihood didn't involve raking up the past.

'So why now, Kit?' she asked. 'After all this time? Why the urgency? Why are you here at nearly one in the morning on New Year's Day?'

He rubbed a hand over his jaw and began to pace and she got the impression he was nervous, which was odd because nervousness wasn't a state of mind she'd ever associated with him. Even when they'd waited for the results of the endless pregnancy tests she'd taken, when she'd been a bag of nerves, gnawing on her nails and practically quaking with hope and dread, he'd sat there stonily tense, looking more impatient than anything.

'Could I get a drink?' he said, suddenly stopping mid-pace and whipping round.

Lily snapped out of it and stood. 'Sure. Sorry. What would you like?'

'Whatever you've got. Something strong.'

She went to the drinks cabinet, took out a bottle of brandy and filled a glass. Then she handed it to him, watched as he knocked it back in one swallow and felt a flicker of alarm.

'That bad, huh?' she said with a small frown, her resolve to stay strong and aloof wobbling a bit at the realisation Kit wasn't quite as in control of himself as she'd thought.

'Pretty bad.'

'Are you ill?' she asked, and braced herself.

'Not exactly,' he muttered.

'What does that mean?'

She held up the bottle in case he wanted another but he shook his head and set the glass down on the table. Then he straightened, shoved his hands through his hair and frowned down at a spot on the floor. 'It's complicated,' he muttered.

Lily stashed the bottle back in the cupboard and stifled a sigh. It always was complicated with Kit, but then she wasn't exactly Miss Simplicity herself. Together, not talking, not listening, not really knowing each other all that well, they hadn't stood a chance.

'OK, Kit,' she said, moving to the sofa and hoping that this wasn't going to be too traumatic and that she wasn't going to regret not standing her ground and sending him away when she had the chance. 'If you want to talk, then talk.'

CHAPTER THREE

IF KIT HAD had any doubt that his troubles were bound up with his ex-wife, it vanished the second Lily sat down on the sofa.

On the drive over he'd told himself that he was wasting his time because why would going to see her work when everything else had failed? What exactly was he after? Forgiveness? Understanding? What made him think she'd grant him either now when she'd been so unforgiving and so *un*-understanding at the time?

She probably wouldn't even be in, he'd thought. The Lily he'd known had been a party animal and tonight, after all, was one of the greatest party nights of the year.

But the soft golden light shining through a gap in the curtains drawn across the window at the front of the house had suggested she was at home. And that was when Kit had sent his driver home because, even though he was most definitely not looking forward to it, having come this far he wasn't about to back out.

It was that thought, along with the strong sense that he was nearing the end of his tether, that had kept him standing there on her doorstep when every defensive bristling inch of her was telling him to go.

It was that thought that had made him ignore her initial reluctance to engage with him, her subsequent spikiness, the occasional flash of temper he caught in her eyes and his strong yet totally irrational and unfathomable dislike of the fact that she was in a relationship.

Everything that had been said or hinted at as well as the simmering undercurrent of tension that had been running beneath the conversation of the last half an hour had taken a back seat to the need to get her to listen and the hope that his 'problem' might be about to be solved.

Now, though, his brain was clearing of that too because Lily was sitting down and settling back and crossing her legs, a move that made her dress ride up and exposed a length of thigh.

And suddenly, the memory of how soft her skin felt beneath his hands and his mouth, how tightly she used to wrap her legs around his waist whenever they made love, flashed into his head and, without warning, a wave of lust crashed over him so hard and fast it made his entire body shudder.

Before he had time to recover from the shock of that he was then hit by a whole load of other things that up until that point he'd been too distracted to notice. Such as the way her dress was so tight that it looked as if not a square millimetre of it could bear not touching her. Such as the glorious sheen of her hair, the mesmerising green shimmer of her eyes, the heavenly curves of her body.

He ran his gaze over her and he jolted as if he'd just been plugged into the national grid. Nerve endings that had been dead for so long tingled and quivered and his head pounded with such need he could barely remember his name let alone what she'd just said.

Clearly expecting him to fill the stretching silence, Lily arched an eyebrow and folded her arms beneath her breasts, pushing them together and up and making them swell over the bodice of her dress.

Kit was mesmerised by the movement. His mouth watered, his pulse raced and the sudden urgent desire to haul her into his arms and tussle her to the floor nearly wiped out his knees.

Just as had happened the first time they'd met.

Lily had been on a skiing holiday with friends and so had he. She'd been whooshing down the mountain like a pro, and he'd found himself watching her from the bottom of the slope in admiration. Until towards the bottom she'd lost control, crashed straight into him and together they'd pitched headlong into a snowdrift.

Winded and stunned, for a second they'd just lain there, struggling for breath, their hearts thumping against each other. After a moment, still sprawled on top of him, her eyes sparkling and her cheeks flushed, Lily had started to apologise, but then her gaze had met his and the apology had died on her lips.

It had been the epitome of madness, but despite the cold snow surrounding them chemistry had taken over, heat and lust had flared between them and within seconds they'd been kissing. Devouring each other. Rolling over so that he was pinning her to the ground, while she wrapped herself around him and nearly made him forget that they were in public.

Now he was remembering how wild she'd been in bed, how responsive, how hot and explosive they'd been together before everything had started to go wrong. And as the memories began to come hard and fast all his blood shot south, and within seconds he was sporting an erection harder than granite.

Great, thought Kit, beginning to sweat as the throbbing in his body strengthened. No proper action in that department for five long, dry, frustrating years, and yet one glimpse of Lily's thigh, a hint of soft, luscious cleavage and there it was. His libido, back with ferocious force.

He shoved his hands deep in his pockets as much to stop them from reaching out to strip that dress from her body and touch her as to disguise the very visible effect she was having on him.

'Well?' she said expectantly, and he stared at her mouth, desperate to find out if she still tasted the same, felt the same.

Which he couldn't do, he realised as common sense made a timely and most welcome appearance. For about a billion reasons. She was his ex. He hadn't thought about her like that for years. She probably still hated him. He didn't think he particularly liked her. They had more history than the Egyptians. She had a boyfriend. He wasn't thinking rationally. Or with his head.

In fact, he should probably get out of here. Now. Before he lost control and did something he'd regret. Which was all too possible given the length of his abstinence and the strength of the assault his body and mind were under.

'I should go,' he said, his voice sounding scratchy and rough.

Lily stared up at him in baffled astonishment. 'What? Go? Why?'

'You were right—we don't have anything to talk about.'

So much for all that nonsense about being able to behave like rational, sensible, civil adults, thought Kit grimly. Right now he was feeling anything but.

'Really?'

'Really.'

She frowned. 'Are you all right, Kit? You seem kind of upset all of a sudden.'

The effort of keeping himself under control what with everything that was raging inside him was making his jaw ache. 'I'm fine.'

'You don't look fine.'

'Leave it, Lily.'

'I don't think I can,' she said. 'You really don't seem well.'

'I'll survive.'

Once he was out of here and out of her head-wrecking orbit and once he had time and space to work out what was going on he'd be absolutely fine.

Probably.

Galvanising into action, Kit grabbed his coat and began to shrug it on.

'Wait,' she said urgently. 'Was it something I said?'

The concern in her voice only made him feel even more confused. 'No.'

'Something I did, then?'

Out of the corner of his eye he saw her frown and bite her lip and he gritted his teeth against the urge to throw himself on top of her and kiss the life out of her.

This was horrendous. Why her? Why now? he wondered, his head pounding. He'd met dozens of women over the last few years. Beautiful, intelligent, fun women. Many just as attractive as Lily. Some even more so. So what the hell was happening here?

'It *was* something I did,' she said, leaping to her feet and taking a step towards him, potentially so close that he violently recoiled before she could touch him.

'Don't,' he snapped.

Lily froze. She paled. Frowned. Then said a bit shakily, 'What's going on, Kit?'

'Nothing.' Why wouldn't she shut up and let him get on with the business of leaving?

'Rubbish.'

Kit ignored her. She could be as sceptical as she liked. He didn't care. He was off.

Not bothering with buttons, he whirled round and made for the way he'd come in, but before he could stride down the hall, through the front door and out into the safety of the dark, cold night Lily had whipped past him and planted herself between him and escape.

He stopped in his tracks while she stuck her hands on her hips and set her jaw, a stance he'd never seen before but suggested she wasn't going to let him go without an explanation. Which he was damned if he was going to give, so if she didn't budge he'd just have to lift her out of the way.

'Move, Lily.'

'No,' she said, her chin up and her eyes glinting in the soft, low light of the hall. 'You show up in the early hours of New Year's Day, make a big deal about wanting to talk and then suddenly you don't want to talk? You're making me worried and I won't let you leave when you're in this sort of state. So come on, what gives?'

Now, clearly, was the time to march forwards, physically lift her aside and make his escape, thought Kit with the one brain cell that was still functioning rationally.

But that would mean being near her, laying his hands on her, he reasoned with the part of his brain that was addled with lust, and once that happened he wouldn't be lifting her out of the way, but pulling her close, backing her up against the door and divesting her of her clothing.

Shoving his hands through his hair, he cursed whatever madness had made him think that seeking Lily out had been a good idea.

And then, beneath his breath, he cursed *her* because why the hell was she making such a big deal about this? Why wasn't she just letting him leave? Why did she care what was going on inside his head?

Come to think of it, why was *he* making such a big deal about this? Why was he getting so wound up by what was happening to him?

He ought to be glad his problem seemed to be solved, that he was 'cured'. He ought to be thanking her and heading to the nearest bar in search of someone with whom he could make up for lost time. Or calling Carla, perhaps.

And so what if he was still attracted to Lily? There was

nothing surprising about that. The chemistry that had existed between the two of them had always been instant, fiery and intense. Even towards the end of their relationship when they'd been too battered by what had happened between them to want to act on it, it had still been there, simmering away in the background.

But what if what he was feeling towards Lily now was more than mere sexual chemistry? Something deeper?

Kit froze as the idea of this stormed into his mind and opened up a whole labyrinth of other possible truths.

What if the problem he'd had sleeping with other women in the last five years didn't have anything to do with guilt or regret or self-recrimination? What if it was down to the fact that he was still hung up on his ex-wife?

He'd assumed he'd got over Lily years ago. But from the moment they'd met she'd got under his skin and been in his blood, like some kind of fever, the sort that was quick, fierce and lethal. And incurable. So maybe she was still there. In his blood. Under his skin. Tucked away in some long-forgotten corner of his heart.

Maybe that was why he'd kept vague tabs on her. Maybe that was why the idea of her having a boyfriend bothered him so much. Why he'd wanted to remind her of the good times they'd had together and had deliberately if obliquely brought up that afternoon in the woods.

Maybe she still felt something too, he thought, his heart hammering while his mind churned. Hadn't she flinched when she'd let him in? Hadn't her eyes darkened and her cheeks reddened when he'd alluded to the al fresco sex?

Despite the cool-as-a-cucumber air she was exuding now, despite the defiant stance, he could hear a slight shallowness to her breathing and he could just about make out a familiar faint flush to the skin of her upper chest. There was also a flicker of heat in her eyes that he didn't think was solely down to her wish to know why he was here.

So maybe, as chemistry didn't seem to have a time limit any more than it had anything to do with liking and trust, she was still as attracted to him as he was to her. Maybe it was something more for her too, despite the existence of a boyfriend.

Maybe he ought to think about finding out.

With his common sense spinning off into the distance and his head swimming with need, Kit abandoned what little remained of his self-control and took two steps towards her.

He stopped half a foot in front of her, so close he could smell her scent, could feel her heat, could feel himself helplessly begin to respond to the magnetism that had always pulled at them.

'Is whoever he is really your boyfriend?' he asked, looking down into her eyes, his mouth dry and his body wound so tightly it was in danger of shattering.

Lily blinked, clearly taken aback. 'Nick?' she said, her breath catching and a pulse hammering at the base of her neck.

'Yes.'

Her eyes widened. 'Is that what this is about, Kit? Do you suddenly have a problem with me moving on or something?'

'Possibly,' he muttered because, as disconcerting and unexpected as it might be, he suspected he did.

And then her eyes narrowed and filled with indignation, and she pulled her shoulders back and glared up at him. 'Well, that's just tough because you don't get to have a say in what I do any more. You don't get to have an opinion. And you certainly don't get to comment on my boyfriends.'

'I know that,' he said roughly, trying but failing to ignore the implication that there'd been a few.

'Anyway, would it be so hard to believe if he was?'

'Not at all.'

'Good.'

'Disappointing as hell though.'

She arched an eyebrow and tilted her head in challenge. 'Oh, really? Why?'

The provocative stance, the energy emanating from her and the flurry of memories that were now shooting round his head killed off the last remnant of his self-control, and Kit felt himself begin to unravel.

'Because even though I know it would be mad,' he said, his voice hoarse with the effort of restraining himself, 'even though I know we haven't seen each other for five years and have enough baggage to sink a liner, I'm this close—' he held his thumb and forefinger a centimetre apart '—to dragging you into my arms and hauling you off to bed. The only thing that's stopping me is this boyfriend of yours and even he's now beginning not to bother me. So if you have any sense of self-preservation whatsoever, if you don't feel the same way, then I suggest you step aside and let me leave. Now.'

As the words sank into her head Lily's mind reeled and her heart lurched. Kit wanted to take her to bed? Could she really have heard that right? Surely she must have got it wrong. Surely his proximity was having such a disturbing effect on her mind and body that she'd misheard or something because the very idea of it didn't make any sense at all.

Kit hadn't given any indication of wanting her earlier. Quite the opposite, in fact. He'd been cool and utterly indifferent to her. Which was entirely to be expected. They hadn't seen each other in five years and didn't even like each other particularly.

But no, she thought, blinking up at him in astonishment. It seemed to be that she hadn't misheard and he really had just told her that he wanted to sleep with her. She could see it in his dark eyes, blazing down at her with barely suppressed desire, and she could feel it in his body, which was radiating heat and vibrating with tension.

And even though it could well be nothing more than a simple case of male jealousy or a misguided attempt at marking out territory or something, whatever it was, for one brief, crazy moment she wanted to throw caution to the wind, fling her arms around his neck and sink into him because it had been so long since she'd had great sex and she missed it more than she'd ever let herself admit.

But she stamped out the temptation, set her jaw and held her ground. She hadn't spent the last five years of her life building up sky-high defences to protect herself against men who could cause her the kind of emotional turmoil he could only to have them annihilated by the very man who'd created her need for them in the first place. She'd trained herself to look forwards, not back, and Kit didn't feature in her present, let alone her future.

She didn't want to sleep with him anyway, she told herself firmly. She was totally over him and completely immune. In fact she rather thought she was appalled, insulted and even disgusted by his suggestion.

Especially if *this* was why he'd come here. Lily frowned as the possibility crossed her mind. Was it? Was he on some sort of booty call or something?

Well, if he was, she thought, her indignation firing, that was just awful. If he was, she'd have liked to be able to turn back time in order to slam the door in his face when he first pitched up on her doorstep.

'You want to take me to bed?' she said, her tone as scathing as she could manage, which wasn't very because in amongst the indignation and shock was something that felt suspiciously like hurt, although what there was to be hurt about she had no idea.

'Very badly.'

'Why?'

'You have to ask?'

'Clearly,' she said dryly. 'Are you lonely for a little company on New Year's Eve, Kit?'

'Perhaps.'

'You must be pretty desperate if you're here.'

'I am.'

'So what is this? Auld lang syne and the remembering of old acquaintances or something?'

'I don't know what this is,' he muttered, shoving his hands through his hair, looking as baffled as she felt. 'I didn't come here to sleep with you, Lily, but nevertheless I want to.'

'Well, I don't, so dream on, darling, because it's never going to happen.'

He nodded. 'Fine. Then move aside and I'll go.'

'Right.'

'You aren't moving.'

'I'm about to.'

But she wasn't. Because, to her horror, her feet refused to move.

A burst of panic exploded inside her and she felt a cold sweat break out all over her skin.

Why wasn't she sending him on his way, as he'd demanded? Why wasn't she moving aside, wrenching the door open and bundling him out? Why was she still standing here, deliberating, struggling with herself?

Struggling with herself?

Oh, no, she thought, her heart hammering. Why was what should be an easy decision a struggle? Why was she dithering? She wanted him to leave, didn't she? She didn't care why he was here, did she? She was over him. Wasn't she?

Kit went very still, alert, like a panther about to pounce. 'You still feel it too, don't you?'

'Feel what?' she said, so poleaxed by the notion that she even had to question her indifference to him after such certainty for so long that for a moment she genuinely didn't know what he meant.

'The chemistry.'

'I don't know what you're talking about,' she said, not altogether genuine now.

'Yes, you do.'

'I'm over you,' she said to convince herself more than him.

'Are you?'

'Totally.'

'Then why aren't you moving?'

'You're in the way.'

He took a step back, but to her alarm it didn't make any difference to her mobility. And he knew it. She could tell by the glint in his eye, and the panic escalated to such a level that she thought the top of her head was about to blow off.

What if she wasn't as over him as she'd thought? What if, despite all this time, despite all the lengths she'd gone to to ensure otherwise, she wasn't over him at all?

Because if she was, she wouldn't have to spend every anniversary drunk out of her mind to avoid the memories, would she?

If she was, she wouldn't have found it so hard to drink out of those glasses.

If she was, she wouldn't be so afraid of mind-blowing sex, and she wouldn't only enter relationships with men who left her body completely unstirred.

If she was she wouldn't have felt so hurt at the thought Kit had just come here for sex.

'Do you want to know what I think, Lily?'

'No,' she said, her voice as croaky as if she hadn't used it for years.

'I think you're as over me as I am over you.'

She cleared her throat and tried to pull herself back on track. 'You can think what you like.'

'Can you honestly say you don't want me?'

No. 'Yes.'

'I don't believe you.'

'Too bad.'

'I want you.'

'Well, we can't always have what we want.'

'Can't we?' he murmured.

She set her jaw because whatever he wanted, whatever she might or might not want—and who knew the answer to that?—them sleeping together would be a disaster of titanic proportions and she had no intention of giving in. 'No.'

He moved closer, his gaze not letting her look away, and beneath its intensity she felt her resolve, her immunity to him begin to crumble. 'Are you sure about that?'

Her heart thundered. 'Quite sure.' And then at the predatory gleam in his eye, she added, 'What?'

'I've thought about you, you know.'

She shrugged as if she couldn't care less but inside she was beginning to shake. 'Have you?'

He nodded, his eyes glittering, and took a step forwards. 'A lot.'

'I haven't thought about you at all.'

'Really?'

She nodded. 'Really. Not once.'

'Don't you remember how it used to be?'

'I remember how it was in the end.'

'Coward.' He reached out and touched her hair while his gaze dipped to her mouth, and despite all her protests she shivered.

'Kiss me and you'll regret it,' she said, unfolding her arms and flexing and curling her fingers in warning, but that didn't seem to stop him.

He tilted his head and looked down at her, his eyes as

black as night and so full of intent and desire that she could barely breathe.

'That's a risk I'm prepared to take,' he muttered, and before she could even think of protesting he slid his hand round to the back of her neck then bent his head and captured her mouth with his.

CHAPTER FOUR

LILY TRIED TO keep her mouth closed and her eyes open, she really did, but the familiarity of Kit, the heat of his mouth, his body and his scent blew away her resistance like a dandelion on the wind, and within a second she found herself succumbing to the drugging desire that swept through her.

Her eyes fluttered shut and she moaned and his tongue thrust into her mouth with devilish intent. The heat and the spark she'd felt earlier and had ignored shot back with a rush and her knees went weak.

Any thought of pushing him away vanished. The fingers she'd been flexing in warning now clutched at his shirt to pull him closer because despite everything they'd been through, everything she'd tried to convince herself of over the years, she'd missed him. So damned much.

She could tell herself that she didn't want and didn't need that spark all she liked, but, goodness, she'd missed feeling like this. The heady, delirious rush of simple, hot desire, without any of the angst and anguish that had blighted the latter months of their marriage. She'd missed this kind of need, primitive, pure and fierce.

Just when she feared her legs were going to give way and she'd either fall into him or collapse into a heap on the floor Kit broke off the kiss and lifted his head.

'So is he or isn't he?' he asked roughly, his breathing all fast and ragged and his eyes glazed.

She stared up at him, her heart twisting and tugging, and she could feel herself falling under his spell just as she had the moment she'd looked into his eyes at the bottom of that ski slope in Italy.

The longer she looked up at him, the more her head began to swim with the emotions that she'd kept buried for so long and were now breaking free. Love, hate, joy, despair, desire.

And bewilderment, because had she spent the long lonely weeks, months, years since their divorce hoping for this? Hoping he'd come and find her? Had she been living a lie the whole of the last five years? And if she had, what did that make her? Nuts? Lucky? A hopeless case?

And what did all of this mean? Did Kit still feel something for her other than lust? Something more? Were there still feelings between them? Did they have a second chance?

Her mind teeming and her heart racing, Lily let the weight of emotion submerge the voice of reason bellowing in her head and warning her to be, oh, so very wary.

There'd be time for talk later, time for analysis and perhaps regret, perhaps hope. Right now, though, she just wanted him.

With excitement rushing through her and her pulse thundering, Lily took a deep, shaky breath, then said, 'Despite what I may have implied earlier Nick isn't my boyfriend, and he isn't going to be.'

Kit was wound so tight with tension and desire and the expectation of a slap across the face that for a moment he couldn't work out what Lily was saying.

And then, when his shell-shocked brain finally got round to working it out, couldn't quite believe it. Couldn't quite believe that the risk he'd taken had paid off.

Yet apparently, against all the odds, it had, because here she was, not moving, not lifting her hand to slap him. In fact her eyes were shining, her chest was heaving and she was giving him the kind of look they'd shared at the beginning of their relationship, the one that was filled with heat and need and desperation and had always made his head spin.

That acting on what was clearly going through both their minds wasn't a good idea didn't seem to matter. That there was so much between them and starting something up again would only make things worse and set them back years seemed an irrelevance.

Kit was drowning beneath a wave of desire that had been absent for so long and lust was hammering through him so strong and hot that it drugged his senses, wiped out his reason and everything but the thought that he needed this and he needed Lily. With a desperation and hunger that was eating him up. And it was the same for her too judging by the way she'd just kissed him back.

With one quick move, before she had time to rethink the wisdom of her choice, Kit had her back in his arms and was then twisting her round away from the door and backing her up against the hall wall. The feel of her, the heat of her blasted into him and a bolt of sheer desire powered through him.

He planted his hands on either side of her head while she threw her arms around his neck and then their mouths met, tongues tangled and his mind went blank.

He'd never met anyone who kissed as Lily did, who threw themselves into it with everything they had and everything they felt. Kissing her had always been intoxicating and it was no different now. It was familiar and hot and made him burn.

As did the little moans coming from the back of her throat and the way she was melting against him.

Moving his hand, he buried it in her hair and angled her head so he could kiss her deeper, harder, and she responded with equal need.

Breaking for breath several long, hot minutes later, Kit pulled back and stared down into her eyes. 'Are you sure about this?' he muttered.

'No,' she said dazedly, her breathing all ragged and harsh. 'Are you?'

'Hell, no.'

'Then what are we doing? What is this?'

'Who knows?' he said, sliding his hand round to her jaw and stroking his thumb over her lower lip. 'Irresistible chemistry. Undeniable attraction. A disaster, probably.'

'You could be right.'

'Want to stop?' It might kill him but if she was having second thoughts he couldn't blame her.

'Don't you dare.'

She pulled his head back down to hers and started kissing him again. And then things switched up a gear because she was making sounds—familiar, encouraging sounds— that he hadn't heard for years, and tugging at his clothes, reaching beneath his coat, pulling his shirt from the waistband of his jeans and pushing it up.

He could feel her impatience, but it wasn't a patch on his, and as she put her hands on the bare skin of his back it sent such a shot of desire through him that Kit couldn't wait any longer.

Breaking the kiss, both of them breathing hard, Kit lowered his hands to her thighs, slid her dress up and wrenched her knickers down, feeling as he did so how wet, how ready for him she was. He released her for a moment so that she could kick them off while he grappled with his belt. Which, with shaking hands, was frustratingly difficult.

'Let me,' Lily muttered, brushing his hands aside, unbuckling his belt and then making swift work of the buttons of his jeans.

As she slipped a hand inside his shorts and caressed the

rock-hard, aching length of him he groaned and nearly exploded right there and then.

'Enough,' he muttered, removing her hand and planting it on his neck.

'Hurry,' she said with an urgency that nearly obliterated his control.

'Hold on to me.'

She did, wrapping her arms round his neck and her legs round his waist as he lifted her, pressed her back against the wall for support, and with relief, desire and heat rushing through him he drove into her.

At the warm, wet feel of her he let out a groan of pleasure, relief and who knew what else.

Lily moaned, dropped her head back but, honestly, he was too far gone to notice much what she was doing. All he could feel, and all he could think, was that he was in absolute heaven.

Then she moved and as heaven came that little bit closer Kit realised he was in deep trouble. Because he wanted to go slow, savour the moment, make sure that she was with him every step of the way, but it had been so long, so incredibly long, and if she didn't hold still he'd lose what little control he had left.

'Stop moving,' he said roughly, his fingers digging into her thighs in an effort to hold her still.

'I can't help it,' she whimpered.

As he gritted his teeth against the pressure she held on to him tighter, pressed herself closer. He could hear her breathing go haywire, could feel her tight around him, hear those little pants and he began to spin out of control.

'Stop it now, Lily.'

'No, it feels too good.'

She tilted her hips, pulled him in deeper and that triggered a primitive need in him he couldn't begin to comprehend, let alone control. His head swam with the urge to take, to possess, to reclaim. His heart thundered and inside him there was simply too much urgency. Too much build-up. Too much everything, and his resistance collapsed beneath the sheer force of it.

His control now history, instinct took over and, with the sound of Lily's whimpers and sobbing moans in his ear, he started blindly thrusting in and out of her, faster and harder, unable to stop or even slow down.

And just when the tightness gripping his lower body became unbearable, just when he thought he was about to implode beneath the pressure, or die from the intensity of the pleasure, he lost it.

With a great groan he erupted inside her, pulsating and spilling into her for what felt like for ever.

As hot sexual encounters went that one hadn't quite delivered on its promise, thought Lily, her heart thumping, her breathing skittery and her body twitching and aching with unfulfilled desire while Kit collapsed against her.

But that was OK. She didn't have to be up until seven and she had plenty of experience at recovering after burning the candle at both ends. Later she had a ten-hour plane ride during which she could catch up on sleep, and Kit spending the rest of the night making it up to her would be well worth any fatigue she suffered.

'I'm sorry,' Kit muttered, his voice muffled against her neck.

'Don't worry about it,' she said softly, stroking the back of his neck and smiling at the thought of what was to come.

'How could I not worry about it? That hasn't happened to me since I was sixteen. I didn't even take my coat off.'

A sense of pride surged up inside her at the memory of how keen he'd been. 'Anyone would think it's been a while.'

'Anyone would be right.'

'Really? How long?' Surely it couldn't rival the eighteen-month drought she'd had.

Not that she particularly wanted to think of him with a string of girlfriends, but the undeniable fact was that he was gorgeous, about to enter some rich list or another and, according to the gossip columns that she definitely didn't read, single. A man like Kit wouldn't lack company.

He sighed and her skin tingled beneath the warmth of his breath. 'Five years.'

Lily stopped stroking his neck, frozen with astonishment. 'What?'

'Don't make me repeat it.'

'You haven't had sex for five years?'

'Not since our divorce.'

'Truly?'

He grimaced. 'You think it's something I'd make up?'

It wasn't. Who would?

And because it wasn't and because of what it meant Lily felt instantly sick. Her blood went cold and her body went numb and her throat went tight.

Not because she'd weakened and let herself fall under Kit's spell. And not because she was feeling twitchy with need and could feel him still hard inside her.

No. What was making her want to throw up, what was making her suddenly all shivery and achy and what was making her suddenly desperate to get him the hell out of her body and her house was the realisation that the last person he had had sex with before her just now must have been the woman he'd picked up at some work do while their marriage lay in ruins.

The knowledge triggered a deluge of memories. The devastation she'd felt when he'd told her what had happened. The excoriating hurt and agonising sense of betrayal. And then the pain and the disillusionment and the realisation that they really were over.

As the memories hit furious and fast she could feel a great wave of emotion begin to roll towards her, could feel herself about to break apart and she had to swallow hard to free her throat of the lump that had lodged there.

Unwinding her legs from around his waist, she shifted herself off him just as fast as she could. How could she have been so stupid? How could she have thrown away five years of protecting herself with such abandon? She'd fallen back into Kit's arms without a care for herself. What the hell had she been thinking? How could she have resisted so little? How could she ever have imagined that they might be able to make another go of things? How could she have even wanted to?

Unable to look at him because God knew what he'd see in her eyes or on her face, she pulled her dress down and then used her fingers to smooth her tangled hair.

'Lily?' asked Kit, the concern in his voice showing that he'd sensed something had changed.

'What?' she said blankly, casting her gaze around the floor for her knickers and dimly aware that he was fixing his clothing and tucking his shirt into his jeans.

'Are you all right?'

She bent down and swiped them up. 'I'm fine.'

As she straightened he reached out to touch her face and she recoiled as if he'd struck her. Frowning, he pulled back and stared at her. 'What's wrong?'

'I think you'd better go.'

She needed space. Time. Privacy to examine the wounds, the scars of which had just been ripped off.

'Not until you tell me what's the matter.'

'Nothing's the matter,' she said flatly. 'You got what you wanted. Now go.'

He blanched at the bite of her tone. 'I'm sorry I couldn't wait.'

As if that was what was upsetting her. 'Forget it.'

'No.'

'Look, I was wrong,' she said, bracing herself and looking up at him. 'This was a mistake. An awful mistake that should never have happened and now I'd really like it if you went. Please.'

He must have heard the finality in her voice, must have sensed her weariness or something else, because for a long time he just looked at her. Then he nodded. 'OK, fine,' he said with a frown. 'I'll call you in the morning.'

And with that, he turned on his heel, opened the door and left.

Lily was avoiding him. That was the only explanation for it.

Kit sat at his desk in his office in the penthouse apartment of his London flagship hotel and the place he called home, and glowered at his phone, which might have been broken for all the use it had been so far.

All morning he'd been trying to get hold of her, but infuriatingly her home landline just rang and rang before the answer machine eventually kicked in, and her mobile went straight to voicemail. The brief email he'd fired off asking her to call him had also gone annoyingly unanswered.

Rubbing a hand along his jaw, Kit reflected back to the way things had ended last night and thought he could sort of understand why Lily might not want to speak to him. He'd had the time of his life and she hadn't. She must have been disappointed. Frustrated. Exhausted. It had sounded as if she'd had a busy night even before he'd shown up, and what with such an anticlimax perhaps everything had simply got too much.

In his albeit out-of-date experience, Lily's way of dealing with an emotional overload had always been to shut down, so actually the way she'd responded hadn't been all that unusual.

Nor had the way he'd responded to her. As he'd done

so often in the past, he'd given her the space he thought she needed and left her to it, even though he hadn't really wanted to.

But that wasn't the right way to play it. With hindsight it probably never had been. It was entirely possible that the fact that she'd always withdrawn whenever things had got too heavy going and he'd basically let her, under the guise of giving her space, was how things had got so bad so quickly between them.

He should have been firmer all those years ago and insisted that they face things together, however hard. Lily had been right when she'd said that they'd neither talked nor listened; they hadn't.

Well, whatever had happened in the past, things were going to be different now, he thought, clicking on his inbox for the dozenth time in as many minutes to see if she'd replied. Now he was going to insist on both talking and listening, and that was why her going off grid was so frustrating.

Because apart from deciding that their inability to communicate needed to be fixed, over the course of the night he'd been struck by a truckload of realisations, reached a dozen new conclusions and had come up with a whole load of questions, some of which he wouldn't mind putting to her.

Such as, what had Lily meant by saying that if he'd asked she might have given him an apology for what she'd done? Why had she let him think that she was going out with someone when she wasn't? And why the abrupt change in her demeanour in the minutes before he left? One minute she'd been all warm and soft and then next she'd gone all cold and frigid on him, and he wanted to know why.

Mainly, though, he'd realised that whatever he felt for her, and whatever she felt for him, they weren't over. Not by a long shot.

Setting his jaw, Kit reached for the phone again and was

about to hit the redial button when he paused as a thought occurred to him. Despite it being a public holiday, maybe Lily was at work. Maybe that was why there was no answer from home. Maybe she was on the tube and her mobile out of range of a signal. Maybe she was in a meeting. It could be that she wasn't avoiding him. Merely busy.

Filling with renewed resolve, he looked up her company's details then punched the number into his phone and sat back to wait while it rang. His stomach churned and his mouth went dry, but that was probably down to the fact that it had been a while since his last coffee and he'd been too preoccupied to bother with breakfast.

'MMS, good morning.'

'Zoe?' he said, recognising the voice of his former sister-in-law.

'Yes. How can I help?'

'It's Kit.'

There was a long silence. Then a faint, 'Oh.'

'How are you?'

'Fine. Yes. Good… Kind of surprised to hear from you, to be honest.'

'It's been a while.'

'You can say that again. How are you?'

'Fine. Happy New Year.'

'You too.' She paused. 'So…were you after Lily?'

'Is she there?'

'No. But then I'm at home. The office is closed today so your call was diverted to my mobile.'

'Right.' He frowned. That blew his theory that Lily was at work out of the water. Of course she wasn't. Who was? It was New Year's Day. So was she avoiding him after all?

'Is there a problem or something?' asked Zoe and he snapped back to the conversation.

'She's not answering either of her phones or replying to emails.'

'No, well, she wouldn't be.'

'Why not?'

'Because she's on a plane.'

Kit frowned, a bit taken aback. A plane? She hadn't mentioned anything about going away. Not that she'd been under any obligation to, but still… 'When will she be back?'

'Not for a couple of weeks.'

A couple of weeks? He wasn't sure he could wait that long. Patience had never been his strong point—probably one more contributory factor to the breakdown of their marriage—and right now it was wearing increasingly thin.

'Right. I see,' he said, switching to his agenda with a couple of clicks and seeing that there wasn't anything that couldn't be moved or dealt with by someone else for a couple of weeks. 'Where is she?'

'I can't tell you that.'

'Why not?'

'Well, for one thing, she's on a job and the work she's doing requires a certain degree of anonymity and a low profile.'

'And for another?'

'And for another I don't think she'd thank me if I told you where she was. Do you really think she wants to see you after everything?'

Kit set his jaw and took a deep breath. 'She was happy enough to see me last night.' Which was a slight stretch of the truth, but desperate times called for desperate measures.

There was a pause. 'Last night?'

'We spent it together.'

'Really?'

'Part of it.'

He heard Zoe blowing out a breath. 'Jeez.'

'I need to talk to her, Zoe.'

'She'll be back in a couple of weeks. You can talk to her then.'

'I can't wait that long.'

'After five years, you can't wait two weeks?'

'No.'

'Why not?'

'I'm not sure.'

'Do you still love her?'

Kit felt the totally unexpected question hit him like a punch to the chest.

Did he?

He'd spent the last five years thinking he didn't, but who knew? Seeing her again last night had thrown everything he'd always assumed about their relationship and his life for the last five years into question, so how he felt about Lily or anything for that matter was now up in the air.

The only thing he *was* sure about was that they weren't done. Quite apart from all the questions he had for her, he hadn't apologised for what he'd done all those years ago and for basically blaming her for it. He hadn't told her of the guilt he carried or asked her for her forgiveness, and the need to put all of this right burned inside him like a hot coal.

Last night had opened doors he'd never imagined would ever open again, and now—even if they were only slightly ajar—he wasn't about to let them close. Not only did he seek redemption, he also had the feeling that he was hovering on the brink of a second chance with Lily here, and even though it had never crossed his mind before, had never been something he'd thought he wanted, he now realised he wanted it more than anything, and if that didn't tell him that he still had feelings for her he didn't know what would.

'I don't know,' he said, erring on the side of caution because how he felt about Lily still needed further analysis. 'Maybe. Maybe not. Either way, there are things we need to figure out. Please, Zoe.'

There was another long silence while Zoe presumably

weighed up the pros and cons of telling him and he held his breath.

'Oh, OK,' she said eventually and Kit felt the tension drain from his shoulders. 'But look, she really is working so you can't go barging in there right now.'

'When, then?'

'She finishes next Sunday. Afterwards she's staying on for a few days' holiday until the following Saturday.'

He rubbed a hand along his jaw while his brain raced. He could wait a week, couldn't he? It would give him time to think. Plan. Delegate. Figure out exactly what he wanted to say and how he was going to say it, and how he was going to persuade her to give them the second chance he thought they had. And actually, neutral territory, without any association to the past, might be just the thing.

'Fine,' he said, 'I'll wait. You have my word.'

'Hmm,' said Zoe, sounding as though she didn't think his word counted for much.

'Where is she, Zoe?' he said, ignoring the sting of his ex-sister-in-law's scepticism because right now he had more important things to focus on.

'On her way to the Indian Ocean. Santa Teresa Island. She's staying at the Coral Bay Lodge.'

'Thank you.'

'Look, Kit, Lily hasn't had a holiday in years. She's really looking forward to it. It took her ages to get over you. Tell me I'm not going to regret having told you where she's going.'

'You won't regret it.'

He'd make sure of it.

CHAPTER FIVE

As JOBS WENT, this one hadn't exactly been a hardship, thought Lily, settling on her sun lounger and preparing herself to test the customer service levels of the beach-bar staff, although this time for her own personal pleasure.

Some were, some weren't. That was the way it went, and had gone, right from the start. MMS had started off offering customer satisfaction surveys before expanding to include services such as employee performance analysis, consumer demographic studies and bespoke training programmes, all in the name of driving service excellence. Their clients came in all shapes and sizes and temperaments.

This particular—easy—client had been with them since their inception and had grown with similar speed. Somehow, as the by-product of a much larger deal they'd ended up with a portfolio of assets that included the island of Santa Teresa. They'd offloaded the assets they didn't want, but had decided to keep Santa Teresa with its once five-star luxury resort to see what they could do with it. They'd hired MMS to conduct a thorough analysis of how to turn the business around on the consumer side of things.

Normally MMS contracted the fieldwork out. In their business anonymity was key, and employing a small band of discreet, trustworthy, reliable freelancers to go wherever they were needed allowed Lily to concentrate on the marketing, sales and client side of the business and Zoe to focus on the numbers and data analysis.

On this occasion, however, the woman they'd hired to spend a week assessing the performance of staff and the overall consumer experience at the Coral Bay Lodge had slipped on ice and broken her ankle over Christmas and couldn't fly. At such short notice, especially over the holiday season, they hadn't been able to get anyone else so Lily had taken on the job.

Actually, she'd been heartily grateful for the distraction. January in London was typically on the quiet side and if she'd been there twiddling her thumbs she'd have had hours in which to dwell on everything that had happened on New Year's Eve. Instead she'd been so busy working, concentrating on the details and reporting back to Zoe with her findings that she hadn't given Kit a moment's thought.

Well, *hardly* a moment's thought, she amended, picking up the cocktail menu and wondering whether five in the afternoon was too early for a sundowner.

He *had* slipped into her head on the odd unguarded occasion, but whenever he did hot on the heels of it came the instant realisation of just what a bad idea Sunday night had been, how much what he'd done still hurt and how stupid and deluded she'd been to even imagine that him showing up on her doorstep might mean anything other than the need to scratch an itch.

Thank goodness the sex had been lousy or she'd be in serious trouble, she reflected, glancing down the long list of cocktails. If it had been as mind-blowing as she knew it could be, she'd now undoubtedly be wondering what she'd been missing all these years. What she'd been thinking when she'd decided to pursue relationships with men who didn't affect her pulse rate.

She might also well be letting good sex get in the way of good judgement and telling herself that maybe she'd overreacted on Sunday night. She might be thinking that perhaps everything that had gone on between them before was now water under the bridge and why on earth shouldn't they try again?

Despite the heat of the day Lily felt a shiver run down her spine. Wow, what a lucky escape she'd had.

And continued to have because thankfully since the day following the night before she hadn't heard from Kit. Oh, that Monday he'd called. Repeatedly. At least, she assumed it had been him; she didn't have his number in her phone, but he'd said he would, and she couldn't think of anyone else whose number her phone didn't recognise who would keep popping up with such persistence.

By the time the tube to Heathrow had emerged above ground, she'd seen she had half a dozen missed calls but, feeling too tired and too emotionally on edge to deal with the conversation she could imagine he'd want to have, she'd switched her phone off.

She'd switched it on twelve hours later and braced herself for more missed calls, but they seemed to have dried up. Which she was delighted by. Really, she was.

Smiling up at the waiter who'd materialised beneath her thatch umbrella as if able to read her mind, Lily ordered a margarita. It wasn't too early and, besides, so what if it was? This was the first holiday she'd had in two years, and she planned to enjoy it.

After all, how could she not? she thought, lying back as the waiter smoothly retreated, putting her sunglasses on and closing her eyes with a deep sigh of satisfaction.

The endless azure-blue sky had been unblemished by cloud for the entire last week and the temperature was on average a perfect twenty-eight degrees. She'd downloaded a dozen books to read and there were miles of white sandy beaches to stroll along should she want the exercise. Ditto the sea, which was clear and turquoise and incredibly inviting. And what with the fabulous restaurant and beach bar she wasn't planning on moving for the entire week.

Lily was on the point of dropping off when the quick tensing of her muscles and the sudden jump in her heart rate alerted her to the fact that someone was standing over her.

The waiter with her cocktail, she thought delightedly, levering herself up, whipping off her sunglasses and opening her eyes.

And nearly passing out with shock at the sight of Kit looming over her, blocking out the sun and holding what looked like her drink.

Oh, no, she thought, her heart plummeting as she stared up at him. There went her plans to relax.

'Hello, Lily,' he said casually, his deep voice sending goosebumps scattering all over her skin.

'Hello, Kit,' she replied, adding a cool smile to show that she could do casual too.

Acting like an automaton, she sat up, swung her legs round and reached for the sarong she'd dropped on the neighbouring sun lounger. With an odd feeling of calm she stood up and wrapped it round her, covering up the bikini that she'd thought modest when she'd put it on this morning but right now felt like the skimpiest thing she'd ever worn.

She tied the ends of the sarong between her breasts and took a moment to arrange her thoughts. Thoughts that actually weren't in nearly as much disarray as they ought to have been, she had to acknowledge. Because the strange thing was in all honesty she wasn't all that surprised to see him. Kit had always been proactive, and what with the way things had been left between them and the way she'd ignored his calls she should have guessed that he wouldn't have let it lie. In fact, she should have realised something was afoot when the calls had stopped.

'Yours, I believe.' He held out her drink.

Lily took it, ensuring that their fingers didn't accidentally brush. 'Thank you,' she said. 'The hotel business not doing too well these days, darling? Having to moonlight as a waiter?'

Kit shot her a smile that despite her intention to stay cool and unruffled made her hot and bothered in a way that had nothing to do with the afternoon heat. 'The hotel business is doing great. And as I was on my way over anyway I thought I'd save him the trip.'

Lily lifted the glass to her lips, swallowed down a massive gulp and winced as the tequila shot down her throat and hit her stomach. 'So thoughtful.'

'I can be.'

She licked the salt from her lips and felt a sharp stab of satisfaction when his gaze dropped to her mouth for a second. 'This is beginning to become a bit of a habit,' she said.

'What is?'

'You showing up unexpectedly.'

'I might be on holiday.'

Yeah, right. 'Are you?'

'Yes.'

'My, what a coincidence.'

'Isn't it just? Do you mind if I join you?'

Yes. 'Not at all,' she said, waving a hand in the direction of the sun lounger to her right as she sat down. 'Be my guest.'

Kit took off his sunglasses, folded them and hooked one arm over the V of his T-shirt. Then he sat down and leaned forwards, resting his elbows on his knees.

As his eyes met hers Lily felt herself beginning to lose track of things, as she often did when she looked into his eyes, and she wished he'd kept his sunglasses on. Instead she put her own back on, and waited.

'I was told you were staying at the Coral Bay Lodge,' said Kit.

'Who by?'

'Zoe.'

Of course. No one else apart from the client knew she was in this part of the world. But what the hell did Zoe think she was doing? Normally her sister was the soul of discretion, so what had happened? How could she ever have thought that Lily would want to see Kit? How had he ever persuaded her to release the details? Had he said something about what had happened between them on New Year's Eve, and Zoe, in her current state of ecstatic happiness and filled with the resultant determination for everyone else to feel the same, was under some warped misconception that she was facilitating a reconciliation?

Whatever the reason, Lily thought darkly, she and her sister would be having words just as soon as she was free to call. 'When did you speak to her?'

'New Year's Day.'

A week ago. 'Right. Why?'

'I rang you, but you didn't pick up.'

'I was travelling.'

'You didn't return my calls.'

'I didn't know it was you.'

He arched a sceptical eyebrow. 'Didn't you?'

'You should have left a message.'

'Would you have called me back if I had?'

'Of course.'

'Sure about that? Because I don't remember getting a reply to my email.'

Lily smiled and shrugged nonchalantly. 'Well, I guess we'll never know, will we?'

'I guess not.'

'So were you worried about me, Kit? Ah, that's sweet.'

'I wasn't worried in the slightest,' he said easily. 'I merely wanted to talk to you. This seemed to be the only way of achieving that.'

'I'm flattered.'

'You should be. You were tricky to track down.'

'I moved hotels.'

'You moved islands.'

Lily took another gulp of her margarita. 'Yes, well, these islands are small. My hanging around on Santa Teresa once my work was done might have looked a bit odd.'

'It took me longer than I'd expected to find you.'

'Are you after an apology?'

'Would I get one?'

'Not this time.'

Kit grinned that heart-fluttering grin of his and her stomach flipped in a way she didn't like at all. 'Didn't think so,' he murmured.

'Couldn't you have waited until I got back? I haven't had a holiday in years.'

'Patience isn't one of my strong points.'

'No.' She paused and then gave it one last futile, she suspected, shot. 'Is there anything at all I can do to make you go away?'

'Not a thing.'

No, she hadn't thought so. Lily sighed and resigned herself to the inevitable. 'OK, fine. You win. But I'm not dressed for a chat.' She certainly wasn't ready.

He ran his gaze over her, so slowly and thoroughly that she felt as if he'd stripped her bare. 'You look fine to me,' he said, a little hoarsely she thought, 'but perhaps you're right. Maybe this isn't the time or the place.'

Never and nowhere would be the right time and place in her opinion, but what could she do? On an island this size she'd never be able to avoid him, and hopping on the next available boat to the mainland wasn't the answer because not only was running away immature, as Kit had just proved, he'd simply come in search of her.

Anyway, it would probably be fine. All they were going to do was talk, and talking never killed anyone, did it?

Besides, on one of the *extremely* rare occasions that Kit had flitted into her head over the last week she'd reflected that she'd been wrong when on her doorstep a week ago she'd told him they'd never been able to talk. Communication between the two of them had always been fine when there wasn't much of import to communicate. The problems had only arisen when the stakes had been stratospheric, when emotions had run high and they'd felt exposed and vulnerable. It was then that they'd both gone into hiding and communication had become a four-letter word.

Tonight there wouldn't be anything at stake. Kit might make her feel a bit on edge, and, God, he looked mouth-wateringly, spine-tinglingly hot in the white polo shirt, khaki shorts combination he was currently wearing, but she wasn't emotionally involved. Not now.

And, actually, if he wanted to rake through the ashes of their relationship, that was fine with her because there were things she needed to tell him. Things she'd come to realise over the last five years. Things that she wanted to get off her chest and he ought to know.

She was much stronger than she'd been all those years ago, and with the exception of the wobble she'd had on New Year's Eve, which had merely been down to shock anyway, he didn't have the ability to hurt her any more.

Therefore, if she was well prepared and stayed focused conversation with Kit would be fine. Cathartic even. 'Shall we have dinner?'

'The restaurant?'

Of course the restaurant; no way was she inviting him to her villa for room service. 'Why not?'

'Eight o'clock?'

Three hours in which to decide her strategy? Three hours in which to don her suit of armour? Or, despite her brave thoughts just now, three hours in which to get completely and utterly hammered? Whichever route she chose to take three hours was perfect.

Draining the rest of her margarita and ignoring the small bundle of nerves beginning to twist her stomach, Lily nodded coolly. 'Eight o'clock it is.'

The terrace where dining took place was everything that could be expected of a luxury four-figure-a-night five-star resort on an island off the coast of Mozambique. Lanterns sat on the edge of the decking, the candles within flickering in the twilight. Tables set with starched white tablecloths, silver cutlery and fine crystal dotted the terrace and the beach. Soft, sultry music drifted from behind the bar into the warm evening air.

Nature lent quite a hand to the feeling of sensuality too. The sea rushed up the sand with a gentle swish and then rolled back. The heady scent of lady of the night drifted through the warm evening air. The palm trees that surrounded the restaurant rustled in the breeze and cicadas chirped in the undergrowth.

Utterly oblivious to the considerable charms of the establishment, however, was Kit, who was standing at the bar and frowning down at his beer as he experienced a rare yet all-consuming moment of self-doubt.

Heading over here had seemed such a good idea last week when he'd put his plans into place. Fired up on adrenalin and the thrill of the chase, and practically burning up with the idea of a second chance with Lily, he'd had his secretary make the travel arrangements while he'd issued instructions to his management team. He'd found himself looking forward to seeing her again and the challenges he knew he could expect. He'd been looking forward to getting everything off his chest and persuading her to give them another shot. More than looking forward to it, if he was being honest.

But now he was here, now he'd seen her clear hostility towards him—which she'd been less successful at hiding than she probably thought—it struck him that maybe he'd been a bit reckless. And maybe he wasn't being very fair.

OK, so he wanted to talk things through and offload, but perhaps Lily didn't. Who was he to insist they rake up the past when, considering the boyfriends she'd mentioned, she'd evidently moved on in a way that he didn't think he had?

By turning up out of the blue like this and demanding they talk he'd put her in an impossible position. He'd probably shot her intentions to relax and enjoy her holiday to pieces. Given what he knew of her he wouldn't be all that surprised if she'd hopped on a boat to the mainland to catch the next flight home. Or at the very least hotfooted it to one of the other islands that made up the archipelago in an effort to put some distance between them and resume her holiday in peace.

Either one of which was looking increasingly likely, he thought, glancing at his watch, because it was now quarter past eight and Lily was never late.

Beating back the disappointment beginning to sweep through him, Kit swallowed hard and forced himself to focus on practicalities. If she wasn't late, if she had gone, what would he do next? Go after her again and this time lock her up or something to make flight impossible? Leave her in peace until they got home? Or give up altogether?

As his stomach began to churn Kit exhaled slowly and told himself to calm down. He'd give her another fifteen minutes, then he'd put in a call, and, depending on whether or how she answered, would take things from there.

Thirty seconds later, however, the doubt over whether or not she'd left and what he'd do about it vanished because despite having his back to the entrance to the bar he knew Lily was there. He could feel it in the way his muscles tensed with awareness, the prickling of his skin, the overwhelming sense of relief that flooded through him.

Deliberately slowly he set down his beer, turned round, and at the sight of her his heart stopped. For a moment he felt winded. Blinded. Stunned. She was wearing a simple floaty black dress and sparkly flip-flops, and she was clutching a small black bag. Her neck was bare but big silvery hooped earrings hung from her earlobes.

Her dress wasn't particularly revealing or overly clingy, yet something about her made his mouth go dry. It was as if she were sort of glowing from the inside out. Her dark hair shone in the soft light of the bar and her eyes gleamed and her mouth was curved into a barely there smile that had his pulse racing.

She looked… He racked his brains for a moment to find the right word. Serene. That was it. She looked serene.

While he felt anything but.

With his heart beating double time Kit watched as she walked over to him and for the first time in years felt a stab of panic because he didn't know whether to kiss her mouth, her cheek, shake her hand or do nothing.

His indecision was as terrifying as the decision he had to make, and his palms went damp in a way that had nothing to do with the condensation that he'd felt on his beer glass.

With every step she took his head swam just that little bit more, until she stopped right in front of him and, thank goodness, took the decision out of his hands by reaching up and planting a soft, light kiss on his cheek.

Then she stepped back and smiled up at him, presumably completely unaware of how she was affecting him.

'You look nice,' she said, giving him a quick once-over that had heat shooting through him.

'You look beautiful,' he replied, once he'd managed to clear his head of her scent and unglue his tongue from the roof of his mouth.

'Thank you.'

He cleared his throat. 'I booked a table.'

'Great.'

'Would you like a drink before we sit down?'

'Would you?'

'If you would.'

'I don't mind.'

Feeling as if a swarm of bees had invaded his body, Kit swallowed hard. For crying out loud, this was absurd. He was thirty-two. He ran a global multimillion-pound business. He was known for being decisive, intuitive and utterly ruthless when the situation called for it. Yet here he was, being rendered practically tongue-tied by the prospect of an evening with his ex-wife. His totally calm and in control ex-wife. Who was expecting not a drooling idiot of a dining companion, but a possibly difficult conversation that he'd insisted upon.

Telling himself he really had to get a grip, with superhuman effort Kit pulled himself together. 'Let's just go straight to the table, shall we?' he muttered, taking her hand and practically marching her across the bar and out onto the sand.

CHAPTER SIX

THIS WASN'T A DATE. This wasn't a date. This wasn't a date.

As she followed Kit to the table that sat at the water's edge and was set for two Lily tried to concentrate on the mantra rolling around her head and not on the electricity that emanated from the connection of her hand with his and was zapping through her, but it was proving no more helpful now than it had when she'd been getting ready.

After going back to her room earlier this afternoon and taking a cold shower, which hadn't done much to obliterate the hundred or so grasshoppers that had seemed to have taken up residence in her stomach at the thought of the date—no, *dinner*—with Kit, she'd decided that while donning armour was a must, mainlining tequila probably wasn't the way to handle the evening. She was in a jittery enough state as it was and with alcohol loosening her already iffy inhibitions who knew what might happen?

Once she'd made that pleasingly mature decision, she'd called her sister and after that, well, she hadn't known what to think about anything.

As she'd dialled the number she'd been planning to tear a strip off Zoe for revealing her whereabouts to Kit of all people. She'd been going to say she understood that her sister was at a heightened level of happiness at the moment, but that she had to realise that not everyone was in search of the same, and that *she* certainly wasn't looking for it with Kit. She'd even been prepared to counter-argue the excuse of Kit's powers of persuasion she was sure Zoe was going to give.

What she hadn't been prepared for, however, was her sister's declaration that she thought Kit still had feelings for her, that he'd said he might still love her and that *that* was why she'd told him where she was. To give them the opportunity to see whether they had a second chance. Or something.

In something of a daze Lily had hung up, and it was then that she'd descended into the kind of emotional turmoil she'd spent so long avoiding, her head teeming with questions such as 'Could he?' 'Did he?' and her heart beginning to swell with what she had the awful suspicion might be hope.

Which made such a mockery of everything she'd spent the last five years trying to convince herself of that it was no wonder she'd worked herself up into such a state. For the best part of the next couple of hours she'd paced up and down her room wondering whether her sister had got it right and then trying to figure out that if she had, what she— Lily—wanted, if anything, and what, if anything, she felt.

Before she knew it it was half past seven and she still hadn't dried her hair. Bafflingly none the wiser about how she felt about any of it, she'd put it to the back of her mind while she got ready, and there it had stayed until she'd seen him standing at the bar, nursing his beer and looking so familiar and so gorgeous that her heart had turned over and her brain had turned to jelly and she couldn't think about anything at all.

So she'd schooled her features into a neutral arrangement that she hoped masked the craziness that was going on inside her head, had taken a deep, steadying breath and told herself to remember what dinner was about.

But, heavens, it was difficult to focus when her head

was filled with the look on Kit's face when he'd turned and seen her. She didn't think she was wearing anything particularly astonishing but from the heat in his eyes she felt as if she were the most beautiful woman he'd ever seen. Perhaps on the planet.

It was even harder to concentrate on the reason they were here when everything about the place, from the lighting to the music and even the positioning of the tables, screamed intimacy, privacy and romance.

They reached their table at the same time as a waiter, who pulled out Lily's chair, waited for her to sit down and then did the same for Kit opposite. He handed them each a menu, took their order for aperitifs and then melted away.

Glancing down at the list of dishes, each of which sounded more mouth-watering than the previous, Lily swiftly made her choice. As did Kit, judging by the way he put the menu down with a brief nod and sat back.

Her eyes met his, their gazes locked and as the seconds ticked by she became achingly aware of the beating of her heart, the sound of her breathing, of every inch of her body come to think of it. The connection between them was as strong as ever, the attraction undeniable, and the tension, the heat and the anticipation still simmered.

'I'm glad you're here,' said Kit eventually, the faint surprise in his voice as much as his words snapping her out of her reverie.

Lily swallowed hard and gave herself a quick mental shake. She had to get a grip. She really did if she was going to make it through dinner. 'What, here on the island?' she asked, which she didn't think made much sense. 'Or here at this table?' Which did.

'Here with me. Now.'

'Why wouldn't I be?'

'It had crossed my mind that you might have used the afternoon to run away.'

Ah, he knew her so well. 'It crossed mine too,' she said with a small smile, 'but then I figured what would that have achieved? Avoidance isn't the way to deal with any of this.'

Kit leaned back and looked at her, a thoughtful expression flickering across his face in the twilight. 'What is?'

She gave a little shrug. 'I'm not sure. Honesty maybe?'

'Honesty works for me.'

He glanced up and smiled his thanks at the waiter who'd set a glass of champagne in front of her and was now doing the same with his beer for him and her breath caught. Goodness, his smile really was something else. She'd been on the receiving end of it so many times but it had never failed to affect her. Still didn't, it seemed, because the waiter was looking down at her expectantly as apparently it was time to order and she couldn't for the life of her remember what she'd chosen.

Indicating that Kit should go first with a wave of her hand, Lily picked up the menu and while he ordered lobster followed by tilapia she found with relief her starter of prawns and main of curried sea bass.

'I'm sorry about New Year's Eve,' said Kit once the waiter had disappeared with their order and they were once again alone.

'New Year's Eve?' echoed Lily, her eyebrows lifting a little. 'Why? What is there to be sorry about?'

'What isn't there to be sorry about?' he muttered, shifting in his chair as if suddenly finding it uncomfortable. 'I turned up out of the blue, virtually forced you to let me in and then behaved like a crazed hormonal out-of-control teenager.'

'Oh, right,' she said, feeling herself flush at the memory of how out of control they'd both been. How reckless and deluded *she'd* been. 'Well, consider your apology accepted.'

'Thanks.'

'You're welcome.'

See, they could be perfectly civilised about this, she thought, taking a sip of champagne, which was cold and dry and utterly delicious. Even if she was a total mess inside.

'I wasn't surprised you threw me out what with the… ah…way things went,' he said and went a little red.

She stared at him for a second and then put her glass down. 'You think I threw you out because I was cross I hadn't, well, you know…?' Neither of them was usually such a prude about these things, but then normally they didn't discuss them in public. At least she didn't.

Now it was he who raised his eyebrows. 'Didn't you?'

'Of course not.'

'Then what happened?'

'When you told me that you hadn't had sex for five years it occurred to me that the last woman you'd slept with was, well, you know…' She braced herself, then in the spirit of the honesty she'd just claimed she believed was the way forwards, said, 'Her.'

Kit frowned. 'I see.'

'It freaked me out. Brought back a time I've spent five years trying to forget.'

He rubbed a hand over his face. 'Of course. I'm sorry.'

'I realise now that I might have overreacted a bit, but in my defence it had been quite an emotionally stressful night, even before you turned up.' She shrugged and shot him a faint smile. 'Anyway, it's not your fault.'

'Isn't it?' he asked, his face dark and his eyes glittering in the twilight. 'Isn't everything?'

And there it was. The moment she could either agree that it was and they'd stay where they were, with Kit in all likelihood heading home and out of her life first thing in the morning, or she could tell him what she'd come to realise and they could both move on, although God knew where to.

Knowing what she had to do for her own peace of mind as much as Kit's, Lily took a deep breath. 'Not really,' she said and felt the release of a kind of pressure she hadn't realised had been building up inside her.

Kit sat up, alert and to all appearances in something of a state of shock. 'What?'

'There's no need to look quite so surprised,' she said, although she couldn't really blame him given how, at the time, she'd totally laid the responsibility for what he'd done at his door. 'I've had plenty of time over the years to think and I've come to realise that what happened between us wasn't your fault. Or at least not entirely.'

'Really?'

She nodded and broke off a piece of bread. 'Oh, I know what I said then, and I know I laid the blame for it all going wrong wholly at your feet, but that wasn't very fair of me.'

'Wasn't it?' he said, his astonishment fading and leaving the expression on his face totally unreadable.

'You know it wasn't. And you told me so, many times. Not that I was willing to listen. At the time all I could focus on was what you'd done and I didn't think about what might have led to it.' She popped the bread into her mouth, chewed for a moment and then swallowed. 'I mean, you're not the cheating sort, Kit, but I was so blinded by hurt, so wrecked by the feeling of betrayal, I didn't see that. I didn't ask myself why you'd done it and I didn't think about my role in everything. As far as I could see I didn't have a role other than as the only victim. I'd been going through hell and you didn't seem to understand.'

'I tried.'

'I know you did.'

'But maybe not enough.'

'Maybe I didn't let you.'

He rubbed a hand along his jaw. 'With hindsight I should have been firmer and I should have made us face things together.' He let out a humourless laugh. 'But believe it or not I wasn't having all that much fun either.'

'I realise that now.' She sighed. 'But the whole IVF thing was so grim and painful and devastating and by its very definition so physically mainly about me that I failed to see it involved both of us. Plus I knew how much you wanted children being an only child and things, and the knowledge that I couldn't have them just about broke me apart. I didn't cope with things very well and I shut you out.'

'I allowed you to.' Kit shoved his hands through his hair and frowned. 'I told myself that I was giving you space but in reality I think what I was doing was avoiding something I didn't have a clue how to handle.'

It was the first time he'd acknowledged his contribution to the collapse of their marriage and it warmed a part of her deep inside that had always been so cold.

'Really we were both victims, weren't we?' she mused, feeling an odd sense of calm spread through her. 'Of something we didn't have the strength or maturity or understanding to deal with.' She paused. 'Of course you topping things off by going and sleeping with someone else didn't exactly help.'

As her words hung between them Kit paled beneath his tan. 'I'll never forgive myself for that,' he said, his voice cracking a little. 'There's this nugget of guilt that's always there and I'm so sorry, Lily. For everything. But particularly for betraying your trust like that.'

'You're forgiven.'

'Am I?'

'Yes.'

'Are you sure?'

'Of course.' She took a quick sip of champagne. 'Five years is too long to be angry and resentful and I think I forgave you ages ago. I get now that you must have been feeling lonely and isolated and all those other things you said at the time,' she said, remembering the endless evenings she'd spent going over it all. 'That doesn't mean what you did didn't devastate me, because it did. But I can sort of see how it happened. I mean, we hadn't had sex for months, had we? And we were barely speaking. We were virtual strangers. Something had to give at some point.'

His jaw tightened and shadows flickered across his face. 'Nevertheless I made that choice to cheat,' he said gruffly. 'I was the one that trampled all over our marriage vows.'

'True.'

'I've regretted it ever since.'

'Did you ever consider not telling me?'

'For about a nanosecond.'

She tilted her head and looked at him. 'Was it really just sex and a one-off?'

'Yes.'

'Then maybe it would have been better if you hadn't.'

'Perhaps.'

'Although our marriage was dead in the water long before that, wasn't it? So the end result would probably have been the same.'

'If I'd thought there was any hope of salvaging it I'd never have done what I did,' said Kit.

'Wouldn't you?'

'No. Not that it's any excuse. Nothing excuses it. Certainly none of the justifications I came up with.'

Lily winced as everything he had accused her of— self-absorption, surliness, lack of understanding among others—all came back. 'I guess we both said things we probably shouldn't have.'

'Probably,' he said with a nod. 'But I've had time to think too and I was too quick to absolve myself of any of the blame. Whatever was happening to us, I should have made us deal with it together. I regret the fact that I didn't.'

For a moment they lapsed into silence, the space between them no longer filled with regret but a sort of tentative understanding.

'Listen to us,' she said softly, 'each trying to take the blame for the way things turned out.'

'Unlike when it actually happened when all we could do was blame each other.'

'Exactly.'

Kit smiled, his eyes glittering in the candlelight. 'Who'd have thought we'd get so wise?'

'Well, I've had a lot of time to think and I ended up figuring that for me it was like someone—you—had died or something because the man I knew would never have done something like what you did. So I kind of went through the whole grief thing, starting with shock and rage. It took me a while and a *lot* of wine to get round to the acceptance and forgiveness stage but I got there. And here we are, I guess.'

Kit didn't say anything to that, but just looked at her for several long, heavy moments, his eyes darkening and the expression on his face changing into something that made her heart thud and her throat tighten.

'What?' she asked, her voice husky.

'You're incredible.'

'No, I'm not,' she said, trying to tamp down the surge of heat rising up inside her and the thudding of her heart. 'Just a bit older maybe and appreciating the benefit of twenty-twenty hindsight. Anyway, it isn't all one-sided. Didn't you say you'd been thinking too?'

'I've had my moments.'

She shot him a rueful smile. 'And it's not like I didn't do things I regret.' Her smile faded and she bit her lip as a familiar wave of shame rolled through her. 'I'm sorry about cutting up your clothes and keying the Porsche, Kit.'

'Don't be.'

'And the email was truly unforgivable. I should never ever have done that.'

Kit shrugged. 'Water under the bridge.'

Not for her. Once the initial surge of triumphant satisfaction had faded she'd felt sick and hollow and riddled with guilt. Still did a bit. 'Did it make things very difficult?'

'Pretty tough.'

She inwardly cringed. 'What did you do?'

'Having been informed of my questionable integrity none of the British banks would lend me anything and the venture capitalists wouldn't touch me with a bargepole so I went to the States.'

'I read that your first hotel was in New York. I wondered about that. Will you tell me how you did it?'

And so, over the course of dinner, Kit did. He told her how after New York he'd moved to Paris and set up a hotel there. And then, most recently, London.

He told her of the satisfaction he felt of realising the dream he'd had ever since his jet-set parents had taken an apartment in Claridges, the dream that had sustained him through his degree in hotel management and his swift climb up the ladder. He shared the obstacles he'd faced and the successes he'd had.

And in return Lily told him how she'd come to start her business, how shortly after their divorce she'd resigned from her much-loved marketing job. How, needing the distraction of a new challenge, she'd hit upon the idea of offering a range of products to help businesses improve their customer experience. She'd put it to Zoe, who'd been keen, and that was that.

She asked after his parents, and he learned that Zoe was engaged. They discussed a few previously mutual friends with whom only one of them had stayed in touch, the places they'd lived, and caught up on as much as they could while skirting round the subject of lovers in her case and lack of them in his.

Dinner was delicious. At least Lily had told him it was. Personally Kit couldn't taste a thing. He was too busy reeling from everything she'd admitted between their aperitifs and the arrival of the food. Too busy recovering from the mind-blowing discovery that she'd forgiven him and that the second chance he'd so badly wanted might be closer than he'd dared hope. Too busy revelling in the sound of her voice and her laugh, watching her expressive face and losing himself in the depths of her mesmerising eyes. And too busy realising that there was no longer any doubt about whether or not he loved her.

He was absolutely nuts about her. She was the strongest, toughest, most beautiful woman he'd ever met and he was a fool to have ever let her go. He'd never fallen out of love with her and he was going to do everything in his power to win her back.

But he couldn't barge in and tell her what he wanted, he thought suddenly, watching Lily drain the last of her coffee and stifle a yawn. He couldn't carry on with the strategy he'd employed up until now. He was going to have to tread carefully. Their relationship was so fragile, their truce so new, and he could so easily screw things up with his impatience, his need to be in control and his continual drive to move things forwards.

It might be the challenge of the century but with Lily he had to switch mindsets. He had to take a back seat and wait. He had to let her come to him, and then they could begin to build their relationship from there.

So there'd be no more chasing. No more persuading her to do things she didn't really want to do. No more doing anything that might scare her off.

Whatever happened next had to be her decision. All he could do was ensure that he did his best to help her make the one he wanted.

Despite her initial misgivings the evening really couldn't have gone any better, thought Lily, walking beside Kit as he escorted her back to her villa, the inky darkness of the night wrapping round them like a warm, cosy blanket.

Once they'd moved on from the difficult topic of their mess of a marriage, accompanied by course after course of heavenly food and delicious wine, the banter had batted back and forth with barely a break for breath. They'd had so much to talk about, so much to find out. It had been just like old times, but somehow better.

As they'd begun to get to know the people they'd become, Lily had found herself liking Kit more and more, and beneath one lethal smile after another she'd felt herself fall deeper and deeper under his spell.

She'd known it was happening, known that she was being foolhardy and reckless in not bothering to resist, but it had been such a long time since she'd felt like this, all relaxed and languid yet buzzing at the same time, that she hadn't been able to stop herself.

And hadn't really wanted to because over the course of the evening the answers to the questions she'd spent this afternoon trying to figure out had become increasingly clear, and now it seemed that the night held myriad possibilities.

Possibilities that had her body thrumming with anticipation and her heart thumping crazily because dinner had cleared the air. Cleaned the slate. Had maybe, even, reset their relationship, put them back at the start and cleared the way for a stab at a second chance together, free from and prepared for all the trouble that had come their way the first time round.

The idea was kind of thrilling, she thought, going all shivery and hot inside. Exciting. And what she wanted.

What Kit wanted, however, was completely up in the air. He'd been silent and thoughtful ever since he'd offered to walk her back, and infuriatingly wasn't giving anything away.

But if he was as achingly aware of her as she was of him

then there was only one logical conclusion to tonight, and even though on some dim and distant level she knew the idea of falling into bed with him again needed way more consideration, the desire simmering inside her was too insistent to ignore.

'You know, if I'd known how cathartic getting all that stuff off my chest was going to be, I'd have been in touch with you years ago,' said Lily a little huskily as they strolled up the path to her villa.

'Would you?' he murmured.

'Absolutely. I feel as if I've spent the last five years carrying this enormous kind of weight that's suddenly gone. I feel lighter somehow. Calmer.'

'I know what you mean.'

'I'm glad we talked. And had the chance to catch up,' she added with a smile.

'So am I.'

At her door she turned to him and lifted her face, her pulse hammering so hard he must surely be able to see it. Would surely act on it.

'So what happens now?' she said, the anticipation and excitement zipping through her making her all trembly inside.

'Now?' he said, reaching out a hand and softly running his forefinger down her cheek.

She nodded and held her breath as every one of her senses focused on him and this moment.

He tilted his head, his eyes dark and unfathomable. 'Well, sweet pea, that rather depends on you.'

'Me?' she echoed softly, the endearment and his touch stealing her ability to think straight.

He nodded and gave her a faint smile. 'That's right. So have a think about it and let me know.'

And just as she was about to ask what he meant Kit bent his head, dropped a light kiss on her cheek and then, to her utter bewilderment, turned and walked off into the night.

CHAPTER SEVEN

LILY DIDN'T SLEEP WELL—largely because she'd spent most of the night tossing and turning while her body hummed with frustration and unsatisfied desire and her mind churned with confusion—and when dawn broke she was still wide awake, the questions that had plagued her all through the night still rattling around her head.

What on earth was Kit playing at? she wondered, staring up at the slowly rotating ceiling fan that hung over her bed and listening to the soft whirr it made.

Last night she could have sworn he'd been as aware of her as she had of him. She'd been convinced that the practically tangible tension and attraction had been mutual. And what with the endearment, the one she hadn't heard for years, and the touch to her cheek, a gesture so familiar and so missed it made her heart ache just to think about it now, she'd been certain he'd ask to come in for a nightcap, and equally certain that she'd say yes.

But how wrong she'd been. How disappointingly, confusingly wrong.

After the urgency of what had happened in her hall last week and the way he'd crossed half the globe to come and find her—not to mention the interest she'd thought he'd displayed over dinner—the fact that he'd suddenly backed off baffled the hell out of her. She hadn't been expecting—or wanting—the restraint she'd got, the chaste little kiss, nor the tossing of the ball neatly into her court.

And what was that all about anyway?

What had he meant when he'd said that what happened next was up to her? Why was it up to her? And up to her how?

What was he expecting her to do? Make a move? Jump his bones or something? Well, that was never going to happen without some kind of signal from him, she thought darkly. Not now. No way. She needed to know how he felt about her before she made herself vulnerable like that again. She needed to know that there was more to this than just sex.

And unfortunately she didn't, because, while last night she'd had all kinds of ideas about how he might feel about her and had been so ready to drag him into her bed, this morning she didn't have a clue. For all she knew the endearment and the touch had merely slipped out of him from habit and meant nothing.

So where did they go from here? Where did she want them to go? Where did *he?*

Bending her head from side to side to stretch out the kinks in her neck, Lily frowned. Gosh, why was this so difficult? So complicated?

With a sigh of resignation and despair because she was now more at sea than at any point since he'd reappeared in her life, Lily swung her legs round and got off the bed.

Whatever was going on, she thought, heading into the bathroom and flicking on the shower, she had no doubt she'd soon find out, because given the way Kit had gone about things so far it was surely only a matter of time before he turned up demanding to know what she was going to do with that ball.

Or perhaps it wasn't.

Two hours later Lily had had breakfast—by herself—and had hovered by the pool for plenty long enough to be found, but to her agitation and disappointment there was no sign of Kit anywhere.

Where was he? Busy? Avoiding her?

Or had he left?

Maybe he had, thought Lily, lowering the e-reader that she'd been staring unseeingly at for the last ten minutes, and frowning with distaste as the idea shot into her head and took root.

Perhaps she'd been too idealistic in her assumption that they'd cleaned the slate. Perhaps her confession over supper put him off or something. She couldn't really see why it would, and the ease of their subsequent conversation hadn't given her that impression, but with hindsight she had rather let it all out without letting him get much of a word in edgeways.

Perhaps their conversation, the understanding they'd reached and the catch-up they'd had was exactly what he'd been after- –closure—and now he'd got it he was done.

Maybe he was after nothing more than friendship or something and he was perfectly happy for her to let him know what she thought about that once back in London.

Maybe the kiss he'd dropped on her cheek had been not one of restraint but one of goodbye.

Her heart squeezed and her throat tightened. Then she gave herself a quick shake and pulled herself together because on the other hand it was entirely possible she was being a bit melodramatic about where he could be.

Surely Kit wouldn't have flown all the way out here just to leave less than twenty-four hours later. Hadn't he said he was on holiday? And surely he'd want to hang around to hear what decision she'd come to, even though she hadn't come to one because she still couldn't figure out what she was supposed to be deciding.

For her own peace of mind, though, and out of respect for the author of the book she was struggling to concentrate on, maybe she'd better go and check if he was still here. Then at least she'd know one way or another and would know how to proceed.

Putting her e-reader down and reaching for her sarong, Lily got to her feet and headed inside.

'Good morning,' she said to the receptionist, with a sunny smile that totally belied the weird kind of tension now clutching at her stomach. 'I was wondering, could you tell me whether Christopher Buchanan has checked out?'

'Not to my knowledge, madam,' he replied.

'Oh, thank God for that,' she said, clapping her hand to her chest and letting out a rush of breath as the tension dissipated and she filled with an overwhelming sense of relief. More overwhelming than the situation warranted, probably, but who cared?

'Would you like to know where he is?'

'I would.' Very much. Because if he wasn't coming in search of her, she'd go in search of him.

'I believe he went to the spa.'

'Thank you.'

Phew, she thought, leaving the main building and walking along the track towards the thatched structure that contained the spa. Kit hadn't gone. He was just having some time out. Relaxing. Doing what millions of people all over the world did on holiday.

Although choosing to do it in a spa did seem kind of incongruous. She'd always thought of him as a man of action and purpose, constantly on the move and unstoppable in his drive for more. He'd never been one for navel-gazing and just sitting around doing nothing, but maybe he'd changed in that respect too. It had been five years after all, and no one— not even Kit—could keep up the kind of level of both mental and physical activity she associated with him for ever.

And even though the idea of him lounging in a steam room or having a massage or something was difficult to reconcile with the Kit she'd once known, she found it surprisingly easy to visualise.

In her mind's eye she could see him sitting on one of the wooden ledges, leaning back against the wall while the steam swirled around him. She could see droplets of water forming on his chest, trickling down over the smattering of hair that covered his skin there, tracing the ripples of his abs and then meandering south before melting into the top of the towel wrapped round his waist.

She could see him closing his eyes and dropping his head back, and her mouth actually began to water as she imagined leaning over and pressing her lips to the skin of his shoulder to catch a droplet and then make the journey it would have made with her tongue.

Right the way down...

At the image of what she might do then, a bolt of heat shot through her, nearly wiping out her knees, and she had to grip the door to the spa for support.

Good Lord.

Feeling faintly dizzy, Lily gave herself a quick shake to dispel the image, determinedly ignored the heat and cleared her throat. She hadn't fantasised like that in years and had no business doing so now. She wasn't seeking Kit out to drool all over him or to melt into a puddle of lust at his feet; she was going after him to see if she couldn't find out a bit more about what he thought was going on here.

Five minutes later she'd found him. Not in the steam room, thank goodness, but in the Jacuzzi. Which actually wasn't all that much better. Because he was naked.

Well, perhaps not entirely naked, she had to concede once her stupefied brain had started working again and the common-sense robbing flush of heat had subsided. Seeing as how the spa was a public space presumably he had swimming shorts on. Not that she had any intention of investigating *that* too closely.

Which was just as well as her eyes seemed to have fixed on his chest and rather worryingly weren't going anywhere, south or otherwise. The way he was sitting, with his arms outstretched and resting on the edge of the pool while water bubbled and popped all round him, displayed it in all its glory, and she couldn't tear her eyes away.

It was a good chest, she thought dazedly, every nerve ending she had tingling with awareness. Better now, if that was possible, than when she'd first become acquainted with it. His shoulders were broader, his muscles looked harder, more defined, and his skin was a fraction darker.

Her head filled with the memory of how he'd felt moving against her, on top of her, inside her and her fingers itched with the need to reach out and touch him and find out if he still felt the same, still responded to her in the same way…

It was only when one of her feet actually inched forwards that she jerked back to her senses.

Honestly, what was going on? This was ridiculous. It was Kit. Her ex-husband. She knew every inch of his body, from the thick dark hair on his head to his toes and everything in between, so why was she lusting over him as if she'd never seen a body like it?

Ignoring the knowledge that it was the bits in between that were causing her such a problem right now, Lily pulled her shoulders back and dragged her eyes up. To find him watching her with an annoyingly knowing little smile playing at his lips, the likes of which made her all the more determined to stay cool and in control.

'Hi there,' she said brightly. Overly brightly possibly.

'Good morning.'

'Did you sleep well?' she asked, and immediately wished she hadn't because all it did was conjure up the memory of her and Kit falling asleep in each other's arms, hot, satiated and limp with exhaustion.

And then another, of her waking up alone and sad and aware that while physically he was just across the hall in the spare room emotionally they were a million miles apart.

'Like a log,' he said with an easy smile that suggested he wasn't nearly as similarly burdened. 'You?'

'Beautifully,' she lied, ruthlessly dismissing the memories and trying to concentrate. 'I didn't see you at breakfast.'

'I had it in my room.'

'Oh.'

'I had some work to catch up on.'

'Right.'

Then her train of thought faded because, gosh, it was hard work keeping her eyes on his and not letting them drift down as they kept trying to do. And verging on impossible to hold back the urge to whip off her sarong and leap into the Jacuzzi with him and make herself stay where she was.

This was absolutely awful, she thought a little desperately. She'd always been drawn to his body, had always known that the magnetism that existed between them was hard to ignore, but what was going on here was another thing entirely. This was an attraction that she could almost taste. It was intoxicating. Addling. Becoming frighteningly irresistible.

'Did you want something, Lily?'

Him. She wanted him. With a need that was almost blinding. And one that she had to resist until she knew how he felt and what he wanted. For her sanity, her self-respect and her sense of self-preservation. But, goodness, it was going to be hard.

'Lily?'

She blinked and came to. 'What? Oh. Yes.' Although right now she couldn't really remember what it was she wanted. Something to do with finding out what was going on in his head, perhaps.

Well, that was clearly out of the question when her own head was such a mess. She could barely think straight. And if she did embark on the kind of conversation she'd been vaguely contemplating she had the horrible feeling that if he admitted they were done, she might well be reduced to begging, which didn't appeal in the slightest.

She needed time to get used to the situation as well as the scorching attraction she felt for him before attempting a deep and meaningful conversation about what he wanted from her. She needed to see how the land lay a little longer and give him a chance to play his hand first.

So maybe now wasn't the time to go in guns blazing.

'I was thinking,' said Lily, feeling a fraction calmer now she'd come to some kind of a decision about how to handle him and the situation, 'when you're done here, what are your plans for the rest of the day?'

'I don't have any.'

She blinked, faintly taken aback because this was the second time that Kit had surprised her recently. He didn't have plans? That was unusual. It seemed to her that recently he had plans for everything. 'None at all?'

'None at all. Why do you ask?'

'Oh, well, I was thinking of going fishing.' Huh? Was she? That was news to her. Given she'd never done it before she didn't even know if she liked fishing.

'That's nice.'

'And I was wondering if you'd like to join me.'

He shot her a friendly, casual smile that for some reason made her want to slap him. 'Why not?'

Fishing went swimmingly. So swimmingly, in fact, that the following day Lily suggested a tour of the island. Which was such a success that the day after that she and Kit went diving.

The experiences were fabulous, exhilarating, fun, the fishing unexpectedly so. The tour of the island had been fascinating, and when they'd gone diving she'd been overwhelmed by the beautiful and exotic marine life she'd never encountered on any of the dives she'd done before.

What was going on between her and Kit, however, was not so fabulous. Or exhilarating. Or fun. Instead it was downright perplexing.

Three days into their holiday, and Lily didn't know what was going on now any more than she had at the beginning of the week. She and Kit spent all day together, ate every meal together, yet went to bed separately, and, while there had been plenty of laughs and endless conversation, the lie of the land hadn't become any clearer and, more frustratingly, Kit hadn't made any kind of a move.

The word she'd use to describe their relationship at the moment, thought Lily, stuffing a towel into her beach bag and scowling, was platonic.

OK, so most of the activities they'd engaged in hadn't offered the kind of privacy or conditions needed to deal with a potential unstoppable overspill of desire. Such as the day they'd spent fishing and then the tour of the island. On both occasions there'd been other guests and guides around. And when they'd gone diving, yes, there'd been times they'd been alone, but that had generally been underwater, and, while the sight of him in just his swimming shorts had made her stomach flip and her temperature rocket, masks and aqualungs were hardly conducive to either conversation or the intimacy she craved.

But there'd been many an opportunity for non-necessary touching and many a chance of a stolen kiss or two over the last three days. None of which, annoyingly, had been taken up.

They'd never done platonic, and Lily didn't think they should because not being able to touch a body she'd once had permanent and all-over access to, not having the right to it, was driving her nuts.

And that was why over breakfast this morning she'd suggested hiring a speedboat and taking a picnic to one of the private, deserted coves she'd heard of on the other side of the island. That was why she'd dressed in her most flattering bikini, had carefully blow-dried her hair even though it would undoubtedly tangle the minute they set off and had buffed and moisturised every square inch of skin and redone her nail varnish.

She was looking as good as she could under the circumstances, the setting was guaranteed to be conducive to seduction and the food bound to be sublime, and if all of that didn't give him the impetus to make a move, she thought, eyeing herself in the mirror and picking up her bag and hat, then nothing would.

Kit, who was in the resort office and filling in the paperwork relating to the speedboat rental that Lily had suggested earlier, was fast running out of patience. Deciding to wait for her to make up her mind about what she wanted and then let him know was all very well, but at no point had he considered the possibility that she might not. Ever.

But it looked as if that was exactly what was going to happen because he'd been as encouraging as he knew how and yet for three days now she'd shown no interest in him whatsoever. At least none of the sexual kind. And so, while the last few days had been fun and Lily had been great company, he'd slowly been going insane.

He'd seen the look in her eye when she'd happened upon him in the Jacuzzi, and, after thanking the Lord that the lower half of his body was submerged beneath the hot bubbling water and therefore out of sight, had seen it as an encouraging sign.

Fishing, he'd thought, had been an odd choice of activity but he'd been looking forward to it. Looking forward to spending time with her and seeing how she'd handle the attraction that sizzled between them.

But unfortunately she hadn't followed up on the promising start, and day three into his holiday Kit was beginning to wonder why the hell he'd embarked on a strategy of letting her come to him in the first place. And why he wasn't simply abandoning it and dragging her into his arms and to hell with it.

But he couldn't, he reminded himself for what felt like the hundredth time. He had his principles. His strategy was a good one. A necessary one because if they stood any chance of making another go of things it had to be on equal terms. She had to want it as much as he did. Want him as much as he wanted her.

So no way was he going to make the first move. He'd made enough of those already and he was feeling too slavishly in thrall to her as it was. He wasn't going to do a thing until he found out how she felt about him, so if Lily wanted him she could come and get him. The beach they were heading to was quiet. Deserted. Private. They had good food, good wine and the entire day together. All she had to do was give him a sign.

With the paperwork finished, the key in his hand and his resolve once again firm, Kit strode down the jetty to where the boat and picnic were waiting. Climbing aboard and with the morning sun beating down on him, he started carrying out the necessary checks, channelling every drop of his focus into the task and putting his frustrations with Lily from his mind.

Which worked like a dream until he felt his skin prickling with awareness and his muscles tensing and he realised that she'd arrived.

Forcing himself to relax, he glanced up and flashed her a quick, cool smile as if the sight of her didn't make his heart lurch and his mind go blank.

But it did because standing there on the jetty she looked absolutely incredible. She was wearing some sort of translucent thing that floated around her body, moulding itself to her with every breath of breeze and hinting at the luscious curves beneath. She looked like something out of an advert. Cool. Gleaming. Gorgeous. And she blew him away.

'Hi,' he said, once he'd managed to regain his power of speech and gathered the wits she'd scattered.

'Hi.'

Realising that he was in danger of gawking and only a stone's throw from abandoning his very well-thought-out and sensible plan, he moved over the deck to where she was standing and held out his hand.

She took it, and despite his principles, despite his strategy, it was all he could do not to tug her towards him and 'accidentally' have to save her as she overbalanced by wrapping her in his arms.

Once she'd boarded he thought about holding on to her a fraction longer than was necessary. Saying something about how beautiful she looked, how sexy he found her. Giving her hand a squeeze and providing her with the opportunity to squeeze back.

But before he could, she tugged her hand free as if he were suddenly burning her or something, tore her gaze from his and then busied herself with stowing her bag beneath the passenger seat, and he mentally cursed both her for her indifference and himself for his moment of weakness.

'Ready to go?' he said, feeling his frustration simmer, his patience thin even more and his mood begin to blacken.

Sitting down and sticking her hat on her head, Lily shot

him a dazzling smile that reminded him he really had to get a grip of himself if he stood any chance of hanging on to his self-control today and said, 'I've never been readier for anything in my life.'

CHAPTER EIGHT

SHE MIGHT BE ready for anything, thought Lily a couple of hours later, but Kit clearly wasn't.

There hadn't been much opportunity for chat when the boat had been speeding through the water, bouncing on the surface, and the wind rushing in her ears, but once they'd dropped anchor and tied up to a buoy, and once they'd waded to the beach, Kit carrying the picnic basket over his head in a particularly manly fashion, she'd thought things would change.

She'd thought that the day would be like the last few days only with an added frisson of tension and anticipation that the privacy of the cove would afford them. She'd thought—perhaps naively—that today would be a good day to initiate a conversation about what they were doing and what they wanted.

But she'd been wrong.

Because judging by the air of surliness that Kit had worn ever since they'd sped away from the jetty and the monosyllabic responses he'd given to her subsequent attempts at small talk he didn't seem up to conversation, let alone the kind of conversation she was toying with.

From time to time, unable to stand the awkward, tense silence, she'd glanced over at him and caught him looking at her with eyes so dark and intense they were utterly unreadable and she'd gone so jittery, breathless and dizzy that she couldn't have spoken even if she'd wanted to.

All in all the morning so far had not been conducive to talking so was it any wonder that every time she'd geed herself up to tackle the conversation she'd planned, she'd chickened out? No, it wasn't.

But perhaps now they'd had lunch he'd be in a better mood, she thought, brightening a little. Maybe he'd just been hungry. Now she thought about it that made a lot of sense because Kit always got grumpy if he was hungry, and it had been quite a while since breakfast. Plus, although he was beginning to stir now, he'd been so still lying beside her, his eyes firmly closed and his breathing slow and deep, she'd guessed he'd had a little sleep, which would surely add to his receptive frame of mind.

So while earlier might not have been the ideal opportunity to talk, maybe now was. Maybe she ought to take the bull by the horns and take advantage of this moment of peace and quiet and seeming calm, and sort things out once and for all.

Lily took a deep breath and summoned her confidence as she rolled onto her side and propped herself up on her elbow. 'Kit?' she said, and smiled at him in what she hoped was a calm, reassuring manner.

Opening his eyes, he turned his head to look at her, ran his gaze the entire length of her and then back up, and abruptly sat up. 'What?' he snapped.

His tone cut through her thoughts, derailing all her plans for talking to him about them and zooming all her attention instead to the look on his face. His features were twisted, as if he were being tortured inside. He looked dark. Wild. Anguished. In agony, in fact.

'Are you all right?' she asked, alarm beginning to shoot through her at the idea that he might be having a seizure or a heart attack or something.

'I'm going for a swim,' he growled, to her astonishment leaping to his feet and striding off towards the sea.

That smile of Lily's would be the ruin of him, thought Kit grimly, slicing through the water in an effort to rid himself of the sizzlingly hot electric energy flowing through him.

All morning she'd been flashing it at him and it had been driving him nuts. Just now, when she'd bestowed it on him again together with that soft murmur and the undulation of her body as she'd rolled onto her side, all gentle hills and tantalising valleys, rises and dips and light and shadow, he'd been within a hair's breadth of reaching for her.

Damn, this whole boat-secluded-beach thing had been such a bad idea. What the hell had he been thinking in agreeing when she'd suggested it? Had he really thought the circumstances would have her throwing herself at him in wild, unbridled passion? Had he really thought he'd have no trouble holding on to his self-control? Hah. What a complete and utterly deluded idiot he'd been. He had no self-control when it came to Lily. He never had.

So what the hell was he going to do now? He couldn't stay out here pounding away at the waves for ever. He had to head back to shore at some point. And what would happen when he did? How was he going to handle this? Did he even want to think about it?

Perhaps it was best not to. Perhaps it was better to just go with his instinct and suffer the consequences. Communicate how he was feeling with actions rather than words. At least then he'd know one way or another how Lily felt, and if she did reject him he could live with it.

With such a strong sense of purpose now calming the heat and tension inside him, Kit turned for the shore. He was halfway there when he stopped for a breath, looked towards the land and saw Lily sitting on the sand in the shallows and clutching her foot, her lovely face contorted in pain.

His blood ran cold and his heart lurched and he started scything through the water just as fast as he could, the desire to find out what was wrong, the need to help her obliterating any kind of other need and desire.

When he reached the shallows he staggered to his feet, his heart pumping and his muscles screaming. Rubbing water from his eyes and pushing his hair back, he stumbled over to her.

'What happened?' he said, dropping to his knees beside her and noting her pale face with concern.

Lily winced and rubbed her foot. 'I was planning to come and join you for that swim but I trod on something sharp.'

'Does it hurt?'

'A bit.' For which he read *a lot.*

'Let me take a look.'

He reached for her foot. He wrapped his hand round her ankle and was about to take her foot in his other when he felt her freeze. He glanced up at her, saw that her eyes were now filling with wariness as well as pain, and he lost what was left of his patience. 'Oh, for heaven's sake, Lily, don't look like that. I'm not going to ravish you.'

'You aren't?'

What did she think he was? Forget communicating with actions rather than words. There wasn't any need for that now. The wariness in her eyes told him everything. She wasn't keen. He got it. Finally. So he'd leave her alone. And not just right here and now. 'Of course not,' he snapped. 'Relax.'

With a nod and a frown she bit her lip and he felt the tension in her muscles ease a little. Dragging his gaze from hers, he gently turned her foot in his hands and tried not to think about the softness of her skin or about how he used to give her foot rubs that frequently turned into something else. He tried not to think about how gorgeous she smelled, how warm she felt or how close her mouth was, so close that all he'd have to do was twist his head, lean forwards and he'd be kissing her.

'Looks like you stood on a sea urchin,' he said, his voice hoarser than he'd have liked.

'Is that bad?'

'I can only see a couple of spines, but who knows?' He racked his brain for what little he knew about the severity of ocean-creature stings and bites but it was hard when his head was filled with nothing but thoughts of what he'd like to do to her. 'Are you having trouble breathing?' He was. In such close proximity to her his lungs seemed to have forgotten how to work.

'No.'

'Chest pain?'

'No.'

'Then probably not.'

He released her foot and got to his feet before he acted on the instinct he'd been favouring only a few minutes ago out there in the sea but was now wholly inappropriate.

'Where are you going?' she asked, squinting up at him.

'There's a bottle of vinegar in the picnic basket. The acid should help.'

She gave him a faint smile. 'Better than you peeing on me, I guess.'

Kit frowned down at her, and thought that despite the stab at humour he didn't like the flush in her cheeks one little bit. 'Don't move.'

'I won't.'

As her foot continued to throb and tiny stabs of pain shot along it Lily watched Kit head over to the picnic basket, her heart contracting and her spirits plummeting.

Her intention to follow him into the sea and continue the conversation she'd barely started might not have worked out as planned, but she'd wanted an answer to the question about where they were heading and now she had it.

Kit wasn't planning to ravish her, and she didn't think he meant simply here on this beach. A minute ago they'd been practically naked and so, *so* close to each other and all he'd shown her was cool practical concern, while she...

She blew out a breath as she watched him hunker down and rummage around in the basket for the vinegar, part of which had dressed the salad and part of which was apparently to dress her, and swallowed back a surge of desire.

Well, she'd lied when she'd told him she wasn't having trouble breathing and didn't have chest pain, although neither had anything to do with standing on a sea urchin.

The minute he'd laid his hands on her and turned her foot with a gentleness she'd never have expected from him her breathing had gone haywire. And then when he'd told her he had no intention of ravishing her her chest had tightened so much her heart had physically hurt.

And now he was coming back with the damn vinegar and she was going to have to employ every drop of self-control she possessed to stop herself throwing caution to the wind and herself into his arms.

Swallowing hard, Lily kept her hands planted on the sand as Kit once again knelt beside her.

'I'll see if I can remove as many of the spines as I can,' he said with a brief smile. 'I'll try to be gentle.'

She didn't want gentle, she thought rebelliously, clamping her lips together to stop the words tumbling out as he held her foot and began pulling out the spines. She wanted rough. Urgent. Desperate. She wanted his hands not touching her in the cool, impersonal manner of a doctor, but stroking her and kneading her and caressing her in the manner of a lover. She wanted hands that would explore her and make her tremble and drive her mindless with desire.

She might have let out a tiny moan. She might have whimpered. Whatever noise she did make Kit instantly stilled, his head jerking up and his gaze locking with hers.

Something flickered in the depths of his dark eyes and her breath caught. For a moment it felt as if the entire world had stopped to see what was going to happen next.

And then he was jerking away from her, snapping the connection of their gazes and shoving a hand through his hair, and the world carried on its business.

'Kit?' she murmured, reeling from the intensity of the moment and the abrupt way it had ended.

'You winced,' he muttered, jamming the lid on the vinegar and standing up. 'I'm sorry if I hurt you. But now you're done.'

'Nothing to worry about,' she said, scrambling to her feet, the pain now wiped out by a wave of mortification and the sting of rejection. 'And thank you.'

'We'd better head back.'

'Good plan.'

Returning from a visit to the clinic, where her foot was checked and given a cleanish bill of health, Lily stalked into her villa, threw her bag on the sofa and then flung herself on the bed, frustration, disappointment and tension practically tearing her apart.

Kit didn't want her. Physically or otherwise. That much was now blindingly obvious. So obvious, in fact, that she was kind of stunned she'd ever got into her head that he did.

How could she have been so stupid, so deluded? Well, her sister had a lot to answer for, she thought darkly, rolling onto her front and burying her head in a pillow. If it hadn't been for that stupid phone call she'd never have leapt to the clearly wrong conclusion that he might still have feelings for her.

Zoe had said she thought that Kit might still love her, but *might* also meant *might not,* didn't it?

And if *that* was the case then she'd been wrong to read so much into the look he'd given her in the bar when she'd first turned up for supper the day he'd arrived. She'd thought she'd seen so much there in his eyes, but perhaps she'd only seen it because she'd wanted to see it. And perhaps she'd been wrong to imagine, wonder, hope even, that things between her and Kit could be anything other than what they were.

Which was absolutely devastating, because while the last few days hadn't resulted in a tumble in the waves, they *had* highlighted all the reasons why she'd fallen in love with him in the first place: his enthusiasm for everything he did; his live-life-to-the-full attitude; the way he made her feel protected and cherished; his generosity and inherent kindness.

They'd also highlighted the fact that despite all her assertions to the contrary, despite everything she'd told herself over the last five long, horrible years, she'd never fallen out of love with him. She knew now that she still loved everything about him. Always had, always would.

While he was completely indifferent to her.

As her heart twisted Lily let out a muffled wail and thumped the mattress with her fists. Oh, what a mess. So much for wondering where they were going, she thought desolately. They weren't going anywhere. Apart from home. Tomorrow. And then on with their lives. Separately.

As a stab of despair shot through her at the futility of it all she rolled onto her back, sat up and looked gloomily out of the window.

At least the weather, having taken a turn for the worse, was vaguely sympathetic to the blackness of her mood.

Ever since they'd got back—and what a hideously awkward journey that had been——the air pressure had been dropping and the temperature had been rising to what was now an almost unbearable level. The clouds that had started scudding across the sky when they'd moored the boat back at the jetty were now so dense and dark it felt as if the island were lying beneath a heavy, hot and humid blanket.

Even though it was only mid-afternoon it felt like dusk. Not the soft, balmy dusk of the last few days, but an edgy, malevolent dusk that was laden with an ominous kind of portent. The wind was whipping up the sea, bending the trees practically double, and the air was crackling with electricity that she could feel vibrating through her too.

She felt weirdly on edge. Prickly. As if a whole hive of bees had taken up residence inside her.

And what exactly was she going to do for the rest of the afternoon? She couldn't read. Couldn't work. Couldn't do any of the activities the resort usually had to offer as everything had been cancelled due to the storm that was brewing. There was the gym, but even if that had appealed Kit had muttered something about heading that way when they got back, which ruled it totally out.

And as for simply lying back and relaxing, well, that was out of the question too because in the absence of anything else to do it seemed that she was going to be spending the afternoon driving herself mad with if onlys and what ifs, wondering what he was thinking, what he was doing and if there was anything she could have done differently to make him want her again. The rest of the time she had left on the island she'd have to spend avoiding him.

Or would she?

A clap of thunder boomed across the sky, rattling the windows and making her jump. And get a grip.

Hang on, she thought, jumping off the bed and beginning to pace as her brain suddenly started whirring. What was she? Some kind of a wimp? Who was this woman who shied away from a challenge? Where was the woman who'd been so determined to have it out with him that she'd accidentally stood on a sea urchin?

Was she really going to meekly accept that they weren't going anywhere and just leave things in the past? Was she really going to give up without knowing for sure that there was no future for them when the opportunity to find out was there for the taking?

No, dammit, she wasn't.

What the hell did she have to lose by confronting him? Her pride? Well, that had gone years ago. Her sense of self-preservation? Hah. She'd been kidding herself that she ever had one in the first place.

And what was she so frightened of? That he might turn her down? Or that he might not?

Lightning split the sky, illuminating the room for a second, and Lily felt her heart begin to race as what she had to do, what she *wanted* to do, became clear.

She couldn't go home not knowing what could have been and she couldn't stand another minute of the uncertainty. And yes, the outcome of what she was about to do was a fairly scary unknown, and yes, the weather was diabolical, but in all honesty, she thought grimly as she grabbed her cagoule and pulled it on, she'd faced far worse.

Making it back from the gym to his villa a second before the heavens opened, Kit strode into the shower room and flicked on the water with perhaps more force than was strictly necessary, but frankly he was all out of patience, and all out of hope.

He'd done his best to get Lily to want him the way he wanted her, but his best simply wasn't good enough. He had to accept the fact that Lily just wasn't interested in him the way he was in her.

The memory of her sitting on the edge of the beach shot

into his head. The moment he'd caught the tiny sound she'd made that could have been pain or something else and their gazes had locked. The highly charged moment in which it had seemed to him that they were teetering on a knife-edge. In which he'd been willing her to take the chance on them. And in which she hadn't.

The moment that had pretty much told him everything he needed to know.

Steeling himself against the stab of pain that struck his chest, he stripped off his gym kit, tossed it into the laundry basket that sat in the corner of the bathroom and stepped into the cubicle.

Switching the water to ice-cold, Kit winced and felt his muscles relax after his workout, but as for the ache in his chest, well, that, he suspected, was going to be more difficult to assuage.

But he'd just have to because he could take a hint. Or lack of. He wouldn't seek Lily out any more. He wouldn't try to change the way things were. It had been a mistake to think that there was any chance of a reconciliation. They had too much baggage and the past should remain right there, in the past.

It had definitely been a mistake to come here, he thought grimly, turning the tap to hot, grabbing the bottle of gel and beginning to lather himself up. With hindsight he'd have stayed the hell away.

But never mind. He only had another twenty-four hours or so on this godforsaken island and then he'd be home. Back to normal. More or less. He'd put Lily out of his mind and get on with his life. He'd move on. Just as he should have once he'd discovered his little 'problem' had been solved. He'd get over the distaste at the thought of meeting someone else. Of course he would. In time.

He'd have to because whatever the future held, one thing was certain: it didn't hold Lily.

What with thunder crashing through the sky, the hammering of the rain on the roof and at the windows and the pelting of the shower over his body—not to mention the rushing in his ears at the acknowledgement that he and Lily really were over—at first Kit didn't hear the pounding on the door of his villa.

Then he did and he frowned because who the hell was out in this weather? And what was so urgent that it couldn't wait until it passed?

With a scowl, he switched off the shower, grabbed a towel and wrapped it round his waist. Feeling so tightly wound he thought he might be about to snap, he stalked out of the bathroom. Headed into the hall.

And stopped dead because—it was Lily.

The last person he wanted to see. The only person he wanted to see.

With an eerie sense of fatalism, Kit walked over to the door, his heart thundering and his stomach churning. He opened it and flinched at the gust of wind that whipped in.

Wearing some kind of waterproof top that didn't have any chance of standing up to the full force of a tropical storm, Lily was sopping wet and dripping onto the step. Her hair was plastered to her skull and her eyes were wild in the dim light of the afternoon. There was a tension gripping her body that drew him. Confused him. Made him wish he were wearing considerably more than just a towel.

Ignoring the disturbing effect she was having on him, he pulled her inside and then with some effort closed the door.

'What the hell are you doing out in this weather?' he growled, deliberately channelling his feelings of frustration and confusion into anger to stop himself from dragging her against him and in all likelihood getting a slap to the face. 'Are you insane?'

'Very probably,' she said with a shiver as she peeled her cagoule off.

He stepped forwards to take it from her and then, before the scent of her could get to him, wheeled off to hang it in the bathroom. He brought back a towel and handed it to her.

She rubbed her hair and all Kit could do was watch and wish he were doing it for her. With his brain a mess and his body a mass of tension and need he didn't trust himself to speak so instead he waited until she was done.

'I knocked for ages,' she said eventually, dropping the towel on the sofa and raking her fingers through her hair.

'I was taking a shower. I didn't hear you.'

'I apologise for the interruption.'

Kit frowned at the shakiness of her voice. It might be hot and humid outside but now he thought about it she sounded cold. Sort of numb.

And then it struck him like the lightning that was now flashing all around them that Lily had always been terrified of storms. At the first crack of thunder she'd always dived beneath the duvet, shivering and sweating and breathing far too fast. The only thing that had calmed her was taking her into his arms and letting her burrow right up against him until it was over.

'Are you all right?' he asked, the desire and frustration hammering through him making way for a thread of concern.

She blinked up at him. 'Of course I'm all right. Why wouldn't I be?'

'You hate storms.'

She stared at him. 'What?'

'You're terrified of them.'

'No, I'm not.'

'You used to be.'

'Oh. Well. Yes. But I saw someone,' she said, linking her hands and, he thought, for some reason holding on tightly. 'Did a course. Got over it.'

'You did a course?'

'Yes.'

'I didn't know that.'

'There are a lot of things that you don't know about me.'

'Clearly.' Such as… 'What are you doing here, Lily?'

For a moment she just looked him. Swallowed. Then pulled her shoulders back. 'OK, well, the thing is…' She paused then took a deep breath. 'The thing is, I want to know what's going on here, Kit.'

At her words Kit went very still and his brain went on high alert. 'What do you mean?'

'With us.'

Wasn't it obvious? He'd thought it was. But maybe it wasn't. His heart began to thump, though with what he didn't know. 'What do you think is going on?'

Lily blew out a breath and threw her hands in the air, as if some sort of dam had burst and she couldn't hold back any more. 'I don't have a clue, do I? First you're all "let me in we need to talk it's urgent" and pushing me up against a wall, next you're rushing halfway across the globe to come and find me, and now you couldn't be less interested. I don't understand it.'

Kit blinked as if he'd just been thumped in the chest. She thought he wasn't interested? Why would she think that when he'd gone overboard trying to show her just how interested in her he was? 'I'm interested,' he said roughly.

She rolled her eyes and crossed her arms beneath her breasts. 'Oh, yes, sure. In a brotherly kind of way.'

His jaw tightened and his eyes narrowed. What the hell? 'You think I'm being brotherly?'

'What else would you call it?' she said, jutting her chin up. 'The constant helping hand and all the buddy-buddy stuff. The sea-urchin-spine-vinegar thing. Not to mention this current seriously misplaced concern for my well-being.'

'Not brotherly,' he said tightly. 'Not brotherly in the slightest.'

'Then what is it?' she said, her cheeks pink and her chest heaving. 'Because it's driving me nuts. Completely nuts. I don't want your help, Kit, and I don't need your concern.'

Kit could feel the rush of blood to his head, the pounding of his heart. 'What do you need, Lily? What do you want?'

'What do you think?'

'Tell me.'

'OK, fine, I miss you.'

He went very still, every cell of his body hovering, waiting. 'We've spent the best part of the last four days together.'

'I miss your touch. I miss your nearness. I miss your kisses.'

'So what's the problem? Sexual frustration?'

'Damn right that's the problem,' she said, her eyes flashing and her breathing going all choppy. 'Partly. You owe me an orgasm.'

'Well, why didn't you say?'

'I'm saying it now.'

He took a step towards her, his eyes not leaving hers. 'Say it all,' he said.

'Everything?'

'Didn't you say that honesty was the best way to deal with this?'

She gulped. Her breath caught. 'These last few days have been hell, Kit.'

'In what way?'

'I want you so badly it's practically eating me up, while you…' She shrugged. 'You just don't seem to feel the same way.'

'I do.'

Her gaze snapped to his. 'You do?'

'Very much so.'

'So what has this all been about?'
'Me needing you to want it as much as I do.'
'I do,' she said, her voice breaking. 'I really do.'
There came a crash of thunder. 'Then show me.'

CHAPTER NINE

LILY DIDN'T NEED telling twice. After all the stress, the uncertainty and the tension that had been churning around inside her, the knowledge that Kit wanted her as much as she wanted him just about undid her, and with her heart pounding madly and heat flooding through her she flew into his embrace.

She threw her arms around his neck and plastered herself against him and held on for dear life as Kit whipped his arms round her waist and crashed his mouth down on hers.

His tongue delved into her mouth, sweeping over hers, tangling with hers, so fiercely, so desperately, that her knees nearly buckled.

As desire rocketed through her she pressed herself close and Kit pulled her even tighter, and she could feel the length of him beginning to harden against her abdomen.

He swept his hand up and buried it in her hair in a move that was so familiar it made her heart ache. Taking matters into her own hands and summoning up the courage to face him had been the best thing she could have done, and battling through torrential rain and gale-force winds, getting soaked, had been worth it. So worth it.

Because she'd missed this so much. Missed him so much. Pressing herself closer, Lily ran her hands down over his shoulders and then his back, tracing the contours of his muscles, feeling him tremble beneath her touch.

Then she reached the towel tied at his waist, and, filling with a longing she could barely contain, she tugged at it until it fell to the floor and he was naked. She dug her fingers into the muscles of his buttocks, pulling him closer and tilting her hips so she could rub herself against him.

Breaking off the kiss and breathing heavily, Kit stared down at her, his eyes hot and dark and glazed with desire, before dropping his hands to the hem of her top and pushing it up. She raised her arms to help him lift it off her and toss it to the floor. And then he was unzipping her skirt and tugging it down together with her knickers and she was stepping out of both and kicking off the trainers she'd donned to make the wet, sandy journey over here.

Pulling her back into his arms, and capturing her mouth with his once again, Kit manoeuvred her round until the backs of her knees hit the edge of the bed and down she went. She fell back onto the soft mattress and he came down on top of her, taking her wrists and pinning her arms to the bed as he kissed her.

She moaned and wriggled but he didn't release her. Instead he tore his mouth from hers and as she panted and gasped for breath he began trailing kisses down her neck and over the slope of her left breast until his mouth closed over her nipple and she couldn't help but abandon all attempts to free herself.

Beneath the force of the electricity and sheer wanton need that was shooting through her, her brain virtually melted and she stopped struggling and simply gave into revelling in the heaven he was taking her to.

Kit moved down her body, his mouth scorching her skin wherever it travelled, until he reached the hot, wet centre of her and she gasped at the heat of his breath over her.

He let go of her wrists, which should have given her the opportunity to touch him the way she'd been so desperate to, but then he was holding her hips still and slowly lowering his head to her and she was going so dizzy with desire that all she could do was clutch at the sheet.

'Hey,' she said softly, hoarsely, trying to make light of what potentially was so overwhelmingly powerful that she feared there might be no going back. 'I thought *I* was supposed to be showing *you* how much I wanted this.'

Instantly stilling, Kit lifted his head, looked up at her and murmured, 'You were. On the other hand, as you so perceptively pointed out, I owe you an orgasm.'

'There is that,' she said dazedly, her mouth dry and her blood roaring in her ears.

'But it's your call.'

As if she were going to stop him now. As if she could move anyway. As if she even wanted to. 'I think I'd better just shut up.'

'Good decision.'

And, boy, it was. As Kit returned his attention to the hot, wet centre of her her eyes fluttered closed and her body vibrated with the sensations rocketing through her.

When his tongue touched her clitoris she arched off the bed with a soft groan. He sucked. Licked. Slid one finger, then another, into her and gently, achingly slowly moved them inside her. Expertly building the tension inside her, knowing exactly how to, speeding up and slowing down until she thought she'd go mad with either desire or frustration.

She moaned. Cried out in desperation. Began to pant and writhe and was practically on the point of begging when Kit combined the licking and the sucking with a clever twist of his fingers and the tight ball of tension deep inside her exploded. And then she was spiralling out of control, hurtling into oblivion and splintering into a billion tiny pieces as she convulsed and clenched around his fingers with his name on her lips.

'That certainly evened up the score,' she mumbled, once

the tremors had subsided, her vision had cleared and she'd got her breath back.

He pushed himself up and took his weight on his elbows as he looked down at her. 'Good.'

'I want more.'

'Demanding.'

She shot him a wicked smile. 'Oh, you have no idea.'

'I'm intrigued.'

'I still need to show you how much I want this. And you.'

'Then what are you waiting for?'

'Absolutely nothing,' she said, curling a leg around his hip and rolling him onto his back.

Straddling his hips, she leaned forwards to kiss him and, taking him in one hand, positioned him and, unable to wait any longer, sank down.

He groaned into her mouth and she gasped at the feel of him stretching her, filling her, so tight, so deep. He began to move but she stilled him.

'Wait,' she said.

'What?'

'Patience, my darling.'

'Not one of my virtues. Although I must say I've astounded myself this last week.'

'Really?'

'Like you wouldn't believe. Not as much as you're astounding me now though.'

'You like this?' she said teasingly.

'I always did. You know that.'

'Me too.'

He reared up then and, clamping one hand to the back of her neck, the other to her hip, held her close. She could feel his heart thudding against her. Inside her. And then unable to help herself she began to move. Rocking slowly against him, rolling her hips forwards as he thrust up.

The rain continued to pound the roof and the terrace, and sweat coated her skin as the heat inside her grew.

Kit brought her head forwards, caught her mouth with his, and she clutched at his shoulders, barely able to stand the pleasure coursing through her. She whimpered. He moaned and she felt the tension, the desperation clawing at her.

'God, Lily,' he said, breaking the kiss for a moment, his breathing harsh and fast and his face tight.

'I know.' She was trembling so much, feeling so much she thought she might burst with the pressure of it.

'I love you,' he said quietly, looking deep into her eyes.

'I love you too.'

And then his grip on her tightened and he was moving harder and faster and she was grinding down onto him and then with one last powerful thrust he buried himself deep inside her. She felt him pulsate and throb, and the vibrations and the words he groaned into her ear tipped her over the edge, her body erupting in ecstasy.

Lying on the sun lounger and gazing up at the canopy of stars with Lily snuggled between his legs, her head resting on his shoulder, both of them wrapped in his sheets, Kit thought it was kind of hard to believe that only a couple of hours ago he'd been considering jacking it all in with her.

At one point he'd been about as low as he could be but now, after the craziest, best afternoon he'd had in years, there were possibilities. Infinite possibilities.

Just as the storm had cleared the heavy tropical air of dust and heat, leaving everything clean and fresh, they'd cleared the air of the doubt and frustration that had lain between them.

Now he and Lily had the chance to make a new start, and he intended to take full advantage of the fact that those doors were no longer merely ajar but wide open.

'Have you really been thinking about this for the last four days?' Lily murmured, cutting into his thoughts as she gently ran her fingers along his forearm, which lay across her beneath her breasts.

'Pretty much every second.'

'I never guessed.'

'Nor I about you.'

'What a lot of time we've wasted.'

Her words held a note of regret and he smiled faintly. 'I don't think so.'

She tilted her head back and round to glance up at him. 'No?'

'Well, put it this way, if we'd done this days ago we'd never have seen or done half the things we have. In all likelihood we wouldn't have left the villa.'

'That's true.'

'I'd never have learnt how good you are at fishing.'

'That was just beginner's luck.'

'We wouldn't have seen the Madagascar anemonefish.'

'We wouldn't. And it was incredible. Still, I'm pretty sure I'd rather have been doing this.'

She had a point. 'Good to see our ability to communicate is as strong as ever,' he said.

'Yeah.'

'When did we get so bad at reading each other?' he murmured, idly stroking his fingers through her hair and feeling her shiver.

'You have to ask?'

He grimaced in the dark. 'Not really.'

More of a gradual descent than a sudden drop, it had started at around the time of the third failed cycle of IVF, he knew. They'd had such hopes. Dashed once again. Unable to deal with the devastating disappointment, Lily had withdrawn into herself, slowly turning into someone he didn't recognise, and as he hadn't had a clue how to help her he'd spent more and more time at work, telling himself he needed to do it in order to move on and up, but, more likely, subconsciously wanting to avoid her, the situation and the disintegration of their relationship.

'Anyway,' she said, pulling him back, 'I think the last couple of hours proved that we've rediscovered the art.'

They had indeed. Their bodies instinctively recognised each other. Moved together as if they'd never been apart. He remembered what she liked with barely any effort of thought and she remembered what drove him wild.

A gentle gust of wind ruffled her hair and he felt it slide against his fingers like silk. 'I like this,' he said.

'My hair?'

'It suits you short.'

'Thank you.'

'When did you change it?'

'Years ago.'

'A new start?'

'Something like that.'

'Why did you never remarry, Lily?'

At his question, Lily went still, tensed a little, then relaxed in the kind of way that felt as if it had taken some effort. 'Oh, I don't know,' she said lightly. Too lightly, he thought. 'Once bitten, twice shy, maybe.'

'That's all?'

Where the question had come from Kit had no idea, but now it was out there he was rather interested, rather hoping she'd admit that she'd never truly got over him.

She sighed. 'No. Not really.'

'Then why?'

'I never met anyone.'

'Seriously?' He found that rather hard to believe. Lily was gorgeous. Fun. Successful. He'd have thought she'd have been snapped up within weeks. Was very glad she hadn't.

'To be more accurate I suppose I never let myself meet ~~anyone~~,' she said, twining her fingers through his. 'At least ~~anyone~~ I could be properly interested in.'

'I gue~~ss~~ed, unable to work that out. 'What do you ship would put ~~me~~ ~~...~~ ~~ed~~ a deep and meaningful relation-didn't—don't—ever wa~~nt~~ ~~vulner~~able position or something. I could lead to the kind of pain an~~d~~ situation again which tion I went through with you. Does that ~~the~~ ~~...~~ and desola-~~...~~ ~~...~~ sense whatsoever?'

'More than it should. So what are you saying? You've been celibate all these years?'

'No, of course not,' she said with a soft laugh that clearly didn't take into consideration the jealousy lancing through him at the thought of her with other men. 'I've been out with guys. Nice guys. Had flings and things. But none of them involved the earth-moving, mind-shattering, fireworks-and-explosions kind of sex we had. It was more a case of the scratching of an itch. Which suited me just fine at the time.'

'But not now?'

She turned her head and smiled up at him. 'What do you think?'

Kit thought that she was never having sex—good or bad—with anyone else ever again.

'Anyway, what about you?' she said. 'Why haven't you ever remarried? You always did want children and it can't have been for lack of opportunity.'

'It wasn't.'

'Silly me for asking.'

The trace of jealousy in her voice made him smile. 'But every relationship I've attempted tended to be hampered by the problem you solved on New Year's Eve.'

'Your impotence?'

He winced. 'Ouch. Do you have to?'

'Sorry,' she said, not sounding sorry at all. 'What ⸳
you call it?'

'A temporary psychological problem to ᵉ years.'
issues relating to intimacy.'

'Not all that temporary if it we⸳

'No.'

'And that sounds lik⸳⸳ ⸳⸳g a therapist would say.'

'It was.'

Shifting ⸳⸳⸳ ⸳⸳is embrace, she sat up and turned round
to ⸳⸳⸳⸳ at him, surprise written all over her face. 'You saw
a therapist?'

'I did.'

'But it didn't help?'

'Nothing did.'

'That must have been frustrating.'

'You have no idea.'

'Well, now you're cured you can go back and take your
pick.'

Kit looked at her thoughtfully. 'I could,' he said eventually. 'But I won't.'

She went very still, not taking her eyes off him for a
second. 'Oh?'

'Because this—us—isn't just sex, is it?'

'I don't think so,' she said, so softly it came out as almost a whisper. 'I've spent the entire last week remembering why I fell in love with you.'

'Ditto.'

'And now I think the real reason that I've never really
had a proper relationship since us is that despite everything I tried to tell myself I never fell out of love with you.'

'And I think that the problem I had with sex, which I
always thought was to do with the guilt I carried at having
that one-night stand, was down to the fact that I never fell
out of love with you.'

She tilted her head, a faint smile playing at her lips. 'What a pair we are.'

They could be a formidable pair, thought Kit. A great pair. And if only she gave him the chance to prove it, he'd devote the rest of his life to making up for what he'd done to her and to them. He took a deep breath, his heart hammering so wildly he could feel it banging against his ribs. 'Lily?'

'Yes?'

'What would you say to us trying again?'

Despite the fact that somewhere in the back of her mind Lily had been expecting something like this, she still had to bite back the 'yes' that was trying to tumble out of her mouth, and she still had to clamp down on the urge to throw herself against him and smother him in kisses.

Because while she'd thought about it quite a lot this afternoon, and fantasised about it before that more than she cared to admit, the reality of them wasn't some kind of fairy tale. It wasn't all hearts and roses, lost love found and a blissful happy ever after.

Once upon a time it had been painful, heartbreaking and soul-destroying. Now it was messy and filled with memories and experiences that were not, perhaps, conducive to a healthy, functional relationship.

So while on one level the idea that they got back together was the best thing she'd heard in ages, on another she had so many doubts and fears about what would happen if they did that she held back.

Ignoring her heart, which was remembering he'd said he loved her, Lily listened to her head, which was insisting she proceed with caution, and sighed. 'I don't know, Kit.'

He frowned, his smile fading. 'What don't you know? You know I love you.'

'And I love you. But we were in love last time and look

what happened. What makes you think it would work this time round?'

'We've changed.'

'Enough?'

'I think so.'

He was right. They had. But still… 'Some things haven't though.'

'Like what?'

'Like the children you've always wanted,' she said, and steeled herself for the dull ache that throbbed through her. Not quite the sharp pain it had been because she'd come to terms with it now, but nevertheless it still hurt a little. 'That's not going to happen with me, because I really don't think I could go through the whole IVF thing again.'

Three rounds had been quite enough and she never again wanted to experience the hope and the despair that the procedures had aroused in her. Never again wanted to be reminded of the pain and devastation of her ectopic pregnancy and her resultant infertility.

'There are other options,' he said, watching her closely.

'Adoption?'

He'd suggested that once before, just after she'd found out that the third round of treatment hadn't worked, and at the time she'd been feeling so like she'd failed in her evolutionary role on the planet, and so unable to believe that he could have brought it up at that time, that she'd yelled at him that he was unthinking and unfeeling and wholly insensitive if he thought that adopting could make up for holding their own child in her arms.

But now, though, she could see that it was an option. The only one they had really.

'We could think about it,' he said. 'At some point. Or not. Whatever you want. I'd rather have you and no children than a family with anyone else. I always did.'

Ignoring the warmth that swept through her at that, Lily

said quietly, 'You say that now, but what if you change your mind?'

'I won't.'

'You might.'

'Trust me.'

'And that's another thing,' she said, frowning as yet another thing to worry about should she agree to try things again flew into her head. 'How do I know I *can* trust you? How do I know that when things get tough, when I go all weird and withdrawn, as I'm bound to from time to time, you won't go and find comfort with someone else?'

He reached out and took her into his arms. Pulled her round and back into him, nestling her head beneath his chin. 'Because we'll talk,' he said against her hair as he held her tight. 'Communicate.'

'Do you think we can?'

'I'll make sure we do. I won't let us not.'

Lily watched a shooting star dart across the sky and felt her heart skip a tiny beat. 'Is it really that simple?'

'It could be if we take things one day at a time.'

At the sincerity in his voice and with the warmth and heat of his body wrapped round her Lily found herself hovering.

Could they make a go of it? Get it right this time? Kit did make it sound simple. And out here, in the velvety isolation of the night, tucked away in their own little bubble, it seemed as if anything was possible.

But what would it be like when they got back to London? Back to life? Real life. Would they be able to navigate the obstacles of their relationship as well as two busy careers? Not to mention manage the expectations of family and friends. Did they have the strength? The commitment? Did they really have the ability to be open and honest when experience suggested otherwise?

'Look, Lily, I'm not saying it won't be hard,' he said

quietly, as if able to read her mind. 'I don't think we're always going to have an easy ride. All I know is that I love you and if I do by some miracle get you back I'll do my damnedest to make it work.'

At the quiet conviction of his words and with the beat of his heart strong and steady beneath her shoulder she could feel herself falling. 'I'd need honesty.'

'You'd have it.'

'Always?'

'Always. And I won't give you any reason not to be able to trust me. Ever.'

'Really?'

'I promise.'

And just like that down she went, head over heels into a future with him. 'All right,' she whispered with her heart in her throat. 'Let's do it.'

CHAPTER TEN

'You look happy.'

Lily dropped her bag on her desk, sat down in her chair and gave her sister a smile that was wide and bright and at the moment pretty much permanent. 'I am.'

And she was. Because despite her misgivings, the last couple of months had been wonderful. Better than she could ever have imagined. And so much fun that every time she thought about the five years she and Kit had been apart she found herself shaking her head in amazement that she'd actually thought she'd been fine.

She hadn't been fine, she could see now. She'd been coasting. Simply existing as the days rolled endlessly by, and living her life in black-and-white. And despite a great social life and her fabulous family, she'd been so very, very lonely.

In contrast, since they'd returned from the Indian Ocean she felt as if she were on fire. She woke up every morning raring to go, brimming with a fizzing sort of energy she could barely contain. The days now whizzed by in glorious Technicolor, the nights were hot and heavy with passion and she'd never felt less lonely or more convinced that choosing to give them a second shot had been the best decision she'd ever made.

Not that everyone thought so. Her parents, for example, had been extremely wary, not wanting to burst her bubble of happiness yet unable to refrain from suggesting proceeding with caution. But that was only natural given that they'd seen the wreck she'd been when she and Kit had parted.

And while most of her friends had been carefully congratulatory, others, who'd also witnessed her falling apart, told her she was mad and wanted to know how she was able to trust him, to which she would shrug and say she just did.

The only person who seemed genuinely delighted was Zoe, who was so loved-up at the moment and so wrapped up in wedding plans that she was delighted by pretty much everything these days.

'Happier than usual, now I come to think of it,' said Zoe, dragging Lily out of her musings and back to the office where she was supposed to be picking up information for her imminent meeting.

'That's entirely possible,' said Lily, reaching for the folder she needed that was lying on her desk and putting it in her bag-cum-briefcase.

'What's happened?'

She zipped her bag. 'Kit asked me to move in with him.'

'And?'

'I agreed.'

Zoe blew out a breath. 'Wow.'

'I know. Great, isn't it? Although I suggested he move in with me. I mean, he lives in a hotel. I rattle round a four-bedroomed house.'

'And he was all right with that?'

Lily nodded and swivelled to her computer to quickly check where she was going. 'Seems to be,' she said, pulling up the maps page and entering the postcode. 'I mean, he has most of his stuff there already and it's not like we haven't done it before. I already know his bad habits and of course I don't have any.'

Zoe grinned. 'Of course you don't. So when does he move in?'

'Next weekend.' And she couldn't wait.

'Things are going well, then?'

'Yup.'

'I'm glad. You know, I always liked him.'

'Did you?' asked Lily, glancing up at her sister and shooting her a quick smile. 'Because I seem to remember you once saying that hanging, drawing and quartering was too good for him.'

Zoe waved a dismissive hand. 'That was years ago in response to a very specific circumstance. Things are different now.'

'They are,' she agreed, thinking that they were different indeed.

For one thing they'd already been through more stuff than most people had to deal with in a lifetime of marriage, and had come through. For another *they* were different. This time round they were their own people. They weren't wrapped up in each other to the exclusion of everyone else, as she'd realised they had been before. They were more mature, more settled, more grounded. Their relationship was now more adult. In more ways than one, she thought, drifting off for a very happy moment to remember some of the new tricks she and Kit had tried in the bedroom, the bathroom, the kitchen…

'Dan likes him too,' said Zoe, snapping Lily out of her delightful little reverie.

'The feeling's entirely mutual.'

Her ex-husband and her future brother-in-law had got on like a house on fire when they'd first met. Now they played squash together on a pretty regular basis, which was faintly weird, although great.

'So what have you got lined up for today?'

Lily sat back, her smile deepening. 'We're going on a date. Kit's off to Rome tomorrow to check out a site for a new hotel so he's taking me to this brand-new restaurant that's opened just around the corner from home. It's very cool and very difficult to get a table.' But he'd done it. For her.

Zoe grinned and rolled her eyes. 'I meant *today* today. As in workwise.'

Lily blushed. 'Of course you did. I knew that.' Determinedly stamping out the heat whipping through her, she pulled herself together and switched into business mode because, honestly, it was high time she stopped feeling like a giggly teenager in the grip of her first crush. 'I have a meeting across town. New client. Very big. Very important. Could be huge for us.' She glanced at her watch. 'In fact, I'd better get going.'

Filling with the familiar buzz she got whenever she pitched for new business, Lily stood up, grabbed her bag and hitched her handbag over her shoulder.

'Good luck,' said Zoe.

'Thanks.'

'Let me know how it goes.'

'I will.'

Sitting in a plush office in London's West End, Lily watched John Burrows, the director of marketing for what was going to be their most high-profile client to date, sign on the dotted line, and mentally punched the air in triumph.

It hadn't been an easy sale. He'd asked tough questions, demanded a lot of information and had driven an extremely hard bargain. At one point she'd thought her pitch had been about to unravel from the sheer pressure of it, but she'd held her nerve, conceded the points she was willing to concede and stood her ground on the ones she wasn't, and eventually they'd reached an agreement.

And now, she thought, smiling as he slid the document back for her to sign, she felt as if she were floating along in some kind of a fabulous narcotic-induced haze. Only she

was high on adrenalin, success, life and love, not drugs.
Her relationship was blooming, business was booming and
frankly, she thought, adding her own signature beside his,
it was pretty hard to see how things could get any better.

'We look forward to doing business with you,' she said,
standing and holding out her hand with a smile.

John Burrows gave it a quick, firm shake and then let
it go. 'Likewise.'

'Just out of interest,' she asked, putting the precious
document away, 'how did you hear about us?'

'You were recommended.'

A wave of satisfaction and pride swept through her, tangling with everything else that was rolling around inside
her and making it a pretty crowded place. Word of mouth
was often the way they got clients, and it was good to know
that they were still rated highly. 'Who by? If you don't
mind saying.'

'I don't mind saying at all. It was Kit Buchanan.'

'Oh?' said Lily, her eyebrows lifting a little in surprise
because Kit hadn't mentioned it. 'How do you know him?'

'I don't,' said John. 'But my wife does.'

'Really?' she asked with a smile. 'How?'

'Paula works with him. She does some of his PR from
time to time. She asked him if he might know of anyone
who might be able to help with what I was looking for and
he suggested you.'

At the mention of PR in connection with Kit, Lily's blood
chilled, all the good stuff draining away and leaving nothing but a hard, cold lump in her stomach. A tremor ran
through her and her memory took her right back to the
night he'd stumbled in in the early hours after that work
night out and had confessed to having just slept with someone who'd worked in the PR department of the hotel where
he was working.

A cold sweat broke out all over her skin and her throat

tightened and for a moment she went dizzy at the sickening thought that Kit still saw the woman he had a one-night stand with.

And then she gave herself a shake and got a grip. She was overreacting. Being absurd. Irrational. Seeing a coincidence where it was highly unlikely that there was one because thousands of people worked in PR, and probably more than half of them were women.

Besides, if Kit had recommended *her* and they'd only been back together for a couple of months, then the chances were that Paula Burrows had only started working with Kit recently.

And finally, Kit would have told her if he actually now worked with the woman he'd cheated on her with, wouldn't he? Of course he would, because he'd promised her honesty and openness and had said he'd never give her any reason not to be able to trust him.

She believed him so she had nothing to worry about. Nothing to fear. She should give him the benefit of the doubt, attribute her bizarre reaction to John's news to her pathetic insecurities and leave it.

Lily left it for the ten minutes it took to wrap things up with her new client and walk to the lift and then the three she spent zooming down twenty-five storeys to the ground floor. She left it for the two minutes she needed to cross the lobby and walk out of the door, and the next two it took to cross the road and enter the garden square.

She left it, in fact, until she was sitting on a bench in the early spring sunshine, digging around in her handbag for her phone and inwardly cursing herself for being so pitifully weak and insecure that she had to check out Paula Burrows for sure.

But what else could she do? she thought, finally locating her phone and hauling it out. For the last five of the seventeen minutes since the suspicion had taken root in her brain she'd been itching to do something about it because she'd realised somewhere between the fifteenth and fourteenth floors that in this case ignorance wasn't bliss. In this case ignorance was a bitch and she'd far rather be in possession of the facts, whatever they turned out to be.

After a couple of taps on the tiny screen of her smart-phone Lily typed in 'Paula Burrows' along with 'PR' and the name of Kit's company.

And up she popped.

With her heart in her throat, Lily braced herself and scrolled through the woman's CV, bypassing the profes-sional qualifications and industry awards until she got to the employment section.

The woman who might or might not have slept with her husband had had an impressive career so far. She'd been working for Kit's PR company for two years. Prior to that she'd worked at another top ten agency. And prior to *that* she'd worked in the PR department at the Brinkley Hotel Group. As had Kit. At the same time.

Which didn't automatically mean that they'd slept to-gether, Lily told herself, frantically trying to cling onto logic as she fought not to hyperventilate, because presum-ably this Paula Burrows, or Barnes as she'd been then, hadn't been the only woman in the company's PR depart-ment.

But nor did it mean they hadn't, she thought, beginning to lose the battle with her breathing and logic. And if by horrible coincidence Kit did now work with the woman he'd had a one-night stand with and hadn't told her, what did it mean? What was going on?

She didn't know. A mere half an hour ago she'd been so certain about everything to do with her and Kit and their fabulous burgeoning relationship, but now with her head pounding with questions and doubts and her grip on her self-control rapidly disintegrating she suddenly didn't know anything any more.

All she did know was that she couldn't go back to the office and face Zoe's inevitable questions and relentless cheerfulness. Not while her thoughts were such a mess and the emotions she was struggling to keep in check were threatening to spill over.

So with a couple of taps and a quick swipe she found Zoe's number and hit the dial button.

'Hey,' came Zoe's cheerful voice down the line.

'Hi,' said Lily, her own voice sounding thick and croaky as if she hadn't used it in years.

'How did it go?'

'Good. We got it.'

'Great. Well done you. I'll put the champagne on ice.'

Lily lifted a hand to her pounding temple and closed her eyes because the last thing she felt like doing right now was celebrating. 'I think I might head home.'

There was a pause. 'Are you all right?'

'Fine. Just a bit of a headache, that's all.'

'Sure? You sound rough.'

'I feel it. But I'm sure I'll be fine in a bit.' Which was a lie because she couldn't imagine feeling fine any time soon.

'OK, well, try to rest.'

'I will.' Not.

'And I'll see you tomorrow.'

'See you tomorrow,' she echoed dully, and hung up.

In something of a daze she stumbled out of the park and hailed a taxi, and when it screeched to a halt gave the driver her address and climbed in.

She didn't notice much about the journey home. Her head was swirling too fast and her stomach was churning too violently.

What should she do about what she might or might not have just discovered? Should she confront Kit? Summon up her courage and ask him outright to clarify things? And whatever his response, should she bite the bullet and ask all those questions about the woman he'd betrayed her with that she'd been in too much of a state to ask at the time but had secretly wanted to ask for weeks—or years, if she was being honest?

Or should she just leave it?

Because she could well be getting the wrong end of the stick here. It could be a coincidence. He could have had the one-night stand with someone else in the PR department. And did she really want to bring the past up? Did she really want to know all the sordid details of what had happened five years ago? For what could possibly be no reason at all other than to satisfy her morbid curiosity?

No, she didn't, she thought firmly as the taxi pulled up outside her house and she got out, handed over a couple of notes and told the driver to keep the change. So she'd leave well alone. Put it to the back of her mind. Forget about it.

Things between her and Kit were good. Better than good. The searing—and probably wholly unnecessary—jealousy would fade. As would the hurt stabbing at her heart. With a bit of effort she could bury the doubt. And in a jiffy she would be back to normal.

Anyway, Kit was going away tomorrow and they had a lovely evening planned, and she wasn't going to rock this boat for anything.

CHAPTER ELEVEN

SOMETHING WAS UP, thought Kit, frowning to himself as he stood back to let Lily into the lift that would zoom them up to his suite. She'd been quiet throughout dinner. Pensive, monosyllabic and weirdly distant.

Given she'd just landed a huge deal, and considering she'd been aching to go to that restaurant since it had opened, her demeanour was unusual, disconcerting. He'd pulled strings and had managed to get a highly sought-after table at relatively short notice, and while he didn't need her gratitude a bit of enthusiasm would have been nice.

And not just about either the restaurant or the deal.

She'd been so excited when he asked her what she thought about moving in together, and so up for it, he'd found her excitement infectious. Earlier this evening, though, when he'd brought it up and made a joke about having to change the habit of a lifetime and start putting the lid back on the toothpaste she'd barely responded. Admittedly the joke hadn't exactly been side-splittingly hilarious but it hadn't even raised a roll of the eyes, and he found the change in her faintly disturbing.

So what was wrong? Was it something to do with work? Zoe? Him? And what was he going to do about it?

The doors swooshed open and as Lily went ahead of him into his open-plan living area, dropping her bag onto a chair and then shrugging out of her coat, for a moment he considered giving her time. Waiting until she sorted it out in her head and then either told him what was up or moved on.

And then he dismissed it.

No, he thought, setting his jaw and striding over to the cupboard in the kitchen that stocked the drinks. He'd made that mistake before and he wasn't making it again. He wouldn't give her the chance to avoid him. Wouldn't let her deflect. Whatever was wrong they could deal with it because so far things between them had been going brilliantly, and he wouldn't let them screw it up.

It was probably nothing more than a blip in any case, he told himself, pouring a whisky for himself and a glass of red for her. Nothing they couldn't sort out together if only she'd let him in.

He slid the glass of wine across the breakfast bar towards her and then leaned back against the counter and looked at her. 'OK, Lily, so what's up?'

She glanced up at him, her eyes weirdly empty, and despite the warmth of his apartment he felt a tiny shiver race down his spine. 'Nothing's up.'

Yeah, right. 'Is it work?'

'Why would anything be up at work?' she asked, knocking back almost half her wine.

Kit frowned because downing alcohol as if she needed the fortification wasn't like her. 'You tell me.'

'Work's fine.'

'Zoe, then?'

'She's fine too.'

That really only left one other option, because he might be many things but he wasn't stupid enough to ask if it was the time of the month, and that option was him.

He took a breath and braced himself. 'What have I done?'

'You? Nothing.'

'Right.'

She shrugged and drank what was left of her wine. 'Forget it. It's late and you have an early start. So let's go to bed.'

Feeling his patience begin to drain, Kit put his glass down and fought to stay calm. 'For goodness' sake, Lily. Don't do this. Didn't we say we'd communicate? Talk? Be open with each other? So tell me what's wrong. Whatever it is, I can take it.'

For a moment there was nothing but silence and as he waited for her to respond he became oddly aware of the beat of his heart, the tingling of his skin. An odd sense of impending doom seeped into him and for the first time since they'd got back together again he felt a flicker of panic.

Then she nodded. Once, briefly, and he didn't know if he was glad she agreed to open up or petrified at what she was going to say because there was an odd stillness about her. An eerie kind of control. The sort of calm that came before a storm.

'OK, fine,' she said, her voice so chilling and her small smile so horribly tight that he began to sweat. 'You're right. You're absolutely right.'

He felt himself tensing and a sudden rush of adrenalin, as if his body was preparing for something, although God knew what. 'So?'

'I have a question for you.'

'Go ahead.'

'Is Paula Burrows the woman you screwed while our marriage was in its death throes?'

As her words echoed through his apartment and shock rocked through him Kit went very still. Of all the possible issues that had been going through his head this hadn't been one of them so where the hell had this suddenly sprung from?

'How did you find out about Paula?' he said with a frown, and then winced because that was the wrong *wrong* way to put it. He'd made it sound as if Paula were a dirty little secret when nothing could be further from the truth. 'I mean, how did you hear about her?'

'My meeting today was with her husband,' she said, still alarmingly calm although a bit paler than she'd been a minute ago. 'He said you'd recommended us.'

'That's right. I did. I'd forgotten.'

'You'd forgotten?' she echoed in disbelief.

'It was a while ago.'

'And the answer to my question?'

Kit swallowed hard and killed the temptation to lie because even though it would be the easy way out of this he hadn't lied to her yet and he didn't intend to start now. He'd promised her honesty and she'd get it, whatever the fallout. 'The answer is yes,' he said, and waited for her reaction, not knowing how the hell he was going to handle it.

Lily went very pale and was gripping the stem of her glass so tightly her knuckles were white. 'I see,' she said with a faint nod. 'So let me get this straight. You work with the woman you cheated on me with. You still see her. And you didn't think to tell me.'

Knowing that if he wasn't careful this conversation could go very badly very easily, Kit decided to stick to the unvarnished truth, however brutal. 'It didn't occur to me,' he said, and inwardly winced because it might be the truth but it sounded wholly inadequate.

Lily stared at him as if unable to believe her ears. 'It didn't occur to you?'

'No. She's worked on a handful of projects for us and I've seen her at the most half a dozen times in the last couple of years.'

'And what do you do when you do? Reminisce about old times?'

'Of course not,' he said, choosing to ignore her sarcasm and remain calm and focused because in the face of her evident anger that seemed the only way to get through this. 'It's just business.'

'But none of mine, it would seem.'

He heard the hurt and the bitterness in her voice and it made his heart contract, but what could he say to that? The truth was that he hadn't thought of Paula as the woman he'd slept with since the morning after that terrible night, when following his confession and the blazing row he'd had with Lily he'd gone into work, resigned on the spot and cleared his desk.

He hadn't thought to tell Lily about her because Paula genuinely hadn't crossed his mind once in the last eight weeks.

Now he wished he had. Now he wished he'd had time to prepare for this because if he had he might have anticipated Lily's anger and her hurt, he might have thought about her insecurities and doubts and how they might make her respond to this kind of news and he might have formulated a strategy to deal with it.

As it was he was navigating unfamiliar and extremely choppy waters and he didn't have a clue what he was doing and he now had the horribly panicky feeling that the longer he said nothing, the worse things were becoming.

'Your silence speaks volumes, Kit,' said Lily with a bitter laugh as she apparently read his mind. 'And you know what? You want communication? Well, this is the way I'm choosing to communicate, you jerk.' And with that, she hurled her glass at him.

With lightning reflexes Kit dodged to the left and the glass flew over his right shoulder, smashed against a cupboard behind him and shattered, and the sound of it jolted him out of paralysis.

She spun on her heel and marched off in the direction of her coat and bag, but within a second he caught up with her, grabbing her wrist and stopping her. She gasped in outrage and he could feel her pulse jumping beneath his fingers but he ignored both as he whirled her round to face him.

'Let me go,' she said fiercely, trying to pull free.

Not a chance, he thought grimly, because whatever happened he wasn't letting her go ever again and they could get through this. They could. As long as he didn't mess it up. 'Why? So you can run away?'

'So I can leave before I do you some serious damage,' she said, her eyes flashing at him.

'That's a risk I'm prepared to take.'

'Fool.'

'Probably. But you don't get to run away from this this time.'

'Well, you don't get to decide what I do.'

That was true, but he did get to decide what *he* did, and if he wanted to fix this he had to start with the honesty and openness he'd promised her. 'Ask me about her, Lily,' he said. 'Ask me anything.'

Lily stopped struggling and stilled. Blinked a couple of times, and he thought he saw some of her hostility ebb. 'Anything?'

He relaxed his hold on her a fraction, but she didn't step back. 'Anything.'

'What makes you think I'm interested?'

'Aren't you?'

There was a moment's silence and he could virtually see the internal battle she was fighting. 'OK, fine,' she said, lifting her chin in challenge. 'What does this Paula person look like?'

'Average.'

She shook her head and glared at him. 'Not good enough, Kit. Not nearly good enough.'

'I mean it. Brown hair. Blue eyes. Around five foot six, I guess. Not fat. Not thin. Really average.'

'And what was she like in bed?' she asked bluntly. 'Better than me? Worse than me? Hotter? Kinkier? More adventurous? More creative? The woman is in PR after all.' She flashed him a look. 'And if you say "average" again I'll thump you.'

Kit ignored the thought that he really didn't want to be having this conversation because he didn't have a choice. Her questions and the insecurities they revealed were natural and justified and he wouldn't ignore them any more than he'd judge them. 'I don't remember.'

Lily rolled her eyes. 'Oh, please.'

'I really don't. I was hammered out of my skull.'

'Then why her?'

'Because she was there.' Inwardly he cringed as for the first time in years the memory of that night flashed into his head, but he didn't take his eyes off hers. 'I was at rock-bottom and she was there.'

'Such a charmer.'

'You wanted honesty, you have it. I'm not proud of what I did, Lily.'

'Does she know you were using her?'

'Yes.'

'You told her?'

'We had a chat the first time she turned up at a project meeting.'

'Cosy.'

'Not particularly. It was awkward.'

'My heart bleeds.'

'Nothing's happened, Lily. Not since that night. And it won't. It was a mistake and we both are more than aware of that. If that doesn't convince you then how about the fact that I'm with you and she's married?'

'So what? That didn't stop *you*.'

'Happily.'

Lily flinched. 'You know her well enough to know that, do you?'

'I asked. We chatted. I apologised. She forgave me. We've moved on.'

He'd thought Lily had forgiven him too because hadn't she said she had way back when they'd first talked? But that clearly wasn't the case, and he'd been a fool not to see it.

He'd thought that their relationship had been going well, but the progress he'd naively assumed they'd made had been nothing more than superficial. Physically things couldn't be better. Emotionally, however, they were still rocky in a way he hadn't appreciated. But now he could see that beneath the surface there'd been an undercurrent of mistrust, and why wouldn't there be because, as he was beginning to realise, he wasn't the only one who had to constantly live with the knowledge of what he'd done.

And he might have nothing to feel guilty about, nothing to be ashamed of this time, but that didn't matter. It was because of what he'd done that Lily was feeling so insecure and hurt and if he wanted to hang on to her he was going to have to do a lot more than simply be open and honest. He was going to have to prove to her that she could trust him and how he was going to do that he had no idea.

Hell, if only he didn't have to go to Rome tomorrow, because he could really do with the time and headspace to think about this properly.

'I thought I had too,' said Lily quietly. 'But it seems I might not be as over all this as I'd thought.'

Kit felt his chest tighten. 'Is it a deal-breaker?'

She shrugged and sighed. 'I don't know.'

'Is there anything I can do to make it right?'

She looked up at him for a couple of long minutes, as if searching his face and eyes for sincerity, bit her lip and then frowned. 'You really want to make it right?' she said, her frown clearing as she pulled her shoulders back and lifted her chin in a way that had wariness trickling through him.

'Of course.'

'Then use another PR agency.'

As her ultimatum sank in Kit went still, his mind reeling and his heart sinking as he realised he'd been right to be wary because of all the things she could have asked of him she'd asked for the one thing he couldn't give her.

He got that this was some kind of test. He got that she wanted him to prove that he meant what he said. And he'd have done just about anything. But firing his PR agency? That he couldn't do. There was no way he was going to let something personal ruin a perfectly good business relationship. Certainly not one that had taken years to build up and now worked brilliantly for both parties.

'I can't do that, Lily.'

She stared up at him in disbelief. 'I thought you wanted to make this right?'

'I do. But not like that.'

'Why not?'

'Because they're the best in the business and we have an excellent relationship. And I can't let something personal get in the way of that.'

'OK, fine,' she said, with a small smile he didn't like one little bit. 'Then ask Paula to resign or switch to a different team or something.'

His heart sank further. 'I can't do that either.'

'Why not?'

'Because she's very good at her job and it would be grossly unfair. If not downright illegal.'

'I see,' she said coolly, but he didn't think she did. 'So you really won't fire them or get rid of her?'

'I won't.'

Lily pushed against his chest and took a step back. 'Then I really don't think there's anything else to be said, do you?'

CHAPTER TWELVE

THE FOLLOWING MORNING Lily stumbled in to work, late for the first time since she and Zoe had begun working together, but that wasn't hugely surprising since she'd only fallen asleep at dawn. She was feeling on edge and cranky and not just from lack of sleep.

'Morning,' said Zoe, looking up from her monitor and shooting her a smile. 'At last. I was beginning to worry.'

'Sorry.' Lily dumped her bag on her desk with rather more force than was necessary and then stalked over to the coffee machine.

'How are you feeling? Headache better?'

'What?' she muttered, stuffing an espresso capsule into the top and slamming the lid shut.

'Your headache,' said Zoe again, only a little slower. 'Is it better?'

'No.' Her head hurt like hell, but then it would given the half a bottle of wine she'd polished off when she'd got home last night.

'Are you sure you should be here, Lily?' said Zoe, concern evident in her voice. 'You look absolutely awful.'

'Gee, thanks,' said Lily, grabbing a cup, sticking it beneath the spout and pressing the button while thinking that however awful she looked it wasn't a patch on how awful she felt.

Last night, that scene with Kit, had been horrible, she

reflected with a shudder. So much for hoping that the unnecessary—she'd thought—jealousy would fade. And so much for being able to ignore the doubts she'd had in that garden square. All afternoon while she'd been sitting at home alone with her thoughts and practically climbing the walls, the jealousy and doubts had been growing, feeding rapaciously off her insecurities and her fears.

But she'd made herself calm down and by the time she'd joined Kit for dinner she'd thought she could contain the swell of emotion. Control it. Ignore it. Clearly she'd been mistaken because he'd pushed and prodded and poked until she hadn't been able to take any more and she'd exploded.

Right up until the point where he'd confirmed what she'd suspected she'd been willing to give him the benefit of the doubt. She'd totally been prepared to accept that she'd indulged her penchant for melodrama and overreacted.

In her heart of hearts she hadn't expected him to admit she was right. Deep down she'd hoped he'd deny it. Tell her she was being an idiot, that the coincidence was just that.

But when he'd confirmed it, well, that had been just awful. That had made a mockery of all the silken promises he'd given her on the island. The promises of the last two months. All that nonsense about honesty and openness and communication when he'd been lying to her from the very moment he'd barged his way back into her life. Or at the very least lying by omission and not telling her something he should have realised she'd want to know.

Once she'd got over the shock of it she'd been so, *so* angry. So deeply hurt and fiercely disappointed and so rocked by the realisation that despite what she'd told him, despite what she'd thought, she evidently hadn't forgiven him for what he'd done, she'd lost control. And that was why she'd done what she'd done and said what she'd said.

Back at home and in bed, her head churning, she'd hardly slept a wink. With time and distance in which to think more objectively than she'd been able to at the time, and with the anger and hurt fading, she'd found herself hating the way she and Kit had argued, wishing she'd held back, wishing she'd been under better control, wishing she hadn't let her emotions get the better of her. Above all she wished she hadn't given into the need to test his commitment to them by issuing that awful, hugely unfair ultimatum.

'No, seriously, Lily,' said Zoe worriedly, 'you don't look well at all.'

'I'm fine.'

'No, you're not. What's happened?'

'I'm hung-over, that's all.'

'Big night?'

'You could say that.'

'How was the restaurant?'

'The restaurant was fine.' The food had been divine. The atmosphere, however, had been positively frosty and things had gone downhill from there.

'And how's Kit?' asked her sister, zeroing in on the trouble with a precision born from experience.

'I haven't a clue.'

'What happened?'

'The honeymoon's over.' She wasn't sure the whole thing wasn't over and her heart actually physically hurt at the thought.

There was a pause while Zoe absorbed this news. 'Huh?'

'We had a row.'

'About what?'

The machine having done its job, Lily lifted the cup and took it back to her desk. 'Remember the one-night stand he had?' she said, sitting down and wrapping her hands round it as if the heat might give her the strength to relive the horrors of last night's scene.

'How could I forget?'

'It turns out she works with him.'

Zoe's jaw dropped and her eyebrows shot up. 'No,' she breathed.

'Yes.'

Taking advantage of her sister's astonishment and speechlessness Lily sipped her coffee and filled her in on the details of how she'd found out.

'What did you do?' said Zoe, once Lily had finished her rundown.

'Lost it.'

'I'm not surprised.'

'I threw a wine glass at him.'

Zoe winced. 'Full?'

'Empty.'

'Classy.'

'I know,' said Lily with a sigh. 'Not exactly my finest moment.'

'I'd say you had provocation, and look on the bright side—it could have been worse.'

'How?'

'You could have taken a key to his car, scissors to his suits and emailed his backers.'

'There is that,' said Lily with a grimace. 'And at least I didn't bottle it all up as usual.'

'You certainly didn't.' Zoe shook her head. 'But, Lil, that ultimatum... Really?'

'I know,' said Lily glumly. 'It was wholly unreasonable. Grossly unfair. I shouldn't have done it. I'm mortified that I did, but I wasn't exactly thinking clearly.'

'So what happens now? Are the two of you over?'

She'd asked herself the same thing all through the night, but still didn't have an answer. 'I don't know,' she said, filling with a deep ache. 'I hope not because I know I overreacted and that it was a heat-of-the-moment kind of thing. Paula Burrows isn't the problem. Kit and I are. Me in particular.'

'Has he called?'

Lily shook her head a bit too vigorously, and despite the coffee her head started pounding again. 'No. And I'm not sure he will.'

'Why on earth not?'

'I think I owe him an apology,' she said, rubbing her temples and grimacing.

'It sounds like he owes you one too.'

'Possibly.'

'So what's stopping you from calling him?'

'He's in Rome.'

'And?'

'It's not the sort of conversation I want to have over the phone. There may be grovelling. From me at least. And it's not going to be pretty.'

Zoe shot her a smile. 'In that case,' she said, 'don't you think the phone sounds rather perfect?'

Zoe was right, thought Lily as she unlocked her front door after getting home from work and went inside. What was wrong with apologising and possibly grovelling over the phone? Nothing. Her blushes, and Kit's, would be spared, and actually it was the only option she had because frankly she didn't think her nerves could stand another night like last night.

She dumped her bag on the floor and hung her coat up and glanced at her watch. In fact she'd do it right now. Strike while the iron was hot and all that. It was seven o'clock, eight in Rome. Too late for a meeting or a site visit, surely. Kit would be having supper. A drink. Working in his hotel room, perhaps.

Maybe even waiting to hear from her.

Brightening a bit at that, she went into the kitchen and poured herself some wine—her hangover having been taken care of earlier by three more espressos and two bags of crisps—then picked up her phone.

Tapping it against her mouth, she wandered into the sitting room and settled herself on the sofa. Right. So. What was she going to say? And how was she going to say it?

Ten minutes later, Lily had a strategy of sorts and a few points jotted down so that she didn't forget them, and she was more than ready to apologise, grovel and do whatever else Kit asked of her. She also had an empty glass of wine and cheeks red with embarrassment at the memory of how she'd behaved last night but that was fine because he wasn't going to get to see either.

With her heart in her mouth she picked up the phone and dialled his mobile. Which went straight through to voicemail without ringing. She hung up. Tried again. But the same thing happened so she left a message asking him to call her when he had a chance. And then texted.

Trying to keep a lid on a simmering sense of frustration, next she tried the hotel he'd told her he was staying at. But there was no answer from his room there either, and the reception desk couldn't help.

Out of ideas, Lily put the phone on the coffee table. Then sat back and frowned as she felt herself sort of deflate. She'd made notes, dammit. Thought about this at length and in detail. She'd also summoned up quite a lot of her courage to call, and after such a build-up the let-down was huge. She felt oddly cheated. And just the teensiest bit put out because after all the lengths—the emotional ones especially—she'd gone to to contact him, the least he could do was be there to listen to what she had to say.

So where was he? Who was he with? What was he doing? And should she be worried?

Of course she shouldn't be worried, she told herself sternly. He was probably out. Or in the shower. The battery of his mobile might be flat. Or he might be somewhere where he didn't get a signal.

On the other hand, their argument last night had been pretty hum-dinging, and she had been kind of unreasonable and irrational, so could she have driven him into the arms of another woman? Someone comforting and amenable, not argumentative and melodramatic.

Lily went cold and her heart slowed right down as her head swam at the thought of Kit with someone else. And then she blinked, gave herself a quick shake and pulled herself together. No. She was being ridiculous. That wasn't at all likely.

Was it?

No. No. No.

They'd had one argument. Big deal. Millions of couples across the globe did. All the time. More often probably. It was normal. Nothing to worry about. She just needed to relax, that was all. Get a sense of perspective. Not leap to wholly unlikely conclusions based on her massive insecurities.

There was bound to be a perfectly rational explanation for why Kit wasn't answering his phone. Absolutely bound to be.

Stifling a yawn because now that he was done for the day the exhaustion he'd been holding at bay since he'd got up this morning was pouring through him like a tidal wave, Kit climbed the steps from the basement restaurant where he'd had dinner and then left his colleagues ordering more drinks, and checked his phone.

Two missed calls. One message. One text. All from Lily.

The desire to call her had been needling him all day. He'd felt the urge to talk to her hammering away in the back of his mind throughout the site visit and the meetings that had taken up the rest of the day. But he'd been unable to do either because he'd barely had a moment to himself to think, let alone work out what he wanted to say to her and how to say it.

Now he did, but it was late. Nearly midnight here and therefore eleven in London. He ought not to disturb her. He ought to wait until morning. On the other hand he didn't think he could stand another night like last night during which his conscience had niggled at him so relentlessly that he'd hardly slept.

What the hell? he thought, tapping the reply button to her text message and typing Too late to call? Nothing ventured, nothing gained.

Then he hailed a passing taxi, and, after it pulled to a screeching halt beside him, climbed in and gave the driver the address of his hotel in his very dodgy Italian. As he sat back and rubbed a hand over his eyes, his phone beeped and he sat up, more alert than he'd felt at any other moment today.

Never was Lily's reply, and within a second he was dialling her number, his heart lurching in a way that had nothing to do with the driver, who clearly thought he was at Monza.

The phone had barely rung before she picked up. 'Hi,' she said, sounding breathy, as if she'd had to run for the phone, which she couldn't have if she'd only texted seconds ago.

'Hi,' said Kit. 'Sorry it's so late. I've only just picked up your messages. I was out for dinner with a couple of people from work. A basement place. No signal.'

He heard her let out a breath and when she spoke again she sounded strangely relieved. 'That's OK. How's it been going?'

'Fine. Good.'

'Good.' There was a moment's silence and Kit was just about to fill it when Lily got there first. 'Look, Kit,' she said, her voice soft and husky and sending a stab of desire shooting through him. 'I'm so sorry about last night.'

Kit nearly dropped the phone. *She* was sorry? 'If anyone should be apologising, Lily, it's me.'

'Whatever for? I was the one who called you a jerk and threw a glass at you. I'm the one who hurled that ultimatum at you, which was utterly unforgivable. Of course I don't expect you to fire your PR agency. I'm sorry I suggested it, and if it's any consolation I'm mortified.'

'You had justification to be angry,' he muttered, not entirely happy about the fact that she thought she was in the wrong. 'I should have told you about Paula. And if it had ever crossed my mind I would have. I never think of her outside the context of her working for me. She genuinely means nothing to me. Please believe me on this.'

Lily sighed. 'I do. I think. And with hindsight I'm not sure that last night was really about her.'

He frowned in the darkness. 'It wasn't?'

'No. Because I've thought about it, and, you know, I *do* forgive you.'

'Then what was it about?'

'I had a little wobble, that's all. Freaked out for a moment.'

'Over us?'

'Maybe.'

'Why?'

There was a brief moment of silence and Kit could imagine her frowning, biting her lip as she worked it out. 'I think I'm a bit scared, Kit. This has all been so fast. It's kind of overwhelming.'

'There's nothing to be scared of, sweetheart.'

'There's me. And then there's this all going wrong and my life falling apart again. Last time I eventually put myself back together again but if everything goes wrong this time I'd be in bits, and the really terrifying thing is that I'm not sure that I'd be able to put myself back together.'

'You won't have to because it won't happen.'

'How can you know that?'

'Because this time whenever you're scared or vulnerable, or whenever you think something's overwhelming you, tell me and I'll be there.'

'I wish you were here now,' she said quietly.

'So do I. But I'll be back tomorrow morning and we can spend the rest of the weekend making up.'

'I can't wait.' For a moment neither of them spoke. Then she said, 'Kit?'

'What?'

'I love you.'

'I love you too, sweet pea. Deeply. I always have, always will. Even when you're throwing glasses at me and issuing unreasonable ultimatums.'

'So are we OK?'

The faint tremor in her voice cut him to the quick and at that moment he knew that he'd do everything in his power to make sure of it. 'Of course we are.'

CHAPTER THIRTEEN

BUT THEY WEREN'T OK. At least Lily wasn't.

At first she'd clutched onto Kit's reassurance that they were fine as if it were a lifeline, and had buried the tiny bubble of doubt somewhere deep inside where it wouldn't bother her.

Which hadn't been all that hard because when he'd got back from Rome everything had been so lovely. After a weekend spent making up as promised, he'd announced that he was going to cut back on work and delegate as much as he could. With the extra time, if she was amenable to the idea, he was going to woo her.

Lily had been very amenable to the idea, and had adored the dates, the dinners and the two minibreaks he'd taken her on. He'd poured every drop of spare energy into them and she'd fallen more and more in love with him every day that had passed.

Which made the fact that the doubt she tried to get rid of kept bubbling away all the more frustrating.

And she did try. Really hard. She tried to focus on the present, on the relationship she and Kit had now and the many, many positives of that. She told herself not to look too far into the future and simply to take one day at a time, as he'd suggested all those weeks ago when they'd been on that island.

But to her despair she kept slipping back into the past.

She kept dwelling on the latter stages of their marriage and reliving all the pain and hurt that she'd suffered.

She didn't know why she did it. She certainly didn't want to. Most of the time she wanted to reach right inside her head and yank out all the thoughts and doubts and fears churning around inside. But she couldn't seem to help it.

Just as she couldn't seem to help the horrible, insidious, burning desire to check Kit's phone whenever he left it unattended. Or the almost irresistible temptation to casually open up his inbox and take a look at his emails whenever he was away from his laptop. Especially after the rare occasion he hadn't been able to delegate and had had to go away.

She hated it. Hated the way suspicion was slowly creeping into everything she did and everything she felt when it came to Kit. She hated the fact that she knew it was happening yet couldn't seem to stop it however much she told herself that they were fine, that things were going great.

Because the truth was things weren't going so great and it was all her fault. As she'd dreaded, she was handling the things that were going on in her head and in her heart really badly. Most of the time she wasn't handling them at all.

Kit was trying his best. In addition to the attention he lavished on her and the way he kept her up to date of everything he was doing and everyone he was seeing he kept sitting her down and asking her what was wrong, telling her that he wasn't going anywhere so she might as well spit it out. But she had the feeling they could have spent a week in the same room with him endlessly attempting to get her to talk and still she wouldn't have been able to explain.

She didn't know what was wrong. She didn't know how much longer she could stand the emotional distance that was beginning to stretch between the two of them. Didn't know what to do about it. Didn't know what would happen if she confronted it. Didn't want to think about what it might mean for them.

From time to time she caught him looking at her. Worriedly, sadly, frequently frustratedly, and she couldn't blame him because the expression in his eyes reflected how she felt. Their relationship was slowly imploding and she couldn't seem to do a thing to stop it, and it was breaking her heart.

By the time Zoe's hen night came around, Lily was so low, so confused and so adrift that she really wasn't in the mood for partying. But what could she do? She wasn't going to back out. What with Zoe's practically non-existent circle of friends, she and Dan's sister, Celia, were the only guests, and she wasn't going to dampen her sister's happiness with her doubts and unhappiness.

So as the trio walked down the stairs into the basement lounge bar in Notting Hill, Lily plastered on a smile, and when the waitress asked what they'd like to drink she ordered a margarita.

Then another.

And another.

And then she started enjoying herself.

Zoe was sparkling like the diamond solitaire that adorned the third finger of her left hand. Celia was wickedly clever and outrageously entertaining. The place was jumping, the tapas-style food delicious and she had a nice buzz. Almost nice enough to forget what a hash she was making of things with Kit.

'Right,' said Celia, once the waitress had returned with a fresh round of drinks. 'So I know this is Zoe's hen night and everything, but to be honest, as that *Mr & Mrs* quiz thing proved, she's so besotted by my brother that that story's boring.'

'Hey,' protested Zoe.

'Well, it is.' With a grin Celia turned to Lily. 'Your relationship on the other hand sounds absolutely fascinating.'

Lily somehow managed to drum up a smile, but it was

hard when despite the uplifting effect of the tequila her spirits plummeted. 'Fascinating is not the word,' she said dully.

'Then what is? Awesome? Steaming? Mind-blowing?'

'Technically mind-blowing's two words,' said Zoe.

'The word you're looking for is hopeless,' said Lily, and to her horror she could feel the backs of her eyes beginning to prickle.

Celia stared at her. 'What?'

'Mine's a study in how not to have a relationship,' she said, the happy buzz now a dim and distant memory as the desolation and loneliness she'd been feeling recently welled up inside her.

'Oh? How come?'

Lily swallowed. 'First time round we screwed it up so badly I shut myself off and Kit had a one-night stand.'

In the ensuing silence Celia stared at her. 'Jeez.'

'I know,' said Zoe. 'Bad, huh?'

Celia frowned. 'But now you're back together.'

Lily nodded and sighed. 'Yes. And making a complete and utter hash of it.'

Zoe gasped. Celia simply shook her head in amazement. 'I'm not surprised, because, really, how could you ever trust him after something like that?'

And just like that Lily froze as the truth of it struck her. Celia had hit the nail on the head. She didn't trust him. At all. 'I can't,' she breathed and, as the knowledge sank in, felt as if a great weight had been lifted from her because suddenly all the confusion and questions she'd been tormenting herself with recently made sense. Absolute and devastating sense.

'What?' said Zoe, looking at her worryingly.

'I don't trust him,' she said, faintly reeling. 'I don't think I have for months.'

'Oops,' muttered Celia. 'I really shouldn't have asked.'

For a split second Lily was tempted to agree with her because part of her would rather have remained in the dark.

Now she knew, though, she had no choice but to admit what she'd probably known every time she'd had to stop herself reaching for his phone or laptop. Every time he'd gone out or away and the niggle of doubt over what he was really doing and who he was really with had returned. Every time she'd secretly wondered whether he was telling her the truth.

Everything that logic would have told her had she not been so deeply in denial.

She didn't trust him.

Her mind spun with the thought of it, the thought of what it meant, which was now blindingly, agonisingly clear. There was only one way for their relationship to go, she realised as her heart wrenched, because she might love him with everything she was and everything she had, but that didn't mean anything without trust.

She had to talk to him. Had to explain. Even if it meant the end. She owed him the truth, however heartbreaking it was going to be, and she owed it to him now.

'Zoe, Celia, I'm sorry,' she said, now feeling as sober as if she'd been drinking nothing but water all night as she got shakily to her feet, her eyes stinging and her throat tight, 'but I've got to go.'

Kit was sitting in the dark in the garden with a half-empty bottle of whisky and a glass when he heard the front door slam.

When Lily had gone out he'd initially been in what was now his study, kidding himself that he was working, much as he'd done every day lately.

But that was a joke, wasn't it, because how could he concentrate on work when his life with Lily was slowly disintegrating? How could he think about anything other than the fact that it was happening again? That Lily was slipping away from him like water through fingers and, once again, he didn't know what the hell to do about it.

He could feel that he was losing her and it scared him witless. Made him ache and filled his heart with pain.

Because he'd tried. So hard. Alone in his room that night in Rome he'd figured out his priorities and had basically changed his entire life for her. He'd decided to put her first, work second and to set about winning her back.

So with the focus and dedication that had built him a successful hotel business in five short years he'd wined and dined her. Reminded her of the man she'd fallen in love with and shown her the better man he'd become. He'd shared with her every detail of what he was doing and who he was with when he wasn't with her. He'd stripped his soul bare for her, told her things he'd never told anyone and trusted her with everything he was.

But it wasn't enough.

Time and time again he'd asked Lily what was wrong, and time and time again she'd looked at him, said she didn't know. He didn't think she was lying. She seemed so genuinely tormented by the question every time he asked that he got the impression that she was as much at a loss to understand what was happening as he was. And, unlike the night they'd argued about Paula, pushing her for an answer wasn't going to work.

He didn't know what would work. All he knew was that she wasn't happy and it was just about killing him.

But what had gone wrong? he wondered, frowning out into the quiet still of the night as for about the billionth time he tried to work it out. He'd thought they'd reached a deeper level of understanding. That this time their relationship was on firmer emotional ground, but maybe he was wrong because over the weeks she'd become increasingly subdued. More watchful and wary somehow. She'd with-drawn into herself, just as she'd done before.

Maybe he'd pushed her too hard, he thought. Maybe moving in together so soon had been a mistake. Maybe she hadn't changed in the way he'd thought—hoped—she had.

Maybe they simply weren't meant to be together.

At the thought of that Kit felt his stomach turn inside out and something deep inside him begin to ache. And then he set his jaw and pulled himself together. No. That was rub-bish. They *were* meant to be together. All he had to do was think of a way to fix this because what they were going through wasn't insurmountable. It couldn't be.

Behind him a light went on inside and as he heard Lily step out onto the terrace, the trace of her scent drifting towards him and every one of his senses zooming in on her, just as they always did, his heart began to thud with renewed resolve because the solution would come to him. Eventually. It had to.

'What are you doing out here?' she said softly.

'Thinking.'

'About what?'

How he could make things between them right. 'Noth-ing much.'

She moved round into his line of sight and his heart lurched crazily the way it did every time he saw her.

But tonight something was different. It wasn't the lack of a smile on her lovely face or the absence of the sparkle in her beautiful eyes because he'd got used to both. It was something about the way she held herself, something in the deadness of her expression, something that made him go icy-cold.

As a ribbon of apprehension and dread wound itself round his insides he felt something inside him wither and all he could think was that somehow it was too late. Somehow they'd got to a point where things couldn't be fixed and he hadn't noticed soon enough.

'You're back early,' he said, swallowing back the sudden lump in his throat.

'Yes.'

'Not much fun?'

'Not a lot.'

She sat down next to him, turned to face him, and Kit wished he could turn back time and not be here when she got back because he didn't want this now. He didn't want this at all. Yet on some dim and distant level he knew it had been a long time coming. Knew it was inevitable. Wished he'd had time to prepare his arguments, wished he had arguments to prepare.

'Want a drink?' he said.

'No, thanks.'

'Mind if I have one?'

'Go ahead.'

He poured himself another glass of whisky and noticed his hand was shaking. 'You're going to say we need to talk, aren't you?'

A flicker of surprise flashed in her eyes and then she nodded. 'Yes.'

'Because this isn't working, is it?' he said, the struggle he was having keeping a grip on his emotions making his voice hoarse.

'No.'

'Want to tell me why?'

Her eyes filled with tears and her chin trembled and it was all he could do not to take her in his arms and tell her everything was going to be all right because he didn't think it was. 'I can't bear to.'

'Tell me, Lily. I won't break.' Although the possibility was there.

'But I might.'

'Come on,' he said, trying to give her a smile but failing. 'Be brave.'

She nodded and blinked, but it didn't get rid of the shimmer of tears and it didn't stop the tremble of her chin. 'I thought I could do this,' she said, her voice breaking. 'But I can't.'

'Why not?'

'Because there's this thing.' She rubbed her chest and frowned as if she didn't totally get it. 'It's so tiny. But it's there. And I just can't seem to get rid of it. That night you went away the first time, after we had that argument about Paula, I couldn't get hold of you and I couldn't help wondering what you were doing and who you were with.'

'I told you what I was doing and who I was with.'

'I know. And I believed you. I still do. But I think it started something and it won't go back.'

'What is it?'

'A lack of trust.'

'You can trust me.'

'Can I?'

'Of course you can.'

'But how do I know that? Tell me, because I desperately want to.'

She looked at him despairingly, as if it was something she'd asked herself a dozen times over, and what could he say? Because she could? What kind of an answer was that? Apart from the only one he had. He'd never do anything to betray her trust, but how could he expect her to believe him when he'd already broken it once?

'Because I love you.'

She put a hand on his cheek and he could feel his skin burning beneath her touch. 'And I love you. More than I ever did before. At the risk of sounding soppy you are my sun and stars. You're the only man I've ever wanted. The only man I've ever loved and probably ever will love. The thought of never kissing you again, never holding you again or never speaking to you again makes me feel physically sick. I have this pain deep inside me, like a hand's reaching right inside and twisting everything inside me into knots.'

'Then don't think about it.'

'I have to.'

'Why?'

'Because without trust loving you isn't enough.' She shook her head and pulled her hand away and the loss of her warmth felt like an icicle through his heart. 'It's not going to work, Kit. It's just not going to work.'

At the sad finality in her voice panic welled up inside him. 'What can I do, Lily? Tell me. Whatever it is I'll do it.'

'There's nothing either of us can do.'

'There must be.'

'There isn't.'

And it was all his fault, he knew. He'd done this to them the minute he'd destroyed her ability to trust him by cheating on her and Kit felt the knowledge hit him as if someone had thumped him in the solar plexus. He didn't deserve her love. He didn't deserve her trust. He wasn't worthy of her. And he had to let her go. 'Lily…'

'I know. I'm sorry,' she whispered, the tears now flowing down her cheeks as she leaned forwards and gently kissed him. 'So sorry.'

He kissed her back, knowing that it was a kiss goodbye, and it just about broke him apart. 'So am I, my darling,' he said. 'So am I.'

CHAPTER FOURTEEN

ON A PROFESSIONAL level the last fortnight had been great for Kit. Plans for the new hotel in Rome were coming along apace and business was booming. To his delight—and no small amount of relief—Paula Burrows had been head-hunted by another PR firm and just yesterday he'd heard that one of his hotels was up for an award.

On a personal level, however, the last couple of weeks had been diabolical. However busy he kept himself, however hard he worked, he couldn't stop thinking about Lily. He couldn't stop wondering how she was and what she was doing, and he'd been going mad wondering if there was anything during their relationship that he could have done differently.

He couldn't seem to get rid of the dull ache that lived deep inside him, the pain that filled every cell of his body or the sorrow and regret that washed over him practically every other minute.

The need to find out how she was drummed through him constantly and the temptation to call her had been so hard to resist that he'd had to delete her details from his phone.

If only it had been as easy to delete her from his memory. But that was nigh on impossible because she was in there all the time. Teasing him. Tormenting him. Driving him pretty much insane.

And making him do all kinds of things he'd really rather

not do. Such as getting up in the early hours and searching the web for news, photos or anything really that might give him a hit of her. Such as composing emails he'd never ever send. Such as on one particularly bad night driving round to her house, parking up outside and waiting for the merest glimpse of her.

It had to stop, thought Kit, rubbing his hand along his stubbly jaw and then across the back of his neck as he sat in his kitchen and brooded. It really did. Quite apart from the fact that some of the things he'd done lately bordered on stalkerish, as painful as it was, as much as his heart was aching, Lily had made it very clear that they were over, and he knew perfectly well that there wasn't a thing he could do about it.

Hadn't he tried during the entire time they'd been together? And then the night in her garden, hadn't he abandoned his pride? Hadn't he begged? Hadn't he very nearly wept, for goodness' sake?

Well, he wouldn't be doing any of that again, he thought with a shudder at the memory of how desperate to hold on to her he'd been and the lengths he'd gone to to achieve it. And he wouldn't be doing any of the other things he resorted to in his wretchedness any more. He'd had enough of the heartache and he was pretty sure that his staff had had enough of his filthy mood. So there'd be no more web searching. No more seeking her out. No more thinking about her. And after this lunchtime, no more playing squash with Dan just so he could pump him for information.

He had to excise her from his memory and his heart because he didn't deserve her and he couldn't have her and he might as well get used to the idea.

Lily stood on the dais in the fitting room of the bridal shop, risked a quick glance in the mirror directly in front of her and practically recoiled in horror at her reflection. She looked absolutely hideous.

When she'd dragged herself out of bed this morning after yet another night of too many tears and too little sleep she'd slapped on some make-up and hauled a brush through her hair and thought she wasn't doing too badly considering how wretched she felt.

But under the harsh bright fluorescent light of the fitting room she saw that she'd been deluding herself. Great grey bags sagged beneath her eyes. There were hollows beneath her cheekbones. Her hair hung limply and dully around her ears, and despite the tinted moisturiser she'd applied—very patchily it seemed—her skin was the colour of wallpaper paste.

Whichever way she looked at it, and given the many mirrors surrounding her that was a lot, she wasn't doing the gorgeous floaty silk dress she was wearing any kind of justice.

But was it any wonder?

The last time that she and Kit had broken up everyone had said that she'd get over it. That all she needed was time. And while she'd been miserable they'd been proved right. But that strategy wasn't working so well for her now and, as she'd feared, it didn't look as if there was any hope that it would.

It had been a fortnight since he'd prised her off him and walked out of her garden, her house and her life, and she was no better now than she had been then. If anything she was worse because she was finding it pretty impossible to see how she was ever going to get over him.

She thought about him constantly. Dreamed about him regularly. Every morning when she woke up she remembered that they were over, and her heart shattered all over again.

Most of Kit's stuff had been gone for days now—

he'd been round when she'd been at work, packed up and dropped the key through the letter box—but every now and then she found something he'd forgotten. A random sock that had made it into her drawer. His toothbrush lying beside the basin. A copy of the *Financial Times* folded in the way that only he folded it. And every single time she'd come across something of his—or even something that merely reminded her of him—she crumpled into a heap on the floor in a flood of tears.

This wasn't like the last time when every time he'd crossed her mind she'd mainly thought 'good riddance' and 'what a relief'. This was hell on earth. Absolute agony. Because, as a result of all their baggage and the way they'd managed to deal with most of it, their relationship this time round had been deeper than before. Closer. And thus the break-up was all the more devastating.

Ending things might have been the only thing she could have done after discovering that she might love him to bits but she just couldn't trust him, but that didn't make it easier to bear. It didn't lessen the pain and didn't make her miss him any less.

This time she knew there'd be no third chance. No trying again. This time, this really was it.

As the reality of what she'd done slammed into her head yet again, Lily could feel the tears welling up again and she sniffed them back because she really couldn't damage this dress. She'd never forgive herself. Neither would Zoe, who'd been sitting on the sofa while the seamstress had rotated round Lily sticking pins into the fabric. Zoe, who was also proving surprisingly unsympathetic about her sister's miserable, agonising plight.

Now the seamstress, having finished her alterations, helped Lily out of the dress and carried it off, leaving Lily to step down off the dais and pull on her clothes aware that her sister was watching her every move.

'What?' she muttered, unable to bear the scrutiny a second longer as she did up her jeans and made a mental note to buy a belt.

'When did you last eat?'

Eat? Had she had a piece of toast last night perhaps? She couldn't remember. 'A while ago,' she said.

'Fancy some lunch?' said Zoe.

Nearly throwing up at the idea of lunch, Lily swallowed back the wave of nausea and shrugged her jacket on. 'Thanks, but I don't think I could stomach lunch right now.'

'Then you can watch me eat.'

'Not sure I want to do that either.'

'Too bad,' said Zoe, taking her arm in a surprisingly firm grip and marching her out of the shop, 'because I'm hungry and we need to have a little chat.'

Five minutes later, Zoe, with a determination Lily would never have expected from her previously non-confrontational sister, had found a pub, ordered two plates of fish and chips and two glasses of white wine and had plonked her down at a table in the corner.

'Right,' said Zoe, effectively blocking her escape by sitting down opposite her and then giving her an oddly fierce glare. 'This has gone on long enough.'

'What has?'

'You. The long face. The wallowing.'

Lily stared at her sister. What the hell? 'I'm allowed to wallow,' she said as her heart gave a great squeeze. 'Kit and I broke up. I'm devastated.'

'Well, get over it, because I'm not having you lose any more weight. This is the second time your dress has had to be taken in in a week. Carry on at this rate and there'll be nothing left of you.'

'Thanks for the sympathy, bridezilla. And come to think of it, where is that anyway?'

'Where's what?'

'The sympathy. You're supposed to be mopping me up the way I mopped you up when Dan ended things with you.'

'This situation is entirely different.'

'Different how?'

'You're being an idiot.'

Lily gaped, the tears receding as indignation took over. 'Excuse me?'

'Well, you are.'

'I can't trust the man I love. I'm heartbroken.'

'That's just it.'

'That's just what?'

'All this nonsense about you not being able to trust Kit is rubbish.'

Rubbish? *Rubbish?* 'It isn't rubbish,' said Lily mutinously. 'It's the crux of the matter. The defining feature of our relationship. Ex-relationship.'

Zoe eyed her shrewdly. 'So go on, then, tell me, what has he done to make you not trust him?'

'You know what he did.'

'I mean recently. Since you got back together again.'

Lily thought about it for a moment, racked her brains and riffled through her memory. And then frowned. 'Well, nothing, I guess.' The opposite, in fact. He'd gone so far out of his way to show her that she could trust him that he was practically in another country.

'Right. I see. So basically Kit made one lousy, brief mistake five years ago and you're still punishing him for it?'

'I'm not.'

'Then what are you doing?'

'The only thing I can,' said Lily, reiterating the mantra that had kept her more or less upright this last fortnight. 'Being sensible. Protecting myself. Surviving.'

'And how's that working out?'

'Not brilliantly,' she had to admit. 'But what else do you suggest?'

'A good long look in the mirror.'

Lily shuddered. 'I did that earlier. Got quite a fright.'

'Look deeper.'

Lily took a sip of wine and sighed. 'What are you getting at, Zoe? And no more cryptic stuff because my brain really can't take it at the moment.'

'What I mean is that you weren't exactly fault free in what happened all those years ago, were you?'

'I know that.'

'Yet when he suggested trying again Kit trusted that you'd have changed, didn't he? So why can't you trust that he has? Seems to me that's not very fair.'

Lily opened her mouth to say something, then closed it again because for one thing here was the waiter with their fish and chips and for another she didn't know what to say to that. Still hadn't figured out an answer by the time the waiter had brought cutlery and condiments and had then retreated.

'And actually,' continued Zoe, picking up the ketchup and squeezing a dollop on the side of her plate, 'if anyone's had their trust broken it seems to me that it's Kit, because from your description of the way things were going before you broke up it sounds like, unlike him, you haven't changed at all.'

Zoe dipped a chip in the ketchup and popped it in her mouth while all Lily could do was stare at her. 'What?'

'You've been doing that tortoise thing again, haven't you?'

'What tortoise thing?'

'The pulling yourself into your shell and hiding while life and its problems go on around you.'

At her sister's bluntness Lily bristled. 'If that was what I was doing, and I'm not saying it was, don't you think it would be understandable? Don't you think some kind of self-defence would be normal?'

'There's no "if" about it,' said Zoe. 'You *have* been doing that, and, self-defence or not, it's a mistake. One you're consciously making.'

Lily looked at her sister in frustration, because Zoe might be all loved-up at the moment, but did she really think it was that simple? Could she really not see how hard it had been for her to end their relationship? How heartbroken she was by what she'd had to do? Did Zoe really think she'd made a mistake by wanting to protect herself from the kind of pain that had torn her apart once before?

Had she really not changed at all?

'I can't just tell myself to trust him and, hey, that's that,' she said, beginning to feel a bit confused because she'd been so convinced she *had* changed.

'Why not?'

'Because it doesn't work like that.'

'Yes, it does.'

'How?' Because she'd dearly love to know.

'Some things, like love, can't be switched on and off,' said Zoe, picking up her knife and fork and levelling her a look, 'but trust isn't one of them. Trust is a choice you can make, Lily, and I think you should think very carefully about the one you've made because Kit's the best thing that's ever happened to you and if you don't sort out what you want and fix things you could blow it for good.'

As Zoe turned her attention to her fish Lily took a sip of wine and tried to unravel all the thoughts that were now churning round in her head.

Was her sister right? Was she still punishing Kit for what he'd done all those years ago? Had she been hiding from everything again? Was she making a mistake? Could she trust him?

As the answers she'd never have expected filtered into

her head the foundations of everything she'd been convinced of recently began to crack.

Maybe she was still punishing him, she thought, her throat tightening as her heart thumped. Apart from that one brief moment, that complete aberration, Kit was the most reliable man she'd ever known. The most sincere. The most loyal. Yes, he'd had a one-night stand but he'd come clean immediately afterwards. Regretted it ever since, he'd said. He might have cheated but he hadn't lied. He'd always been totally honest with her. Been so open he was practically transparent.

But she hadn't been, had she? She'd asked for openness from him but she hadn't reciprocated. Instead she'd gone into denial. Unable to cope with what she was feeling, she'd shied away from it instead of confronting it. And then she'd run away like a coward in case she got hurt again.

Right now, though, the only person hurting her was herself and that was something she could fix because Zoe was right. Trust *was* a choice she could make and there was no one more deserving of it than Kit.

She'd been such a fool. She'd had no reason not to trust him, a billion reasons why she should and why she could, and instead she'd allowed herself to take the easy way out and run away, while he'd abandoned his pride and almost begged her to reconsider.

'What if I already have blown it, Zoe?' she said, shame and regret making her voice hoarse.

In the process of stabbing a piece of her fish with her fork Zoe stilled, glanced up and said, 'Then I suggest you make your way PDQ to the Fitness Rules gym next to Kit's hotel, where I happen to know he and Dan are playing squash, and unblow it.'

CHAPTER FIFTEEN

'WELL, THAT WAS quite a game,' said Dan, rubbing his neck and wincing as he rolled his shoulders. 'I'm not sure I'm ever going to recover.'

Feeling a stab of guilt, Kit wiped the sweat off his forehead and then threw the towel round his neck. 'Sorry,' he muttered, gloomily reflecting that if he'd known he was going to take his mood out on his squash partner he'd have cancelled this afternoon's game. Probably should have cancelled it anyway because maintaining a friendship with a man who was soon to be Lily's brother-in-law was hardly conducive to his intention to move on, however much he liked him.

'Not a problem,' said Dan easily. 'I can take losing once in a while. You look like hell by the way.'

'Thanks.'

'Anything you want to talk about?'

'Not particularly,' said Kit, stuffing his racket into its case and then slinging his bag over his shoulder.

'Right. Good.' Dan picked up his own bag and together they walked from the court in the direction of the changing rooms. 'So I heard that you and Lily had split up,' he said conversationally and the pain that shot through Kit made his breath catch.

'Yeah,' he said casually, as if it didn't rip his heart to shreds just to think about it.

'Want to know how she is?'

Desperately. 'I couldn't care less.'

'No. Right. Well, I guess that's understandable seeing as how she dumped you.'

Kit flinched and ruthlessly obliterated the sudden memory of that night in the garden when he hadn't been able to fix things.

'But if you did,' Dan continued, 'I'd have to tell you that she's a heartbroken wreck. Zoe's words, not mine. I'd also have to tell you that she looks like death warmed up. But you don't care, so I won't.'

At the knowledge that Lily sounded as miserable as he was, Kit felt something inside him collapse. All that drivel about wiping her from his life and his heart, probably, because who had he been kidding? There was absolutely zero chance of that happening.

Grinding his teeth against his pathetically weak willpower when it came to Lily, Kit gave in to the need to talk to someone and maybe get a different take on the situation because he hadn't exactly been doing brilliantly on his own. 'Did you know she doesn't think she can trust me?' he said, dumping his things on a bench and sitting down in case his limbs gave out.

'I had heard.'

'Any thoughts as to what I can do about that?'

'No idea. Can she trust you?'

'Yes.'

'Have you tried telling her?' Dan asked, opening his locker and taking out a towel before stashing his bag and racket.

'Many times and at length. It didn't make any difference.'

'Do you want her?'

'More than I want my next breath,' said Kit. 'But five

years ago I did something stupid. Something I've regretted ever since.'

'I heard about that too.'

'And it's turned out to be too great an obstacle to overcome.'

'So we all make mistakes,' said Dan, now armed with a bottle of shower gel as well as a towel.

'This was some mistake.'

'Yeah, but it was a while ago, wasn't it?'

'Five years.'

'And has Lily never made a mistake?'

Kit frowned as all the mistakes she'd made filtered into his head. 'Plenty.'

'So stop beating yourself up and do something about it. Marry her or something. Bind her to you so she can't escape and prove it over and over again until she has no choice but to trust you. Bit drastic, I know, but what else are you going to do?'

As Dan strode off and shut himself in one shower cubicle Kit stashed his things in his locker, grabbed a towel and headed for another, his mind beginning to race.

Was Dan right? he wondered, turning on the tap and feeling hot needles of water pummelling his skin. Was he beating himself up unnecessarily about the mistake he'd made? Had he let Lily dictate the way things had gone out of some kind of sense of inadequacy? Had that been totally the wrong thing to do?

Maybe it had, because Lily wasn't perfect, was she? For the last few weeks he'd been tearing himself apart with remorse and guilt over what he'd done, but what about Lily? Hadn't she reverted to type when the going had got tough? She had. And while he'd made huge changes and sacrifices for them she'd hardly done a thing.

So maybe he wasn't blame free in their break-up this time round, but neither was she. Just like before. They were equals. They always had been. Which meant that he *was* worthy of her, dammit. He *did* deserve her. They deserved each other.

He shouldn't have let her get away with ending things between them, he thought, turning off the water and grabbing his towel. That had been a mistake. One he wouldn't be making again because he loved her and she loved him and he was, well, he was wasting time.

Having abandoned Zoe in the pub after her sister had told her to go and then heading straight to the gym, Lily didn't have a plan. She hadn't had the time to formulate one. Nor had she had the mental space because her head was so full to the brim with the realisation of what a foolish idiot she'd been and her heart was pounding with so much love and hope and regret at the way she'd behaved that there wasn't room for anything else.

So when she pushed through the door of the gym and saw Kit striding purposefully across the lobby for a split second she didn't know what to do. For a moment she just watched him, her heart swelling because he looked so gorgeous, so familiar, and she loved him so damn much.

He also looked like she felt. Drawn. Haggard. Unkempt. As though basic self-maintenance was simply too great a challenge to face these days. Which was something of a boost to her pretty shaky confidence because if he'd looked clean-shaven and crisp, as if he hadn't been pining for her the way she had for him and was totally over her, she'd have been straight out of the door.

As it was, when he saw her he stopped dead, stared at her, his face totally unreadable, and she didn't know whether he was glad to see her or surprised or appalled. All she knew was that her heart was thundering so loudly it was a miracle no one else seemed to be able to hear it and her body was straining to throw itself at him and she wasn't going anywhere.

Literally. However hard it was she was staying right where she was because there'd be no throwing of anything anywhere until she'd said what she had to say, whatever that was.

'Hello, Kit,' she said, aiming for breezy nonchalance but, she suspected, failing.

His brows snapping together in a frown, Kit stalked over to her and stopped about a metre away. 'You're here,' he said.

'So it would seem,' she said, a bit breathless as her lungs were having trouble functioning in his presence.

'Why?'

'I wanted to talk.'

'Seems to be the fashion at the moment.'

'What?'

'Never mind,' he muttered.

'I thought we could go to your hotel. Maybe a meeting room or something.' Not his apartment though. No. Way too many disturbing and distracting memories there.

'Good idea,' he said, taking her arm and wheeling her round. 'You'd better come with me.'

He marched her out of the gym at such a rate that she had to jog to keep up. He held her tight as he led her into his hotel and across the lobby and she tried not to respond to the feel of him that she'd so badly missed. When he by-passed the ground-floor meeting rooms and took her to the lift she protested but her protest went unnoticed.

By the time they reached his apartment Lily was out of breath and her stomach was fluttering because Kit had a kind of energy about him, a sizzling sort of tension and a sense of purpose that she'd never seen before and it was doing crazy things to her heart.

He dropped his things on a chair, then thrust his hands

deep into the pockets of his jeans and turned to face her. At the fire in his eyes and the intensity of his expression, Lily's knees nearly gave way and a flicker of hope at the thought that she might not have screwed things up for good began to burn deep inside her.

Kit raked his gaze over her. 'Dan was right,' he said flatly. 'You do look awful.'

'So do you.'

'Yes, well, I feel it.'

'Me too.'

'But I'm glad you're here,' he said, flashing her a quick, lethal smile.

Oh, thank goodness for that, she thought, letting out a breath of relief because he was acting so oddly she hadn't been sure. 'You are?'

Kit nodded. 'Saves me a journey.'

'Where were you going?'

'To come and find you.'

Lily felt her heart turn over and that little flame of hope began to burn a little more fiercely. 'Oh.'

'So my carbon footprint thanks you.'

'It's welcome. But now can I tell you what I came to say?' she said, feeling so encouraged by the fact that he hadn't ignored her or turned her away that she was now practically exploding with the need to fix what she'd done.

'In a moment,' he said. 'Sit down.'

'I don't want to sit down.'

'Sit.'

She sat, even more bemused and now quite a bit more turned on by his dark, edgy demeanour. 'Are you all right, Kit?' she asked, leaning forwards and looking at him closely. 'You seem, I don't know, a bit weird.'

'I'm fine.'

'Sure,' she murmured, and then couldn't quite remember what she'd been thinking because Kit was fixing her with a look that had her heart thumping and her mouth going dry and her head swimming.

'OK, so here's the thing, Lily,' he said, and for some reason she shivered. 'Despite what happened a fortnight ago, we are not over.'

As his words hit her poor, battered brain her heart tripped and then swelled to bursting. 'You have no idea how glad I am to hear you say that, because—'

But he held up his hand and cut her off. 'Let me finish. I love you, Lily, but you are as far from perfect as I am.'

'Oh, you're so right,' she said with heartfelt conviction. 'I'm not perfect at all.'

'And, yes, I made a mistake but it was years ago and I refuse to carry the guilt around any longer.'

'Good, well, about that—'

'You've made many more mistakes than I have.'

She nodded. 'I know. I know.' She'd made tons.

'I thought I wasn't worthy of you. But I am.'

For a moment she reeled. How could he ever have thought that? Had *she* made him think that? 'You are,' she said with a stab of shame.

'We need each other, Lily,' he said, his eyes dark and intense and focused wholly on her. 'We love each other and we deserve each other.'

'We do.'

'So here's how this is going to go. We're going to get married, you and I, after which I plan to devote the rest of my life to proving to you how much you can trust me. We're going to communicate. Talk. Be a proper partnership. We're also going to adopt a brood of children and be extremely happy.' He arched an eyebrow as if challenging her to object. 'So what do you think about that?'

But why would she object when it was everything she wanted? Filled with so much relief, happiness and love she couldn't speak, instead Lily just walked over to him, put her arms around his neck, pressed herself against him and kissed him.

And damn it felt good because it had been such a long, miserable time since she'd been in his arms, but now she was because he was hauling his hands out of his pockets and putting them on her back, pulling her tight to him and kissing her back equally fiercely.

Free from all the insecurities that had plagued her these last few weeks, all the doubt and confusion that had so troubled her, and filling with the absolute certainty that she and Kit were going to be all right, she kissed him long and hard and with everything she felt. And when they broke for breath, his breathing was as ragged as hers, his heart was thundering as hard and fast as hers and his eyes were blazing as fiercely as she could imagine hers were.

'I'm taking it that you're not averse to the idea,' he said hoarsely.

'I couldn't be more for it,' she said with a giddy kind of smile. 'Although that bit about devoting the rest of your life to proving to me how much I can trust you? You don't need to do that.'

He frowned. 'I don't? Why not? I was looking forward to it.'

'I don't know how I could ever have thought I couldn't trust you, Kit. I'd trust you with my life. I'm so sorry for doubting it.'

'You trust me?' he said after a moment's pause. 'Since when?'

'Since about an hour ago.'

'What happened an hour ago?'

'I came to realise that trust is a choice, and I guess before I chose not to trust you. I don't exactly know why. Because I was scared maybe? Because it was all going too fast and I panicked? Because I could feel myself retreating and I couldn't stop it?'

'And now?'

'Now I want to trust you and I do. With everything I am and everything I have, because when have you given me reason to doubt it? You haven't. Not once. And you won't. I know that.' She shook her head in despair. 'I was such a fool. I went back on our deal to communicate and shut you out again. But I promise that that won't happen again because I'm done with denial. It's the coward's way out and I don't want to be a coward any more. I'm sorry if I made you think you don't deserve me because if anything I don't deserve you. And I'm sorry for breaking up with you. It was just about the worst thing I could have done. This last fortnight has been horrible. The worst of my life.'

'Mine too,' said Kit, his voice rough. 'I thought I'd lost you for good.'

'No, no,' she said. 'I was the one doing the losing.'

He tilted his head and looked down at her, his eyes filled with warmth and love and the promise of a future. 'I'm pretty sure it was me, but do you really want to argue about this?'

'Not really.'

He gave her a soft smile and his eyes took on a gleam. 'Because you know there are far better things we could be doing,' he said, his hands slowly sweeping up her back to her shoulders and making her shudder with longing.

'Like what?'

'Like you agreeing to marry me. Will you?'

Lily felt the backs of her eyes begin to prickle because how many people got a second chance? How many people were that lucky? 'Yes,' she said, blinking a bit. 'Because I want to, obviously, not because you scared me into it with all that "this is how it's going to go" thing.'

Kit's smile deepened and what with the way he was now stroking the skin of her shoulders her stomach practically dissolved. 'I'm sorry about that,' he murmured. 'But I wasn't taking any chances.'

'Don't be,' she said breathlessly. 'It was very assertive. Very dynamic. Very alpha male.'

'I'm delighted you think so.'

'And attractive.'

He slid his hands beneath the spaghetti straps of her vest top and slowly inched them down. 'How attractive exactly?' he asked softly.

'Extremely,' she said, beginning to tremble.

'So about these other things we could be doing...'

* * * * *

SEVEN NIGHTS
WITH HER EX

BY
LOUISA HEATON

Louisa Heaton lives on Hayling Island, Hampshire, with her husband, four children and a small zoo. She has worked in various roles in the health industry— most recently four years as a Community First Responder, answering 999 calls. When not writing, Louisa enjoys other creative pursuits, including reading, quilting and patchwork—usually instead of the things she ought to be doing!

To my husband, Nick, who offered to take
me to Yellowstone Park as a research trip.
(But we never did get there…sigh…)

CHAPTER ONE

Wow! This place is amazing!

Dr Beau Judd drove her hire car into a vacant space outside the Gallatin Ranger Station in Yellowstone National Park. Silencing the engine, she looked out of her window and let out a satisfied sigh.

This was *it*. This was what she'd been looking for. A return to nature. The vast open expanses of the American wilderness. Huge sweeping plains of golden-yellow wild flowers, ancient stone outcrops, forests of pines and fir trees, beautiful blue skies and the kind of summer weather that people back in the UK could only dream of.

She grabbed her guidebook and flipped through the pages, determined to take every moment that she could to learn about where she was. Those golden flowers—bursting skywards like mini-sunflowers—what were they called? Beau flicked through to the flora and fauna section of her book and smiled.

Balsamroots. Perfect.

Her gaze fell to the text beneath the picture and her smile widened.

Native Americans would often use the sap of this plant as a topical antiseptic.

Now, wasn't *this* what she was here for? To learn? And that plant was a perfect start to her new learning experience on the Extreme Wilderness Medical Survival Course. She'd spent too long cooped up in hospitals, on wards, in Theatre. Standing for hours, operating in the depths of a patient's brain, gazing for too long at X-rays or imaging scans, stuck in small rooms passing along bad news, living in a sterile environment, never seeing the sky or enjoying the fresh air.

Her *life* had become the hospital. She'd even begun to forget what her flat looked like. There'd been too many nights spent sleeping in the on-call room, too much time spent with patients and their families, so that she hardly saw her own. Hardly had any friends apart from her work colleagues. Hardly saw anyone she cared about at all.

This next week would all be about Beau reclaiming *herself.* Getting back to grassroots medicine. Getting back to hiking—which she'd used to love, but she hadn't worn a set of boots for years. Not unless they had a heel anyway.

She was one of the top neurologists in England. Had spent years building up her reputation, skill set and repertoire.

Now was the time to take some time out. For herself. Regroup. Do what she loved. Learn and hike in some of the most beautiful country on the planet.

Beau got out of the car and sucked in a lungful of fresh mountain air. Then she popped the boot so she could get her backpack out. She'd bought all new kit—tent, clothes, equipment, walking poles. All colour-co-ordinated in a gorgeous shade of red. *Matches the hair*, she thought with a smile as she tied a bandana around her head to keep her long auburn hair off her face.

The first day's hike started today. She wanted to be ready. She didn't want anyone having to slow down because of her. Here she would make friends—hopefully for life—and with this experience under her belt perhaps she could start thinking about doing that season at Base Camp, Everest. Her ultimate goal.

She slung the backpack over her shoulders, adjusting the straps, then closed the boot, locked it. Lifting her sunglasses, she strode over to the ranger station, ready to check in and meet the other hikers. Hopefully she wasn't the last to arrive. She'd left Bozeman a whole hour earlier than she'd needed to, but still… She'd find out when she got inside.

It took a moment for her eyes to adjust to the interior of the log cabin, and then she noticed the receptionist standing behind the counter.

'Hi, there! I'm Dr Judd. I'm here for the Extreme Wilderness Medical Survival Course.'

'Welcome to Yellowstone! And welcome to Gallatin. Let me see here…' She ran a finger down a checklist. 'Sure. Here you are.' She ticked Beau's name with her pen. 'The others are waiting in the back. Go on through and help yourself to refreshments. They'll be the last you'll see for a while!'

Beau smiled her thanks and headed over to the door, from where she could already hear a rumble of voices in the next room.

This was it. The moment everything about her life would change! She would enjoy great new experiences. Get back to the basics of medicine and enjoy some survival training.

Plastering a huge smile on her face, she opened the door and scanned the room of faces, ready to say hi.

The smile froze on her face as she realised who was in the room with her.

A man whom she'd hoped *never* to see again.

Gray McGregor.

How was he even *here*? In this small ranger station? In Yellowstone Park? In America? What the heck was he doing? Why wasn't he back in Scotland? In Edinburgh, where he was meant to be?

This had to be some sort of double. A doppelgänger. *We all have one, right?*

The smile left her face and unconsciously she let her hand grip the door frame to keep her balance, wrong-footed suddenly by the shock of seeing him. Her centre of gravity was distorted by the backpack, but also by this imposter—the image of the man who'd broken her heart—standing in front of her.

Of all the parks in all the world, he has to be in mine.

The real Gray she'd not seen for... She thought quickly, her mind stumbling as much as she was, over numbers and years that suddenly wouldn't compute. Her brain had flipped in a short circuit. Frozen. The ability to add up basic numbers was beyond her at this terrible moment in time.

And the clone just stood there, the smile that had been on his face before he'd become aware of her presence disappearing in the same way that clouds covered the sun. His eyes widened at the sight of her, the muscle in his jaw clenching and unclenching.

It is *you.*

The noise in the room quietened as the other backpackers sensed a change in the atmosphere, but then rose again slightly as they all pretended not to see.

It was all flooding back! All of it. The day she'd dressed in white *for him*. The hours spent getting her hair done at home, giggling and laughing excitedly with her hairdresser. Then the hour spent with the beautician, getting her make-up looking perfect. Putting on *that dress*, attaching the veil, taking hold of her bouquet and glimpsing herself in the mirror before the photographer had been allowed in to take pictures.

The joy and excitement of the day had been thrumming through her veins as with every picture taken, every smile she gave, every pose she stood for, she had imagined walking down that aisle to be with him. Anticipating the look on his face, the way he would smile back at her, the way they would stand side by side in front of the vicar...

Only, you weren't there, were you, Gray?

The *heartache* this man had caused...

He looked a little different from the way she was used to seeing him. Back then he'd been fresh-faced, his dark hair longer and more tousled. Today his hair was cut shorter than she remembered, more modern, and he had a trim beard that was as auburn in colour as her own hair. And he was staring at her with as much shock in his own eyes as she was feeling.

But I'm not going to let you see how much you hurt me!

Deliberately she tore her gaze from him, tried to ignore her need to hurry to the bathroom and slick on a few more layers of antiperspirant, and walked over to one of the other hikers—a woman in a dark green polo shirt.

'Hi, I'm Beau. Pleased to meet you.'

She turned her back on him, sure that she could feel his gaze upon her. Her body tensed, each muscle flooded with more adrenaline than it needed as she imagined his gaze trailing up and down her body.

Resisting the urge to turn around and start yelling at him, she instead tried to focus on what the other hiker was saying.

'…it's so good to meet you! I'm glad there's another woman in the group. There's three of us now.'

Beau smiled pleasantly. She hadn't caught the woman's name. She'd been too busy trying not to grind her teeth, or clench her fists, whilst her brain had screamed at her all the horrible things she could say to Gray. All the insults, all the toxic bile she had once dreamed of throwing at him…

All the pain and heartache he'd caused…she'd neatly packaged it away. Determined to get on with her life, to forget he'd ever existed.

What was he even *doing* here? Surely he wasn't going to be on this course, too?

Of course he is. Why else would he be in this room?

Months this trip had taken her to plan and organise. Once she'd realised that she needed a change, needed to escape that cabin fever feeling, she'd pored over brochures, surfed the Net, checking and rechecking that *this* was the perfect place, the perfect course, the perfect antidote to what her life had become.

It was far enough away from home—from Oxford, where she lived and worked—for her to know that she wouldn't run into anyone she knew. Who did she know anyway? Apart from her family and patients? And her colleagues? How many of *them* had planned a trip to Yellowstone at the same time as her? None. The chances of *him* doing the same thing, for the same week as her… Well, it had never even crossed her mind.

Why would it? She'd spent years forcing herself to not think of Gray McGregor. The damned Scot with the irrepressible cheeky grin and alluring come-to-bed eyes!

Eleven years. Nearly twelve. That's how long it's been.

Eleven years of silence. Why had he never contacted her? Apologised? Explained?

Like I'd want to hear it now anyway!

Outwardly she was still smiling, still pretending to listen to the other hiker, but inwardly... Inwardly a small part of her *did* want to hear what he had to say. No matter how pathetic it might be. Part of her wanted him grovelling and on his knees, begging for her forgiveness.

I'll never forgive you, Gray.

Beau straightened her shoulders, inhaled a big, deep breath and focused on the other hiker—Claire. She was talking about some of the trails she'd walked—the Allegheny, the Maah Daah Hey.

Focus on her, not him.

'That's amazing. You walked those trails alone?'

'Usually! I think you can take in so much more when you've just got to entertain yourself.'

Was he still looking at her? Was he thinking of coming over to speak to her? Beau stiffened at the thought of him approaching.

'What made you come on this course?' she asked.

'Common sense. A lot of walkers I meet on trails are...shall we say, *older* than me? And when I was walking the Appalachian, this guy collapsed right in front of me. In an instant. I didn't know what to do! Luckily one of his group was an off-duty responder and he kept the guy alive until the rescue team arrived. You never know when you're gonna be stuck in the middle of nowhere with no medical assistance!'

Beau nodded.

'What about you, Beau? What made you come on this course?'

'I just wanted to get out and about, walking again. Somewhere beautiful. But somewhere I can still learn something. I want to work in the hospital tent on Everest at some point.'

'Oh, my Lord! You're braver than me! Are you a nurse, then?'

'A doctor. Of neurology.'

'My, my, my! You'll no doubt put us all to shame! Promise you won't laugh at my attempts to bandage someone?'

Beau didn't think she'd be laughing at anyone. The mood of her trip had already changed. Just a few moments ago she'd been carefree and breathing in the mountain air, assuring herself that she'd made the right decision to come here. But now…? With Gray here, too?

She would make him see that she was not amused by his presence. She wasn't *anything*! She had no energy to waste on that man. He'd been given more than enough of her time over the years and her life had moved on now. She was no longer the heartbroken Beau whom he had left standing at the altar. She was Dr Judd. Neurologist. Recommended by her peers. Published in all the exclusive medical journals. Award-winning, innovative and a leader in her field.

She would have nothing to do with him this next week, and if he didn't like her cold shoulder, then tough.

Beau slipped off her backpack, put it to one side and went to make herself a cup of tea at the drinks station. It would probably be the last decent cup of tea she'd experience for a while, and she didn't want to miss having it. They had time before they set out.

She kept her back to the rest of the room, studiously ignoring Gray.

He would have to get used to it.

* * *

Yellowstone National Park. Over three thousand miles away from his native Edinburgh. He'd travelled over the North Atlantic Ocean, traversed mile upon mile of American soil to make it here to Wyoming, this one small spot on the face of the *whole planet*, and yet... And yet somehow he had managed to find the one small log cabin in the huge vastness of a national park that contained the one woman he could not imagine facing ever again.

Why would he ever have expected to find her *here*? This wasn't her thing. Being outdoors. Hiking. Roughing it in tents and having to purify her water before drinking it. Beau was an indoors girl. A five-star hotel kind of girl. Life for her had never been about struggle and survival. This should have been a safe place to come to. The last place he would have expected her to be. Wasn't she a hotshot neurologist now? Wasn't she meant to be knee-deep in brains somewhere?

Seeing her walk into the room had almost stopped his heart. He'd physically felt the jolt, unable to take in oxygen. His lungs had actually begun to burn before he'd looked away, breaking eye contact, his mind going crazy with questions and insinuations as heat and guilt had seared his cheeks.

You broke her heart.
You never told her why.
You deserve to suffer for what you did.

And he *had* suffered. Hadn't he?

If only she knew how much he longed to go back and change what happened. If only she knew how much he'd hated himself for walking away, knowing what it would do to her but unable to explain why. If only she knew of how many nights he'd lain awake, thinking of how he could put right that wrong…

But how to explain? It was easy to imagine saying it, but actually having her here, right in front of him… All those things he wanted to say just stuck in his throat. She'd think they were excuses. Not good enough. Was she even in the right frame of mind to want to talk to him?

Beau had turned her back. Begun talking to another hiker. Claire, he thought she'd said her name was.

He took a hesitant step forward, then stopped, his throat feeling tight and painful. He wouldn't be able to speak right now if he tried. She clearly wanted nothing to do with him. She was ignoring him. Spurning him.

I deserve it.

Other people in the room were milling about. Mixing, being friendly. Introducing themselves to each other. Gray allowed himself to fall into the crowd. Tried to join in. But his gaze kept tracking back to her.

She still looked amazing. Her beautiful red hair was a little longer than he recalled, wavier, too. She'd lost some weight. There were angles now where once there'd been curves, and the lines around her eyes spoke of strain and stress rather than laughter.

Was she happy in life? He hoped that she was. He knew she was successful. Her name had been mentioned in a few case meetings at work. He'd even suggested her once for a family member of an old patient. His own work in cardiology didn't often give him reason to work with neurology, but he'd kept his ears open in regard to her. Keen to know that she was doing okay.

And she was. Though she had to have worked hard to have got where she had. So had he.

He watched from a distance as she mingled with

the others, placing himself in direct opposition to her as she moved. The room was a mass of backpacks, hiking boots, men slapping each other on the back or heartily shaking each other's hands as they listed their posts and achievements to each other. Two women at the back of the room sat next to each other, their backpacks on the floor as they sipped at steaming cardboard cups. The last taste of civilisation before they hit the wilds of America.

But all Gray could concentrate on now was Beau. And his own overwhelming feelings of regret.

Would simple words of apology be enough?

Would telling her about the many times he'd picked up the phone and dialled her number even be adequate? Considering that he'd never followed through? He had always cancelled the call before she'd had a chance to answer. And all the emails he had sitting in his 'Drafts' folder, addressed to her, in which he'd struggled and failed each time to find the right words... The times he'd booked to go to the same medical conference as her, hoping to 'accidentally' bump into her, but had then cancelled...

She'd just call me a coward. She'd be right.

He had been afraid. Afraid of stirring up old hurts. Afraid of making things worse. Afraid of hurting her more than he already had...

Time had kept passing. And with each and every day that came and went, it had become more and more difficult to make that contact.

What would have been the point? He could hardly expect forgiveness. Or reconciliation. An apology would mean nothing now. He'd broken things so irrevocably between them. How could he fix them now? He had nothing to offer her. Not then and certainly not now. He was broken himself. And even though he'd known that, years ago, he'd still asked her to marry him! He'd forgotten himself and what he actually was in the madness of a moment when he'd felt so happy. He'd believed anything was possible—got carried away on the *possibility* of love.

But he didn't expect her to understand that. They'd come from two separate worlds and she'd known nothing of his family life. Of what it was like. He'd deliberately kept her away from his poisonous family. Kept her at a safe distance because she was so pure, so joyful, so full of life, believing in happy-ever-after.

She still wasn't married. And that puzzled him. It had been all she'd ever wanted back then. Marriage. And children. It was what she had thought would complete her. After all, she'd said yes to his proposal and then just weeks later had started talking about children.

That was too much. That smacked the reality right back into me.

That was when the full force of not having thought through what he'd done had come to the fore. That was when he'd realised he couldn't go through with it.

For a man who was an expert in hearts, he'd sure been careless with hers.

And it had almost killed him to know that he was doing it.

The tea wasn't great. But she kept sipping it, swapping hands as the heat from the boiling hot water burned through the thin cardboard cup.

She was beginning to get over the shock and was now feeling calmer. She could even picture in her mind's eye dealing with him quite calmly and nonchalantly if he decided to speak to her. She'd be cool, uninterested, dismissive.

That would hurt him.

Because Gray liked to be the centre of attention, didn't he? That was why he'd done all that crazy adrenaline-junkie stuff. He'd passed it off as doing something for charity, but even then he'd wanted people to notice him, to say he was amazing or brave. That was why he'd done Ironman competitions, bungee jumps, climbed mountains and jumped out of planes. *With* a parachute, unfortunately.

He had always succeeded. People had *always* clapped him on the back and told him he was a great guy and he'd thrived on that. Had lived for that, doing more crazy things despite her always begging him not to. Had he listened? No.

So her ignoring him? Choosing not to notice him? That would have to sting a little.

Gray was an attractive man. Usually the most attractive man in a room. And he wasn't just a pretty face, but a brilliant cardiologist, too—getting his papers published in the most prestigious medical journals, trying out new award-winning surgeries, being the toast of the town.

He could at least have had the decency to fail at *something*.

And not once had he called, or apologised, or explained. Even his family hadn't had a clue—not that they'd spoken much to her. Even *before* the wedding. Perhaps that had been a clue?

Beau risked a quick glance at him, feeling all the old hurts, all the old pains, all the grief that she'd tried so unsuccessfully to pack away come pouring out as if they'd had the bandages ripped from them, exposing her sore, festering wounds.

She swallowed hard and looked away.

I will not *let him see what he's doing to me!*

A rage she had never before experienced boiled over inside her and she suddenly felt nauseous with the force of it. She turned away from him, her hand trembling, and took another sip of her tea. Then another. And another. Until her stomach calmed and her hand grew more steady.

She let out a breath, feeling her brain frazzled with a million thoughts and emotions.

This course was meant to be an enjoyable busman's holiday for her. Could she do it with him here?

There's thirteen of us, including the guide. Surely I can just stay out of Gray's way?

Beau had been looking forward to this adventure for ages. This was the moment her career and her life would take another direction and lead her to places she had never dared to go.

She'd thought about it carefully. Planned it like a military exercise. She'd excelled in her hospital work and was top of her game in neurology. Other neurologists who felt they could do no more to help their patients would suggest *her* as the patient's next course of action. She was very often someone's last chance at life.

And she excelled, knowing that. She lived for it. The staying up late, the research, the practice, the robotic assistance that she sometimes employed, the long, *long* and challenging surgeries. The eye for detail. The precision of her work.

Awards lined her office walls at home in Oxfordshire. Commendations, merits, honorary degrees. They were all there. But this…

This was what she craved. A week of living by her wits, experiencing medicine in the wild, using basic kit to attend to fractures, altitude sickness, tissue injuries, whilst hiking through some of the most stunning scenery on the planet.

Forget technology—forget the latest medical advancements. There would be no security blanket here. No modern hospital, no equipment apart from a few basics carried in a first aid kit and what she could find around her.

It was perfect.

Even if *he* was here.

High grey-white mountains, lush expanses of sweeping green and purple, firs and shrubs, thickets of trees hiding streams and geysers. It was a vast emptiness, an untamed wilderness in all its glory, and *she* would try to beat it. No. Not beat it. Work *with* it, around it, adapt it to her needs so she could succeed and get another certificate for her wall. Another trophy so that she could think about applying for Base Camp, Everest. So she could work at the hospital there.

That small medical tent, perched on the base of one of the world's greatest wonders—that was her real aim. Her next anticipated accomplishment.

And there was no way she was going to let all that be ruined by the one man she'd once stupidly fallen in love with and given her heart to. The one man who had broken her into a million pieces. Pieces she still often felt she was still picking up.

She was still trying to prove to the world that she *did* have value. That she was the best choice. The only choice. His rejection of her had made her a driven woman. Driven to succeed at everything. To prove that

he'd made a mistake in his choice of leaving her behind.
To prove her worth.

*Because I'm worth more than you, Gray. And I'll
prove it to you.*

'Yellowstone National Park is a vast natural preserve,
filled with an ecosystem and diverse wildlife that, if
you're not careful, is designed to kill you.'

Mack, the ranger leading their group, tried to make
eye contact with each person standing in the room.

'There is danger in the beauty of this place, and too
many people forget that when they come here and head
off-trail. They're so in awe of the mountains, or the
steaming hot geysers, or the dreamlike beauty of a wild
wolf pack loping across the plains, that they forget to
be *careful*. To look where they're going. We are going
to be traversing land millions of years old, trying to be
at one with nature, but most of all we are here to learn
how to look after one another with the minimum of re-
sources. Yes, this could be done in a classroom, but...'
he paused to smile '...where would be the fun in that?'

There was some laughter, and Gray noticed Beau
smile. It was exactly the way he remembered it, lighting up her blue eyes.

'Each of you will be issued with a standard first aid
kit. When you receive it, you need to check it. Make
sure it's all there. That's *your* responsibility. Then we're
going to buddy up. The buddy system works well. It en-
sures that no one on this adventure goes anywhere in
the park alone and that there is always someone watching your back.'

The likelihood of Gray being paired up with Beau
was remote. And he certainly wasn't sure if it was something he wanted. But he caught her glancing in his gen-

eral direction and wondered if she'd thought the same thing. Probably.

Mack continued. 'Today we're going to be hiking twelve miles across some rough terrain to reach the first scenario, where we will be dealing with soft tissue injuries. These are some of the most common injuries we see as rangers, here or at the medical centres, and we need to know what to do when we have nothing to clean a wound or any useful sterile equipment. Now, one final thing before we buddy up… We will *not* be alone in this park. There are wild animals that we're all going to have to learn to respect and get along with or stay out of their way. I'm sure you all know we've got wolves and grizzlies here. But there are also black bears, moose, bobcats and elk, and the one animal that injures visitors more than bears…the American bison.'

He looked around the room, his face serious.

'You see one of those bad boys…' he pointed at a poster on the wall behind him '…with his tail lifted, then you know he's going to charge. Keep your distance from the herds. Stay safe.'

Gray nodded. It wasn't just bison he'd have to watch out for, but Beau, too. She didn't have horns to gore him with, but she certainly looked at him as if she wanted him dead.

She was angry with him, and for good reason. He had walked away from their wedding and it had been one of the hardest things he'd ever done. Knowing that she would be left with the fallout from his decision. Knowing that he was walking away from the one woman who'd loved him utterly and completely.

But life had been difficult for him back then, and there was a lot that Beau didn't know. All she'd seen—all he'd *allowed* her to see—was the happy-go-lucky, carefree Gray. The cheeky Scot. But the man she'd fallen in love with hadn't existed. Not really. It had been a front to hide the horrible atmosphere at his home, the problems within his own family: his father's drinking, his mother's depression, the constant fights...

Gray's parents had *hated* each other. *Resented* each other. His mother had been trapped by duty with a man she detested. With a man who had suffered a tragic paralysing accident on the *actual day* she'd decided to pack her bags and leave him.

Being in the same house as them had been torture, watching and listening as they had systematically torn each other apart. Each of them trapped by marriage. An institution that Gray had vowed to himself *never* to get involved with.

'Love fades, Gray. Once that honeymoon period is over, then you see your partner's true colours.'

He could hear his mother's bitter words even now.

So why had he ruined it all by proposing to Beau? He hadn't wanted to get married—ever! And yet being with Beau had made him so happy.

The day he'd proposed they'd been laughing, dancing in each other's arms up close. Her love for him had been beaming from her face, her sapphire eyes sparkling with joy, and he'd wanted... He'd wanted that moment to last for ever. The words had just come out.

Will you marry me?

'We've got one hour before we're due to depart, so take this time to check your pack, check your first aid kit, use the bathrooms, freshen up—whatever you need to do before we set off. Let's meet back here at one o'clock precisely, people.'

Mack headed out of the room and a general hubbub

began as people began to talk and check their bags and equipment.

Gray had already checked his bag three times. Once before he'd set off from Edinburgh, a second time when he'd arrived in America and a third time when he'd first arrived at the park. He knew everything was as it needed to be. There was nothing missing. Nothing more he needed to do.

Technically, he could relax—and, to be quite frank, he needed a bit of breathing space. He headed outside to the porch of the ranger station and sucked in a lungful of clean air before he settled himself down on a bench and took in the sights.

It was definitely beautiful here. There was a calmness, a tranquillity that you just didn't find inside a hospital. Hospitals were clean, clinical environments that ran to a clock, to procedure, to rules and regulations. As busy as a beehive, with people coming and going, visitors and patients, operations and clinics.

But here…here there was peace. And quiet. And—

The door swung open with a creak and suddenly she was there. Alone. Before him. Those ice-blue eyes of hers were staring down at him. Cold. Unfeeling.

He got to his feet, his mouth suddenly dry.

'I think it's time I made some rules about the next week.' She crossed her arms, waiting for his response.

'Beau, I—'

'First of all,' she interrupted, holding up her hand for silence, 'I think we should agree not to speak to each other. I appreciate that circumstance may not always allow that, so if you *do* speak to me, then I'd prefer it was only about the course. Nothing else. Nothing personal.'

'But I need to—'

'Second of all…you are to tell no one here what happened. I will *not* become the subject of idle gossip. And thirdly…when this is over, you will not contact me, you will not call. You will maintain the silence you've been so expert at keeping for the last eleven years. Do you understand?'

He did understand. All too keenly. She wanted nothing to do with him. Which was fair enough. Except that he felt that now she was here, right in front of him, this week might be his chance to explain everything. Forget a pathetic phone call or a scrappy little email. That had never been his style. He had seven days in which to lower her walls, get her to accept his white flag of truce and ask her to listen to him.

But he didn't want to become the subject of gossip, either. He didn't want to fight with her. Nor did he want to share so much that she found out about his injury. But time would tell. They had a few days to cool down. They'd get to talk. At some point.

'I do.'

Her lip curled. 'You see? That wasn't too hard to say, was it?'

Then she pointed her finger at him, and he couldn't help but notice that her hand was trembling.

'Stay out of my way, okay? I want nothing to do with you. *Ever.*'

He nodded, accepting her rules for the time being, hoping an opportunity would present itself to allow a little bending of them.

They would have to talk eventually.

Beau checked her first aid kit against the checklist— gloves, triangular arm bandage, two gauze pads, sticking plaster, tape, antiseptic wipes, small scissors, one small saline wash, a safety pin. Not much for a medical emergency, but she guessed that was part of the challenge. The other part of the challenge for her was going to be a mental one.

Ignore Gray McGregor.

How hard could it be?

She retied her hiking boots, used the ranger station bathroom and then grabbed something to eat, forcing herself to chat pleasantly with some of the other hikers. No one else had a medical background, it seemed, apart from her and Gray. The others were experienced walkers, though, used to long treks and mileage, so she hoped they could all learn something from each other.

At one o'clock precisely Mack came back into the room, followed by another ranger. 'Right, everyone, gather round. I'm going to issue the buddy list. Now, remember, your buddy is more than just your friend. They're your safety net, your lookout, your second brain. You don't go anywhere without your buddy, okay?'

He awaited assent from the group.

'Now, we've tried to divvy everyone up equally and pair people with similar interests, so here goes.' Mack picked up his list. 'Okay, let's see who we have here. Conrad and Barb—you guys are married, so it makes sense to buddy you guys up... Leo and Jack—you guys are both from Texas... Justin and Claire—you guys mentioned you've met before, walking the Great Wall of China... Toby and Allan, both ex-Forces personnel...'

Beau shifted in her seat. There were only four of them left to name: her and three guys, one of whom was Gray.

Please don't pair me with Gray!

But what did she have in common with the other

two? They were brothers, and surely Mack was going to pair brothers. Which meant… Her heart sank and she began to feel very sick.

'Dean and Rick—brothers from Seattle, which leaves our UK doctors, Beau and Gray. Welcome to America, guys!'

Beau couldn't look at Gray. If she looked at him, she'd see that he was just as horrified as she was about this.

Was it too late to change her mind and go home? Go back to the hotel in Bozeman and stay there for a week?

No! You've never backed away from anything!

Looking around the small room, she saw that everyone was pairing with their buddy, shaking hands and grinning at each other. Reluctantly she let her gaze trickle around the room until she locked eyes with Gray. He looked just as disturbed as she was—uncomfortable and agonised—but he seemed to be hiding it slightly better. She watched as he hitched his backpack onto his back and came across the room to her, looking every inch the condemned man.

Staring at him, she waited for him to speak, but instead he held out his hand. 'Let's just agree to disagree for the next week. It should make this easier.'

Easier, huh? He had no idea.

She ignored his outstretched hand. 'Like I said, let's just agree not to talk to each other *at all*. Not unless we have to.' Her voice sounded shaky, even to her own ears.

'That might make things difficult.'

'You have no idea what *difficult* means.' She hoisted her own backpack onto her shoulders and tightened the straps, turning away from the muscle tightening in Gray's jaw.

'I think I do, my lass.'

Her head whipped round and she glared at him. 'Don't call me that. I am *not* your lass. You know nothing about me now.'

'You want me to talk to you like you're a stranger?'

'I don't want you to talk to me at all.'

'I'm not going to be silent for a week. I'm not a monk.'

'Shame.'

'Beau—'

She glared at him. *Don't say another word!* 'Let's get going…*buddy.*'

He took a step back, sweeping his hand out before him. 'Ladies first.'

Beau hoped her stare would turn him into stone. Then she followed Mack and the others out of the ranger station.

CHAPTER TWO

BEAU MARCHED ALONG at the front of the pack, as far away from Gray as possible. She knew he would be lurking at the back. She walked beside Barb, her nostrils flaring and her nails biting into her palms.

She was beginning to get a headache. Typical! And it was all *his* fault. And she had no painkillers in her first aid kit. No one did. She had to hope that it would pass soon. The whole point of this course was to make her think differently. To use what was around her to survive.

Beau thought that she already knew quite a bit about survival. About not giving up when everything was against her. About not allowing herself to succumb to the void.

Since the day Gray had left her standing at the altar, she'd become a different person. Stronger than before. Driven. Her eyes had been opened to the way men could hurt her.

And to think that I solemnly believed that he wouldn't do that to me.

She'd allowed herself to feel safe with Gray. Secure in the knowledge—or she'd thought so at the time— that he loved her as much as she loved him.

Beau ground her teeth. Perhaps she'd been naïve. Perhaps she'd been cocky. She'd told everyone back then how Gray was her soulmate, her one true love. That he was the most perfect man and she was so lucky because he wanted *her*. There had been one time she remembered sitting in the kitchen with her mum, waxing lyrical about how wonderful he was, how happy *she* was and how she couldn't believe she'd found a man who wanted all the same things she did.

Her mum had listened and smiled and rubbed her arm and told her daughter how happy she was for her. How this was what life was all about. Finding love, settling down, creating a family of your own. That it was all anyone needed.

Beau had almost not been able to believe how lucky she was herself. But she'd believed in *him*. Almost devoutly. Her faith in their love had been undeniable, and when Gray had asked her to marry him, she'd been the happiest girl in the world.

She'd thought no one could be happier than her. She'd thought she was going to marry the man she was head over heels in love with and that they would have children and a brilliant life together, just as her parents had done. They'd be strong together, united, and when the time came for them to be grandparents, their love would continue to grow. It had all been mapped out in her mind's eye.

But then he'd destroyed everything she'd believed in and she hadn't even got an apology! Not that it would mean much now. Too much time had passed. The time for an apology had been eleven years ago. Not now.

But there was nowhere for her to escape him here. They were stuck together. Buddied up, for crying out loud! She must have tutted, because Barb turned to look at her as they slowly marched up a steep, rocky incline.

'Mack mentioned you're a doctor?'

Brought back to reality, she tried to push her anger to one side so that she could speak politely to Barb. 'Yes, I am.'

'Do you have a specialty?'

She nodded and smiled. 'Neurology.'

'Ooh! That sounds complicated. They say there's so much about the brain that we don't know.'

'Actually, we know a good deal. Technology has advanced so far nowadays.'

'You know, I think I saw a documentary once where there was a brain operation and they did it with the patient wide awake! I couldn't believe it! This poor man was having to identify pictures on flash cards whilst the surgeons were sticking God only knows what into his brain!'

Beau smiled. 'It's called intraoperative brain mapping.'

Barb shuddered. 'Have you seen it done?'

'I've done it. I'm a surgeon.'

'Ooh! Con—you hear that? Beau here's a *brain surgeon*!' Barb grabbed her husband's arm to get his attention and Conrad nodded at Beau.

'Well, let's hope we don't need your services during this next week, Doctor.'

She laughed, a lot of her anger gone. The married couple seemed nice. They were both middle-aged, though Conrad's hair was already silvery, whereas his wife's perfectly coiffed hair was dark. They reminded her slightly of her own parents. Happily married, easy in each other's company and still very much in love.

Despite everything, it made her smile. 'How long have you two been together?'

Barb glanced at her husband. 'Thirty-five years this August.'

'Wow! Congratulations.'

'Thank you, dear. I have to say it's been wonderful. We've never had a cross word and we've never spent more than a night apart.'

'How do you do it? Stay so happy, I mean?'

'We pursue our own hobbies, but we also make sure we follow an interest together. Which is why we're doing this. We both love walking and seeing the country. Though last year Con had a few heart issues, so we thought we'd come on this course. Combine an interest with a necessity. Sometimes you can be out in the middle of nowhere and it can take hours before you get medical attention. We both thought it a good idea to get some medical basics under our belts.'

Beau nodded. It *was* a good idea. For a long time she had thought that basic first aid, and especially CPR, ought to be taught in schools. So many more people would survive accidents or sudden turns of events in their own health if everyone was taught the basics.

'Good for you.'

'What made *you* come on this course? This kind of stuff must be old hat to you.'

Beau looked across the plateau they'd reached, at the glorious sweeping plains, a patchwork of green, grey and purple hues, and the mountains in the distance. The open expanse. 'I got cabin fever. Needed to get back to nature for a while.'

'And the other doctor? The Scottish one? It looked like you two know each other.'

There was so much she could have said.

Why, yes, I do *know that lying, conniving, horrible Scot...*

'Briefly. A long time ago. We haven't seen each other for a while.'

Barb peered at her, her eyebrows raised. 'Parted on bad terms, did you?'

She smiled politely. 'You could say that.'

'Aw…' The older woman patted her arm. 'Life's too short for holding on to anger, honey. When you get to our age, you learn that. Our son Caleb, bless his heart, always jokes that Con and I are *on the coffin side of fifty*'!' She laughed out loud. 'And he's right—we are. People waste too much time being angry or holding on to resentments and it keeps them stuck in one place. They can't move forward, they can't move on, and they lose so much time in life, focusing on being stuck in the sad when they could be focusing on being happy.'

Beau appreciated what Barb was trying to say, but it didn't help. There was still so much anger inside her focused on Gray. Suddenly she realised that until she heard some sort of explanation from him, she didn't think there was any way for her to move forward. She knew an apology wouldn't help—not really. But maybe she'd like to hear it, see him wriggle about on the end of his hook like the worm that he was.

Gray McGregor owed her *something*, and until she heard it, she wasn't sure what it was. But she wouldn't let it bother her. She told herself she didn't care. Even if she *was* still trapped in the past when it came to Gray. She might have grown up, found herself a stellar career and proved to her peers that she was one of the top neurologists in the country, but in her heart she was still a little girl lost. Hurt and abandoned.

Her heart broken in two.

And there was only a certain Scottish cardiologist who might be able to fix it.

* * *

Gray replayed in his mind his recent words with Beau. He kept his gaze upon her, walking far ahead of him, wondering how she was feeling.

Those dark auburn waves of hers bounced around her shoulders and gleamed russet in the sunshine. He could see her chatting amiably with Con and Barb and wished she could be as easygoing with him. It would make the next week a lot easier for both of them if they could put the past in the past and just concentrate on enjoying the hike and the medical scenarios.

But the sweet, agreeable Beau he'd once known seemed long gone, and in her place was a new version. And this one was flinty, cold and dismissive.

He wasn't sure how to handle her like that, and he'd already been feeling enough guilt about what he'd done without her laying it on thick to make him feel worse.

I know I owe you an explanation.

So many times he'd thought about what he needed to say to her. How he intended to explain, to apologise. Always, in his own mind, the conversation went quite well. Beau would listen quietly and attentively. Most importantly, she would understand that the decision not to turn up at their wedding had hurt him just as much as it had hurt her.

But now he could see just how much he'd been wrong. Beau would not sit quietly and just listen. She would not be understanding and patient.

Had *he* changed her? By walking away from her, had he changed her personality?

So now he chose to give her space. Letting her walk with Barb and Conrad, staring at the back of her head so hard he kept expecting her to rub the back of it, as if the discomfort of his stare would become something physical.

And he worried. There was strain on her face, a pallor to her skin that reinforced the brightness of her freckles and the dark circles beneath her eyes.

Surely *he* wasn't the cause of that? Surely she'd just been working too hard, or for too long, and wasn't getting enough sleep? He knew she worked hard. He'd kept track of her career after medical school. She was one of the top neurologists in the country—maybe even in the whole of Europe. That had to take its toll, right?

But what if she's ill?

A hundred possibilities ran through his mind, but he tossed them all aside, believing that she wouldn't be so silly as to come out on a trek through the wilderness if she was ill.

It had to be stress. Doing too much and not eating properly.

He hadn't seen a ring on her finger. As far as he was aware, she wasn't married, and the hours she worked would leave hardly any time for dating. Unless she was seeing someone at work? There was always that possibility...

He shifted at the uncomfortable thought and tugged at the neckline of his tee shirt, feeling uneasy. Hating the fact that the idea of her being with someone else still made him feel odd.

Yet she was never mine to have. I should never have let it get so far in the first place. I was wrong for her.

'Here you go...have a pull of this.' Rick offered him a small flask. 'It'll keep you going. Always does the trick for me at the start of a long hike.'

Gray considered the offer, but then shook his head.

'No, thanks. Best to stick to water. That stuff will dehydrate you.'

'What do you think I've got in here?' Rick grinned.

'It's a whisky flask, so I'm guessing…alcohol?'

'Nah! It's just an energy drink my wife makes. It's got guarana in it. It's good for you!'

Gray took the flask and sniffed at it. It smelled very sweet. 'And how much caffeine?'

'Dunno. But it tastes great!'

He passed it back without sampling it. 'Do you know that some energy drinks can trigger cardiac arrest even in someone healthy?'

Rick stopped drinking and held the flask in front of him uncertainly. 'Really?'

'If you consume too many. The high levels of caffeine mixed with other substances can act like a drug, stimulating the central nervous system to high levels when consumed in high doses.'

'You're serious? I thought all that pineapple and grapefruit juice was *good* for me.'

'It can be. Just don't add all the other stuff. Do you know for sure what's in there?'

Rick shook the flask, listening to the swish of the liquid inside. 'No. But she spends ages in the kitchen making it for me and it always seems to help.'

Gray grinned. 'I'd stick to water, if I were you.'

'How do you know all this?'

'I'm a cardiologist. I've operated on a fair few people who've ended up in the ER because of too many energy drinks.'

Rick began to pale. 'Wow. You think something's good for you…'

'Sorry to be a party pooper.'

'Nah, you're all right.' Rick tipped the flask upside down and emptied the juice out onto the ground. 'Doesn't make sense to carry the extra weight, does it?'

Gray looked up at Beau and considered all the extra emotional weight he was carrying. 'It doesn't. It doesn't help you at all.'

They'd been walking for a steady hour, and by Beau's reckoning—not that she knew much about these things—they'd walked about three miles into the park, all of it uphill. Her calf muscles burned and she was beginning to feel sore spots within her new hiking boots. She hoped she wasn't getting blisters.

The hillside had produced a plateau, a wide expanse of grasslands, and eventually they'd passed through a grove of lodgepole pine trees—tall and slender, the bark looking almost white from a distance, but grey up close.

Mack stopped them as they got near. 'You'll see a lot of these throughout the park. They're a fire-dependent species, and the seeds you can see, once fallen, provide a natural foraging source for grizzlies as we pass into fall. So you see this tree, then you look for the bear that goes with it. Luckily there isn't one here today.'

He smiled as everyone looked at each other and laughed nervously.

'But this is one example of always needing to be prepared. If you're walking in a new area, know the ecology, the flora and fauna—it can help you stay safe. Today there's no reason not to know. The Internet can tell you in an instant. There are books. Read. Research. It could save your life. Medically, indigenous tribes have used the lodgepole pine for many ailments—they steam the pine needles and bark to help with lung issues, and they also use it for bronchitis, fever and even stomach ache treatments. You can make a pitch from the pines and use it as a plaster for infections, burns and sores.'

Beau looked up at the canopy of the tall tree and was amazed. Working in a hospital, with the technology and advancement that came in the present day, it was easy to forget that all medicine originated from the use of plants, trees, shrubs and flowers. But it was important and not to be forgotten. She got out her compact camera from her pack and took a picture.

Mack walked them on and the plateau soon began to dip down towards a narrow rocky stream. The sound of running water was refreshing in the day's heat and Mack encouraged them all to take in some liquid refreshment and eat a small snack.

Beau perched on a large stone and nibbled on a flapjack she'd brought, avoiding Gray's glance and hoping he would stay away from her for a while longer.

Irritatingly, he sat down opposite her.

'How are you enjoying this so far?' he asked in his lilting Scottish burr.

'It's wonderful. Especially when I don't have to look at *you*.'

He glanced down at the ground. 'There's no need to attack me all the time, Beau. I feel bad enough as it is.'

'Good.'

He let out a heavy sigh, looking out across the stream bordered by rocks and grassy banks. 'I suppose you want me to go away?'

She didn't look at him. 'Or just be quiet. Either would do.'

He pulled some trail mix from his pack and offered it to her. 'Nuts?'

She glanced at him to see if he was making fun of her or being insulting. 'No. Thank you.'

'You know you're stuck with me, hen?'

She put away her flapjack, annoyance written all over her face, and refastened the buckles on her backpack. 'I'm not a hen.'

'Sorry, lass.'

She stood up and heaved the pack onto her back. 'Wow. An apology. You *do* know how to make them, then?'

Gray looked up at her, squinting in the sun. 'Aye.'

'And...?'

'And what?'

'Where's my *real* apology? The one you should have made eleven years ago?'

He cocked his head to one side and pulled his sunglasses down over his eyes. 'I'm saving it.'

'Saving it? For what?'

He looked about them before getting to his feet and leaning in towards her, so that his face was up close to hers. It was unnerving, having him this close. Those moss-green eyes staring deeply into her soul and searching. His breath upon her cheek.

'For when you're actually ready to listen. There's no point in me trying to explain whilst you're like this.'

'I'm not sure it's important, anyhow. Too little and too late.'

'And that proves my point.'

He walked away to sit down somewhere else.

Beau began to breathe again. Their brief conversation had unsettled her. Again. Plainly the way she was reacting to him was not working. Open hostility towards Gray was like water bouncing off an umbrella. It made no difference to him at all. He quite clearly was not going to apologise to her unless she got herself together.

Irritating man!

Most irritating because she was stuck with him for a week!

She had to be realistic. They were here. Together. And, worst of all, they were *buddied up* together. She knew from the itinerary for the trip that there would be paired activities where they would have to work with each other away from the main group. Orienteer themselves to another part of the park. Which meant time alone.

They had to start working together. Whether she liked it or not.

She turned to look for him and saw him standing with Mack, chatting. Beau headed over and plastered a charming smile onto her face. 'Excuse me, Mack, could I have a quick word with my buddy here?'

'Absolutely. Glad you're here, Gray.' He slapped Gray on the arm before walking away.

Gray looked at her curiously. 'Yes?'

'You're right. We need to be working together for this next week and, as buddies, we need to be strengthening our working relationship. I'm not prepared to fail this course, and with that in mind I'm willing to put our past to one side in the spirit of cooperation and… peace. What do you say?'

She saw him consider her outstretched hand. Saw the question in his solitary raised eyebrow, saw the amiable smile upon his face before he reached out and took her hand.

A charge shot up her arm as her hand tingled in his. The strange yet all too familiar feel of his hand on hers was electrifying and thrilling. Her instinct was to let go. To gasp for oxygen. To rub her palm against her khaki trousers to make it feel normal again. But she did none of these things because her gaze had locked with his and she'd stopped breathing anyway.

Who needs oxygen?

Gray's leaf-green eyes bored into hers with both an intensity and a challenge, and Beau felt as if she'd been pulled back through time to when they'd first met on a hospital rotation.

They'd been so young, it seemed. All the students had been fresh-faced and eager to learn, eager to start their journeys. The girls smartly dressed, professional. The boys in shirts and ties as yet unwrinkled and sweat-free.

She'd noticed him instantly. The gleam in his eyes had spoken of an ambition she'd clearly been able to see. And had held a twinkle that had spoken of something else: his desire to stand out, to be noticed, to be cheeky with their lecturers. The way he'd pushed deadlines for work, the way he'd risked failing his assessments—that side of him that had been an adrenaline junkie, carefree and daredevilish.

His mischievous, confident grin had pulled her in like a fish to a lure and she'd been hooked. His attitude had been so different from anyone she already knew—so different from that of any of the men in her own family. He'd been that breath of fresh air, that beam of light in the dark, that sparkling, tempting palace in a land of dark and shadow.

He'd shaken her hand then and introduced himself, and instantly she'd heard his soft, lilting Scottish burr and been charmed by it. The very way he'd said her name had been as if he was caressing her. He'd made her feel special.

She'd not wanted to be dazzled by a charming man. Not at the start of her career. But family, love and marriage were high on her agenda and she'd desired what her parents had. A good, steady partner, with a love so deep it was immeasurable. Beau had had no doubt that she would find it one day.

She just hadn't expected to find it so soon.

Gray had stuck to her side and they'd worked together, played together, studied together and then, after one particularly wild party, slept together. It had seemed such a natural step for them to take. He'd filled her heart with joy. He'd made her feel as if she was ten feet tall. Every moment with him had been as precious as a lifetime. She'd wanted to be with him. She'd wanted to give him everything—because that was what love was. The gift of oneself.

And he hadn't disappointed her.

Afterwards, as she'd lain in his arms, she'd dreamed about their future. Wondering about whether they would get married, where they might live—not too far from her parents, not too far from his, so their children would have a close relationship with each set of grandparents—and what it would be like to wake up next to him every day for the rest of their lives together.

She'd liked the way he acted differently with her—calmer, more satisfied, considerate. *Relaxed.* He'd been a hyperactive buzzing student when they'd met, full of beans and so much energy. He'd exhausted her just watching him. But when he was with her, he wasn't like that. As if he didn't need to be. And she had found the side of him that she could fall in love with...

Gray smiled now. 'I hear you. Cooperation and peace. Seems like a good start to me.'

Beau chose not to disagree with him. It was already looking as if it was going to be one very long week ahead, and this adventure was going to be uncomfortable enough as it was.

I'm letting go of the stress.

So she smiled back and nodded.

Mack suggested that they all get going again, if they were to get to the first scenario and have enough extra time to pitch their tents for the evening.

They walked through scrub brush, conifers and thick deep grass. The overhead sun powered down upon them and Beau stopped often to drink and stay hydrated. At one of her stops Gray came alongside and waited with her.

'How are your parents?'

Beau fastened the lid on her water bottle. It was getting low. Hopefully there'd be a place to refill soon. 'Not that they're any of your business any more, but they're good, thanks.' She answered in a clipped manner. 'Yours?'

No need for her to go into detail. What could she say? That they hadn't changed in over a decade? That they still went to church every Sunday? That they still asked after him?

'They're fine.'

'Great.' These personal topics were awkward. Perhaps it would be best if they steered away from them? Gray's parents had always been an awkward subject anyway. She could recall meeting them only a couple of times, and one of those occasions had been at the wedding! They'd been a bit hard to talk to. Gruff. Abrupt. Not that keen on smiling. She'd babbled on *their* behalf! Chattering away like a radio DJ, musing on life, asking and answering her own questions. She'd been relieved to leave them and go and talk to others, and had just hoped that they'd liked her.

They'd turned up to the wedding anyway. Mr McGregor in his wheelchair, his face all red and broken-veined.

They trekked a bit further. Beau snapped pictures of columbines and hellebores and a herd of moose they saw in the distance. Then Mack brought them into a large clearing that had a stone circle in the centre.

'Base Camp Number One, people! I'll teach you later how to safely contain your campfire, but first we're going to get working on our first medical scenario—soft tissue injuries. As I said before, these are some of the most common injuries we get here in the park, and they can be minor or major. A soft tissue injury is damage to the ligaments, muscles or tendons throughout the body, so we're looking at sprains, strains and contusions. This sort of damage to the body can result in pain, bruising or localised swelling—even, if severe, loss of function or blood volume.' He looked at each of them with determination. 'You do *not* want to lose either. So what can we do out here with our limited kit? Gray? Care to enlighten us?'

'Normally you'd follow the PRICE protocol—protection, rest, ice, compression and elevation.'

'Perfect—did you all hear that?'

The group all murmured agreement.

'Now, unless you're in the North or South Pole, you aren't going to have any ice, so you might have to skip that step, but can anyone think of an alternative?'

Beau raised her hand. 'If you have a sealable bag, you could fill it with water from a stream and rest that over the injury.'

'You could. What else might happen with a soft tissue injury? Someone without a medical degree care to hazard an answer?'

No one answered.

'You'll need to stop any blood loss. And you have minimum bandages in your first aid kit. So, I want you all to get into your pairs and have one of you be the patient, with a lower leg injury that is open down to the bone from knee to ankle. The other partner needs to use whatever they have to hand to protect the open wound. *Go!'*

Beau looked up at Gray. 'Doctor or patient?'

He shrugged. 'Ladies' choice. You choose.'

She smiled. 'Then I think I'll have to be the doctor.'

Gray nodded and plonked himself down on the ground, then looked up at her, squinting in the sun. 'Can you help me, Doctor? I've got a boo-boo.'

CHAPTER THREE

SHE WATCHED AS he reached forward to raise his trouser leg and tried not to stare.

His leg was thick with muscle and covered in fine dark hair, and she swallowed hard, knowing she would have to touch his skin.

Distracted, Beau opened her first aid kit and tried to concentrate. For an open wound she'd have to use the gloves, the saline wash to clean away any dirt in it, two gauze pads, the triangular arm bandage, tape and maybe even the safety pin. Almost all of the equipment in her first aid kit.

She looked up at Mack, who was wandering through the group, watching people's ministrations. 'If we use all of this on one wound, Mack, that only leaves us plasters, antiseptic wipes and scissors for the rest of the week.'

Mack grinned back at her, mischief in his eyes. 'So what do you want *me* to do? You're out in the field—technically I'm not here. You two need to survive. You need to bandage his wound.'

'Because of blood loss and the risk of infection?'

'So what are you going to do?'

'Use it.'

Mack grinned again.

'But that doesn't leave us much if there's going to be another injury.'

'Well, if you didn't clean the wound properly or stop the bleeding, what would happen to your patient?'

'He could lose consciousness. Or it could become septic.'

'So you have your answer.' He walked on, pointing things out to others, showing some of the less well-trained how best to use the triangular arm bandage.

Beau squatted beside Gray and considered his leg. 'Okay, I'll flush the wound with saline first.' She put on the gloves and cracked the end of the small container, allowed the saline to run down Gray's leg, watching as the rivulets separated and dribbled along his skin.

'You could use drinking water, too.'

'Yes, but keeping you hydrated would be a strong reason to save as much water as possible, in case I can't light a fire to boil some more.'

He nodded and watched her.

'Gauze pads next, along the shin line.'

'Should I yell? How much acting do they want us to do?'

Beau gave a small smile. 'Whatever you feel comfortable with, I guess.' She looked around her and picked up a short thick stick, proffered it towards his mouth. 'Do you want to scream?' She grabbed hold of his shin and calf muscle and deliberately pushed her thumbs into his pretend open wound.

He grimaced. 'I might have to dock you points for being a sadist.'

She grinned as she pulled open the packing around the triangular arm bandage, then gently and delicately draped it over his shin and tied it as neatly as she could behind the leg, creating some constriction to prevent blood loss, but not making it too tight to restrict blood flow.

'How's that, Mr Patient?'

'Feels great. I can sense survival already.'

'Good.'

'You *do* have a gentle touch.'

'You see? There's a lot you don't know about me.'

She sat back on her haunches and looked around the rest of the group to see what everyone else had done. Justin and Claire hadn't used their gauze pads, but everyone had used the arm bandage.

Mack was nodding his head in approval as he walked amongst them. 'Good. Good. You've successfully treated the wound—but what do you need to be aware of whilst you wait for recovery or help?'

Beau raised her hand. 'Whether the patient can still move his toes—and look for signs of infection, too.'

'And how would we know there are signs of infection without undressing the wound?'

Again, Beau answered. 'Signs of fever, pallor, increase of pain in the affected limb, loss of function, numbness, unconsciousness, rapid breathing.'

Mack nodded.

Gray leaned in and whispered, 'Still the teacher's pet?'

She glanced at him. 'I like to learn. I like to know that I'm right.'

'Still, you're a doctor. You need to give the others a chance to answer a few questions. Perhaps they'd like to learn, too?'

She almost bit back at him. *Almost.* The temptation to answer him sharply was strong. To tell him to mind his own business, let him know that he couldn't tell her what to do. But she was also mindful that she'd agreed to a truce and, not wanting more confrontation, she nodded assent.

Mack continued to walk amongst the group. 'What would you do if blood began seeping through the bandage?'

Beau almost answered, then bit her lip as she felt Gray shift beside her. *Let someone else answer.*

'Would we replace the bandage?'

Rick answered, 'No. We could tear strips of clothing and add it on top of the bandage.'

Mack nodded, smiling. 'Good. Okay. You all did quite well there. Now, let's think about setting up camp—and then we're going to tackle recovery position and CPR.'

Gray began to remove the bandage and then rolled his trouser leg down.

Beau watched him, then gathered up the bits and pieces they'd used. 'What shall we do with these, Mack? There aren't clinical waste bins out here, either.'

'We'll burn them on the fire once we get it going.'

Right. She supposed that seemed sensible. All the others were starting to get out their tents and equipment, so Beau turned to her own backpack. This was the part she'd been dreading. Putting up a tent. She'd never done that before.

All part of the learning experience.

'Look at you. Reading the instructions like a real Boy Scout.' Gray appeared at her side.

'I like to be prepared. Proper planning prevents poor performance. I'm not like you. Spontaneous. Off the cuff. I like to know what's happening. The order of things. I don't like surprises. You should know that.'

He shook his head. 'I disagree. I think you take risks, too.'

'Me?' She almost laughed at his ridiculous suggestion. 'I don't take risks!'

'No? Who chose to come on the Extreme Wilderness Medical Survival Course on an active supervolcano?'

Beau opened her mouth to speak but couldn't think of anything to say.

'And the Beau I know wouldn't do any of this if it wasn't part of some bigger plan—am I right?'

She closed her mouth, frustrated.

It was so maddening that he could still see right through her.

Gray hadn't brought a tent like everyone else. He had a tarpaulin that he'd propped up with a couple of walking poles, spread over a hammock that he'd attached to two sturdy tree trunks. It took him a matter of a few minutes to get his pitch all set up, and once he was done, he was eager to get his boots off and relax.

But he couldn't concentrate.

Beau was opposite him, on the other side of the campfire, trying—and failing—to put up her tent. She was *inside* the tent now, and he could hear her muttered cursing.

After one particularly loud expletive he chuckled and went over. 'Er…knock-knock?'

There was a pause in the muttering and angry swearing and eventually her head popped out of the tent. Her face was almost as red as her mussed-up, statically charged hair. *'What?'*

Gray knelt down beside the tent entrance so that he was level with Beau's face. 'Do you want a hand?'

She looked at him, her brow creased with frustrated lines. 'From *you*?'

'Tent erection at your service.'

He watched as she blushed deeply before looking at everyone else around the camp, who all seemed to be managing at a reasonable rate compared to her.

'You know, I could have just let you get on with it. I'm being kind here. Offering a branch with pretty little olives on it.'

She bit her lip. 'Okay. But this is the only kind of erection I want from you.'

He smiled. 'Okay.'

She nodded and crawled out, huffing and puffing, standing tall and then letting out a big sigh as the tent collapsed onto the ground beside her like a deflated balloon. 'It was meant to do that.'

He managed not to laugh. 'Of course. Have you… erm…ever put a tent up before?'

She pursed her lips before answering and he tried his hardest not to focus on the fact that she looked as if she was awaiting a kiss.

'No. I've never camped before. But I read the instructions and it looked quite simple.'

He held out his hand. 'Give me the instructions.'

Beau pulled them from her back pocket and handed them over. They were folded up and creased.

Gray thanked her, pretended to look at them briefly and then threw them onto the campfire.

'*Gray!*' She stared after the instructions open-mouthed as they were eaten up by the orange flames. She turned back to him.

'You don't need the instructions. Tents are easy.'

'Oh, *really*? Easy, huh?'

'Absolutely.'

'Well, be my guest.' She looked around for a seat but after finding none just sat on the ground with her arms and legs crossed. She looked smug, almost as if she expected him to fail and become as frustrated as she'd been when she'd tried.

Gray grabbed the poles he needed, from where Beau had laid them out on the ground in logical order and size, and instantly began threading them through fabric tubes and forming the outer shell of the tent.

He heard her curse and tried not to smile at his own smugness when he saw the look on her face. He picked up the pegs and pinned the tent to the ground. Within minutes he had it ready.

Wiping his hands on his trousers, he turned to her with a happy smile. 'There you go. The best erection in camp.'

'How did you…? Where did you…?' She sighed. 'How…?'

Gray shrugged. 'A gentleman never tells.'

She cocked her head to one side and smiled. 'I'm not asking a *gentleman*.'

'Ouch!'

'Come on…how did you do that so fast?'

He considered the tent briefly before he replied. 'I've got one of these.'

She looked at his tarp. 'But not on this trip?'

'I prefer the bivvy and tarp during the summer months.'

'Okay. Well, thank you very much. I appreciate it.'

He could tell that it had taken her a lot to thank him. He simply smiled and let her get her equipment into the tent, even helped her roll out her sleeping bag. Once they were done, they both stood there awkwardly, staring at each other.

Gray felt so tempted to tell her everything there and then, but something inside told him that now was not the right time. Beau was still suspicious of him. Trying to show that she was indifferent to his presence. Which obviously meant she was still angry. Perhaps he would talk to her in a few days. Give the shock of them both being here a chance to pass away. Give her time to cool down and be receptive to what he had to say.

Perhaps if he showed her during this course that he was a good guy—reliable, dependable, someone she could trust with her life—then maybe by the end of the week she'd be much more amenable to hearing what he had to say. And they could put the past to rest.

Mack made his way over. 'Hey, Gray, you're rostered for cooking duties tonight. Feel like running up a culinary masterpiece with some beans?'

Cooking? He didn't feel confident about that. And not for other people! Not if they wanted to stay alive. He could perform heart transplants or bypass grafts or even transmyocardial laser revascularisation—but cook up something tasty? That was edible? That didn't require its film to be pierced and to be shoved in a microwave?

'Er…sure, Mack.'

Beau stood watching him now, her arms crossed, one hip thrust to the side and a grin on her face.

'Problem, Gray?'

Of course she would remember his fear of the kitchen. When they'd been together, Beau had done all the cooking after his one disastrous attempt at a beef stroganoff had resulted in a weird brown splodge on their plates that had tasted, somehow, of nothing.

He'd never learnt from his mother. The kitchen had been her domain—the one place she'd been able to escape from the men in her family and know they wouldn't disturb her. The mysteries of the kitchen and its processes had always eluded Gray, but that had always been fine with him. The hospital had a canteen, and when he wasn't there, he ate out.

'Maybe.'

'I thought you'd camped before? Whatever did you eat?'

'I brought army ration packs. They were self-heating. I didn't have to do anything.'

'Okay...what ingredients do you have to work with?'

Beau headed over to the bags Mack had pointed out and rummaged through the ingredients. There were butter beans, tomatoes, potatoes and a small can of sardines.

'That's not a lot for thirteen people,' she said.

Mack grinned. 'Well, this *is* a survival course. Be thankful I'm not making you forage for ingredients. Yet.'

Beau's face lit up. 'Of *course*!' She disappeared into her tent and came back out holding her guidebook on Yellowstone. 'This will tell you what we can eat. We could get some of the others to forage for foodstuffs and add them to the pan. You stay here and chop up the potatoes. Leave the skin on, Gray—the most nutritious part of the vegetable is just under the skin.'

'Is that right?' He was amused to see her so energised. It reminded him of the sweet Beau he'd used to know so well. 'Are you chaining me to the kitchen sink?'

She shrugged. 'Stops you running away.'

Then she headed off to clear her plan with Mack and gather some of the others to help find food.

He watched her. Asking Mack for advice on foraging and safety. Organising people. Arranging them into teams. Showing them what they might be able to find. One pair was dispatched to gather more firewood. Another pair to collect water for purifying.

She was in her element.

Gray sighed, sat down by the potatoes and grabbed a small, short knife, ready to start chopping.

Considering she hadn't even been able to bring herself to even look at him earlier today, they had already taken huge steps towards bringing about a ceasefire. Maybe soon they could have those peace talks they so desperately needed.

While everyone waited for dinner to cook, Mack began teaching the recovery position.

'If you come across a casualty who is unconscious and breathing, then you'll need to put them into the recovery position. Anyone tell me why?'

Beau's hand shot into the air and Gray smiled.

Mack looked for someone else to answer, but when everyone looked blank, he allowed her to. 'Yes, Beau?'

'Rolling a patient onto their side stops the tongue from blocking the airway and also helps prevent choking in case of vomiting.'

'That's right. Beau, perhaps you'd like to be our pretend patient?'

She nodded and went over to the ranger and lay flat on her back on the pine-needle-covered ground.

'Before we put the patient into the recovery position, what should we check for?'

'Check breathing again?' suggested Conrad.

'You could. But let's assume she's still breathing. You'll need to check to make sure there's nothing in her pockets that will jab into her when we roll her over. So, things like car keys, pens, pencils, sticks—things like that. We should also remove the patient's glasses and turn any jewelled rings towards the palm.'

He demonstrated by sliding a ring round on Beau's hand.

'There's also a little poem you can remember to re-mind yourself of what you need to do here. *"Say hello and raise my knee, then take my hand and roll to me."*'

He placed Beau's hand palm-up by her face, as if she was saying hi, and then grabbed her trouser leg and raised the knee of the opposite leg, so that her foot was downwards on the forest floor. Then he grabbed her other hand, put it by her face and, using the trouser leg of the raised knee, rolled Beau over onto her side, adjusting the hand under her face to open the airway.

'Simple. Okay, tell me the poem.'

"'Say hello and raise my knee, then take my hand and roll to me."'

'Good. You need to keep repeating that to yourself. It'll stand you in good stead. Always remember to po-sition yourself on the side you want the patient to roll onto. Now, what if your patient is pregnant?'

'You'd need to roll them onto their left side,' said Gray.

Mack nodded. 'Absolutely. Why?'

'Less pressure on the inferior vena cava.'

'Thank you, Gray. Now, I'd like you all to get into your buddy pairs and practise this. Take turns at being the patient. Off you go.'

Gray stood over Beau and smiled. 'Want to stay there?'

'If I must.'

He knelt beside her and awkwardly patted her pock-

ets. He hadn't expected to be *touching* Beau. Not like
this. Not holding her hand in his and laying it by her
face. It was too much, too soon.

Talking to her he could handle. Joking with her and
keeping the mood light he could handle. But this en-
forced closeness…? It reminded him too much of the
past, when touching her had been easy and pleasurable
and had made her eyes light up.

Not now, though. Now she lay stiffened on the floor,
uncomfortable and gritting her teeth. Was it that awful
for her? Him being this close? Was she hating every
second of it?

Once she was in the recovery position, she leapt up
and brushed herself down. 'My turn.'

Disarmed, he lay down and closed his eyes, not wanting to see the discomfort in *her* eyes, not wanting to
make this any more difficult for her than it plainly already was.

Beau got him into the recovery position quickly.
'You're all done.'

He got up and brushed off the pine needles and they
stood there awkwardly, staring at each other, not knowing what to say.

Clearly the activity had been difficult for both of
them and Gray couldn't stand it.

'I'll just check on the food.' He went over to the
cooking pot and gave it a stir. It didn't look great, but
it did smell nice. Mack had shown Beau and the others where to find some small bulbs of wild garlic, and
they'd added that to Gray's dish.

He glanced through the simmering steam at Beau
and began to wonder just how the hell he was going to
get through this week.

Mack got everyone up. 'Okay, folks, that's it for today. The rest of the evening is your own. Gray is our chef this evening, so let's all keep an ear out for him ringing the dinner bell.'

Gray had no idea when it would be ready. Claire came over and asked, and when he shrugged, she stuck the small paring knife into the potatoes to check.

'Seems good to me.'

'Yeah? I'd better dish up, then.'

Gray served them all a portion that was quite meagre, even with the additions. It actually tasted nice, which was a surprise. The others made satisfactory noises whilst eating it anyway, so he could only hope they weren't just being polite.

Afterwards Gray was ready for bed. His foot was starting to trouble him and he ached in places he hadn't been expecting. Not to mention that his nerves were still on edge from the recovery scenario.

He had to get around the way it felt when he touched her. He had to forget the softness of her skin, the smooth creaminess of it and the knowledge that he knew exactly how the rest of her felt.

It would feel so good to caress her again.

He sneaked a glance at her whilst she was talking to Dean and Toby. He saw the twinkle in her eyes, her joyous smile. Heard her infectious laughter. She looked relaxed, as if she was enjoying herself.

I want her to be that way with me.

Later, Gray and Beau carried the pile of tin dishes down to the creek and laid them beside the shallow running water, trying to rinse them in the darkening light. Beau was struggling for the right thing to say. How could she start a conversation with the man she'd once thought she'd known inside out…?

But he started it instead. 'I'm glad we're both making the effort to try and get along.' He paused to glance at her. 'It's good.'

'It's easier than trying to ignore you.'

He smirked. 'I'm in joyous rapture about that.'

The dishes rinsed well in the stream, and Beau figured the small particles of food that were getting rinsed off would hopefully feed some of the fish or wildlife further downstream.

'Your cooking has improved.'

A smile crept across his face. 'A compliment? I'll take it.'

'No, really. It was a nice dinner. Considering.'

'Considering it was cooked by me?'

She nodded and laughed.

He smiled at her, as if pleased to hear her laugh again. 'Thank you. I'm just glad everyone was able to eat it without choking. No one's been taught the Heimlich manoeuvre yet.'

She laughed again, her gaze meeting his, and then suddenly she wasn't laughing any more. She was caught by the deep mossy stare of his eyes, the longing she saw within them, and by her own fear as old feelings came bubbling to the surface.

She stood up abruptly. 'We ought to head back. It's dark. Who knows what's out here with us?'

He stood, too. 'Yeah, you're right.'

The deepening shadows around them just served to make his eyes more intense as he looked at her. She could feel old urges reasserting themselves, and memories of how easy it had once been to be with this man—

how she'd loved him so much she hadn't thought there was anything left of her own soul that was just her.

Beau bent to gather the dishes. Gray helped, and both of them were careful not to touch each other before they headed back to camp. Walking a good metre apart.

CHAPTER FOUR

SHE'D COME A long way since her arrival at the ranger station that morning. If anyone had told her that by the end of the day she'd be sharing a meal with her ex-fiancé and washing dishes by a stream with him—whilst *smiling*—she would have told them that they were crazy. No chance.

But she had. And now she sat across from him, with the campfire crackling away between them as night fell, catching glimpses of his face in the firelight.

He was still the same old Gray. Slightly more grizzled, slightly heavier set than before, but still with the same cheek, the same nerve. The other hikers all seemed to like him. But he'd always had that effect on people. Dean and Rick, the brothers from Seattle, were currently seated on either side of him, and beyond them everyone seemed to be listening to the story Gray was weaving.

He was a born storyteller, enamoured of holding everyone's attention. It was probably why he'd chosen cardiology, she thought. Heart surgeons always seemed to act as if they were the best. Because without the heart the body wouldn't work at all.

Well, Gray, without a brain the heart doesn't stand a chance, either.

That was the difference between them. She could see that now. Beau had always been the steady influence—the thinker. The planner. Everything meticulously detailed. Whereas Gray had always been the rash one, the passionate one, the spontaneous, carefree daredevil.

Initially she'd been excited by those qualities in him. His indifference to planning the future, his studies, his life. She'd loved the way he could get excited about one thing and then develop a passion for something else entirely further down the line. How he could be thrilled by new technologies, new inventions, new medicines. Whereas *she* had always been cautious—researching new methods, new techniques, checking the statistics on their success, talking to the people involved about their experiences, making sure everything was *safe* before she considered using anything in her work.

Beau did not like surprises. Especially unpleasant ones. And Gray had caused her the most unpleasant surprise in her life so far by not turning up to their wedding. A wedding could be planned in advance, carefully thought-out, with alternatives arranged, waiting in the wings, to prevent any last-minute hitches. You planned the day meticulously so that you didn't have to worry about it running smoothly, so that it *just did*. And on the day itself you were meant to just turn up and go with the flow. Put on your dress, do your hair, do your make-up, smile for the camera and *enjoy*.

And because she'd planned her wedding so well, she'd not expected anything to go wrong at all. She'd been naïvely blissful, secure about her feelings for her husband-to-be, anticipating the joy that their marriage would bring, knowing the happiness they already had was growing and growing with every day.

So when he hadn't shown up, it had felt as if she'd

been punched in the gut! A blow that had come out of nowhere. And her heart...? It had been totally broken.

And then the questions had flooded her mind. Why had he abandoned her? Had she been wrong? Had it all been one-sided?

Looking at him now, adored by his fellow hikers, she still found it hard to tell herself that he had actually just left her there. Without a word. Without a hint of concern.

Had there been signs in the days *before* the wedding that he'd planned to run out on her? She couldn't recall. He had seemed a little distant occasionally, when she'd gone on about the arrangements, but weren't all grooms-to-be like that? Surely it was the bride's prerogative to go overboard when planning her perfect day?

The pain had been incredible. It had made her doubt their love. Made her doubt *herself*. She'd spent weeks worrying that there was something wrong with *her*. That she was lacking something—that there was something Gray needed and couldn't get it from her.

But what? She was a nice person. Clever. Kind. Friendly. Loving. She'd never been shy in showing him her affection. Their sex life had been great! *Hadn't it?* Of course it had been. No man could make a woman feel like that and then say things were lacking in that department.

He hadn't said much in the days leading up to the wedding, she supposed. He hadn't said much in regard to their marriage, or his hopes and dreams, so she'd talked about hers, hoping to draw him out. But he'd never said anything. Just smiled and looked...nervous.

Beau poked at the campfire with a long stick and watched as the embers collapsed and spat heat upwards and outwards, tiny flecks of flame bursting forth and disappearing into the night sky above. The dark blue of the night revealed the sparkle of stars that she could never have hoped to see from her home town of Oxford. Even from the hospital roof you couldn't see a sky such as this.

The vast openness of Yellowstone made her realise that there was so much she wasn't used to seeing. Or noticing. It made her aware that she wouldn't know if something else was out there until she made the time to look for it.

Was there something about Gray that she'd not known about?

She glanced up at him once more and caught his gaze upon her through the heat of the orange flames. He looked pensive, and he rubbed at his jaw before he turned to answer Rick, who'd asked him a question.

He looks weary.

She wasn't used to seeing him look worn down. He'd always looked sprightly. Ready for anything. Raring to go.

Had today done that to him? Had *she*? She didn't like how that made her feel, how uncomfortable she suddenly was, and her stomach squirmed at the notion.

Perhaps there was more to this situation between them? Something she'd not been aware of because she'd never thought to look for it. Was it something obvious? Was it staring her in the face? Like the stars—always there, but not always seen?

Was I so wrapped up in the wedding that I forgot to focus on us?

Beau threw her stick into the fire and watched as it got swallowed up by the flames. She knew with certainty now that this week was going to be one hell of a learning experience.

And not the kind that she'd been expecting.

Beau had spent an uncomfortable night in her tent. Before the trip she'd bought a decent one, and a groundsheet, a sleeping mat and a sleeping bag, and had thought that would be enough for her to get a decent night's sleep. But the ground had been hard and unforgiving and she'd tossed and turned, worrying about being away from her patients, being here with Gray— not to mention the possibilities of insect invasion—before she'd finally fallen into a broken sleep at about five o'clock in the morning.

Unfortunately Mack had woken them all up around seven by banging a tin bowl with a rock right by the entrance to her shelter, and she'd woken blearily, feeling as if her body was bruised all over.

'Okay, okay… I'm awake,' she'd moaned, rubbing her eyes and blinking thoroughly until they seemed to operate correctly.

Now she sat up, stretching out her back muscles and rolling her stiff shoulders and noting, with some small satisfaction, that her tent had not filled with ants overnight. *Perhaps it's safe to sleep on the ground after all?* Then she pulled herself from her sleeping bag, put on a fresh set of underwear, the clothes she'd worn yesterday, and put her hair up into a ponytail and unzipped her tent.

'Morning, Beau.'

Gray was already up, looking freshly groomed, his eyes bright and sparkly.

She groaned. Used to her normal schedule, Beau was not a morning person. She needed a good-sized mug of coffee, a Danish pastry and a blast of loud music in her car to wake her properly before she got to the hospital, and she guessed she wouldn't get that here.

She peered gloomily at the pot that Barb was in charge of. 'What's for breakfast?'

'Oatmeal.'

'Porridge? Great,' she replied without enthusiasm.

It wasn't exactly a buttery, flaky pastry delight, but never mind. It would have to do. She warmed her hands over the fire and then ducked back into her tent to grab her toothbrush and toothpaste. She stood and cleaned her teeth and rinsed her toothbrush with the last of her bottled water.

'I've got a pot of boiled water cooling down already,' Barb said when she returned. 'Have you got your purifying tablets?'

'I've got a filter.'

'Brilliant.'

Beau was quite pleased with her state-of-the-art filter. It meant that she could collect water from any source, pour it through, and all protozoa and bacteria would be removed, including giardia and cryptosporidium, the two biggest causes of infection in water. It saved having to boil water and wait for it to cool before it could be put into containers. It had been one of her new purchases, thoroughly researched and tested, and she'd even looked up reviews from previous customers to make sure it was the best for the job.

After she'd put her toiletries away, she stretched her back once again and took in the view. Now that she was more awake, she could appreciate where they were. High up on a mountainside, on a grassy plateau, surrounded by nature, with not a building, a towering spire nor a frantic cyclist in sight. Just clear blue skies, promising the heat of another day, the sun, a gentle warm breeze and the bright, cheery sounds of birdsong lighting up the morning.

'It's gorgeous, isn't it?'

'It certainly is.'

Gray smiled down at her, making her jump. She sat up.

'What are we doing today?'

'Mack said we need to cover CPR, as we missed it last night, and then we're heading higher up to cover altitude sickness.'

She nodded. 'Right. How far up do you think we already are?'

'Four or five thousand feet?'

'And altitude sickness sets in at…what? Eight thousand or more?'

'Depends on the climber. Could be now.'

'Mack won't want to take us up that far, will he?' she asked, feeling the pain in her calf muscles from yesterday's climb.

'No, I won't,' Mack answered as he came out of his tent. 'It's a survival course, not a medical experiment.'

She smiled at him. 'Glad to hear it.'

Barb gave the oatmeal a stir. 'This is done. Everyone hungry?'

Everyone nodded and grabbed their metal dishes to receive a small helping of breakfast before sitting down around the fire to eat quietly.

Porridge wasn't her thing, but Beau ate it anyway, and Justin and Claire offered to get everything washed up before they packed up camp.

They soon covered the CPR training—how to do it effectively without defibrillators. Two breaths to thirty compressions in two rounds, before checking for signs of life—breathing, pulse rate, chest rise and fall. Mack showed them all how to find the right spot on the chest for compressions. How to place their hands. What sort of rhythm they needed and how fast. Showed them that even if they did it properly they might hear ribs break—which made everyone cringe at the thought!

Then there was a short break before Mack showed them how to put out the fire safely, and once they'd packed up their tents and equipment, they all set off once again on the next hike.

Gray fell into step beside Beau and she noticed that he was limping.

'Blisters?'

He didn't quite meet her gaze. 'Er…no. Not really.'

'How did you sleep?'

'Well, thanks. The hammock was great.'

'Lucky you. I barely got forty winks before Mack's alarm. The ground mat I bought felt as thin as tissue paper.'

He smiled. 'That's why I brought a hammock. Off the ground is better. Even the most comfortable bed is on legs.'

'The voice of experience?'

'Most definitely.'

Mack led them up a stony trail. Like a line of ants they began their ascent, and in the early-morning warmth they were all soon puffing and panting, stripping off layers as they got higher and higher. Beau focused on one point—the shirt of the person in front. Her mind was blank of everything as she simply concentrated on putting one foot in front of the other. Plodding on, climbing bit by bit, until they reached a lookout high on the side of the mountain.

Mack indicated a rest stop by dropping his backpack to the floor. 'Let's take an hour here. Get fluids on board, and then we'll start our next lesson from this beautiful viewpoint.'

Beau slipped off her backpack and used it as a seat as she took a drink of water from her bottle. She was hot and sweaty, totally out of breath, and the muscles in her legs *burned*. She stretched her legs out in front of her and counted her blessings.

This was what she had come here for. To find nature. To escape the confines of the hospital. When had she last climbed anything? She didn't even climb stairs any more—she changed floors at the hospital by using the lift, and the same at home. Her flat was on the sixth floor and the lift worked perfectly every time she needed it. She *needed* this sort of workout. Blowing away the cobwebs on muscle groups that she ought to have been using. Using her body and not just her brain. Breathing in this fresh, crisp mountain air and feeling alive!

She watched a large bird, far out above the canyon, circle effortlessly in the air. 'Now, *that's* the way to climb to new heights.'

Gray squinted up at the sky. 'I wonder if birds get altitude sickness.'

'Or have a fear of heights. Can you imagine?'

'We humans think too much. We worry and fret, build our anxieties on imagined threats. If you think about it, animals have it easier.'

She took another drink of water. 'What worries *you*, Gray? You never struck me as a worrier.'

He stretched out his legs. 'I worry about lots of things. I just choose not to show it.'

Leo came over and rested against the rocks next to them. 'You're a surgeon, though, aren't you? You can't show your patients that you're worried. They'd have no confidence in your abilities if you did.'

Gray nodded. 'That's right. It's a strength not to wear your heart on your sleeve. Patients need to see that you're confident and sure.'

But Beau was thinking about their past. 'And what if you're *not* sure about something?' she asked, her face curious. 'Do you talk to them about your concerns? Do you ever share your doubts so they know the full picture?'

It was obvious he knew she wasn't just referring to his work. 'I always let my patients know the full picture. They always understand the risks. Letting them know about dangers and possibilities doesn't stop you from being confident.'

'But what if you're *not* confident in an outcome? What then?'

He stared at her, long and hard. 'Then I don't proceed.'

She nodded, her face stony. 'You don't move forward?'

'No.'

Leo looked between the two of them, clearly puzzled at the tone of the conversation and at the way they were looking at each other. He took a bite from his trail bar. 'Looks like Mack's about to start the next lesson.'

He was right.

Mack gathered them all round. 'Okay, I'm sure that as we made the climb up here we all noticed we were getting a little out of breath. Now, imagine being like that all the time…not being able to breathe, feeling like there isn't enough air, struggling to take in enough oxygen. How do you think that's going to affect you on a day-to-day basis?'

Rick put up his hand. 'You'd struggle.'

Mack nodded. 'Too long in too high an altitude, without a period of adjustment, can affect thinking skills and judgement calls, and it leads to hikers and climbers taking risks. Luckily here in Yellowstone we don't have the extreme elevations that provoke serious cases of altitude sickness, but we do have heights over eight thousand feet, and as soon as you go beyond this number, you'll start to see symptoms. Now, can anyone tell me what those symptoms are?'

Beau was itching to answer, but she thrust her hands in her pockets and bit her lip to stop herself from speaking.

Conrad suggested an answer. 'Dizziness?'

'That's one. Can you give me another?'

'Nausea?'

Mack nodded. 'Most people complain of a headache first. They get nauseous, feel exhausted. Then they might be short of breath, might get nosebleeds, muscle weakness. So what do we do to alleviate the condition?'

Beau gritted her teeth, let Mack continue.

'We descend. Height creates the problem, so going back down to where it's easier to breathe solves it. People *can* adjust, though. This is why on mountain climbs—and specifically when tackling Everest and those sorts of places—climbers ascend and then come down for a bit. Then they go up again—then down. It's a back and forth dance. Two steps forward, one step back. It acclimatises them to the new altitude. It allows their bodies to get used to the thinner air.'

Everyone nodded.

'The air itself still has oxygen at about twenty-one per cent. That doesn't change as you go higher. What *does* change is the air pressure, and that's what causes altitude sickness. Unfortunately we can't tell who will succumb. Some of you may even be feeling it now.'

He looked around at them and Claire raised her hand and mentioned that she had a headache.

He nodded once. 'So we start to head down. Let's go!'

They all got to their feet and slung on their back-packs wearily. The air did seem thinner. Everything seemed so much sharper up high. But the trail Mack led them down quickly led them into a beautiful green valley where they had to wait for a herd of moose to pass by.

Beau got out her camera. They were magnificent animals! As tall as she was, heavyset, with brown-black coats and long, horse-like faces. There was one with huge cupped antlers, and he stood there proudly as his herd passed the hikers, heading for a crop of willow trees, where they stopped to graze.

She took shot after shot, excited by getting her first close-up with an animal she hadn't a chance of seeing in the wild in the UK, and when she finally put her camera away, Gray smiled at her.

'What?'

He laughed. 'You're still the same.'

She shook her head, disagreeing with him. 'I'm older. Wiser, I hope.'

'I grant you that…but you still have that joy in you that I saw all those years ago. You always saw the joy and goodness in everything.'

'That's my problem. I *thought* I saw it in you once, but…I was wrong.'

He stopped walking and sighed. 'You weren't wrong.'

'Then why did you hurt me so badly?' She stopped

to look at him directly. The others were ahead. They couldn't hear.

Gray looked down at the ground. 'That wasn't my intention. I was trying to stop you from being hurt further down the line.'

He passed her and began to walk to catch up with the rest of the group.

Beau watched his retreating form and felt the old hurt and anger begin to rise. She pushed it down, refusing to show him that he could still press her buttons.

She hurried to catch up, too, and as she passed him, she muttered, 'Just for your information…it didn't work.'

Gray stopped and stared after her.

They walked for a few more hours. They passed through rocky canyons, small copses and grassy open plains. They followed the Gallatin River, passing a few men who stood in it in waders, fly-fishing, and giving them a wave.

Gray could feel the weariness in his legs—particularly his left leg—and ached to stop and stretch out, but he said nothing, preferring to soldier on.

They were all alert and on the lookout for bears, knowing that these mammals were keen on fishing themselves, but they saw none, and Mack soon led them off the popular trail and deeper into wilder country.

Just as Gray was feeling the familiar pinching pain in his left calf that told him a cramp was about to set in, he heard crying and groaning. His ears pricked up at the sound and his doctor radar kicked in. Someone was afraid and in pain. And then suddenly, there before them, in a clearing, were three people lying on the ground with blood everywhere.

Adrenaline shot through his system. The cramp was forgotten as he raced past the others in his group with Beau to attend the casualties before them.

There were two men and a woman. First he needed to assess them all, find out who was in the most medical danger, and he knelt by the first patient—the woman—who lay on her back, clutching at a bleed in her thigh, hopefully not her femoral artery. Out here, a bleed like that could be fatal.

'Lie back! Can you tell me what happened?'

He went to check the leg, already pulling off his belt so that he could create a tourniquet, and then he noticed that there was no wound. No tear in the fabric. And the blood was fake. He looked up at the others, to see Beau looking confused, too.

Mack knelt down beside him, grinning. 'Pretend patients! The wounds aren't real, but you might come across people on your travels with serious injuries. I want you to work in groups of four. Each group take a patient. Assess the injury, ascertain what happened, and then I want you to tend to that patient. We'll feed back to the group what we did and why. Gray, you work with Beau, Conrad and Barb. Jack and Leo—you're with Dean and Rick. The rest of you, tend the third patient.'

Gray had already got fake blood all over his hands and he let out a huge breath. *Thank goodness it's not real!* It had really got his own blood pumping, though.

Beau knelt beside him and Conrad and Barb gathered round.

'Barb and I will let you two take the lead, Doc,' said Conrad. 'We're sure you know more than us.'

'Maybe, but you need to learn. Let's see what our "patient" can tell us.' He looked down at the woman on the ground. 'Can you tell me what happened to you today?'

'We were camping when we were attacked.'

'By animals?'

'No, some lads came into our camp. They were drunk and waving knives around.'

Gray nodded. He'd actually been in a similar situation once before, hiking in the Peak District. A group of rowdy teenagers had wandered into his campsite, drunk and disorderly, and had become very threatening. Luckily he'd managed to talk them down and send them on their way—but not before one of them had tripped over his guy rope and broken his nose.

'Was your leg injured with a knife or something else?'

'I'm not sure.'

He nodded, then looked up at Conrad and Barb. 'What do you think we should be thinking about doing here?'

'Stopping the bleeding?' Barb suggested.

'Good. How?'

'We could apply some pressure? Raise the injured limb?'

He nodded. *Good. They knew some basics.* 'What else? What if it was an arterial bleed?'

'Pressure and a tourniquet?'

'Good—but you'd have to be quick. Arterial bleeds spurt, and with force. The area around the wound will get messy quickly and the patient can lose a large amount of blood in a short time. What else do we need to do?'

Conrad and Barb looked blankly at each other. 'We're not sure, Doc.'

Beau smiled at them. 'Once you've dealt with an

arterial bleed, and it appears to be under control, you need to do two things. Find a way of getting more help, but also look for further injuries. Too many people assume that if a patient has one major injury that's all they have to look for. But patients can quite often have more possibly fatal injuries, so you need to assess your patient properly once the bleeding is stemmed and under control.'

'What if the bleeding doesn't get under control?'

'Then your patient could go into hypovolaemic shock. If they don't get help, they'll die.'

Barb paled slightly and Conrad put a comforting arm around his wife's shoulders. 'That's terrible.'

Gray showed the couple how to check for further injury, and how they could assess their patient's level of consciousness, then Mack gathered them all together.

The three 'patients' stood and had a bit of a stretch, grinning.

'Okay, so what did we all learn?'

Gray gave a brief rundown on what they'd covered with Conrad and Barb. One group had dealt with a venous bleed to an arm; the other had dealt with what had looked like a simple contusion—or bruising—to the abdomen.

Mack focused on this last one. 'Who else thinks that this was just a simple case of bruising?'

Beau put up her hand.

'Yes, Beau?'

'There could be internal bleeding. A bruise is the definition of an internal bleed, in fact.'

'So what could happen to our patient if this is ignored as a minor injury?'

'He could die. There are multiple major organs in

the abdomen, all at risk—the liver, the spleen, the pancreas...'

'Dangers of internal bleeding, please?'

'Exsanguination—possibly a tamponade on the heart.'

'Which is...?'

'A closure or blockage. Fluid collects around the heart, between the organ and the pericardial sac, and surrounds it, applying pressure and preventing it from beating.'

Mack looked at the group. 'Do we all see how different injuries—even ones that *seem* minor—can have devastating effects on a patient?'

The group nodded and agreed.

'And can we all agree that when you've been hiking for a long time—when you're exhausted, maybe sleep-deprived, hungry or starved of air, perhaps in a dangerous situation—how easy it might be to miss something important when assessing a patient or to make a mistake?'

Again there were murmurs of assent from them all.

'Out in the wilds you need to be on your game. You need to see the present danger, but you also need to be looking three steps ahead. Keeping your wits about you. Not making avoidable mistakes. Now...the likelihood of getting help immediately can be small. You might find yourself on your own, needing to get help and having to overcome obstacles to find it. Everyone get ready—I'm about to show you how to cross a river safely. Without a bridge.'

Gray raised his eyebrows. Surely everyone was exhausted? They'd hiked miles today and barely eaten. Though he guessed this was all part of the package. Trying to replicate the environment people might find themselves in and show them how easy it was to make a mistake.

He knew all about mistakes.

He'd made plenty.

He fell into step beside Beau and found himself drawing into himself. As always, when he focused on medicine he could exclude every other worry or emotion in his head—but when he wasn't, and real life had an opportunity to take residence, there was nothing to distract him.

Beau's presence had shaken him. With her here, he couldn't ignore what he'd done any more. Every time he looked at her it was a reminder of the pain he'd caused, even though at the time he'd told himself he was doing it to save her greater pain in the long run.

Beau had had aspirations for their future. It wasn't just going to be marriage for them—it was going to be a whole life together. Children. Grandchildren. *Great-*grandchildren. That was what she'd seen for them when she'd said yes to his spur-of-the-moment proposal.

She hadn't just said yes to him, but yes to all that, too. She'd seen years ahead of them, spent happily in each other's company as they went on holidays or had romantic weekends away, had picnics in the park, ice creams on the beach. She'd seen cosy chats, the pair of them snuggled under a quilt, holding hands, kissing, enjoying being with each other. Snatched kisses in the hospital as they passed each other on their way to work.

She'd only ever seen joy…

How could he ever tell her that he'd seen something different? How could he tell her that if he'd married her it might have been okay to start with, but then there would have been little differences of opinion? Silences and resentment and screaming arguments. How could he say he had known how their fallouts would turn into sleeping in separate rooms? That they would go without talking for days or, if they did talk, would only snipe at each other and resent the other person for making them feel so bad? How could he tell her that he saw slamming doors and broken plates as well as broken hearts? How could he begin to tell her that he wouldn't have—*couldn't* have—brought a child into all of that?

Marriage had meant something different to them both and she'd had no idea. There'd not been any way for him to tell her that marriage for him meant torture and ruination. How could you show that sort of vision to someone who viewed everything as though the world was only full of good things? Of hope and promise and happily-ever-afters.

Beau had been the light to his dark. The sun to his shadow. She had always been better than him. She'd had such a pure outlook and he hadn't wanted to spoil her beliefs. Dilute her sunshine and make clouds cover her world.

He'd walked away that day, knowing he couldn't face marriage. That he just didn't have it in him to stay and say those vows when he didn't believe they could be true. To love and to cherish? Maybe to start with. For better, for worse? Definitely too much of the latter! Until death do us part? Why would he want to put either of them through *that*?

Marriage to Beau should have been the greatest thing, but he'd been unable to see past his dread. He'd been a child of a loveless marriage. He knew what it was like to be forgotten. Unwanted. Not loved as a child should be loved, but *used*.

He could almost feel another wound ripping across his heart at the thought of it. His love for Beau had meant he'd tried to do the decent thing. He'd wanted her to be married. Happily. To someone who could give that to her and who stood an equal chance of believing in the same possibility of happiness. There had to be a man out there who thought the same as Beau. Who wanted the same things.

And yet... And yet Beau was still single. Alone. Her career was her shining light. Her joy.

They were both in their thirties now, and Beau still hadn't any children. What was that doing to her? It had been her dream to have kids...

Gray closed his eyes wearily and rested against a tree for a moment to catch his breath. His leg—his *foot*—hurt physically. Trying to ignore it, trying to gather his mental strength, he opened his eyes to carry on—but stopped as he noticed that Beau had come to stand by him.

'Are you okay?' she asked.

He tried to gauge if she really was concerned. But the look in her beautiful eyes was enough to convince him that she was truly worried. Her brow was lined with worry. She'd even reached out her hand to lay it on his upper arm.

He nodded. ''Course. Just trying to ignore something that's not there.'

Beau looked puzzled. 'Are you in pain?'

He shrugged. 'A little.'

She tried to make him hold her gaze. 'Anything I can help you with?'

Gray let out an angry sigh. He was angry with himself. Angry at having got everything so wrong. Angry at hurting Beau. For still hurting her even now. And she was being *nice* to him. Showing care and concern when she had every right in the world to be ignoring him still.

But when he looked into her eyes, he got caught. He was trapped and ensnared by her gaze. Her concern and worry for him was pushing past his defences, sneaking around his walls of pretence and bravado, reaching around his heart and taking hold.

Hesitantly he reached up and stroked her face. 'You're so perfect, Beau.'

She stiffened slightly at his touch. Was she afraid? Shocked? But then she began to breathe again. He saw the way her shoulders dropped, her jaw softened.

She gazed right back at him. 'Just not for you.'

'But we were so close, weren't we?'

She nodded, a gentle smile curling her mouth. 'We were.'

He took a moment just to look at her. At the way the sunshine reflected off her hair, at the way the tip of her nose was beginning to catch the sun. The way the smile on her face warmed his heart…

Gray looked away. He had no right to enjoy those feelings any more. He tried to cast them aside, to stand straighter, to concentrate on the task ahead—the walking, the hiking. He couldn't start to feel that way for Beau any more. He'd only ended up hurting her in the past. He'd not been able to offer her what she'd needed then—and now…? Now he had even less. He wasn't even a whole man. He was broken. His mistake had been to think he had been whole in the first place.

He stepped past her, feeling her hand on his arm drop away as he moved out of reach. His heart sank. He had to be firm with himself. It was at moments like these when he might all too easily slip into thinking about another chance with Beau.

What would be the point? Where would it lead?

To a relationship again?

No. We'd just end up in the same place.

Gray almost let out a growl of frustration. Instead he gritted his teeth and pushed through the pain he was feeling.

CHAPTER FIVE

THE RIVER GENTLY flowed from east to west and was about twelve feet wide, with gentle ripples across its surface. On the other side their campsite waited for them, taunting them with its closeness.

They were all tired. It had been a long day—first hiking up the mountain and then their rapid descent, with the medical scenario on the way down. Beau was beginning to see how people might make mistakes with their decision-making when they were tired, hungry and sleep-deprived. It would be easy to do when you just wanted to be able to settle down and rest but knew you couldn't.

Now Mack stood in front of them, before the river, giving his safety lecture.

'Whenever you need to cross water, my advice is to always travel downstream until you come to a bridge. *That's* the safest way. But sometimes there may be an occasion where you need to cross without one, and you need to know how to do this safely. I would never advocate that you do this alone. It's always best to do this with someone else, and if possible with ropes.'

He pulled some ropes from his backpack and lay them out on the forest floor.

'Basic instructions are these—when you cross, you

cross the river by facing *upstream* and slightly sideways. You lean *into* the current, because this will help you maintain your balance. You do *not* want to be swept off your feet.'

Beau glanced at the water. How deep was it? It looked pretty tame, but she guessed that there might be hidden currents, rocks beneath the innocent-looking water or even a drop in the riverbed's level.

'You shuffle your feet across the bottom. You do *not* take big steps and lift your feet out of the water. You do *not* cross your feet over, and your downstream foot should always be in the lead.' He demonstrated what he meant before turning around and staring intently at them. 'Do you all understand? Okay—practise that step on dry land.'

Beau imitated what he'd shown them. It seemed simple enough, but she could imagine that in the water it would feel different. She glanced at Gray and could see a worried look on his face. Why was he so concerned? Surely this was a thrill for him? The kind of thing he found a challenge?

'If there is a long stick available—a tree branch, a walking pole, something like that—you can use it for extra balance and to feel beneath the water for obstacles. If you find an obstacle, you'll need to put your feet upstream of it, where the water will be less powerful.'

She was getting nervous now. This was a lot more complicated than she'd thought.

'With a stick or pole, you can place that upstream, too. You move the pole first—then your feet. If the water gets higher than your thighs, and there is more than one of you crossing, you'll need to link arms and lock your hands together. This is called chain crossing. The biggest team member should be upstream,

the smallest member downstream. You'll then move
through the water using the same principles, parallel
to the direction of the current.'

'What if it's too deep for that?'

'Then we use ropes, if available.' He began to lay
out the instructions for using rope to cross water. He
showed them how to anchor it, how to use a hand line,
how to use a second rope as a belay and all the safety
concerns involved.

It all got quite serious, quite quickly, and they were
soon forging into the water to test its depth.

Considering the warmth of the day, the water felt
cold, and Beau gasped as it came to just above her
knees, soaking through her brand-new boots and socks
and quickly chilling her to the bone. It was an odd sensation, being so cold below the knee but quite warm up
top, and the sensation made her shiver and shake a little.

The water's current was deceptively strong, and she
could feel it pushing and shoving hard against her legs
like a persistent angry child. She was now shaking so
much it was hard to tell where her feet were in the
water, and feeling a rock beneath the water, she instinctively lifted up her foot to step over it, forgetting
Mack's warning.

In an instant the current took her—unbalancing her,
sweeping her off her feet.

She was down, with the water closing over her head
in a frightening wave, filling her mouth, and she felt the
cold suck at her clothes and body as the current tried
to push her downstream. Gasping and spluttering, she
tried to rise upwards, to find her feet and grab hold of
something—anything—so that she could regain control and stand up. But the sheer coldness of the water,
the disorientation she was feeling from being hungry,

exhausted and sleep-deprived, meant she didn't know which way was up.

She opened her mouth to breathe, but it just filled with water. Beginning to panic, she splashed and opened her mouth even more to call for help—only to feel two strong arms grab her around the waist and pull her upwards.

'I've got you!'

She blinked and spluttered, gasping for air, wiping her wet hair from her face, and saw that Gray had her in his arms. She was pressed against him, soaking him through, but the joy of feeling her feet against the solid riverbed floor once again, and being upright and out of the cold, stopped her from feeling awkward.

She coughed to clear the water from her throat and clung tightly to him. 'Thanks.'

'You okay?'

She pulled a piece of river grass from her mouth and looked at it for a moment, disgusted, before throwing it away. The other hikers were looking at her with concern, still making their way across the river. It was then that she realised just how up close and personal she was with Gray.

Pushing herself away from him, she felt heat colour her cheeks—before she shivered slightly and recoiled at the feel of her wet clothes clinging to her body.

'I'm fine.' Why was he looking at her like that? There was far more than just concern in his eyes and it made her feel uneasy.

Anxious to get out of the water and to the campsite to dry off, she made her way across the river and clambered onto dry land with some difficulty. Her boots were full of water and her backpack had got soaked in the water, too. It would take her ages to dry everything off! Though she supposed the hot June weather might help, if she laid her things out on some rocks…

Once the others were all safely across, Gray insisted on putting her tent up for her quickly so she could get changed. As she'd suspected, everything in her pack was wet, but Claire kindly lent her some spare clothes to wear whilst her own were drying.

Mack was stern, giving her what felt like a lecture, and feeling like a naughty child, she sat by the river alone, her chin against her knees as she looked out across the innocent-looking water and thought about what might have happened.

She didn't have too long to think about it before Gray came to sit alongside her.

'How are you feeling?'

She shrugged, not willing to answer right away. Her fall in the river had disconcerted her. She *never* got things wrong. She always got things right—picked up new things quickly, learnt easily. Fording the river had shown her that control of things could all too easily be taken away from her when she wasn't expecting it. She'd thought she could handle the river—she'd been wrong.

And she'd thought she could convince herself that her feelings for Gray were those of uninterest and anger. She'd told herself that she didn't care about him any more. She'd been wrong on that count, too.

The way he'd rescued her in the river…the way she'd felt talking to him again…it was confusing. This was a man she should be *hating*! A man she should be furious with. Not even *talking* to. But being around him was stirring up feelings that she'd told herself she would *never* feel for a man again.

Gray jilted me! Rejected me!

And yet it had felt much too good to be in his arms again. Much too comfortable to be pressed up against him…much too familiar and safe and…and *right* to be that close to him again.

He'd felt solid. Sturdy. Strong. A safe haven. A certainty. And for a long time she'd tried to tell herself that Gray was an *un*certainty. An unstable individual who had always been a risk to her security and happiness.

How could she be getting this so wrong? Why was she so confused about him?

Even now, as he sat next to her on the rocks, she could feel her body reacting to him. To his presence. It was almost as if it were craving his touch again, and to be honest it was making her feel uncomfortable. It wasn't just the discomfort of being in someone else's clothes, or the knowledge that she'd made a mistake in the river and might have drowned, but also the discomfort of knowing that the chapter in her life which concerned Gray was not as closed as she'd once thought it was.

Somehow he was breaking back in and opening that door again.

'I was really worried about you.'

She didn't want to hear that from him. 'Don't be.'

'I saw you go under. I… My heart almost stopped beating. You just disappeared under the water like you'd been swallowed up by a beast.'

She could hear the pain in his voice. The fear. It was tangible. Real. She had no doubt he meant every word he said.

But I can't allow myself to react to him. Gray's no good for me.

'But you caught me, so everything was all right in the end.'

She refused to turn and face him. She couldn't. If she did turn—if she did see the look in his eyes that she knew to be there—she would be lost. She needed to fight it. Fight *him*. And her reaction to him. Her desire to feel him against her again. It had to go.

She stared out at the water, cursing its calm surface, knowing of the torrent below.

'If you had been swept away—'

'But I wasn't! I'm okay.'

She glanced at him. Just briefly. Just to emphasise her words—she *was* here, she *was* safe. Then she turned back to the river, her stomach in turmoil, her whole body fighting the desire to turn and fling herself into his arms again.

He didn't speak for some time and she could sense him looking out at the river, too.

'Are you cold? Would you like my jacket?' he asked eventually.

His jacket? The one that would carry his scent? What was he trying to do? Drown her in *him* instead? How would she even be able to *think*, wrapped in its vast depths, with the echo of his warmth within them?

'No, I'm good, thanks,' she lied.

'You're still shivering.'

'I'm not cold. It's just…just shock. That's all.'

'Well, shock isn't minor, either. We need to keep you warm, hydrated. Come and sit by the fire—we can get some hot tea into you.'

'Honestly, Gray, I'm fine.'

It was killing her that he was trying to take care of her. It would be easier if he left her alone for a while. Allowed her to gather her thoughts. To regroup and rebuild those walls she'd built for the past eleven years. Because somehow, in the last few hours, they'd come crumbling down and she felt vulnerable again. Vulnerable to *him*. And that was something that she couldn't afford.

'Come and sit by the fire, Beau. I insist.'

He grabbed her by the arm and gently hauled her to her feet. His arm around her shoulders, he walked her over to the fire and sat her down on a log next to Barb. Then he disappeared.

Just as she thought she could relax again, he came back. She tensed as he wrapped a blanket around her shoulders.

'How's that?' He rubbed her upper arms and knelt before her, staring into her eyes.

He was close enough to kiss.

She tried not to think about it—tried not to look down at his mouth, at those lips that she knew were capable of making her shiver with desire. She tried not to notice the way he was looking at her, the way the lines had increased around his green eyes, the way his beard emphasised his mouth—his perfect mouth—the way his lips were parted as he stared back at her, waiting for her response.

I could just lean forward...

She closed her eyes and snuggled down into the blanket. *No.* She couldn't allow herself to do that. It was wrong. *He* was wrong. What the *hell* was she doing, even *contemplating* kissing him?

Beau scrunched up her face and gritted her teeth together before she opened her eyes again and looked directly back at him. She nodded to indicate that she was fine, but she wasn't.

She was fighting a battle within herself.

And she really wasn't sure, at this moment in time, which side would win.

* * *

Rick was next on the rota to make a meal, and Mack provided him with a small amount of rice and some tins of tuna. It wasn't great, but it was protein and carbohydrates—both of which they all badly needed—and despite its blandness, despite the lack of salt and pepper, they all wolfed their meal down, hungry from restricted rations and exhausted from the long, tiring day.

Except for Beau.

She toyed with her food, pretending to eat, but in reality she was just pushing it round her dish, trying to make it look as if she was eating.

Gray sat next to her, put down his dish. 'You need to eat.'

'I'm not hungry.'

'You've had a shock. You need to eat for strength. You're too thin as it is.'

She could hear in his voice that he was concerned about her. Could hear that he had good intentions. But she didn't want to hear them from him. She didn't want to be reminded that he cared, because if she acknowledged that, then she would need to accept that *she* still cared about *him*, too.

'I'm fine.'

'No, you're not. You're hardly eating and you're as thin as a stick of rock.'

She sucked in a breath, trying to not get pulled into an argument. 'Honestly, Gray—just leave it, will you?'

'Beau, I care about—'

She stood up and cast off the blanket and walked away from the campfire, aware that everyone would be wondering what the hell was going on, but not having the energy or the inclination to explain. Irritated, she stamped over to the riverbank and checked to see if her clothes had dried on the rocks.

Luckily for her they were almost dry, the heat of the sun having done its work, and she scooped them up and headed to her tent to get changed. Clambering in, she turned and zipped up the tent beside her, shutting out the outside world before she collapsed on the ground, trying her hardest not to cry.

How dare he show me that he still cares? Does he not understand what that is doing to me?

Just a couple of days ago, safe in her work environment, if one of her colleagues had asked her how she felt about Gray McGregor, she would have been able to answer calmly and easily that he meant nothing to her any more. That she hardly ever thought of him, and that if she did, it was only because of a vague curiosity as to what he might be doing now.

That would have been true. But *now*?

Now she felt all over the place. Confused, upset, *disturbed*.

I wanted to be in his arms! I wanted to kiss him!

She'd only been with him for two days. Two days into a week together! What on earth would she be like at the end of it? Beau had thought she was strong. She'd thought—she'd assumed—that she was resolute in her feelings towards the man. That those feelings wouldn't change…that she'd be able to carry on with her life and every day would be the same as the one before it. Just the way she liked it.

Only, Gray being here had changed everything.

She pulled off the clothing that Claire had let her borrow, and as she sat there in her underwear, she heard Gray clear his throat outside her tent.

'Ahem…knock-knock?'

Just hearing that lilting Scottish accent, purring away so close to her, sent shivers of awareness down her spine.

Gritting her teeth, she pulled her tee shirt over her head and retightened her ponytail. 'Yes?'

'I've come to see if you're okay.'

Growling inwardly, she lay flat to pull herself into her khaki cargo pants and zipped them and buttoned them up before she yanked open the zip to her tent and stuck her head out.

'I'm fantastic.'

His head tilted to one side and he raised a questioning eyebrow. 'You sound it.'

'Good. Then maybe you'll leave me alone.'

'So you're angry with *me*?'

She scuttled out from within her tent and stood up, straightening her clothes. 'Yes—and don't say that I don't have good reason.' She knew she sounded petulant, but she didn't care.

'I'm sorry. I didn't realise that asking if you were all right was a capital offence.'

She didn't answer him, just knelt down to gather up Claire's clothes so she could return them.

'Only if *you* do it,' she said eventually.

He shrugged and squinted into the bright sun. 'My apologies, then. I was just trying to show that I care.'

'Well, you can't.'

'Why not?'

She turned to him, exasperated, but kept her voice low so as not to share their argument with the whole camp. 'Because it's *you*, Gray. You. I put my life in your hands once before. I gave you everything and you abandoned me. And…' she raised a hand to stop him from interrupting '…just when I thought I knew where to place you on the evolutionary scale—which, for your information, was somewhere below pond scum level—you turn up here and you're nice! You're *annoyingly* nice and pleasant and charming, and then you have the nerve to save my life and make me feel *grateful*! Do you know what happened to me the last time I was grateful to you, Gray? Hmm…?'

All through her rant, all through her rage and exaspration, he'd stood there, staring calmly back at her, not saying anything. Just listening. Just being *gracious* about the whole thing, for crying out loud!

'I was just worried that you weren't eating enough.'

'That's for *me* to worry about, Gray. Not you. *I* get to worry about me. You don't get that opportunity any more—do you understand?'

He nodded once. 'Okay. If that's what you want.'

She let out a pent-up breath. 'That's what I want.'

'Okay. Well, I figured you might want this. I sneaked it into my backpack and I was saving it for a special occasion, but…but I think you might need it more than me.'

He reached into his pocket and pulled out a chocolate bar. Not just *any* chocolate bar, but her *favourite*.

She blinked uncomprehendingly. Then she reached out and picked it up, almost not believing it was really there until she held it. Her anger—which had been simmering quietly ever since she'd stepped foot into that ranger station and seen him there—disappeared.

'I love these.'

'I know.'

'But…but you didn't know I was going to be on this course.'

'No, I didn't. But I've always bought them. Ever since…' He stopped talking and looked down at the ground. 'Anyway, you can have it. Seeing as you skipped dinner.'

He walked back to the campfire and joined the others, his back towards her.

She stared at the chocolate bar, which was slightly crumpled and soft from where it had been tightly packed into his bag, and felt her heart melt just a little bit more.

He still bought them. Even after all this time.

And I've just said all those horrible things…

Beau swallowed hard. Now she felt guilty. Guilty for being so harsh towards him just because *she'd* been feeling confused. Was it *his* fault that she felt that way? No. She should be in greater control of her feelings. Hadn't she always been before? Since he'd left her, she'd kept a rigid control over everything. Even down to making sure there were no unexpected surprises during her day. Her life had been timetabled to within an inch of its life. Knowing what would happen and when had kept her safe for so long. Had kept her from being hurt again.

But maybe…maybe surprises could be a good thing? Maybe a little uncertainty, a little risk, was okay? Didn't babies learn to walk by falling over? They didn't expect the fall, but they learnt from their mistakes.

Perhaps I need to let myself make a few mistakes? Take a few risks? Maybe there might be a little something out there for me, too.

She peeled open the chocolate bar and took a small bite.

The next morning Mack woke them early again and began teaching them another lesson. The topic this time was fractures.

'You have to know, even as a layman, how to evaluate an injury—either for someone else in your group or yourself.'

Beau could appreciate that. She was having a hard time assessing herself right now.

'You need to consider three things—the scene, a primary survey and a secondary survey if you're to come to the most accurate conclusion and assist yourself or another hiker out in the wild.'

'What's a primary and secondary survey?' asked Leo. 'I always get confused about those things.'

'Good question. A primary survey means looking at your patient and checking for life-threatening injuries or situations. So ABC. *Airway.* Is it clear? If not, why not? Can you clear it? *Breathing.* Is your patient breathing? Is it regular? Are there at least two breaths every ten seconds? And last of all *circulation.* Is there a major bleed? What can you do to stop it? That's your primary survey.'

'And if there aren't any of those signs?'

'Then you do your secondary survey. This also consists of three things. Remember with first aid and CPR there's generally a rule of three—ABC is one set of three. Scene survey, primary survey, secondary survey is another. If you remember to check three, you can always feel secure in knowing that you've checked everything. The secondary survey includes checking vital signs, taking the patient's history into account and a full head-to-toe body exam.'

'I'll never remember it all!' declared Barb.

'You'd be surprised,' Gray said.

'Once you've checked their vitals are okay, you can ask if they have pain or an injury. Find out how that injury occurred. Does it sound like there was enough force to create a fracture? Then you check the body, feeling firmly for any pain or deformities. But remember—even if the patient seems okay, their condition could change at any moment. You need to be alert. You may miss an injury because the patient is focusing on the pain from a bigger injury. And then what? Beau?'

'Then you swap hats,' said Beau, happy to answer. 'You take off the hat that states you're treating a fracture and put on the hat that says you're treating someone who's unconscious—you put them into the recovery position. If it gets worse again, you put on the CPR hat.'

Mack nodded. 'So, now let's focus on the fractures themselves. You look for the signs and symptoms of a fracture. Gray, can you tell us what they are?'

'Inability to bear weight on a limb, disabled body part, obvious deformity, pain, tenderness or swelling, angulation or bone protruding through the skin or stretching it. The patient might also mention hearing a crack.'

'Good. Did you all get that? You need to treat all possible skeletal injuries as if they are fractures. Even if you suspect a sprain or a dislocation, treat as a fracture until proved otherwise.'

'Okay, so how do we do that with no splints available?' asked Rick.

'There's always something you can use,' Gray continued. 'You've just got to think outside the box. Splinting is correct. It stabilises the break and helps prevent movement on the splintered ends—which, believe you me, can be excruciatingly painful.'

He rubbed at his leg, as if remembering an old injury.

'If you don't splint an injury, it can lead to further damage—not just to the bone, but to muscle, tissue and nerves, causing more bleeding and swelling, which you do *not* want.'

'So what do we do?' asked Rick.

'You need to get the bones back into the correct anatomical position. Which means traction—which means causing yourself or your patient *more* pain. But you must do it—particularly if you're hours or even days from medical help.'

Claire grimaced. 'I'm not sure I could do that.'

'You'd have to. It can be upsetting, but it's best for the patient. Causing pain in the short-term will help in the long-term.'

Claire nodded quickly, her face grim.

Mack took over. 'Let's imagine a break on the lower left leg, near the ankle. This will be the most common injury you'll come across. People hiking and trekking across strange open country, falling down between rocks, not putting their feet securely down—all that contributes to this kind of injury. Claire, why don't you be my pretend patient?'

She got into position before him.

'You need to grasp the proximal part of the limb— that means the part of the limb closest to the body— and hold it in the position it was found. Then, with your other hand, you need to apply steady and firm traction to the distal part of the limb—this is the furthest point—like so.'

He demonstrated by gripping above and below Claire's 'fractured' lower leg.

'You do this by applying a downwards pull, and even though your patient may cry out, or try to pull away, you *must* slowly and gently pull it back into position. This will help relieve the patient's pain levels. Okay?'

Everyone nodded, even if they were looking a bit uncertain about their ability to do it in a real-life situation.

'Before you apply a splint, there's a rule of three

again. You need to check CSM—their *circulation*, their *sensation* and their *movement*. Can you feel a pulse below the injury? In the case of this one, can you find a pulse in the foot?' He demonstrated where to find it. 'Is the skin a good colour? Or is it pale and waxen, indicating that the positioning may still be off? Does the patient feel everything below the injury? Can they wiggle their toes? If there's anything restrictive, like a tight boot or socks, you can remove it to help reposition the limb properly.'

'What if the break is inside the boot?' asked Rick.

'You leave the boot on. The boot itself can act as a splint around the ankle sometimes—it's for you to judge what needs to be done.'

'What if we do something wrong?'

'You might never know. Or the patient might get worse, in which case you'll assess and treat accordingly. You can use sticks for splints, or walking poles, backpacks, snowshoes, the straps off your packs—anything that will provide a steady and supportive purpose.'

Rick nodded. 'Okay, but when we put a splint alongside the injury, how exactly do we attach it? In the middle? Where the injury is?'

'No. Fasten the splint above and below the suspected fracture.'

'Right. And what about an open fracture? Do we bind it? Compress it?'

'No. Leave it uncovered before you splint, and if you can find enough splints to go around the injury on all sides, that's even better. Use padding, if you need to, to prevent discomfort—torn clothing…whatever you can find. But remember to keep checking it afterwards, because the wound may cause swelling and the splinting may then be too tight. You need to assess frequently and often. Have you all got that?'

They nodded.

'Right. Now the practical. With your buddy, I want you to practise assessing for and splinting a left ankle break. Remember to do a scene survey, and a primary and secondary survey. Remember your rules of three and use the environment around you to find and locate splints. Patients—give your doctor a few surprises. I'll come round and assess when you're done.'

Beau looked to Gray. It was his turn to be the patient. But for some reason he looked extremely uncomfortable, and she wondered briefly what it was that was worrying him. He'd seemed fine just a moment ago.

Was he thinking of a way to surprise her? As Mack had suggested? If he was, then she was determined to be ready for him.

CHAPTER SIX

'MAYBE I SHOULD be the doctor for this one,' Gray suggested.

'No. You've already rescued me. It's your turn to be the patient.'

'I was the patient for the leg wound. It's your turn.'

She looked at him, feeling exasperated. Why was he getting antsy all of a sudden? Why didn't he want to be the patient? He'd get to sit down and have a rest!

Beau decided to give him 'the look'—the one that told him, *Sit down right now. I don't have time for this!*

Gray cursed silently, his lips forming expletives she couldn't hear, before he shook his head in defeat and sank down to the floor.

'Do my right ankle.'

'Mack said the left.'

'Well, I'm surprising you. I broke my right one.'

'Gray, what's the matter with you? Now, first of all the scene survey. It's safe for me to approach you…there are no hazards.' She knelt down beside him and smiled broadly. 'What seems to be the problem?'

Gray tried his best glare, but when he could see that it wasn't having any effect on her, he resigned himself to what was about to happen. 'My ankle hurts. I think I've broken it. I heard something snap.'

'Uh-huh. Which one?' She smiled at him sympathetically and saw his face soften under her onslaught of sweetness.

He let out a breath. 'My left.'

She nodded, glad he was finally playing ball. Though why on earth he'd wanted to swap ankles was beyond her. She *had* noticed that he had been limping slightly. Perhaps she was about to find out that he really did have blisters and hadn't been looking after them properly.

'Okay. So, primary survey—your airway is clear, you're breathing normally and there don't appear to be any bleeds. Do you feel pain anywhere else?'

'Only in my pride.'

She laughed, puzzled by the strange discomfort he seemed to be displaying. 'Okay...so, secondary survey. Lie back—be a good patient.'

Gray lay back on the ground, but she could see he wasn't relaxed at all. He looked tense. Apprehensive. It was odd. This was a simple scenario—he should be fine about all of this.

'Okay, and on a scale of one to ten, with zero being no pain and ten being excruciating pain, how would you rate it?'

'Definitely a ten.'

'And how did you damage your ankle?'

'I slipped. I wasn't concentrating.'

'Uh-huh. Okay, I'm going to check the rest of you and make sure there are no other injuries. Just relax for me, if you can.'

She felt around the back of his neck and pressed either side of his neck vertebrae. No reaction. Then she felt his shoulders, checked his clavicle, then ribcage.

There was plenty of reaction. In her own body!

Touching him like this, enveloping the muscle groups

as she checked both his arms, patted down his hips and applied a small amount of pressure on the hip bones, aware of how close her hands were to his skin, was almost unbearable. Her hands encompassed the thick, strong muscles of his thighs, moved past his knees down to his...

Huh? What was that?

She sat back and frowned, staring at his lower leg, then glancing up at his face in question. Waiting for him to answer. To explain.

'What is that, Gray? A brace?'

Had he hurt his leg? Had he been hiding an injury all this time? What had he done to himself?

Gray sat upright and his cheeks coloured slightly. His brows bunched heavily over his eyes and the muscle in his jaw clenched and unclenched before he answered her, without meeting her gaze. 'It's a prosthetic.'

She felt a physical shift in her chest, as if her heart had plummeted to the dirty ground below, and her stomach rolled and churned at the thought that he'd been so hurt somehow. That Gray—her once beloved, powerful and strong Gray—had been hurt to such an extent that he had physically lost a part of him.

'A what?' she asked in an awed whisper, not wanting to believe him.

The word 'prosthetic' literally meant an addition. An attachment. An artificial piece that replaced a missing body part. Something lost from disease, or a congenital condition, or trauma.

She could feel herself going numb. Withdrawing, almost. If she heard his answer, it would make it even more real.

Gray sighed and lifted up his left trouser leg, looked

at her directly this time. 'I lost my foot, and some of my leg below the knee.'

She stared at it. Watched as he peeled off his boot and then his sock and revealed it to her in its full glory. The shiny plastic exterior...the solid metal bar from mid-shin down to the ankle, where the fake foot began.

'Gray...'

'Please don't, Beau. Don't tell me you're sorry. There's no need to be. I can still do what anyone else does. People have climbed Everest with a prosthetic.'

'I know, but...'

'You always told me—always warned me—that I took too many risks and, well...here you are. You were proved right. I did something stupid.'

She reached out to touch it, then stopped. She had no right to touch him there. Or anywhere, really. Her hand dropped back to her lap. 'Are you okay?'

'Apart from missing half a limb?'

'How did it happen?'

He pulled his trouser leg back down. 'It's a long story.'

'I want to hear it.'

'Why? We're not together any more—you don't have to prove you care.'

'Gray—'

'Please, Beau, leave it. Just splint the ankle.'

'Are you sure? I could just—'

'Just...splint it.'

She looked at his downcast face, the anger in his eyes, and her heart physically ached for him. To see him like this—bared and open...wounded. Not the strong Gray he'd always shown the world, but having to—being forced to—reveal a weakness... Beau knew how that must be making him feel.

But it didn't matter. His prosthesis didn't make him any *less*. He was still Gray. And he was right. People today could do anything with a prosthesis. Look at all those athletes. Or any ordinary person, carrying on with life. He was still a top cardiologist. It didn't stop him from operating. It didn't stop him from saving people's lives. But how to say that to him without sounding preachy? He knew it already. Surely?

He's still the same Gray. Life tries to strike you down, and though it feels, at the time, like it's the worst thing you'll ever have to get through, like you'll never survive...well, you do get through it. You do *survive. You're changed. You're different. But you survive.*

She knew Gray must have gone through a period of grieving for his lower leg and foot. A part of him truly *was* missing. But he was strong. Resilient. She had to believe in that. He was *here*, wasn't he? Hiking across Yellowstone for a week. You didn't do *that* on a prosthetic unless you were determined and believed in yourself.

Beau began to look around her for something to use for splints. There was plenty of wood, but she needed to find something sturdy enough to support a joint. There were some thick pieces of wood over at the treeline and she gathered them and came back to Gray. She silently began attaching them, using the bungee cords from her backpack. She fastened them, checked to make sure they weren't too tight, then knelt back and waited for him to look at her.

'Please tell me how it happened.'

For a moment she didn't think he was going to speak at all, but then he began.

'There's a place called St John's Head on the Isle of Hoy, in the Orkneys. Have you heard of it?'

She shook her head. 'No.'

'It's considered the world's hardest sea cliff climb and I wanted to give it a try.'

She nodded. Of course he had. That was what he'd always been like. Pushing the envelope. Pushing boundaries. Seeing how far he could go.

'You're not just fighting the heights and the rock there, but the gale-force winds, the rain, the birds dropping…' He paused for a moment to think about his choice of words. 'Dropping *stuff* on you. It's a sheer rock face, with almost no fingerholds. There's a route called the Long Hope. It's amazing. You have to see it to believe it.'

'It sounds…exposed.'

He gave a laugh. 'You have no idea. When you're up there, you feel like you're the only person in the world.'

'You went alone, didn't you?'

He nodded. 'I was trying to free climb it. No ropes, no equipment. This other guy managed it a few years ago. I'm an experienced climber—I'd done free climbing before—I thought I'd be okay.'

'But something went wrong?'

Gray nodded. 'Before I knew what was happening, I was falling. I hit the rocks below, broke my leg in three places, fractured my pelvis, had an open fracture of the ankle. Luckily I had my phone. More importantly, I had a *signal*. Mountain Rescue and the coastguard joined forces and got me to a hospital.'

'Did they try and save your leg?'

'They tried. I had three surgeries. But an infection set in and they had to amputate. It wasn't the fall that lost me my foot—it was bacteria.'

She felt sick. It was awful. Yet he'd got himself back

up, carried on with his demanding work, come on this course...

'Is that why you're here? To prove to yourself that you can still achieve things?'

Gray shifted on the ground and fidgeted with the splint she'd assembled on his lower leg. 'Maybe.'

'You're still *you*, you know? Just because there's a physical piece missing, it doesn't mean you're any less than who you were.'

She was a little shocked that she hadn't realised he was injured in this way. She'd noticed the limping, but it hadn't occurred to her that it might be something so significant. What else had she missed about Gray?

'I know that. I was mad at myself for making a mistake on the cliff. Even now I can't pinpoint what went wrong, and that irks me. But I knew if I got one of the more expensive prosthetics I could still do things like this. Still have my adventures.'

She smiled at him. That was better. The fighting spirit she knew and...

She glanced at the ground, feeling her cheeks colour. 'Go on, then—tell me. I know you're dying to. What are the specs on this thing?'

He gave a sheepish grin. 'It's got a tibial rotator, which allows the leg to rotate even when the foot is placed firmly on the ground. It also helps prevent skin irritation in the socket, where there's an extra gel padding cuff for hiking trips. The foot itself is multiaxial, so it can tilt and rotate over uneven ground.'

'Sounds top of the line.'

'It is.'

'I'm glad you're out here.'

Gray looked surprised, then reached out and laid his hand on hers, curling his fingers around her palm and squeezing back when he felt her hand squeeze his. 'Thank you, Beau. I don't deserve you. I never did.'

She didn't know what to say. He was wrong! He *did* deserve her! Even now she could feel...

Beau swallowed hard, trying to find an anchor in this sea of swirling emotions she was reeling under. She wanted to wrap her arms around him and hold him. She wanted to press him close. To feel him safe in her arms. But another part...a much smaller part...told her to keep holding back. Told her that this was *Gray* and she was crazy even to be thinking of giving this man comfort.

Instead she concentrated on the feel of his hand in hers. Its steady strength. Its warmth. The solidity of him near her. His presence—all too real and all too confusing.

Why couldn't she have been there to help him during his time of need?

Would I have gone if he'd called me and asked?

Yes. I would have.

They sat quietly, holding hands, until Mack came alongside them to assess Beau's splinting skills and medical surveys. They dropped each other's hand like a hot coal at the ranger's approach. Only once Mack had given Beau a big thumbs-up and suggested that they swap roles did they manage to look at each other again.

Something had changed between them.

Something weird and almost intangible. Whatever it was, it had strength and influence, and Beau lay on the ground and tried to ignore the feelings raging through her body as Gray assessed her for injury and applied a splint to her left ankle. Her cheeks kept flushing, she felt hot, her stomach was turning and spinning like a roulette wheel, and she tried to tamp down the physical awareness she felt with every touch of his hands.

When Mack called for a break, and told them all to make camp and put up their tents, she hurried over to her backpack and put her tent up quickly, eager to get inside and just *hide* for a while. Gather her thoughts. Regroup her emotions. Wipe away the solitary tear that rolled down her cheek at the thought of Gray broken and alone at the base of a sea cliff.

What does all this mean?
Am I in trouble?

It was Leo's turn at the cooking pot, and he had rustled up a spicy potato dish. Gray had no idea what had gone into it, just knew that it tasted good and he wanted more. But, as always, Mack had limited the rations so that they were always just the empty side of full, burning more calories in the day than they were able to take in, so they could see how hunger might affect their choices.

Tomorrow would see the start of the paired orienteering—sending the buddied couples out into the wild on their own, to see if they could navigate to a particular spot, make it safely and deal with any issues on the way. It had been the part of the week that he'd been looking forward to the most—surviving on his own wits with just one other person. But now...now he wasn't sure.

Now Beau knew about his leg. He'd tried his hardest to hide it from her, feeling a little foolish about it at first, but now he'd come clean and she wasn't fazed at all.

But I still feel incomplete. Is it just my leg? Or is something else bothering me?

If he'd ever felt he might stand another chance with her, that feeling had died when he'd fallen from that cliff and lost that part of his leg. It had been a physical manifestation of the fact that he wasn't whole. That he wasn't the complete package. That he couldn't offer her what she wanted from life. And that realisation still hurt like hell. He might have a new bionic foot and ankle, capable of coping with any terrain thrown at it, but what about *him*? What could *he* cope with?

Beau had meant everything to him. She'd made his heart sing and he'd been able to forget all the drama and misery of his own home when he'd been with her. She had brought him comfort and repose. A soft place to fall. *She* had been his home.

But he'd ruined it. That tiny slip, that tiny lapse of concentration, and he'd blurted out the one question he'd never thought he'd ask… *Will you marry me?*

It had changed everything. Turned his happiness upside down, put a deadline on his joy. No, not a deadline—*a death sentence*. Marriage would have killed who they were. Their happiness at being in each other's presence would slowly have been eroded and familiarity would have bred contempt. Living in each other's pockets would have caused them to seek time apart, space from one another, just so they could breathe again. They would have grown to dread being in each other's company, started to hate the way they ate their food, the way they fought about who wanted to go out and who wanted to stay in, whether they squeezed the toothpaste tube right… *Every tiny thing* would have been used as a stone to throw at the other.

He'd lived it. He'd seen it. Been stuck in the middle of two warring factions—both sides of which he loved for different reasons, both sides of which he stayed away from for the same reasons…

It was a fact that children imitated their parents. Gray might try not to be like them, but he was sure little things would sneak through. Sure, he might just have little quirks that at first Beau would find amus-

ing, and then irritating, and then soon she'd be so opposed to them she would threaten to leave him unless
he changed his ways…

Marriage was only possible for people who knew
what they were doing. Who were emotionally available.
Who had the strength to get through it. But for him and
Beau…? *No.* He was damaged goods. He'd been broken
before they'd even got started.

He knew he should have spoken to her earlier, but
she'd seemed so happy, so confident in their happiness.
Had he been wrong to try to let her be happy for as
long as she could? Not to decimate her dreams? She'd
even started talking about how after the wedding she
would come off birth control so they could try for a
child straight away…

That had been terrifying. Being responsible for
bringing another child into another potential battle-
ground? No. He couldn't do it. He'd *been* that child
and look at what it had done to him.

The problem was whether Beau would understand
all this. Her world was perfect, and her parents—the
strangest couple in the world, who actually seemed still
to *love* each other after many years—had been a different example entirely. There were no broken marriages,
as far as he knew, on her side of the family, so *some*
people got it right, but…

Beau was in the dark regarding his experience. She
couldn't possibly know how he felt about marriage. The
fear it engendered in him. That pressure to get it right
when he had no idea how.

When everyone had finished eating, he volunteered
to wash the dishes in the river and noticed after a few
minutes that Beau had joined him.

'Hi,' she ventured.

He glanced at her—at the way her beautiful wavy hair tumbled around her shoulders, at the way her eyes glinted in the evening sunshine. She was still the most beautiful woman he had ever met. And then some.

'Hi.'

'Want a hand?'

'I've got two of those, thanks. Do you have a foot handy?' He laughed gruffly at his own joke and carried on swirling the dishes in the crystal-clear running water.

'Only my own. I don't think you'd want one of them—they've got sparkly pink nail varnish on the toenails. But I'd give it to you if you needed it.'

She took the dishes from him as he finished and began wiping them with a towel.

'You never know. My prosthetic has got all the latest tricks and flicks, but it doesn't have sparkly pink nail polish. I think that may be the latest upgrade it needs.'

She smiled at him. 'You know, I've been thinking about your accident…'

He paused briefly from his washing. 'Oh?'

'Just wondering who…who supported you through all that.'

'I got myself through it.'

'What about your family?'

He shrugged. He'd refused to lean on them for any kind of support. 'Well…'

'Did you tell them?'

'Not at first…'

'But they *do* know?'

'They do now. I told them after it was all over. Once I'd healed.'

'Why didn't you tell them?'

He shifted his stance, switching his weight from one

foot to the other. 'We aren't that close. Never were. And my mother had enough to do, looking after my dad, so...' He trailed off, not wanting to say more. He'd always protected her from the reality of his family and it was a hard habit to break.

'You know, one day you're going to have to tell me. I'm not going to let this rest.'

He nodded. 'I know. When I'm ready.'

Beau gazed at him and smiled. 'I can wait.'

Perhaps she was nearly ready to listen? He let his fingers squeeze hers, acknowledging her support. For a moment he couldn't speak. He was so taken aback that she was saying these nice things. They'd both certainly come a long way in the last few days.

'And, you know...apart from the fact that you've got a body part that will *never* wear out...you'll make a cracking pirate if you choose to put a wooden peg in its place!'

He smiled. 'Of *course*! Stupid me for not seeing the best of my situation.'

'Well, you've always been guilty of *that*, Gray.'

His smile dropped. 'What do you mean?'

She looked up at him, startled by his reaction, realising she'd said more than she should. She'd answered too quickly. Without thinking.

'Erm... I don't know... Forget it.'

'No. You meant something when you said that— what did you mean?'

Beau looked uneasy, shifting her eyes away from his. 'Just that...back then...well...you had *me*, Gray.'

Her gaze came back to his, slamming into him with a force that almost knocked him off his feet.

'I thought we were happy together. That we had

something special. That our love was stronger than anything else!'

The tears beginning to run from her eyes were real. Knowing that he was still causing her pain almost ripped him in two.

He cradled her hands against his chest. 'It *was*!'

She shook her head. 'No, it wasn't. You didn't love me enough—you let your doubt, or whatever it was, tell you to abandon me. Leave me. Without a word. Not a *single* word!'

'Beau—'

'I wasn't enough for you. Our *love* wasn't enough. You focused on something else. Something that tore you away from me. And do you know how that made me feel? *Worthless!*'

He pulled her towards him, into his arms, pressing her against his chest, hoping to dry her tears, hoping to show her that she could never be worthless to him. But feeling her against him, feeling her cry, woke something in him that he'd buried deeply. Buried so far down he'd thought it could never be found again. He'd found it now, though, and it had him in its grip.

He pulled back to look at her, to make her look him in the eyes, so that he could tell her that she was the most important person who had *ever* been in his life...

But as soon as his eyes locked with hers, he was mesmerised. Her shimmering sapphire eyes were staring back at him with such pain in them that he felt compelled to take that pain away, and before he knew what he was doing—before he had a chance to think twice—he lowered his lips to hers and kissed her.

It was like dropping a lit taper into a fireworks factory. There was a moment of shock, of disbelief and wonder at what he was doing, and then—*boom!* He lost control. All those years of being without her, all those years of never allowing himself to *feel*, came crashing down and his body sprang to life. It was as if she was a life-giving force and this was the kiss of life.

His arms enveloped her and pressed her to him. He couldn't get enough of her. He *had* to feel her. All of her—against him. Her softness, her delicate frame was protected by him. Her lips were against his, and the way she gasped for air and breathed his name was like oxygen feeding his fire.

It could have become something else, something… *more*, but just as he thought he couldn't resist her, couldn't resist the desire to feel her flesh against his own, the others in the group started catcalling.

'Get a room, you two!'

They broke apart and stared at each other, shock in their eyes, both of them not quite sure how that had happened.

Then Beau walked away, pulling open the flap to her tent and darting out of sight.

Gray gathered the dishes and took them back to camp, where he received many pats on the back from the other men and some raised eyebrows from Barb and Claire, whom he glanced at sheepishly.

'Well, that explains a few things,' Barb said. 'I *knew* there was something going on between you two. Feel better now?'

He didn't answer. He wasn't sure. The kiss had been amazing. More than amazing. But what was Beau thinking? She'd said some things… Had he made things worse? Had he made things better? Surely she wouldn't be in her tent if he'd helped in any way. He wondered if he should go and talk to her.

He glanced over at her tent, but Barb shook her head. 'I'd leave her a while, if I were you. It looks like you woke something up between the pair of you and she needs time to get used to it.'

'But shouldn't I—'

'Give her space, Gray. You'll have more than enough time on the orienteering hike, alone together, to talk out any last wrinkles. For now, give her time to absorb what's happened.'

'Shouldn't I at least go over and apologise?'

She cocked her head at him. 'You're *sorry* about kissing a girl like that?'

He thought for a moment. 'No.'

Barb grinned. 'Good! The world would be a lot better if husbands kissed their wives like that a bit more, I can tell you. Con? You listening to this?'

'Sure, honey.' Conrad, who was tending the campfire, turned and grinned at them both.

'Pah! You old romantic! Anyway, if you ever kissed *me* like that, I think I'd drop dead from the shock—and I ain't ready to go yet.' She laughed. 'But, Gray, listen to me—and listen good. You and Beau look like you have something special going on. Something deep that comes from *here*…' She pointed at her heart. 'You don't let that go. Not ever. That kind of love is the stuff that gets you out of hot water.'

He frowned. 'How do you mean?'

'You don't need no old lady telling you how to live your life, but if I had one piece of advice to give you, it'd be to tell yourself every day just *why* you love that other person. What you're grateful for. What they do to make you feel loved and special. Because if you're busy focusing on the good stuff all the time, the bad times, well…they can seem a lot easier to get through.'

He nodded to Conrad by the fire. 'Is that what you do?'

'Sure is!' Barb leaned in, speaking in a mock whisper. 'Or I'd have killed him already! The man could snore for America!'

Gray glanced over at Beau's tent. *Was* it as simple as that? Just thinking of the good things? Reminding yourself every day why you loved that person? Reliving moments like that kiss they'd just shared? *Could* it be that easy?

He didn't know. He wasn't sure he wanted to admit that it could, because if he did, then the pain he'd put them both through had been for nothing. If he believed that, then everything could have been avoided if only he'd had enough faith in his love for Beau being stronger than any day-to-day drudgery trying to ruin it all.

Did I ruin our lives because I didn't think I was strong enough? No. I thought I was protecting her. Protecting me. I couldn't bear the idea that she could ever hate me.

But hadn't that happened anyway?

Gray rubbed his hands over his face and groaned. Why couldn't this be easy? A case of two plus two equalling four? Why did life have to have so many twists and turns, dead ends and multi-car pile-ups?

He stared at the entrance to Beau's tent, willing her to come out.

CHAPTER SEVEN

THERE WAS ANOTHER breakfast of porridge the next morning. Beau had suffered a long, uncomfortable night, having stayed in her tent for most of the previous evening, only coming out when Claire and Barb had called for her. She'd grabbed her toiletries bag and hurried away with them, her head downcast, ensuring she didn't make eye contact with Gray.

They'd kissed!

And she'd forgotten how wonderful kissing Gray had been. Her feelings had been all topsy-turvy, her heart hammering, her pulse pounding and her brain bamboozled and as fragile as a snowflake above a firepit as she'd fought to decide whether she should continue with it or fight him off. But it had been too delicious to stop.

I certainly didn't fight him off!

No. She'd breathed his name, gasped it, making those little noises in her throat that now made her feel so embarrassed as she thought of them. Had he heard her? *Of course he had!* He would have had to be deaf not to, and there was nothing wrong with his hearing. Or any of his other body parts…

She tried not to recall the sensation of him pressed hard against her.

And now I'm sitting here, around a campfire, eat-

ing porridge that's as difficult to swallow as week-old wallpaper paste, trying not to look up and catch his eye. What am I...? A mouse?

She gritted her teeth and looked up. He was opposite, talking to Mack in a low whisper, and by the way Gray was pointing at his leg, she assumed they were discussing his prosthetic. Or maybe the accident that had caused it? She supposed Mack must have known about the prosthetic beforehand. Health and safety—these were the all-important buzzwords everywhere these days. Surely Gray had *had* to declare it beforehand? He might not have been allowed on the course otherwise.

Gray glanced over and caught her gaze, smiled.

Quickly she looked away. This was going to be awkward. Today they would be splitting up into their pairs for the orienteering challenge, after one final lesson around the campfire with Mack. She and Gray would be alone together. Just the two of them. Hiking through Yellowstone to a pre-approved grid reference, where apparently there would be a checkpoint to collect supplies before they headed to another grid reference, where they would find the ranger station. They would have to talk. There would be no escape for either of them.

And we're hardly going to be able to get through it in silence, are we?

Silence would be nice after that kiss. Preferable, actually.

No, forget that. Not coming on this trip would have been preferable.

But she had. So had he. And they'd kissed. And it hadn't been one of those polite kisses you gave at family gatherings, either. That polite peck on the cheek for a family member you hadn't seen for a few months.

It had been hot. Passionate, searing, breathtaking, goosebump-causing...

He had to have felt something, too. A reawakening. A refiring of something that had once burned so hot. That *unfinished* feeling between them... That entwining of souls—the kind of feeling that was so intimate it touched your heart.

Beau knew she had to get a grip. Take control. Let Gray know that, yes, she acknowledged something had happened between them, but that was all it could be— *something*. An undefined moment. And there was no need to explore it further. She had to make it very clear that they should leave it alone and get on with finding their way back to civilisation, thank you very much.

The situation they were in was so intense. It was risky. People got close to each other in this kind of situation because that was what happened in a high-pressure moment. It created a false reality. And when life returned to normal afterwards, the feelings just weren't there...

He *had* to know that this didn't mean anything for them. She'd come on this course alone and, damn it, she was going to leave it alone, too. There would be no need for further contact. She wouldn't be exchanging telephone numbers or email addresses with him. He would go back to Edinburgh and she would return to Oxford and life would continue. Everything in its neat little box, the way it always had been. In *her* control.

The reason the kiss had happened in the first place was because the whole thing had got *out* of her control. This wasn't reality.

But something *had* changed between them, and she'd learnt more about him in the last few days than she'd ever known before. She knew that there was so much more to understand about her enigmatic ex-fiancé. And that wasn't all. Though she hated to admit it, her lips still tingled from his kiss.

Her senses had gone into overdrive since, and though she'd been huddled in her tent, preferring to believe that she'd caught some sort of strange disease and was suffering from a weird kind of fever, she'd been aware of exactly where Gray was outside her tent. Whenever he'd come close or walked by, she'd known. Whenever he'd spoken during that evening, she'd frozen, just so she could listen to what he said. Her body had ached for him.

Ached!

She hadn't wanted someone this badly since...

Since Gray.

If she could have, she would have groaned out loud, but instead she shoved in another spoonful of the dreadful porridge. She filled her mouth with the soft mush just to stop herself from crying out.

Are you kidding me?

She sat there, miserable in her silence, staring at Gray, all rumpled and tousled opposite her, wanting both to kiss him and beat her fists against his chest in equal measure.

'Okay, everyone. Last-minute stuff before I send you off in your pairs out into the big, wide world. You remember what I said about the big animals in the park, yes?'

They all nodded.

'Well, now you need to know about the smaller beasts. They may be lighter than a two-thousand-pound bison, but they can still knock you off your feet if you're not careful.'

'Such as...?' asked Claire.

'Snakes, for one. There have only been two recorded snakebites in this area, and your main culprit is the prairie rattlesnake. You'll find her in dry grasslands and the warmer river areas. You all know what a rattlesnake looks like? Sounds like?'

Again, they nodded sagely.

'You hear that rattle—you head in the other direction. You give her a wide berth. Usually they rattle to warn you, before you get too close, but not always—so be on your lookout when you walk.'

'Are they always on the ground?' asked Gray.

'Mostly. But they have been known to climb trees, or rest in crevices between rocks, so always check your surroundings. There may be the rare occurrence of a snakebite, and a rattler bite will inject you with plenty of nasty stuff—hemotoxins that cause the destruction of tissue. If you don't have a reverse syringe handy—which you don't—you need to keep your patient calm and still, and wrap the affected limb tightly. Apply a splint and get yourselves some medical help as soon as possible.'

'Shouldn't we attempt to suck out the poison with our mouths?'

'Technically, it should be safe to suck out the venom if the person doing the sucking doesn't have an open wound in their mouth. Poisons only affect you if you swallow them. But we're not dealing with poison here— we're talking *venom*. Venom is toxic only when it's injected into the lovely soft tissues of the human body and its rich bloodstream. So if you suck out venom from a snakebite, you *should* be okay—but we don't advise it any more. My advice? *Don't do it*. The human mouth isn't that clean, either, and you're just as likely to introduce bacteria into the wound and do as much damage as the snake did.'

He looked at their sombre faces.

'Walk with a stick when you're out in the wilds alone. You can tap the ground before you, and if there is something you've missed, the stick is more likely to get attacked before you.'

'And that stick will come in handy for a river crossing—let's not forget!' said Conrad.

Everyone smiled and the sombre mood was lifted.

'The next thing is stating the obvious—you need to keep an eye on your buddy. Heat exhaustion and dehydration can set in quickly. This time of year it's hot—you're sweating constantly and you'll need to keep up your fluid intake and stay out of the midday sun for as long as is possible. Beau, do you want to let people know the signs?'

She coloured, feeling Gray's eyes upon her, and her answer, when it came, was not given in her usually confident voice. 'Erm…you might feel weak, thirsty. When you go to the loo, your urine might be only a little amount, deep in colour, or it might even hurt to try and pass water… Erm…'

Gray helped her out. 'You might feel drowsy, tired, dizzy, disorientated. Faint when you try to stand. These are all signs of it getting worse. You must keep putting the fluids in, even if it means stopping to purify water. Water should be your top priority.'

Mack nodded. 'Then there are the mosquitoes, the leeches, the spiders, the ticks. These could all just be minor irritants, but long-term might lead to other problems. Tick bites, especially, could lead to Lyme disease.'

'Ooh, that's *nasty*. My cousin has that,' Barb said.

'I know you've all got bug spray, and some of you

have citronella. These are all good repellents, but you need to check each other at every stop for ticks. If you get one, don't just try to pull it out. You need to remove them by twisting them out with tweezers or proper tick removers.'

He smiled and stood up.

'Right! Let's pack up camp, douse the fire, and then I'll hand out your coordinates and maps. You'll each be given a different route to follow, but we should all arrive at the ranger station by Heart Lake sometime tomorrow afternoon. When we do, you can all tell me how wonderful I've been whilst you sip real drinks and eat a proper meal. Sound good?'

They all cheered, and he nodded and headed over to his own tent, started to take down the guy ropes.

Beau helped Barb wash the breakfast dishes. 'Are you nervous about heading into the wild with just you and Con?' she asked.

'No. I know he'll look after me and I'll look after him.' She looked up at Beau. 'You nervous?'

'A bit.'

'About the wildlife problem or the cute doctor problem?'

Beau blushed. 'One more than the other.'

'Oh, don't you worry, honey. That man has got your back. And maybe some time alone together is just what you two need. A romantic walk together… A campfire beneath the stars all on your own…'

'But what if it *isn't* what we need? What if we find ourselves alone and it all turns bad? What if we really hate each other?'

Barb tilted her head as she gazed at Beau. 'I don't think that's going to happen. Do you?'

Beau wasn't sure. Having the others around had pro-

vided a security she hadn't realised she'd been rely-
ing upon. Now they were all about to go their separate
ways and she'd be on her own with Gray… Well, there
were enough butterflies in her stomach to restock a zoo.

When the dishes were done and packed away, she
headed over to collapse her tent—only to find that most
of it had been done already and Gray was kneeling on
the pine-needle-littered ground, putting her rolled-up
tent back into its bag.

'Oh! Erm…thank you.'

'No problem. I saw you were busy, so…'

She nodded. 'I can take over now.'

She held out her hands for her things and took the
tent from him, started to rearrange her pack. Keeping
her back to him, she breathed in and out slowly, trying
to keep her heart rate down. But it was difficult. He was
so close! So near. Watching and waiting for her…ready
to say goodness only knew what when they were alone.

Perhaps she could pre-empt him. Let him know there
wasn't going to be a continuation of what happened yesterday. Because if there was… Well, she wasn't sure her
senses and her heart would survive the onslaught. Gray
was like a drug to her. She could feel that. The effect
he had on her was as if she *had* been bitten by a rattlesnake! With her body turning to mush and her ability
to think shot to pieces…

She had to let him know where she stood. Where
they stood.

Beau turned and faced him, squaring her shoulders
and standing her ground as if she were about to go
into battle. 'Gray? You need to know that after…after
last night…what happened…I… It won't be happening
again. We can't let it happen. We can't.'

Try to look him in the eyes!

'But we do need to work together to get back to the ranger station, so can you promise me that you won't do anything? You know…won't provoke something of a similar nature?'

The corner of Gray's mouth turned up in a cheeky way. '*Provoke* something? What do you mean?'

Beau looked about them. Was anyone listening? She leaned into him, closer, so that she could whisper. 'I mean the kissing! Please don't try to do anything like that again!'

Gray stared deeply into her blue eyes, searching for an answer he obviously couldn't see. But he must have heeded her words, because he stepped back and nodded. 'I won't start anything. You have my word.'

'Thank you.' She felt her cheeks flush with heat again at the relief.

'But only if…'

'Only if what?'

'Only if *you* can keep *your* hands to *yourself*.'

He turned away from her to haul on his backpack, and when he turned back to face her, he was grinning widely. He really was maddening!

'I'm sure I'll try to restrain myself.'

A few hours later they had been given their coordinates and were walking to their first checkpoint. Or so Beau hoped. Gray was the one reading the map and leading the way and she was putting her trust in him totally.

Feels familiar. And look where it got me before!

'Er… Gray? Could I just glance at the map?'

'Well, that depends…'

'On…?'

'On how often you've used a map to navigate across country.'

She let out a tense breath and glared at him. 'I made it from Oxford to Heathrow in one piece.'

'By GPS?'

'It can't be that hard! Could I just have a look?'

He handed her the map with a smile on his face. 'There you go. You're in charge.'

She nodded with satisfaction and glanced at the map. She'd expected a few place names, splodges of green for woodlands and trees, maybe patches of blue to mark out lakes and blue lines for rivers. This map *had* all of those things—but it also had other lines that went all over the place. And where were the grid references...? 1...2...3... It was all numbers!

She bit her lip, her eyes scanning the map, looking for some sort of point of reference that was familiar with their surroundings. 'Is this even the right map?'

'You have to know our longitude and latitude to start with.'

'Which is where again?'

She wouldn't look him in the eye. So he stood by her side and pointed at a small spot on the map. 'Just there.'

'And we're heading to...?'

'Over there.' He pointed again. 'Our first checkpoint.'

'Right.'

It wasn't getting any clearer. What were all those other lines? Elevation? That seemed about right...

'So we need to take this trail ahead of us until we reach this...' There were a lot of lines all tightly together. 'This high spot?'

He nodded and smiled. 'Looks like it. We should make it there by nightfall. Camp overnight and then tomorrow we need to cross another river.'

Now she looked at him, feeling the cold memory

of her previous accident shiver through her body. She wasn't looking forward to that. What if it was deeper and more dangerous than the last one?

'Oh…'

'But we should be able to get to the ranger station by lunchtime. Just imagine—tomorrow we can be drinking real tea and tucking in to a restaurant meal with all of this behind us.'

'Sounds simple.'

'Should be.'

She passed him the map. 'Maybe you *should* have this.'

They'd parted company from the rest of the group—everyone with nerves and butterflies in their stomachs, everyone hugging each other, whispering words of encouragement into each other's ears before setting off—turning around occasionally until the others were out of sight.

Each pairing had been given a different checkpoint to reach, and then from that checkpoint they all had to navigate their way back to the ranger station. Nothing too arduous, but enough of a toe in the water to prove to themselves that they *could* do it, that they'd survive and, if need be, could cope with any injuries on the way.

Beau had learnt a few things on this trip so far. She'd learnt that she could cope with being around Gray. With talking to him. Being civil. They'd even got…*close*… and she'd discovered her feelings for him were still very much up in the air. He was maddening and gorgeous and frustrating and sexy and… Had she mentioned gorgeous?

He still bought her favourite chocolate bars. He'd been incredibly hurt and had survived alone. The idea of him lying there, broken and hurting, at the bottom of that remote sea cliff had been nauseating. Heartbreaking. What had he thought of as he'd lain there? Had he thought he was going to die? Had he had regrets?

Was I one of them?

Beau had never rested. Since the day he'd left, she'd pushed herself. Striving, challenging herself, working harder and harder, until the hospital had become the only thing in her life worth a damn.

But there was always a part of me missing...and that part was Gray.

She'd never had any closure. She'd never found out the reason for his disappearance.

There were a few clues now. Maybe it was something to do with his family? Had someone warned him *not* to marry her? It certainly couldn't have been anyone from *her* family. They'd all been so pleased for her when she'd announced their engagement.

Beau glanced at him as they walked, admiring the cut of his jaw, the stubbornness there in the line of his mouth, his tightly closed lips, his lowered brow as he slowly led them up an incline.

And he was doing all this with a prosthetic leg! He was amazing. He was still the man she'd known all those years ago, still challenging himself, pushing the boundaries, taking risks.

I'd be a fool to get involved with him again.

Gray held out his arm in front of her chest and Beau walked straight into it, frowning.

'Hey!'

'Shush!' He held his finger to his lips and pointed ahead through the treeline. 'Look...a herd of bison.'

Bison?

She stared hard, feeling the hairs rise on the back of her neck as the huge beasts passed them.

It was a large herd. Easily a hundred or so animals, maybe more. It was made up of mainly adults, as tall as her and Gray, with a few youngsters trotting alongside. They were thick, broad animals, with shaggy fur, some of it clumped, accentuating their humped backs as they ambled along, in no hurry at all. Several of them nibbled at the ground, others were snorting and looking around, keeping watch.

Instinctively Beau and Gray knelt out of sight by a large rock at the side of the trail. Beau's legs felt like jelly, but she drew on the reserves inside her that she always drew from. The reserves that had got her through sixteen-hour surgeries, nights on call and the all too numerous occasions when she'd had to sit at a family's bedside and deliver bad news, trying her hardest not to cry alongside her patients' relatives.

She'd had to stay strong. She'd made a profession out of it. Forcing herself to stay dry-eyed, forcing herself to stay on her feet, to answer one more patient call, to do one more consultation, perform one more surgery.

Shifting her feet, she glanced at Gray, excited at having seen these amazing animals up close. 'Should I take a picture?' she whispered.

'Does your camera have a flash?'

'I can switch it off.'

He nodded and she struggled to get her camera out of her fleece pocket. Once she'd deactivated the flash, she pushed herself up onto her knees and peered over the top of the rock. Breathing heavily, she used the zoom to focus in on one particular specimen that was snorting, using its tail to bat away flies as it scanned the horizon, alert for any danger.

'Wow…'

Back down behind the rock, she showed the digital picture to Gray and he smiled and whispered, 'It's good. But no more. We don't want them to know we're here.'

'Surely they can smell us?'

'Maybe. But I think we're upwind, so I'm going to go with no. Let's stay out of sight until they've passed.'

They sat with their backs to the rock and got some fluids on board.

Beau glanced at Gray. 'I don't suppose you've got another chocolate bar stashed away in those pockets?'

He smiled. 'No. Sorry.'

'Trail mix it is, then.' She rummaged in her pack for the small resealable bag and pulled it out, offering him some.

'No, thanks.'

She shrugged. 'More for me.' She ate a mouthful. Then another, savouring the taste of rich nuts and dried fruit, regretting that none of them was covered in chocolate. 'You know…you surprised me a lot the other day.'

He turned to her, an eyebrow raised in amusement. 'On which occasion?'

'The chocolate. That was my favourite bar. The kind you always used to buy me whenever you passed the shops on the way home from a shift. You said you still buy them. Why?'

Gray shifted on the hard ground, as if it had suddenly got a lot more uncomfortable in the last few seconds. 'Because…' He let out a heavy sigh. 'Every time I pass a store, every time I have to shop, I buy them. Eat them. They remind me…'

'Of me?'

He gave a smile. 'Of some happier times. I have this image in my head of you curled up in the corner of the sofa, your head buried in a pile of medical texts, nibbling away at a bar, one piece at a time, savouring each block before you ate the next. I don't know…it probably sounds stupid…but having them, eating them, makes me feel…closer to you.'

Beau stared at him, her heart thudding away in her chest. That was so sweet. That he still bought those bars. And for him to openly admit… She wondered if he would talk to her about his family, open up more if she asked.

But she didn't. This moment wasn't the right time. Now was the time for being honest—but not in that way. It was not the moment to bring up painful stuff that could turn all this on its head. And she didn't want this going wrong. They were heading in a good direction. Communicating. Opening up about little things. It was a start. And she liked it. Liked talking to him. Right now they were building bridges. They were forging new pathways ahead of them and they were doing it together. That was what was important.

So instead she smiled at him. 'We're close now.'

She reached out and took his hand, squeezing it, looking up into his eyes and feeling warmth spread within her, as if her heart was opening up and letting him in again. It was scary, but strangely, suddenly, it felt so right.

Their kiss now seemed like a dream, and she began to wonder how it would feel to kiss again—but this time when she was ready for it. Prepared. Able to appreciate it properly. Even instigate it?

Perhaps she ought to take a leaf out of Gray's book? Be daring. Take a risk. Put herself out there on the ledge. Make that leap of faith.

To where, though? Where do I want us to end up? If I kiss him, what message will that send?

Gray smiled at her, then laid his head back against the stone and closed his eyes.

I could kiss him now, but...

Something held her back. She stared at him for a moment longer and then let out a breath, the tension leaving her chest, her shoulders relaxing. Now was not the time.

They continued to wait for the herd to pass. Gray with his eyes closed, resting. Beau just watching him, taking in all the details of his face, questioning her heart's desire.

After the last of the bison had gone, they forged onwards until they reached their checkpoint—a tree marked with a wooden first aid box. Upon opening it, as instructed, they found the extra 'luxuries' that Mack had promised them would be in there. They'd daydreamed about what they might be. Food? Chocolate, maybe? Perhaps even a small bottle of wine to celebrate?

But no. Upon opening the box they found a standard first aid kit, a roll of toilet paper and a tick remover.

'Great...maybe we can eat those?' Beau suggested wryly. 'What *is* the correct way to cook loo roll? You're meant to boil it, right?'

Gray smiled, then they got to work setting up camp for the night. He successfully lit a small fire that they edged with rocks and they ate a rather tasteless lentil broth, their thoughts drifting to dreams of the next day, when they would be back at their luxury hotels. Though even that dream was tempered by the sour note that by then they would have parted ways, and there was still so much they hadn't said...

Beau gazed through the flames to look at Gray. He

was looking straight back at her, but this time she didn't look away. She held his gaze, thinking of how they'd once been with each other. The way he'd made her feel. How happy he'd made her. Before their wedding day anyway. She'd loved him so much.

She swallowed hard, determined not to cry over something she'd shed enough tears over. That had been then. This was now. They'd both changed and here they were, in the heart of Yellowstone Park, beneath the stars, sitting around a campfire, with just the sounds of crackling wood and distant insects, the air scented with woodsmoke and pine.

'At any other time I would say this is quite romantic.' She smiled.

He smiled back. 'But not this time?'

Now she felt awkward. She didn't know how she should reply. She wanted to keep the good mood. Keep the good feeling they had. She'd missed it. The *ease* of being with him. And she didn't want to let it go. She wished they were sitting closer. Not separated by the flames.

'Well.' She shrugged and grinned, feeling her cheeks flush with an inner heat. 'It's kind of awkward. Don't you think? If we were still together, we'd take full advantage of this moment... The stars, the campfire beneath the moon, just the two of us...'

He nodded, agreeing. 'But let's not forget that I promised to keep my hands to myself.'

She matched his nod. 'Yes, there's that, too.'

They stared at each other across the fire. Smiling. Breathing. Keeping eye contact.

Beau felt a strange awareness inside her. She could feel the weight of her clothes against her body. The tightness of the tops of her socks, her waistband digging into her stomach. She felt uncomfortable. Keen to move.

She stood up and nodded some more. 'I think I ought to go to bed.'

Gray stood, too. 'If that's what you think is best.'

'I do.'

There was a tense silence. The air was charged with a heat that did not come from the flames below.

Beau kept remembering the way he'd kissed her the other day. How it had felt to be back in his arms. That ease of being with him that she'd never felt with anyone else. He was so close now! So available. But was she brave enough to start something?

'Right, I'm going, then.'

'All right. Goodnight.' He slipped his hands into the pockets of his jacket, his jaw clenching and unclenching in the moonlight.

'Goodnight.' She stared at him, unwilling to walk away. Not really wanting to go to bed. Not alone. Anyway. 'Gray, I—'

She didn't get to finish her sentence.

Gray stepped forward, and for a brief moment she thought he was going to take her in his arms—but, disappointingly, he didn't. Instead he began to speak.

'We need to talk.'

Beau sucked in a breath. *Okay.* This was going to be one of those moments, wasn't it? One of those life-changing moments when your path in life forked and you could choose to go left or right.

'All right.'

He reached out and took her hand, enveloping it in both of his, gazing down at them as he stroked her skin, inhaling deeply, searching for the right words to begin.

'I need to be honest with you. If anything is to…happen…between us, then we need to be honest with each other. That's what destroyed us in the past. Secrets. I *did* want to marry you, Beau. I need to say that. Right at the start. Because you *must* believe it. I did. I wanted you to be mine for ever. I wanted to know that you'd be there for me every single day of the rest of my life. I loved you. Deeply. Do you believe me when I say that?'

She searched his face, saw the intensity in his eyes, felt the way he squeezed her hand whilst he waited for her answer. Yes. She believed him.

'I do.'

'Good. That's good. The wedding…the actual day itself…that would have been easy for me. That wasn't why I left—the pressure of the day. That wasn't the bit that worried me. It was the next part I was worried about.'

'The honeymoon?'

She didn't understand. How could he have been worried about that part? She'd spent many a night with Gray McGregor and he certainly knew what he was doing. This man had made her body *sing*. He had made her cry out in ecstasy and shiver with delight. She'd used to lie in his arms and fall asleep, feeling secure, loved and cherished. He had been her other half. The part that had made her whole. She'd never found that since. With anyone. Connections she had made had seemed…wanting. Unreal. There'd always been something missing.

'No, not that. The *marriage* part.'

Oh. Beau frowned. She didn't understand. 'Why?'

'You were right when you said that there was something about my family you didn't know. There was something…*is* something. Even now.'

She remained silent, waiting for him to explain, but she stroked the back of his hand absentmindedly, being supportive, as much as she could be, whilst he told her his story. She was apprehensive, too. For years she'd wanted to hear his explanation, and now that it was here, well…she wasn't sure if she could bear to hear it. What if it was terrible? What if it was something sad? What if all these years he'd been hurting, too?

'When my parents first met, they were madly in love. They were like us. Young. Hopelessly enchanted with each other. All they could see was a bright future ahead of them. They thought that no matter what happened they would face it together and they would be *strong*. That's what they believed.'

She smiled at the mental image, picturing it perfectly. But her smile faltered when she remembered that something had then changed.

'But…?'

'But that didn't happen. They got married, yes, but they were poor. Jobs were scarce. My mother got a job in a factory, part-time, just as she learnt she was pregnant with me. My father was working as a mechanic in a garage, fixing and tending buses for the council. He worked incredibly long hours. She hardly saw him. But he had to work to bring in the money. Especially when she stopped working to have me.'

She nodded, understanding their financial struggle. Even though it wasn't anything she'd experienced herself, she had seen it in others. 'It must have been difficult for them.'

This was all new information for Beau. She'd known almost nothing about Gray's family. Just that his father was in a wheelchair, paralysed from the waist down, and that his mother hardly spoke, her face for ever shut in a pinched, tight-lipped, sour way. Their early years together sounded like a tough time.

'It was. And I was a difficult bairn. Mum found it hard to cope. Dad couldn't help—he was always at work. When he got home late each evening, he was exhausted, barely having enough energy to eat before collapsing into bed each night.'

She squeezed his hand.

'Mum begged him to help more at home, but he had no time. He was afraid that if he took time off work he'd lose his job, and they couldn't afford that. She started taking in sewing and ironing to earn a few extra pennies, and they simply began living separate lives. I had colic. I barely slept, apparently. Crying all the time and nothing would soothe me. My mother felt like a single parent. They became true ships that passed only in the night.'

She felt his pain but wondered what this had to do with *their* relationship. 'What happened?'

'I don't know… My mum would bad-mouth him to me all the time. Say that he was useless, that he was a waste of space. He wound her up. The way he was never there. The way he irritated her when he *was*. The way he never lifted a finger to help her at the weekends. She even suspected there might be something with another woman. The receptionist at the garage. I didn't know if he was having an affair, but my dad would go on at me the same way. Say that my mother was a harridan, a nag, that she couldn't leave a hard-working man in peace.'

Beau felt uncomfortable. How awful that must have been—to be stuck between two warring parents. The two people you relied on and loved most in the whole world.

'Their verbal battles sometimes got physical. He didn't hit her or anything, but they both threw things. The soundtrack to my childhood was yelling and hearing ceramics hitting the walls. I even ended up at the doctors once, after accidentally treading on something sharp that had been missed in the clear-up afterwards.'

He let out a deep breath and his face brightened just slightly.

'That was where I began to love medicine. It was the only place where I'd been tended with real care and compassion.'

His eyes darkened again.

'My parents hated each other. Despised each other. The slightest thing would set them off. A look. The way the other one chewed their food. Whether they snored. Anything. And I was left as a go-between. Used like some pawn in a battle that I didn't understand. Then one day my mum decided she'd had enough. She packed her bags and waited for him to come home so she could tell him she was leaving.'

Beau was shocked. 'Without you?'

He nodded. 'The time he should have been home came and went. She got furious because she thought he'd gone to the pub with the other woman, spending money we couldn't spare on booze, and said that he was preventing her from giving him the performance of a lifetime. She'd planned on telling him once and for all how he was a good-for-nothing husband and she was leaving, But then the phone rang. He'd had an accident. A bad one.'

Beau felt sick. 'The one that paralysed him?'

He nodded again. 'A bus had come off a raised ramp and rolled over him, crushing his spine and pelvis. I'll never forget the look on my mother's face as she heard the news. Shock…disbelief…and then a deep sadness. Resignation. We went to the hospital, but he was in surgery. The nurses were very good to me—loving, caring.

It was there I decided I wanted to be like them. Nothing like my parents. I wanted to become a doctor. We learnt later that Dad was paralysed.'

Beau could picture it all. The shock of the accident. The complete one-eighty that Gray's mother must have had to do...

'And then your mother felt she *couldn't* leave?'

'That's right. She unpacked her things whilst he was in the hospital and I've never seen a sadder woman since. They just get on with things now. She helps him. Cares for him. But they barely talk. They just exist in the same house. Despite what had happened, what they'd gone through together, they've become more separate. Their marriage has become a prison. Each is saddled with the other for eternity. And to think they once loved each other so much...'

He couldn't look at her, his eyes downcast, lost in the painful past.

She was silent for a moment. Taking it all in. What had happened to his parents was awful. The way their relationship had crumbled under tough times. The accident... The paralysis... The way his mother must have felt obligated to stay... The way his father must have felt, stuck with a nursemaid wife he could barely tolerate speaking to...

'That's horrible, Gray. And I can't believe I'm only hearing about it *now*. Why didn't you tell me before?'

He looked at her then, sadness in his eyes. 'I've *never* known them to be happy, Beau! Not *once* can I see, in any part of my memory, either one of them smiling, or laughing, or being happy! I grew up in a dark, stormy world, full of crazed arguments, broken china and tense silences you'd need a machete to cut through! I loved being at school because I was *away* from them. I stayed away from home as much as I could because it was the only way I could be happy—without *them* dragging me down, dragging me into their battles. And when I met *you*…my sweet, beautiful Beau…I couldn't believe that a man and a woman could be so happy together! You were a breath of fresh air to me—the first hint of spring after a lifetime of bitter, endless winter…'

She could hear that he was trying to explain how he'd felt when he'd met her…but he'd *left* her. Surely it couldn't be true that their perfect future had been ruined because of what had happened to his *parents*?

'But, Gray, how could you have left me because of *them*…?'

Beau stared up at him, tears burning her eyes. Her hurt, her humiliation from all those years ago came flooding back again. The pain was fresh once more. All those years she'd thought there'd been something wrong with *her*. Something she'd been lacking. Something missing that had made him walk away. Maybe into the arms of another woman? And she'd racked her brains, trying to think of how she could have been *more* so that he would have stayed. Had pushed herself ever since, trying to prove that he'd been wrong to walk away and give her up.

'Gray, I'm sorry your parents had an awful time, but it hurts to see that you let that impact *us*. So your parents gave you a bad example…? Mine gave me a *great* example of what marriage could be.' She smiled through her tears. 'They still do. After all this time. Are you saying that my experience of *my* parents' marriage is wrong? *Why* couldn't you believe in a happy marriage? With their example?'

He shook his head. 'Because your family was the exception to the rule. Everywhere I looked I saw married couples barely getting along. Couples who had nothing to say to each other after many years. Couples who could only talk about their children. Couples who did things separately. Who took time apart, holidayed on their own. Couples who looked like all joy of life had left them.'

'You thought that would happen to *us*?'

She almost couldn't believe it. His parents' story was tragic, and she felt for him that he had been trapped in it. But that had been his parents' pain. Not *theirs*. She and Gray had been happy. Strong.

'I feared things would end up that way. Because I couldn't be honest with you about this before we got married, so what you saw in me was a lie. I was a lie. *We* were a lie. We wouldn't have survived! I accept the fact that leaving you at the church like that was a cowardly thing to do, and I should have turned up to tell you to your face that I was leaving. But at the time I was so racked with guilt, so broken in two at knowing that I *had* to walk away from you—away from the woman I truly loved so that I didn't take her into a tortured future—that I wasn't thinking clearly. So I'm sorry I left you at the altar, Beau, but if I hadn't, then you would have left *me*. At some point.'

'I would *never* have left you.'

Tears flowed freely down her cheeks now. His pain was so raw. His suffering so real she couldn't imagine how he had managed to keep it so contained. And how had she not known? How had she not noticed?

'I should have pushed for more. I should have made you tell me back then. We could have avoided this.'

'We couldn't. Because we were based on a fantasy. *You* thought we were perfect.' A pained look crossed his face. He didn't want to hurt her. 'We *weren't*. I couldn't tell you because you didn't want to hear it. You didn't ask about *me*. All you could see was the romance and the fun and the laughter.' He stared hard at her. 'You didn't want the reality of me. You were so caught up in the wedding preparations you couldn't see what was right in front of your eyes.'

Her cheeks were wet. She could feel the drips of her tears falling from her jawline. 'What? Are you saying that I…I *failed* you somehow? That I didn't listen? That I didn't give you the chance to tell me what you needed to say?'

It hurt to think he might believe that. *Had* she been at fault?

'I wasn't ready, Beau. I had doubts. A real fear as to what awaited us in the future.' He sighed heavily, as if worn down by the argument. 'I wanted to love you for ever, Beau. I really did. But I knew it couldn't happen. Unless we were honest. You weren't ready to hear that, so I walked away.'

She looked out across the plateau at the mountains in the distance, now dark with greying shadow as the sun set. The sky was filled with glorious tones of orange and pink. It all looked so pretty. So wonderful. But how could this sunset be so beautiful? So warm? There were blooming flowers in the distance. The crackle and pop of burning wood and the scent of woodsmoke drifting past them. The last of the day's bird chorus slowly fading to nothing.

Was she also to blame for their relationship failing in the way that it had? And if that was the case, didn't she need to take some of the responsibility for everything that had gone wrong? For the fact that what they'd had in the past had all been *fake*?

She pulled her fleece jacket around her. 'I loved you. That part was real…'

She looked away, her bottom lip trembling. She feared that maybe he'd never loved her. That their relationship had never been what she'd thought it was. She tried to pull her hands free of his, tried to separate herself from him, acknowledging that she had somehow always imagined things wrongly. That their past relationship had been some sort of dreamworld she'd been living in. Had she been deluding herself that he loved her?

But Gray wouldn't let her get away. He held on tight, pulling her back and making her look him in the eyes.

'I loved you, too. More than *life*! And I refused to put you through that. I refused to let us go blindly into the future with you thinking that everything was fine when I knew that it wasn't.'

'Our love was real?' Her bottom lip trembled.

He nodded and pressed his lips to her forehead before looking down at her. 'It was. I couldn't lie about that.'

'But—'

'Beau, look at me.'

She looked up at him with eyes glistening from salty tears, with her heart almost torn in two by the heartbreak of knowing that she'd caused him pain and that she'd kept him *silent*. Unable to tell her what he needed. She so badly wanted to put that right. So she would listen to him now. Hear what he had to say.

'Yes?'

He stared deeply into her eyes, as if searching for something. 'We had something special, but it wasn't our time then.'

'Is it our time now?' she asked, with hope in her heart.

Gray swallowed, cupping her face, his hands so tender, warm and soft, and then he took another step towards her, breathing heavily, lowering his head until their hungry lips met.

She sank into his embrace. Against his hard, solid body. Tasting him, enjoying him, her hands up in his hair, grasping him, pulling him towards her, desperate for his touch. Remembering, recalling *this*—how good it had always felt to be with him. How special.

Their past was forgotten in that instant.

She *needed* Gray. Had missed him so much it was painful. But now he was back in her arms and it felt so good. She didn't want to let him go. She wanted to enjoy the moment, and to hell with the consequences, because right now she needed this. *Him*. It didn't matter what he'd said. All that pain he'd shared. Because *this*—this was what was important. Being with him. Reconnecting.

Her fingers fell to the hemline of his top and she began to lift it, to pull it over his head, so that her hands could feel the touch of his skin, his broad shoulders, his taut chest, that flat stomach she remembered so well. His sleeve caught on his chunky wristwatch and she had to give it a yank, but then it was gone, discarded.

For a moment she just looked at him, taking in the beauty of his body, the solidity of his muscles, his powerful frame, and then she was pulling off her own top, kissing him again as he unclipped her bra in a fervour. She wriggled her arms so it would fall to the forest floor. Gasped as his hands cupped her breasts and brought them to his lips. So in need for the feel of his hot lips against her skin.

The touch of his tongue tantalised her, causing her to gasp and bite her lip. She felt as if she was on fire. Her whole body a burning ember. A delicious liquid heat seared from her centre right through her body, inflaming every nerve ending, every sensation, every caress, stroke or lick, driving her insane with need.

'I want you, Gray.' She made him look at her as she spoke, wanting him to know in no uncertain terms what she wanted him to do.

He stared back into her heavy eyes and nodded, then took a step away from her.

She almost cried out, fearing that he was going to stop, leave her in her fevered state, that he was going to humiliate her just as she'd laid herself bare.

But no. He was grabbing a groundsheet, a blanket, and then he took her hand and pulled her towards it.

Hungry for him, hungry for more, she moved to him and felt the core of her burning with need as his fingers began to unbutton her trousers. Hurriedly she kicked off her boots, then her trousers were cast aside, and she hopped from one foot to the other as she removed her socks, before throwing herself back into the safety, security and heat of his embrace.

She wasn't cold. It was a perfect summer's evening. The air on her body felt like a lover's caress in itself, and there was something thrilling about that. As Gray lowered her gently onto the blanket, his hand drifted up the length of her thigh and then delicately began to stroke the thin lace of her underwear before reaching down to feel the heat between her legs.

Yes! Touch me there...

She breathed heavily, her eyes open, gazing upwards at the stars, as she felt his fingertips drift lazily over her body, felt his gaze roaming the expanse of her nakedness, his lips tenderly kissing the underside of her breast, then her waist, her belly button.

And then... Then his mouth drifted downwards,

towards the lace, towards the place she wanted him the most.

Beau closed her eyes, her hands gripping his hair, and gasped.

They slept under the same canvas that night. Naked, entwined, they lay together, his body wrapped around hers, until sleep and exhaustion claimed them.

Gray woke first. He was glad. It gave him a chance to put his prosthetic back on. Beau hadn't really seen him without it yet, and after what they'd shared last night, he didn't want to spoil what had happened with the sight of his stump over breakfast.

He'd grown used to it. Accepted it. But still, sometimes when he saw it, he remembered what his leg had looked like before, what it had felt like to be whole, and he hated the reminder.

He could spare Beau that, at least. Hadn't he shown her enough last night? He'd hurt her with his words. With his confession. He knew it deeply. He'd seen it in her eyes. She'd started to question herself. Look back. He'd hated seeing her pain, but maybe now, after last night, they could move forward?

Their relationship had died a death before because he'd never been honest with her about his family. About his fears of what might happen to them if they married. But last night…last night had been *amazing* and he wanted that to continue. For them to be together again. He and Beau were a good match.

His finger gently swept up the length of her bare arm and he smiled as she groaned slightly and shifted in her sleep, pressing her body against him.

The length of her, naked and warm, was nuzzled

into him, and he looked down at her face, soft in repose against his shoulder.

Why had he ever listened to that infernal internal voice? To the voice of logic and reason that had kept niggling away at him? Telling him it would all go wrong, that they would end up behaving exactly like his parents' in a toxic marriage.

Thinking of his parents made him remember his father at his stag party, when he'd said, 'You'll regret it. You mark my words, son, you're about to ruin both your lives…'

He grimaced, refusing to hear those words again. He was not going to let thoughts of his father's bitterness ruin what he had at this moment. This perfect moment—holding the woman he had once loved so much in his arms.

Could we start again with a clean slate?

His heart agonised over the possibility.

But he didn't have long to argue with himself.

Beau blinked open her eyes and smiled as she looked up at him. 'Morning.'

'Good morning. Sleep well?'

'I did. The first time in ages. You?'

He nodded. He *had* slept well. And he was in no doubt that it was down to being with Beau. He didn't want to move. Didn't want this moment to end. Could they possibly lie here for ever?

'Would you like breakfast?'

She smiled and gave him a brief kiss. 'Depends what's on the menu.'

He laughed and pulled her onto him, feeling his body spring into life for her once more. 'I think I could possibly find something a bit more interesting than oatmeal.'

Beau grinned. 'Really? I—' She stopped, tilting her head at a funny angle. 'Can you hear that?'

He wasn't sure he wanted to listen to anything. But to humour her he remained silent and tried to listen. He could hear birds singing and... He squinted and sat upright, his hands still holding Beau to him. Was that...*snuffling*?

'Stay here.'

He slid Beau to one side of him and pulled on his trousers and then, hurriedly, his socks and boots. Quietly he slid the zip down on the tent and looked out. There was nothing he could see in front of the tent. He popped his head back inside.

'I don't think there's anything there, but just to be on the safe side get dressed and we'll go and take a look.'

The snuffling noise was definitely there, and it sounded as if it was *behind* the tent, where they couldn't see without stepping outside.

Gray didn't think it was a mountain lion, and wolves were dawn and dusk creatures. It was now—he glanced at his wristwatch—nearly eight in the morning. When Beau was dressed and had put her boots on, he took her hand and then slowly stepped out, peering over the top of the tent.

And froze.

Behind him Beau was crouched, unable to see what was happening. 'What is it?'

'It's...er...something.'

Beau pushed past the tent flap and came out of the tent to peer past Gray. The second she saw the herd of bison she also froze, feeling her blood run cold.

Mack had warned them. Bison were dangerous. They'd seen that herd last night—they should have *thought*, should have considered that they might still be in the area. But they hadn't. They'd had…*other things* on their minds.

'Gray, what do we do?' she asked in a whisper.

There was nowhere for them to go. The bison herd filled the whole plateau around them. The only place for them to go was the cliff edge.

Where a river ran far below.

About a forty-foot drop.

Gray turned slowly to look at her. 'The tent won't protect us, and these animals can be dangerous.'

'Perhaps they don't even know we're here!'

Gray glanced over and caught the eye of a bull, which peered at them, snorting through its nose. Was he the leader of the pack?

Gray watched in silent dread as the tail of the bison began to rise.

'It's going to charge!'

'What?'

'We need to jump.'

'Please tell me you're joking.'

'Nope.'

He grabbed her hand in his and made a quick run to the cliff edge, where they stopped to look over at the drop.

It was dizzyingly high. Precipitous. And he could feel the pull of gravity as he looked over the edge. He was used to heights. To climbing. To the risk of a fall. But Beau wasn't, and he needed her to jump without hesitating.

A quick glance back at the bison told him it was starting to head their way. Without doubt the animal was going to charge them. Protect its herd. There was nowhere else to go.

'On three…'

'Gray…' She gripped his arm in fright.

'One…two…*three*!'

He held her hand tight and took a leap off the edge, feeling her jump with him, hearing her scream filling the air as they fell, with the water rushing up to meet them.

CHAPTER EIGHT

HER SENSES WENT into overload. Her scream was whipped away by the passing air as she looked down at the terrifying sight of the water rushing up to meet her.

She was falling fast. The air rushed past her mouth before she had time to inhale, her stomach was rising into her chest cavity, and her limbs were flailing madly, trying to find something—anything—to grab on to in mid-air. But of course there was nothing. It was terrifying.

I'm going to die!

The river that had at one point seemed so far away was getting disturbingly close, and then suddenly, *splash*! Her body hit the water, which smacked her in the face as if she'd just been hit by a heavyweight boxer, making her gasp. Water flooded her mouth, her nostrils, her ears, as she struggled against it. Her body stung from the impact, every nerve ending screaming, but somehow there was an even more important agony she had to contend with—the need for oxygen.

It hurt to look about under the water, and all she could see beside her and below were dark shadows, whereas above her there was light. Sparkling sunlight glittering on a surface that didn't seem that far away. She began to swim, her lungs stretched to breaking point.

And just when she thought she wouldn't make it, just when she thought the surface of the water had just been a mirage, she broke the surface, coughing and spluttering as she gasped for air and tried not to swallow more water.

Inhaling deeply and quickly, wiping her wet hair out of her face, she trod water, turning and twisting, trying to get her bearings.

Where was Gray?

He suddenly popped out of the water next to her, his hair plastered over his forehead, looking for her, and he gave a relieved smile when he saw she was right next to him. 'You okay?'

'I'm all right. Are you okay?'

He nodded and looked up. 'Can you believe that? We did it!'

She blew water from her lips and nodded. Yes, they had done it. And now she was treading water in her clothes and the water was colder than it looked.

She could see a bank further downstream, where they'd be able to crawl out and get on dry land, and she pointed at it. 'Over there.'

She tried to swim, trying to remember how to coordinate her limbs for the breaststroke. The current wasn't too strong and she made it easily, clambering from the water like a sodden sheep, the weight of her clothes dragging her down, cold and shivering.

Slumping onto the ground, she turned to wait for Gray, who crawled from the water beside her before flopping onto his back and letting out an exhausted breath.

Beau swallowed hard and lay back against the dirt, exhausted. There was probably mud getting in her hair, but she didn't care.

I jumped off a cliff!

'I can't believe we did that.'

He turned to look at her and grinned. 'Well, we did. You did great.'

Her gaze drifted to the clifftop, where their camp had been. 'All our things are still up there.'

Gray nodded and let out another sigh. 'But the most important thing is down here. With me.'

She met his gaze and smiled, and then she rolled towards him and planted a kiss on his lips. 'Thank you.'

'What for?'

'Saving our lives.'

'I made you jump off a cliff.'

'Yes. But as we are *not* currently a bison's breakfast, I'd still call that a save.'

Gray frowned. 'I don't think bison *eat* people.'

'Maybe not, but they sure as hell can flatten you if they want, and I don't know about you, but I quite like to have my body in full working order.'

Gray looked away and then sat up, running his hand down his left leg towards his prosthetic.

Oh. I shouldn't have said that. I didn't think.

She bit her lip. 'Sorry.'

'It's fine.' Gray got to his feet, testing it out. 'Still works.'

She stood up beside him, looking around them. The river flowed downstream away from them and on either side were gorse bushes and trees and mountains rising high. 'Are we lost?'

He looked at her briefly before turning, scanning their surroundings for himself. 'I don't think so. If I remember correctly, Heart Lake is fed into by this river. If we follow it we should make it back to the ranger station in a few hours.'

She nodded. 'Okay. Should we try and find water, or do you think we can make it without?'

'It's getting warm, but we should be fine if we keep a steady pace.'

She bit her lip and he reached out a hand to grab hers.

'Hey, we'll be fine.'

Beau hoped he was right.

Gray trudged on, leading the way. Apart from being hungry and thirsty, he wasn't sure what to feel. Last night had been bittersweet. He and Beau had become close again last night! And though he'd loved every second of it, he still wasn't sure they'd resolved anything by this morning. Kissing her, then making love to her, had distracted their thoughts, and though he had wanted to lie in her arms for many more hours, enjoying that blissful moment when it had seemed the rest of the world had stopped turning, he'd been well aware that the issues between them were still there.

Jumping off that cliff with her, her hand in his... He remembered with a cold shudder how it had felt to hit the water, to feel his prosthetic weigh him down. He had struggled to swim, to get to the surface. Beau had let go of him and for a moment—a brief, terrifying moment— he'd thought she'd been swept downstream. Until he'd broken the surface and seen her there next to him. Safe.

But only just. How could he look out for Beau when he could barely survive himself?

If he had a magic lamp and he could make a wish, then he'd wish for a long, happy life with Beau. No doubt about that. But...

What could he offer her now? He'd told her the truth at long last, there was that, so they had honesty now— and, yes, there was still that intense heat between them.

But relationships had to be more than just sex. There had to be trust, intimacy, love, compassion. There had to be give and take. Compromise. Teamwork. They had to be a unit. A solid couple. He had to feel as if he could protect her and love her in the way she deserved. In the way she wanted. She *needed* that happy-ever-after, but was he the man who could give it to her?

Did he deserve another chance with her?

They didn't live near each other. They each had a career in different parts of the country. They each worked really long hours. Beau had her family in Oxford—his were in Edinburgh. What did he have to give Beau apart from their painful, disappointing past? And although she'd said his leg didn't bother her, it *did* bother him. He wanted to be perfect for her. Whole. If she took him on, she'd be taking on his leg. The phantom pains he still got…the possibility of getting early osteoarthritis in his good knee because of the amputation. She had to accept that he was disabled—like his father.

Did she deserve that? Want that? There were so many men out there who had all four functioning limbs and hadn't hurt her in the way that he had. Men who hadn't let her down.

He didn't want to burden Beau the way his own mother had been burdened—with a disabled man whom she'd grow to resent.

He knew that she wanted him. He'd seen it in her eyes. In the way she'd listened to him reveal his soul and the way she'd looked as they'd made love. She had feelings for him still—he could see it. And he couldn't deny the way he was feeling about her.

The only problem was he wasn't sure if they should pursue it. Because if they gave things another go and it all went wrong, the heartache of losing her again would be too much.

Not worth going through for anything.

Perhaps walking away would be the kindest thing after all?

Around them Yellowstone Park was glorious, dressed in its summer colours: bright blue skies, wispy white clouds drifting past, trees adorned with many greens, from the darkest pine to the lightest willow, blue-white columbines attracting butterflies of every shape and size amongst the yellow cinquefoil flowers like buttercups.

They ambled through the landscape together, breathing heavily under the oppressive heat, until around midday, when Beau had to stop and sit down. Collapsing to the floor, she sucked in oxygen, exhausted. She was as thirsty as anything, her mouth dry as dust.

When had she *ever* felt this spent? She'd been on her feet for only a few hours. She'd had much longer shifts in hospital. But at least then she'd had access to drinks. The river trickling alongside them almost seemed to mock her. All that water...

All that campylobacter. All that giardia. Drink that and you certainly will be in hospital. With sickness and diarrhoea.

She swallowed and tried not to think of a nice cold glass of iced water. Instead she decided to focus on something much better. The fact that she and Gray had grown close again. That they'd overcome the barrier of their past. Gray had shared his concerns and fears. They'd made love under a starry sky and she'd slept in his arms and felt happy again for the first time in an age.

After everything, it seemed things were going *right*

for her with Gray, and she'd thought she'd never be able to say that. *Ever.* Yet here they were. Together. Supporting each other, protecting each other, looking out for each other. This was what couples did. They worked as a team. They were strong. United.

Her feelings for him were very strong. She still loved him. She knew it in her heart. She'd been struggling against it ever since she'd walked into the ranger station just a few days ago. Her love for him had never gone away and he was the only man who could make her feel this way.

Last night had been a revelation. A new chapter for them both. She'd been grateful for his honesty. For his making clear that which had been blurry. Explaining the pain. Explaining his reasons for walking away.

It had hurt to feel that she'd been to blame for some of it, but truth sometimes did hurt. She'd listened to it, acknowledged it. Accepted it. *Some of it was my fault.* But then they'd slept together and he'd held her in his arms, and she'd felt so good to be there. She just *knew* she could never let that go again.

'Do you think there's much further to go?'

He ran a hand through his hair. 'Couple of miles, maybe. Not far.'

'We might run into the others soon. They might have water! You know...if they didn't have to jump off a cliff.'

He smiled at her. 'Maybe.'

'I'm glad I'm here with you, Gray. Doing this. It wouldn't have been the same without you. Us meeting again. Getting close again. Opening up. It's been good for us, don't you think?'

Gray nodded and looked about them. 'Ready to go again?'

She stood and slipped her hand into his, surprising him. 'I'm ready.'

He said nothing, just started to walk.

Then, within the hour, they met some familiar faces.

CHAPTER NINE

BARB AND CONRAD waved to them and they hurried over to meet up with the older married couple, who both looked quite fresh and not at all trail-weary.

The two women hugged and the men patted each other on the back—until Barb frowned and looked at them both. 'Where's your gear?'

Beau grinned at Gray. 'A bison took it.'

'Oh! Really?'

'We woke this morning and we were surrounded. One started to charge and we had to jump into a river to escape.'

Barb looked at her husband. 'You weren't hurt? Con, get these people some water.'

But Con was already doing that, and he handed over their flasks to let them both take a long, refreshing drink.

'Oh, wow—that tastes so good!' Beau wiped her mouth and handed it back, but Con waved it away.

'You keep it. We're nearly back to the ranger station. Look over there—through the trees. See that strip of blue? That's Heart Lake.'

Beau squinted and shielded her eyes—and, yes! There it was! They'd made it back, safe and sound, and their friends were okay, too.

Barb threaded her arm into Beau's and walked with her, whilst Gray walked behind them with Con.

'So how did you two get on?' she asked.

Beau smiled and nodded. 'It was good. I think it might just be okay for us.'

'Oh, honey, I'm so pleased to hear that! You two look made for each other.'

It felt good to hear someone else say that. It reinforced everything that Beau had been thinking. She'd made some mistakes in the past. She'd taken Gray's feelings for granted. Had not given him the opportunity to share how he truly felt. She'd been caught up in her romantic tale of love, of how they'd had the romance of the century, but none of it had been true. Well, almost none. They *had* loved each other. But the foundations of their relationship had been shaky.

She'd not known the full truth about her then husband-to-be, but now she did. She'd been so busy trying to have what her parents had that she hadn't realised that he'd been trying to steer them away from what *his* parents had.

But it's settled now. We're nearly back to civilisation. We can make this work. Somehow.

She supposed they'd have to travel to see each other at first. Maybe one of them could try to get a job in the other's hospital. There was always a need for a good neurologist or cardiologist. Then, being close, they could work on just being together again. It was scary— being back with Gray, taking a risk—but it felt *right*. As if she was home.

The brain had two hemispheres and there were connections—neural pathways that connected the two, making the brain a whole so that it worked to perfection. Being separated from Gray had been like having only one hemisphere. She could survive, but there were deficits. She'd known something was missing. That she wasn't whole.

Now they were coming back together and everything was slowly becoming *right*.

The rest of the group began to emerge from different directions as they got closer and closer to the ranger station. Seeing each other's faces brought comfort and joy, and when they were all back together again, they walked into the ranger station with the biggest grins on their faces. Their happiness in their joint achievement filled the room with its glow as they each told their stories—the funny moments, the scary moments. How they'd survived.

Beau listened to it all, her heart full.

As the chatter died down, Mack congratulated them all on getting back safe and sound, and after a quick debrief they all started to decamp. To gather their things and get ready to catch the minibus that would take them back to Gallatin and their own cars. Where they would all part ways.

Seeing as Beau didn't have any gear to sort through, she located Gray and waited for him to end his conversation with Toby and Allan. The guys were promising to keep in touch.

Afterwards, when they'd left, he turned to her and smiled. 'You okay?'

'I'm good! I'm great, actually. Looking forward to getting back to my hotel and changing my clothes. Taking a hot shower. I thought that maybe you'd like to join me?'

It was forward, she knew, but she wanted this good feeling to continue. To make sure he knew they could work on this relationship and make it succeed this time.

Now she knew what he had feared, what he'd worried about before, they could move on.

But Gray's face was blank. 'I'll be heading back to my own hotel. I've got a flight to catch tomorrow and I'd like to get some rest.'

Oh.

'Are you sure? I thought that we—'

'This isn't what you deserve, Beau.' He lowered his voice and moved her away from the others. '*I'm* not. I can't love you the way you want me to. I think it's best if we close the door on what we had and just move on.'

Beau stared at him, feeling sick. Was he really saying this? But they'd shared so much!

How could I have read you so wrong?

Gray walked away from her once more, his feet leaden, his heart weary. Every step he took became more and more painful as he increased the distance between them.

It was tempting. So tempting to turn around and go back to her, give her what she wanted, but he couldn't. He needed to get away from her. Create some space. He couldn't think when he was this close to her. He couldn't think when she looked at him like that. With *love* in her eyes.

It was like stepping back in time. Right back to where they started! Surely she could see that he was doing this for both of them?

'*Gray!*' She grabbed his arm and spun him round. 'What are you *doing*?'

'We're still in the same place. It's eleven years on, and we're in a different country, but we're still stuck in the same place!'

'No. It's different now.'

'Is it? You still see the sweetness and light in everything. Despite what I've told you. Despite knowing I can't protect you. Can't love you the way that you need. Can't offer you anything but a disabled partner who sure as hell doesn't deserve a second chance.'

'It won't be that way—'

He pulled his arm free. 'Please, Beau! I can't think when you touch me! I can't think with you around. It's too much. Believe me, it's better this way.'

'For who? For *you*? Because it isn't easy for *me*!'

'I just…need some space. Please, Beau, will you let it go? I can't be who you need.'

She looked up at him with sadness. 'Who are *you* to know who I need?'

He couldn't speak then. He couldn't reply. He couldn't *think*. Seeing the tears fall from her eyes was so hard. But what could he do? The feelings that had resurfaced when they'd made love had shaken him. He wasn't prepared for this! He'd expected to apologise, he'd expected her to listen grudgingly, but so much else had happened. Emotions were getting involved again— love and longing, hurt and pain. He couldn't see what he needed to do.

Gray needed her to go.

Gritting his teeth, he turned his back on her and waited for her to walk away.

He hadn't sat next to her on the bus. It had been like a slap in the face. Instead he'd walked past her and gone to sit at the back with Dean and Rick.

So she'd sat there alone, behind the driver, trying her hardest not to turn around and look at him in case everyone else saw the heartbreak on her face.

Where had it gone so wrong?

They'd talked. They'd made love. That night had

been exquisite. The sensations he had made her feel had made her...euphoric. He'd been tender, caring, passionate. They'd lain together afterwards, entwined. He'd smiled at her that morning, had kissed her—he'd seemed fine. They'd jumped off that cliff. Survived the fall without injury. Got out of the river without being swept away. They'd both been so happy and exhilarated at what had happened, and then...

He'd gone a little quiet on the trek back—but then again, they both had! They'd been thirsty. Talking had just seemed to make her mouth drier. But whilst she'd allowed herself to think everything was different, had got carried away with imagining the glorious future they could have, he'd been thinking...what?

'I'm not what you deserve. I can't love you the way you want me to.'

How was it *his* choice to decide what she deserved? She deserved *him*! He was her soulmate. Her better half. Her match. In every way. She *needed* him.

She loved him.

Did I do it again? Did I get carried away with a romantic fantasy?

Maybe he was right. Maybe he *could* see right through her. Perhaps he was right not to rush into anything? Could he see that she was falling into old habits?

'I can't love you the way you want me to.'

She just wanted to be loved by *him*. He was the only man who would do. Who would fulfil the need she felt every day. To be touched by him. Loved by him. Held in his arms. She'd had eleven years to realise she wouldn't be able to find that with anyone else. Not the way she felt when she was with Gray. That sense of completeness.

When he got off the bus, if he left without her, he would be taking her heart with him.

Beau wiped away a tear and looked out of the window.

The minibus trundled along the park's roads, past sights they hadn't seen. Glaciers. Geysers. She saw some elk, and high above some birds circling on the thermals in the blue skies. The raw beauty of the place hurt her eyes. It was too beautiful to look at when she felt so ravaged, so she closed her eyes and laid her head against the window, allowing the motion of the vehicle to rock her to sleep.

She dreamed. She dreamed that she was in the water again, after the jump, and that she'd just exploded to the surface, gasping for air, looking about her for Gray. Eventually his head popped up out of the water, further downstream, and though she called for him, though she waved to show him where she was, he simply got washed downstream, disappearing from sight...

She woke with a jerk, sitting bolt upright, aware that people were getting off the bus. Looking outside, she could see the car park of the Gallatin Ranger Station, and over to her right her rental car. Had it been only five days since she'd parked it there? So much had happened...

Beau stood up, determined to speak to Gray, to not let him get away without a word as he had once before. She turned around to face the back of the bus, where he'd been sitting.

He was gone.

She looked out at the others, still gathering their bags from the bus's storage compartments, but he wasn't there, either.

Beau clambered down the steps and grabbed Barb's sleeve. 'Where's Gray?'

'I think he went into the ranger station, honey. You have a good sleep?'

She didn't answer. She raced for the station, blasting through its doors and scanning the room, then darting past the receptionist into the room in which she'd first seen him. He had to be there! He had to be with Mack or someone.

But the room was empty.

She shot back outside to check the toilets, but they were empty, too. Desperate now, she headed back to the receptionist. 'Has Gray McGregor been in?'

'He collected his car keys just a few minutes ago. I think he's gone.'

No!

She darted outside, aware that the others were looking at her strangely, but not caring. All that mattered was finding Gray. She couldn't see him in the car park and there was no car leaving. Had he already left? Had she missed him?

As Rick passed her, she grabbed his arm. 'What hotel was Gray staying at? Did he mention it?'

'Sorry, Beau, he didn't.'

'But he gave you his number? To keep in touch?'

'Yeah, but it's a UK number.'

'Not his mobile?'

'His cell? No, sorry.'

She almost cried out. How could this be happening? How could he do this to her again?

She stood in the middle of the car park for ages. Con and Barb picked up their car and waved to her as they passed by, as did the others. She stared at nothing.

Thought of nothing but her loss as the cars drove past her, some tooting their horns.

She didn't move until her bladder began to scream at her. Only then did she slowly plod over to the bathroom and relieve herself, before going into the station and collecting her car keys and belongings.

The luxury of the car felt wrong. The leather seats, the air conditioning. That new car smell. It all seemed so false. So manufactured. She'd become used to nature in that short week. The fresh, warm air. The smell of pine—*real* pine. Not that stuff that was made in a factory and created from chemicals.

She started the engine and entered the address details for her hotel into the GPS system, began to drive. She drove almost on autopilot, getting back to her hotel, barely remembering the drive at all.

When she'd checked in to her room, she dropped her keys onto the dresser and turned on the shower, shedding clothes in slow motion, feeling as if she was moving through thick treacle, stepping under the warm spray and closing her eyes, trying to feel nothing. Trying not to think.

But it all became too much.

And she sank into the corner of the shower and began to cry.

His hotel room was a world away from the last week's experience. Had it really been just a week? The room, though familiar, looked empty—dry of life. Not real. A false environment. A place that was meant to make him feel as if he were at home, but was so false it almost made him feel sick to be there.

Home was where Beau was.

It always had been. And it had ripped him apart to

walk away. Again. But how could he throw himself into their relationship? He loved her. With all his heart and more. But he wasn't *right* for her. If they tried to make it work, one of them would have to give up their career at their current hospital and move. That bit might not be so bad, but what about when the thrill of being back together again wore off? What happened when reality sank in? What if they decided to have children?

He couldn't do it.

All that time, all those eleven years he'd spent away from her, he'd struggled to feel satisfied or happy with anything. And finding Beau again, in Yellowstone, of all places, had made him realise just what he'd been missing.

She had always had his heart. From that very first day when he'd spotted her at medical school—that gorgeous, long-limbed, elegant woman with the flaming red hair—his breath had been taken from him. He'd tried to use his old, familiar chat-up lines and they'd had no effect on her. She'd laughed them off, almost disappointed by his attempt at using them. And so he'd tried a different tactic.

He'd been as genuine as he could. He'd listened to her. Studied with her. Helped her revise. He'd been content with just *being* with her. Basking in her glow. Enjoying the warmth that she'd created in his cold, empty heart. The first time he'd kissed her... Well, that had been something else!

After that he'd been unable to tear himself away from her. Beau had been his bright star, his happiness. His joy. His deep love. He'd never known it was possible to love another person so much. Whenever they'd been apart, he'd thought of her. Whenever he'd been on a day shift and she on a night shift, and they'd met like ships in the dawn of the early morning, their time together had been too short. Bittersweet.

Sometimes they'd meet in the hospital cafeteria and just drink coffee silently together. Happy to be next to each other. They hadn't needed words. They hadn't needed grand gestures to show the other how much they meant to them. They'd just been happy to *be*. Sitting opposite each other, holding hands.

He refused to end up hating her. His heart, his logical brain, told him he wouldn't do that to himself. They'd met again. Cleared the air. Shared a wonderful few days together. And it was best to leave it at that. With good memories. Ending on a high.

So why do I feel like this?

His heart physically ached. He was fighting against the urge to throw caution to the wind and go and find her again. To feel her in his arms just one more time…

But what good would it do? It would hurt them each and every time they had to part ways.

But what if it could work?

The devil's advocate part of his brain kicked in. Presented him with images of them happy together, surrounded by a brood of happy, red-haired, green-eyed children. Mini-versions of him and Beau. Having the kind of marriage people dreamed of.

Some people managed it, didn't they? He'd read about them in the news. Couples celebrating fifty, sixty, seventy years of marriage and giving their advice for a long, happy marriage:

Never go to bed on an argument.

Enjoy each other's company.

Be honest.

Be realistic.

It was that last one he'd held on to. Surely he *was*

being realistic? Over fifty per cent of marriages *failed*, and those couples that stayed together he knew were doing it for reasons other than love. They didn't want to be alone. They were staying together for the sake of the kids. It was a habit they couldn't break. It was too expensive to separate...

Which of them were *truly* still in love?

It was hard to admit that he was afraid, but he knew he was. Afraid of hurting Beau. Afraid of having her hate him. Afraid of having her resent him. Afraid of her looking at him the way his mother looked at his father...

He sat on the end of his hotel bed and held his head in his hands.

Trying to convince himself he was doing the right thing.

It didn't help that there was a voice in his head screaming at him that he was doing the *wrong* thing.

He needed some space.

He needed some calm time.

He needed to *think*.

She'd kept herself busy—reading books, magazines, the newspapers. Watching television. Well...telling herself she was reading. Telling herself she was paying attention to the screen. All so she didn't think about Gray.

It wasn't working.

He was in her thoughts constantly, and her mind was churning with all the possibilities. Perhaps he'd done a good thing for them both by walking away. Because what if he was right? What if they *were* doomed to a future of having one of those relationships where people put up with what they'd got because the alternative was too terrible?

Being alone...

I'm alone now, aren't I? And it sucks!

He was wrong. They were stronger than that. Their love was stronger than that. Because it had lasted for the eleven years they'd been apart—always there, burning away quietly in the background and then roaring back into full flame when they'd met up again.

There was no point in fighting it. When she got back to the UK, she would go to Edinburgh. She would find his hospital and she would wait in his surgery until there was time for him to see her. He *would* see her. He would do her that honour. And it didn't matter if he listened and then told her he couldn't do it, she had to at least *try*. He had to know that she wanted to be with him. Had to know how much she loved him. Wanted to be his partner, his lover, his soulmate. She was all those things already—it was just that he was refusing to see it!

Could she convince him that there was another kind of future for them? Let him know that there was an alternative? That they could be happy, like her parents? People who had such a deep love for each other were strong enough to get over any day-to-day upsets. Get through the rigours of life. People *succeeded* at marriage! Those couples who were determined to make their vows mean something. Who solved their problems before they became big issues. It was impossible to get through a marriage without there being ups and downs, but it *was* possible to do it without hating each other— and they had a love strong enough to do so.

He needs to know that I won't give up on him this time.

He'd shocked her, and there'd not been a chance for her to say what she needed to say. Well, he'd had *his* chance. And soon, back home, she would have hers.

* * *

The plane home was delayed by two hours, so Beau waited in the airport lounge, sipping coffee and finally—*finally!*—able to get her hands on a beautiful, flaky, buttery Danish pastry. She could almost feel herself salivating at the thought of it, but when it arrived, when it came to eating it, she found it difficult. Dry. Cloying. Tasteless.

She left it, pushing her plate away and swallowing the last of the coffee. Just as she was doing so she heard the boarding call for her plane.

She'd got an aisle seat and she settled down, anxious to get her feet back on British soil, where the air would be refreshingly damp and chill and the only animal likely to make her jump out of the way would be her neighbour's overenthusiastic Red Setter.

She sensed rather than saw Gray arrive. She'd not even been looking at the passengers getting on the plane, but she'd felt someone brush by and suddenly she *knew* who it was. The cologne, her awareness of his proximity—it all pointed to the one man she'd thought she'd never see again.

'Gray...' She almost choked on his name as she stumbled to her feet. It was so unexpected to see him here. On *her* flight.

'Beau. You're looking well.'

He looked washed out. As if he hadn't slept. His eyes were reddened and there was a paleness to his skin, despite their days in the American sun.

'I am. Thank you. You're on *this* flight?'

She winced. What a stupid question! Of course he was!

'Row J.' He pointed to his row, unable to take his eyes off her, then reluctantly moved on. The passengers behind him were getting impatient that he was blocking the aisle.

Beau sank back into her seat, her heart racing, thudding in her chest. She closed her eyes and tried to take a deep, steadying breath. This was it. Her chance. Her opportunity to speak to him. Eight hours' worth of opportunity, before they touched down in the UK. No need to track him down—no need to chase after him. Fate had given her this gift.

She was suddenly afraid. Her stomach felt cold, solid, like a block of ice. Fear was pinning her limbs to her seat.

This is one of those turning points in life, isn't it? Do I want to give us another chance? I really do!

She really wanted a spot of Dutch courage.

Where are those flight attendants when you want them?

Beau blinked and thought of what her life would be like if she didn't go and talk to him. It was too horrible to imagine. She'd be alone again. Driven only by work. Her life empty. Feeling as if she was waiting for something that never came. In limbo. Her life on pause. And though she loved her job, she knew she loved Gray McGregor more. She *needed* him. More than she needed oxygen.

She closed her eyes and tried to breathe.

CHAPTER TEN

THEY'D BEEN IN the air for an hour before she finally got up the nerve to go and talk to him. An hour of letting her stomach churn, of gripping her armrests till her knuckles turned white, before she finally unclipped her seat belt and got up out of her seat. Her legs were like jelly, her mouth drier than a desert.

Instantly his gaze connected with hers, and she saw him suck in a deep breath, too.

Good. He was just as nervous as she was.

If it goes wrong, then fine. I'll just walk away, sit back in my seat, and I'll never have to see him again. But what if it goes right...?

Unsteadily, she walked down the aisle and stopped by his seat. The two chairs next to him were empty.

'Mind if I take a seat?'

'Be my guest.' He got up so she could sidle past him, and waited for her to sit before he sat down himself.

She sat in the window seat, so that there was a gap between them. She didn't want to be too close. She had no idea how this conversation was going to go.

'How have you been?'

He glanced at her, then away, his jaw muscles clenching. 'Okay, I guess. You?'

This was her opportunity. Her chance to tell him how

in torment she'd been since he'd left her at the minibus. Since he'd crushed her heart by telling her that he didn't deserve a second chance with her.

'Not bad.' She paused. 'Actually, I've been...thinking.'

He raised an eyebrow. 'Thinking?'

She nodded quickly, her blood zooming through her veins, carried along on a jet stream of adrenaline. 'About you.'

'Oh?'

He wasn't making this easy for her. But maybe he was afraid, too? She saw him swallow. His Adam's apple bobbing up and down as he thought for a moment. Was he anticipating what she was going to say? She could see fear and doubt playing across his face as he sought to find the best way to remain calm whilst she said whatever she had to.

But she was impatient. Nervous. 'You don't have to say anything. I'll speak first. I think that I should.'

He met her gaze and stared. For just a moment. The intensity in his eyes made her temperature rise and her heart pound. 'Okay.'

How to start?

'I'm sorry, Gray. I'm sorry that I wasn't there for you before. That I didn't make you feel that you could talk to me. I'm sorry for the way I treated you when we met again. I'm sorry that it's taken this long for me to be able to see what was wrong. And where the blame lay.'

'Beau—'

'Let me finish.' She smiled, her mouth trembling with nerves. 'I need to say this. Because if I don't say this right now, then...then I'll never be able to say it, and I think we owe it to each other to be honest.'

It was hard not to cry, too. She'd worked herself up

so much that the need to say everything, to get everything out so that he'd hear how she felt, was just overwhelming.

He stared at her, his feelings written across every feature. The concern in his eyes…the tenseness in his mouth…that beautiful mouth. His tight jaw…

'I loved you. I *still* love you. I always have and I always will—whether you allow me to do so or decide you never want to see me ever again. I love you. I think we could work. If you gave us a chance, I think we really *could*. We know who we are. We've put everything out there. Nothing's hidden.'

She reached for his hand and took it in hers, clasping it tightly, hoping he wouldn't be able to tell how much she was shaking.

'I know about your leg and it doesn't bother me. It doesn't stop you from being *you*. I know about your family. What you went through. I know that you think marriage is some sort of prison, but that's not how *I* see it. I see it as a journey.' She laughed nervously and hoped he would laugh, too. 'Yes, I used the J-word!'

He smiled. But he seemed too far away. He still wasn't quite with her. So she got out of her window seat and into the seat directly next to him.

She looked at their entwined hands and felt her barriers breaking down. She wanted this so much! But she was afraid of getting her heart broken again, and now her fear was making her hesitate.

'I want to be with you, Gray. Married or not. I don't need a perfect man. I don't need someone who will never argue with me or grow frustrated with me, because that happens anyway. But what I *do* want is *you*. Gray McGregor. Faults and all. We can do this. We can get it right this time—I know we can—because we both care enough to get it right, and…'

She almost ran out of words. Almost. She looked into his green eyes for inspiration and saw them smiling back at her. She fought back her tears.

'You told me that I deserved someone who could love me the way I want to be loved. You told me that you didn't deserve a second chance with me. But…but you're the one that I want to have loving me. You're the only one who can love me the way that I want. *I'm* the one who deserves a second chance with *you*! Can't you see that? I love you, Gray McGregor. Can't you love me, too?'

Gray brought her fingers to his lips, closing his eyes as he sucked in a breath and inhaled the aroma of her skin before he began to speak.

'I used to fear that our being together would turn us into different people who couldn't stand to be near each other…but being *away* from you makes me miserable. Sadder than I've ever been in my life. When I fell from that sea cliff and lay on the rocks waiting for help, all I could think of was you. I thought that if I died, then at least it would take me away from the torment of not being with you. But now we have this second chance and…and I *want* to take it. I *do*! I thought…I thought that I didn't deserve another chance and so I walked away again. Just for a moment. I needed to get my head straight. I needed to know that I was thinking clearly about us. That I'd rid myself of all that old clutter, that old pain I used to carry inside. I used to hide behind it. Using it as an excuse. Believing it—allowing it to twist me into this man who was too afraid to be with the woman he loved in case it all went wrong. But…'

He smiled at her and wiped a tear from her soft, soft cheek.

'I know what love is. I know that it's what *we've* got. Something special. We're a team, you and me. We always have been. We've shared our fears, our hopes. Our love. You know everything about me and you still love me anyway. Do you know how amazing I find that?'

She nodded, her tears turning to tears of happiness.

'I got off that bus and I had to drive away. Being around you…I couldn't think straight. But back at the hotel I could. I told you that I was scared of what might happen to us, but that was wrong. I was running away from love because I'd never truly felt it. Not until you came along. And suddenly everything was moving too fast! Marriage? Talk of having kids?'

He shook his head at the memory.

'My mother didn't want me. My father barely knew me. I was just a messenger boy. A pawn in their horrible game. And whilst I loved you, *wanted* to be with you, I was terrified of doing so in case I got it all wrong. I didn't know how to be loved like that. So strongly. Living apart from you, just dating you, I could hide from that. Disguise it. I thought that if we got married it would expose me for the fraud that I was. It wasn't you. It wasn't us. It was *me*. But now I know I'm stronger. You *make* me stronger. All that we've been through tells me we can do this.'

A stewardess came by with her trolley, offering drinks, but Gray waved her past.

'I accused you of not living in reality, but I was doing the same thing. I was living in a future that hadn't happened. We have no idea of how this will go, but I think—I *know*—the two of us will make it the best it can be. The strongest it can be. And…and I know that

I love you, too. That I'm miserable without you. That my life is *nothing* without you in it.'

'Gray…'

'Fate threw us back together, but even if it hadn't… I would have found you anyway. I can never be apart from you again.' He smiled, his face warming with the strength of it, happiness gleaming from his eyes. 'Beau, you are the most beautiful woman I know. The strongest woman I know and I want you in my life for ever. Will you do me the honour of making me the happiest man in this world and marrying me?'

'*Marrying* you?'

Did I just squeak that? Since when do I squeak?

He nodded. 'I want to marry you, Beau. I want you to be my wife. I want us to be together through good times *and* bad. In sickness and in health. Till death do us part. Dr Beau Judd, my beautiful neurologist…my other half…'

A kiss.

'My soul…'

Another kiss.

'My heart…'

And another.

'Yes!' She nodded, grinning like an idiot and not caring. He loved her! *Loved her!* It was real this time. 'Yes! Yes! *Yes!* I will. Are you going to kiss me properly now, or just keep staring at me?'

'I'd like to kiss you.'

He leant forward and their lips met.

This was it. Their first kiss on the path to true love. His lips were warm and soft, and they caressed hers so expertly that she felt like a molten ball of fire. Her insides were liquid. Her hands scrunched tightly in his hair and she pulled him against her and kissed him back as if her life depended upon it.

And it did.

She knew she was nothing without this man. She had a home, a career and a family. She should have been content with just those things. But having Gray in her life made everything so much better. Brighter. Riskier, yes, but brighter.

She stroked his face, feeling the softness of his fine beard beneath her fingertips. 'I love you so much.'

He reached for her other hand and kissed her fingertips. 'And I love *you*. We made it off that clifftop—we can make it on solid ground.'

Joy beyond measure was hers. Her happiness scale exploded and blew off its top as she sank into Gray's arms and accepted his love.

But he shifted slightly, reached into his pocket and pulled out a small velvet box. 'I can't believe I had a whole other speech planned for when I tracked you down in the UK. It wasn't very good, but...everything's worked out bonny in the end. You said yes. So...this is for you.'

She took the box and glanced up at him. He looked nervous. It had to be a ring. He'd bought her one before and it had been stored in her jewellery box for too many years. Now she was getting another. But this one *meant* something more.

Beau opened the box. Inside lay a beautiful diamond set in a platinum band. It glittered and caught the light against its velvet nest and she beamed a smile through her happy tears.

'It's gorgeous.'

Gray took it from the box and then took her left hand, sliding it onto her finger. It was a perfect fit.

She kissed him again. As his fiancée. A perfect kiss. A loving kiss.

'I love you, Beau,' he whispered in her ear.

And she whispered back, 'And I love *you*, Gray McGregor.'

EPILOGUE

SHE WAS READY. Her hair was done. Her make-up was done. The dress fitted perfectly. She picked up her small posy of peonies and made her way downstairs, to where her father waited for her, dressed in smart tails and holding a top hat.

'How do I look?' he asked.

'Very handsome.' She smiled.

'You don't think I should have gone with a kilt, like Gray?'

She shook her head. 'No one but Mum needs to see *those* knees, Dad.'

He reached for her hand and let out a steadying breath. 'The car's here. Are you ready?'

There were nerves and excitement in her stomach. Her heart was pounding and her mouth was dry with anticipation. But, yes, she was ready.

'I am.'

Outside, all her neighbours were standing and watching, and there were a few 'oohs' as she came out and they saw her dressed in white.

A silver-grey car, sleek and exclusive, adorned with white ribbons, awaited her, and a chauffeur in a grey suit and cap stood by the open back door, smiling as she approached.

She waved at her neighbours, at the people who'd witnessed her devastation before, knowing they were truly happy for her. That finally she was getting her dream come true. And as they drove to the church, she clutched her father's hand tightly.

'Nervous?'

She nodded. 'A bit.'

'He'll be there, you know.'

'I know he will.'

She wasn't nervous about that at all. She could tell that this time it was different. Gray was a completely different man, a completely different groom-to-be this time. Eager to join in with wedding arrangements, making his own suggestions, telling her how he'd like the day to go. He'd been just as excited for the day as she had. There'd been no doubt. No cold feet. At all.

Just excitement. Just joy at finally getting the day— the *marriage*—they both wanted. Had both dreamed of. The marriage that they knew was now within their reach.

Everyone else was waiting at the church. Her mum had travelled earlier on, with the bridesmaids. All the rest of her family were there, most of them already inside. As she got out of the car, she saw Gray's mother and father go in, too.

The photographer wanted some pictures before she went in and dutifully she posed, her excitement building, her desire to see Gray as she walked down the aisle becoming almost unbearable.

She wanted to see his face. She wanted to hold his hand. Say her vows. Promise to be his for evermore.

The music began and she lowered her veil and took one last deep breath. She'd been here before. She'd just never got this far.

She took her father's arm and nodded.

I'm ready.

And then the doors were open, the congregation stood and she began her walk down the aisle.

She saw Gray at the other end. Beaming with joy as the wedding music soared, almost crying at the sight of her as she walked down the aisle towards him. She could hardly take her eyes off him. He looked so handsome in his red-and-green kilt, his black jacket and brilliant white shirt. Those green eyes were smiling as she drew close, and he reached out to take her hand from her father's.

'You look so beautiful,' he said.

She couldn't speak, she felt so happy. She just took his hand and smiled shyly at him.

As the music died down, the vicar came to stand in front of them and began the service.

Beau and Gray made their vows. Gave each other a ring. And were soon declared husband and wife.

'You may kiss your bride.'

Gray smiled, lifted up her veil and pulled her towards him for their first kiss as a married couple.

After they'd signed the register, they headed outside for more photos, and when they were standing in the glorious sunshine, waiting for the photographer to organise them into another pose, they kissed some more.

And then they heard an American voice interrupt them. 'Er…guys, I think we told you to get a room!'

Beau laughed and turned to see all their American friends from the Yellowstone trip—Mack, Conrad, Barb and the others. All there. All happy to be sharing their wedding day.

'Don't worry. We will,' said Gray. 'Later.'

'Who'd have guessed it would be the honeymoon suite, though?' asked Mack.

Barb looked at Beau and winked. 'Oh, I think we knew. Deep down, we always knew.'

Beau smiled and then kissed her husband.

* * * * *

If you enjoyed this story, check out these other great reads from Louisa Heaton

ONE LIFE-CHANGING NIGHT
A FATHER THIS CHRISTMAS?
HIS PERFECT BRIDE?
THE BABY THAT CHANGED HER LIFE

All available now!

BACKSTAGE
WITH HER EX

BY
LOUISA GEORGE

I've been very lucky to have made some amazing friends over the years—some older, some younger, some wiser and some…not so (but we had a lot of laughs getting wise, usually after the event!).
You know who you are. And if you're wondering… Does she mean me? Yes, I do.

This book is dedicated to you all, with heartfelt thanks for the wild ride, and lots of love.

xxx

CHAPTER ONE

HIDING OUT IN the gents' toilets backstage at the London Arena was not one of Sasha Sweet's personal highs. VIP toilets they might have been but, gold taps be damned, she wanted to go home.

I'll kill you, Cassie.

Bad enough she'd let herself be harangued into this ridiculous exercise, but ducking into the men's room in a moment of rare claustrophobic panic? All kinds of embarrassing.

A whoosh of air and a wall of encroaching noise announced the arrival of someone else in the room. Thank God she'd found an empty cubicle.

She checked the state of the wall before she slumped against it. Grateful to be in an empty cubicle? In the men's room? *Could my life get any worse?*

She held her breath to listen, knowing if she was discovered in here, flouting all security rules, she'd never achieve what she'd set out to do. And the dreams of fourteen kids would literally go down the pan, along with her professional reputation.

Plan A should have worked just fine: approach someone in authority, ask politely, make an appointment. Not hide out like a weird stalker. *In a cubicle.* While thousands of fans charged the backstage corridors wanting a piece of the notoriously damaged, famously over-sexed rock deity, Nate Munro.

Where was Plan B when she needed it?

A deep American accent bounced off the tiled walls. 'Quick, Nate. In here. Give us five minutes 'til they've been herded out. There's a car on its way to pick you up out the back.'

No. Sasha's shoulders crept towards her jaw, tightening the muscles around her neck like a noose. Not Nate. Not here. Not in this bathroom.

'What happened to Security? They're crazy out there.' Sure enough, it was Nate's voice now, much deeper, richer than she remembered, but unmistakably his. Tinged with his working-class roots and a smattering of amusement, but refined by maturity and years of stateside living.

The American voice responded with an air of glee, 'Crazy for *you*. They love *you*. The world loves you, Nate. You are gold.'

True enough. Aeons ago in Sasha's smitten seventeen-year-old eyes being with him had felt as if she'd been sprinkled with gold dust. *Nathan Munro.* Her eyes fluttered closed at the storm of innocent memories. A young singer desperate to be heard. Night after night of listening to his songs, songs he'd written about her.

He'd scaled the heights against the odds. She'd watched his life spiral out of control, as Chesterton had turned its back on him. And she'd been as scathing as the rest.

But now… Wild boy turned out-of-control rock star. Sold out across the globe on his five continents Hall of Fame tour, catapulted to the top of the charts with his husky sultry songs and edgy dark style. The devil with a god's voice.

And powerful too. What he wanted he got and to hell with the consequences.

So what the heck she thought she'd achieve by asking

him for help now, she didn't know. But Sasha inhaled, renewing her resolve. It had been for ever ago. Ten years. He'd probably forgotten about her, about *them*. Or hated her, still.

No matter. She would find a way to ask him for help, and make good on that promise to her kids—that was what was important, not their past history. But she couldn't face him here, after all this time, not in a loo. Even she wouldn't be able to take herself seriously surrounded by pipe work and the cloying smell of pine.

No, she was a music professional and she had standards. She'd find another way: phone his agent, bribe him into submission. Beg. Something.

So just leave. Please.

The American spoke again. 'You want me to find you someone for tonight? There're plenty of women out there. Your usual? Blonde? Tall? Big—'

'Sure. Whatever.'

'I'll get the guys onto it.' The crackle of a walkie-talkie split the room.

'But only for an hour or so. I've got a date later and I don't want to be late.' Nate's voice was laced with irritation.

What? Sasha's shoulders hiked to her ears again. He was planning a one-nighter *and* a date?

Well, the man had stamina.

And no morals.

And that was none of her business.

She'd got over him a long time ago. Hard not to with his colourful love life splashed front page most days of the week. Supermodels, actresses, singers hung off his arm at every opportunity. She just hoped he wasn't planning on entertaining in here; she had things to do.

'So you're not going to the afterparty?' the American asked. 'Twelve months of non-stop touring and you're going on a date instead of getting loose? She must be special.'

'I'll come along to the party later.'

'So who is it this time? Not Cara again? She's trouble, you know. Two stints in rehab. Possession. You've got to steer clear from girls like that.'

'But she did my sales a heap of good. She was good value.'

'Nice thinking, Nate. Point well made. Keep your options open. A pretty lady on your arm keeps the rest of your fans hopeful. But remember, don't do anything stupid—stay away from the two cardinal sins: drugs and marriage. Drugs bring their own problems, pal, but cosy is the kiss of death to your career.'

'I had a lucky escape with that fiasco of an engagement. I'm never going there again.'

Sasha's frown deepened. Did she detect a tinge of boredom in his voice? Something not right in Nate's opulent successful world? And since when was marriage part of the axis of evil?

He'd clearly changed beyond anything she remembered. The Nathan she'd known at first had been sweet and kind and hadn't thought of women as good value. But then, she'd witnessed the beginning of that change: the way he'd morphed from sweet teenager to brooding, angry young man.

Seemed that downward trajectory hadn't stopped.

Suddenly the shrill blare of a text message made her jump.

Shoot! No. *No!* She clamped a hand to her mouth. Had she said that out loud?

Fumbling into her bag, she fell against the wall, dropped her phone and then watched in silent Slow... Motion... Horror. It bounced and slithered across the tiles, under the cubicle door, and out to the other side.

Crouching down, she watched, mortified, as her bright sparkly purple cell finally came to a stop next to a pair of battered black biker boots.

So yes, it seemed her life could get much worse.

Silence reverberated around the room for two long seconds, save for the hard thump of her heart against her ribs. And the shuffle of heavy feet.

'What have we got here?' The American voice deepened as a hand reached for her phone. He read the message out. '"*Target located? Is he still to die for? What about that ass?*"' He laughed. 'Hey, Nate, either you've cornered the gay military market, or we have ourselves a desperate female admirer.'

Desperate?

A loud hammering on the cubicle door rocked into Sasha's body as a rash seeped through her skin, burning bright and hot. 'Hey. You. This is VIP access only…and the men's room. Get out here now before I call the cops.'

No, thanks. Standing in front of an assembly hall full of disenchanted teens was less terrifying than coming face to face with an ex like Nate.

If he remembered the way things had ended between them he definitely wouldn't want to answer her cry for help, but she had to try. She couldn't face the kids on Monday and say she hadn't asked him. In reality, this could be her only chance and it wasn't as if she had any sentimental feelings for him—time had certainly filled that well. Finding her courage again, she inhaled. Maybe asking him in a loo wouldn't be so…degrading.

So be a grown-up. Steadying herself, Sasha pulled back the lock. Sometimes, being a grown-up sucked.

Before she could speak the door slammed open and a blur of dark suit brushed against her, jamming her arm behind her back and her cheek against the wall. He patted her hands, her pockets and legs. The voice in her ear was hard and unforgiving. 'There you go, darling. Take it easy.'

'Let go of me. Let go now. Or *I* call the cops. Harassment. Assault.'

'She's clean.'

'Of course I'm clean. What is this?'

'Can't be too careful, ma'am. We meet all sorts of weirdoes in this business.'

'And that's just the people who work in it, right?' Shoving out of the bear's hold, she straightened her clothes then turned, slamming body-to-body with Nate.

His jaw tensed, and his stare deepened as he took her in, recognition clearly filtering through his brain as he swept his glance up and down her body.

In response she froze, unable to take her eyes from him. Sure, she'd seen the pictures, had some old grainy ones of her own, she'd even stolen quick glances at the rock magazines' centre spreads, heck she'd just watched him perform two hours of perfect harmonies and slow sexy dance moves in the final concert of his tour. But nothing had prepared her for the real thing up close.

He seemed taller, definitely broader, not the teenager she'd once fallen in love with. He was one hundred per cent man. All sex, with his wavy chocolate-coloured hair dipping lazily to one side. She remembered the soft just-washed feel of it, the faint scent of apples.

Her gaze ran across his face, past those famous soft-caramel eyes, the refined cheeks peppered with his trademark stubble, the perfect curve of his lips.

But she couldn't stop there. After all, he'd always been a feast to her senses. She imagined the ruffled feel of his shirt, and the hard muscle underneath. His smell of leather and man. Remembered the long legs for ever encased in black denim, rough against her juvenile skin. The arrogant stance that told the world he didn't give a damn, when she knew he'd cared deeply. Deeply enough to be hurt by the rejection, to leave town altogether and never look back.

And yes, thank you, Cassie, his ass was still to die for.

He stared right back at her, stepping back, palm up in a question. 'Sasha? Sasha Sweet?'

'Nathan—' She started to explain, but suddenly she was grabbed by the bear, who shouted into his walkie-talkie, 'Now. Now. The car's leaving. Go, Nate. You want this one too?'

This one? What was she? A toy? A groupie? 'Wait, no. You've got it wrong. I'm not—'

'No?' The minder grinned and shook his head. 'Had a change of heart, sweetheart? There's plenty more who'd take your place.'

Oh, merry hell. The bear really did think she was a groupie. Nate must have muttered something, or nodded, and she'd missed it before he disappeared into the melee outside.

But at that same moment two more security guards burst into the room, grabbed her by the waist and ran her out through the corridor in a blur of clamouring, screaming women tearing at her hair, her clothes. The chant of *Nate, Nate,* Nate, ringing in her ears.

'Nathan…Wait—' Her voice mingled with the rest, and got lost. Watching his leather-jacketed back disappear into a blacked-out limousine, she breathed out a hiss of irritation. That was that.

He was gone. And now no result for the school; she should have found her nerve and asked him.

Then she felt someone touch the back of her head and push her into the plush car seat opposite Nathan.

He slowly leaned back and grinned, almost oblivious to the two giggling peroxided semi-naked women who had draped themselves over him and now appeared to be cleaning out his ears—*with their tongues.* The door slammed closed.

And with a jerk the car eased towards the arena exit to the accompaniment of bright flash photography. On the way to who knew where, with the ex she dumped, an audience of twin pipe-cleaners on legs, and a whole lot of explaining to do.

CHAPTER TWO

WELL, WELL. THIS was interesting. Ten years in the business and Nate had had a lot of surprises. Some good. Some not so. Some pretty painful and costly. But a flame-haired ex with a penchant for kicking first and asking questions—er, never…wasn't one of them. Until now.

He watched her struggle with the every-day reality of his chaotic life on the road, her shock at the girls in the car. Meanwhile some weird emotion played Dixie with his gut. Was he pleased to see her? That, he hadn't had time to compute.

But images of the last time he saw her flickered through his brain like a bad black and white film. Rain. Tears. Hurt. A big fist of anger that had lodged in his chest, and taken months to shake.

But it was all a long time and countless liaisons ago. He couldn't remember the last time he'd given her any thought at all.

Waving a hand to the girls to let up, he leaned forward. 'Hello, Sasha. To what do I owe this…pleasure?'

'Where exactly are you taking me? I need to get out. To my sister. She's waiting for me back at the arena.' Shaking her mane of soft red curls, she frowned, her lipstick-tinged mouth forming the pout that swung him back through the years. The punch to his chest was surprising. 'That bear of a thug, your security guy, he thought…I don't want…you know. I'm not a…groupie.' Her eyes narrowed even more as she glanced towards the girls.

And for a second he felt a strange ping of shame. Fleeting. Then gone. After all, Sasha's betrayal had been one of the reasons he'd moved on in life anyway. And boy, was life good now. 'But you used to be my groupie, Sasha. And, if I remember rightly, you used to like it.'

Although back then sex had been a solemn promise for the future, not a reality.

At her quick blink he felt the laugh rumble up from his chest, heard the high-pitched giggles from the girls against his neck. Sasha didn't crack a smile.

Okay. So this was clearly going to be important. Or why else was she here?

He tapped on the window for the driver to pull over, slapped each of the girls on the backside and let them out into the following entourage cars.

Meanwhile Sasha shook her head in that way schoolteachers did when you disappointed them. He recognised it because he'd experienced it often enough. 'And just like that they disappear. Everyone does exactly what Nate Munro says?'

He shrugged. 'Sure. I thought you'd prefer to do this… whatever it is…in private. Just you and me. Unless you're into threesom—'

'No!'

'Relax, Sasha. It was a joke.' She was too easy to wind up. 'I don't want to get naked with you either.'

Liar. Post-show sex was as habitual as coffee in the mornings. And right now her navy-blue eyes and feisty spirit sparked the right amount of interest. He watched in amusement as she gripped the strap on her bag. No wedding ring. Interesting. Still, that meant little these days. And why had he looked at her fingers?

A purely male instinctive reaction. Right?

But everything he remembered about Sasha Sweet was laced with regret. Not just the one that got away, she was the one who had stamped hard on his heart.

'Now I know everything the papers say is true. You're just a good-time guy. Shallow. Over-sexed...'

'Oh? You've been reading up about me?' Stretching out his legs across the lush thick white carpet, he grinned, slow and lazy so she'd understand just how good his life had been. After her. 'Believe me, it's been infinitely better than anything they print.'

'I have not been reading up about you.' She rolled her eyes. 'I just happened to notice some headline about your crazy life in the States. It's certainly a far cry from Chesterton.'

'And then some.' He shuddered at the mention of the place that had cut ties with him. That had branded him with the same tarnish they had his no-hope father. A hooligan, out of control. Bad to the bone. And no one, not even Sasha, had ever come to his defence.

'Leaving Chesterton was the best thing I ever did. And yes, there are some mad parties in LA. It comes with the territory.' The press had wasted no time covering the best bits—it just happened the best bits were also the worst. Drunk and debauched had been one hell of a ride.

She tugged at his arm. 'Nate, I need to—'

'I know. Here.' He felt in his pocket for her phone. 'Text her back. I presume the Cassie ID refers to your little sister?'

She looked surprised. 'Yes. Of course. You remember Cassie? Although, she's not so little these days, at twenty-five.'

'How could I ever forget the infamous Sweet sisters?'

Even though he'd long since put their failed relationship down to innocent first-love infatuation, he hadn't forgotten the details. Three feisty red-headed girls who had set the fragile hearts of every nubile boy in Chesterton racing. With Sasha, the middle sister, the only woman who'd ever said no to him.

And here she was, all grown-up and seriously hot.

The freckles he'd loved to count and kiss way back in the Dark Ages were still there on her fresh lightly made-up face. Her spirit, clearly, hadn't diminished. Neither had the curves highlighted by the tight capri trousers and dark mesh top, making her look as if she'd just walked out of a fifties' movie set, or the translucent skin that had sent shivers down his adolescent spine. But he'd got steel in there now.

Working in a business of backstabbing and greed, he was used to people trying to piggy-back on his success. He'd been taken for a ride too many times to count and wouldn't be doing it again; a costly separation had taught him that lesson.

So why his interest was piqued by this particular old girlfriend he didn't know. He might as well just get the cheque book out now. Far easier than going through a messy conversation.

Grabbing the glittery phone from his outstretched hand, she glanced at the screen and visibly cringed. 'I'm sorry about that. Cassie might be an adult, but she hasn't fully grown up yet.'

'And what are you going to reply to her?'

'Oh…I don't know.' She looked up through thick dark eyelashes, her lips pursed, teasingly. 'That you're still obnoxious and full of yourself.'

'And with an ass to die for?'

'See? Obnoxious.' She flashed a smile, which did something funny to his heart. He put it down to being on the road for too long.

'I aim to please. And it seems to work for the most part. I have to admit, you surprise me, Sasha. I never thought you'd do something like this. You always played everything

so safe.' He returned the smile with one of his own as he
undid the top button on his shirt, ready to have a little fun.

Instead of the flustered reaction he'd imagined, she sat
forward and pinned him to the seat with an ice-cool gaze.
'I did not.'

'Yeah? Grade-A student, always toed the line. Never
broke the rules—at least never broke them for me. So what's
changed? Why are you in my car en route to a fancy hotel?'

'Hotel? Oh, for goodness' sake, get over yourself.' She
blinked quickly, the cool fading into fluster. 'I…I said, I'm
not here for sex.'

'Oh, yes, and I remember you saying that before too. But
I never did quite believe you.' He leaned forward, met her
almost in the middle of the seat, caught a glimpse of fire
in her eyes before she turned away.

She'd been saving herself for when they were married
or some such foolish idea. At least, until they were engaged. He wondered, fleetingly, who had taken his place,
been her first time.

He shook that thought away along with the accompanying uninvited tension that zipped through his veins. And
fought back an urge to run his fingers through a curl, see
if it was as soft as he remembered. 'Your body always did
give you away.'

'Not any more. I have full control.'

'Really?' He focused on her legs, did a slow journey
up to her breasts, her throat, her mouth. Awareness crackled around the car sucking out the oxygen. After five long
seconds he met her gaze. 'You want to put it to the test?'

'Absolutely not. You should save your energy for someone who'd be more…grateful. Like the poor misguided
gruesome twosome you just had in here.' She glared at him.
But he didn't miss the flash of heat in her eyes. 'Look, this
has been a mistake.'

And the blushing was still the same; she never could control that. A full peachy rash bloomed in her cheeks, spread to her neck and disappeared into that midnight-blue top.

Dragging his eyes away from her, he tried to breathe out the weird emotions thrumming in his chest.

Outside, the city lights illuminated Marble Arch, traffic slowed even at this time of night.

London.

For the first time in years, he was back home. At least it used to be. Home now was a sprawling Malibu mansion overlooking the ocean. But sometimes he missed the vibrancy of this city, the exciting pulse that emanated from the streets and throbbed through his veins, mixing with the comforting feel of the familiar.

Or was that just his strange reaction at seeing Sasha Sweet again?

She looked out of the window, too, for a few moments until her surprisingly girly phone signalled a new message. When she'd finished reading she tilted her head in his direction. 'Can you drop me off now? Cassie's going to meet me. I'll get the tube from here.'

'Are you serious? You used to cling to me on the tube. You hated it—all those crowds, all that danger hidden in dark corners. The rush of hot air. The noise. Rats.'

'Well, looky here, things move on. I have.'

'Clearly. If you're sure.' He tapped on the screen to alert his driver, then turned back to face her, still confused as to why she was here and why his body was so stirred up by her. 'But what's going on, Sasha? We both know this isn't about my backside or any kind of sexual intent. "Target located," Cassie said. Why am I your target? What do you want?'

'It doesn't matter. Seriously, forget it. All this…' She gestured to the car, to the unopened bottles of champagne in the console. 'You're way too busy, and…different from how I remembered.'

'I hope so.'

'I didn't mean it was a good thing.'

'Champagne is always a good thing. As is success.' In truth, he didn't have time for another sob story. He already had sacks full of begging letters at his manager's office.

But her eyes drew his gaze and he was fixed there with a strange need to prove he could do something she hadn't— listen. 'Okay. I'm probably going to regret this, but I've got five minutes. Try me.'

As the car drew to a halt he watched her take a slow deep breath then exhale the way they'd all been taught back in form four music class. Sing on the out-breath. So he knew if she needed to keep her voice steady it was something important.

'I'm a teacher now, Nate. Music. And my show choir has reached the finals of a national contest. Problem is, we can't afford the fares up to Manchester, the hotel costs, costumes and everything. We need your help.'

As he'd thought. Just someone else asking for a hand-out. Disappointing. 'You want a cheque? Cash? We could stop by a cash machine.'

'No. Part of the contest is about raising the money, not just digging deep into our own pockets—not that we could if we wanted to. It's all about the process—teaching the children about community spirit and involvement, you know the kind of thing. You don't get handouts, you need to work hard to achieve...' As she spoke about the project her eyes blazed with a mesmerising fervour.

Immediately he was thrown back to a time when they'd had their future ahead of them, when they'd believed they could do anything. Be anything they dreamed of. Together. He remembered getting lost in her excitement, in that thick luscious hair, in her. Until the day that fervour in her eyes had mingled with disappointment and distrust.

'We thought about holding a concert at the school to get some funds, but few people around our neighbourhood could afford to come even if they wanted to. No one wants to pay to see a bunch of kids singing and dancing, not...' she fixed him with hopeful eyes '—unless we had a guest star. That would raise a lot of interest from everywhere else too, and, bingo, we get our much-needed cash. I figured we could pay you a fee out of the door money, fifty-fifty.'

He laughed. Loudly. 'A fee? You have to be joking. You couldn't afford me in a million light years.'

'Yes, well, like I said, coming here was a mistake. Why would you want to help us? There was a time when you'd have done this kind of thing for free but I guess we're too late.'

'About a decade or so.' So that was that—he was off the hook from her crazy idea. But one thing niggled him. 'And you stowed away in the men's toilet just to ask me this?'

'I did not stow. Stowing is not my style. It was an accident.'

'Sasha, no one accidentally finds themselves in the men's room. Come on, if you want me to help you, you have to at least be honest.'

She shrugged. 'A friend of Cassie's got me backstage, but I wasn't sure how you'd react at seeing me again, and then when all those fans broke through the barrier and surged down the corridor I thought I was going to get crushed. I panicked.'

'And then played jack-in-the-box in the loo? To be honest I'd have preferred you jumping out of a cake semi-naked, or something.' Now that was an entertaining thought. He'd gone from never thinking about her at all, to imagining her half dressed. How did that work? 'You always did like to make a show of things.'

'I did not.'

'No? Remember that night you borrowed your sister's

new bra and padded it with tissues to see if I'd notice—' He
laughed as his hands curved in front of his chest. 'I noticed.'

She clearly did remember if the new flush on her cheeks
was anything to go by, and how he'd told her she was perfect without any trimmings or falseness. Their last night.
When they'd almost lost control of their agreed celibacy.

Their heated innocent fumblings swarmed back in a
cloud of memories. He'd needed her, needed a release, an
escape from the realities of his life. And they'd been so
close to sealing their love.

Low in his abdomen something tightened and prickled
hot. The jolt of his body's response jarred. He so wasn't in
the mood for a trip down Memory Lane or the unwelcome
feelings she invoked. In his experience women were trouble, particularly exes. 'Why all the cloak and dagger stuff?
Why didn't you just get hold of my manager?'

'Oh duh. Why didn't I think of that?' She smacked the
palm of her hand against her forehead. 'You, Mr Out of
Touch with Reality, have no idea how hard that is. We tried
calling, letters, emails. The kids even sent in a video. But
nothing. No reply from your office. And now the deadline's looming.'

'I see. So desperate measures, eh?' That tingling zipped
through his body again. He liked the idea of Sasha desperate. Images of her youthful body lashed against his mixed
with the full-woman curves in front of him now. One thing
was for sure: she'd always had an effect on him.

God, he needed to get laid. Soon. And not with her, because he never did reruns of his mistakes.

Which was why his indignation grew as he watched her
scrape her hair back into an untidy ponytail, with a hair
tie she kept on her wrist, not caring how she looked. He
couldn't help watching her, unable to remember the last
time he'd been in the same room as a woman who hadn't
continually looked in a mirror or asked for reassurance

about her appearance. Sasha was a breath of fresh air in his world of fakery, but she was trading on their past and that hurt.

'London is awash with Z-list celebrities desperate to raise their profiles. Why not ask one of them? Why me?' He didn't know what he wanted her to reply. That she'd never stopped thinking of him? That this was a way of connecting with him again?

'Aside from the fact you're the only successful person I know, or that came out of Chesterton High?'

'And that was despite it. Did you think I'd be an easy target? Or is it because of our history?'

'I wouldn't use that, Nate.'

'Isn't that exactly what you're doing?'

He watched as she struggled to maintain calm. 'No. I didn't want to dredge up the past, but somehow Cassie managed to convince me to try to get hold of you. This is all about helping the kids out. They don't know about what happened between us—very few people do. What we had was…well, I guess it was special. It was private.'

'So special you refused to hear my explanation. So special you turned your back like everyone else. So damned special you couldn't even look me in the eye.' But he'd looked into hers. Right when he'd willed her to speak up for him, to serve as character witness or do something to save him, the way he'd have done anything for her.

She gripped the door handle. 'You hit someone, Nathan. You told me you had. I wasn't going to lie and say you hadn't. The police were hammering on the door screaming that you'd had to be hauled off the poor kid before you killed him. You were all shouting. I was seventeen and scared as hell by the aggression—from you all. I wouldn't have been heard even if I'd wanted to.'

Which she hadn't. He hadn't told her why he'd hit Craig.

Why he couldn't stop. She'd noticed his raw knuckles and he'd told her just enough to stop her asking questions.

But ancient history didn't matter; he'd put it so far behind him he could barely remember it.

So why the tightening in his chest?

He shook his head. 'Just forget it.'

'You always were trouble, Nathan Munro, and don't deny it.' Her lips stretched into an upwards curl. She might well have developed into a stunning ardent woman, but the smile was still very youthful, teasing. 'And it looks like you still are.'

'I try my best.' Trouble, and never good enough for her and her family. Even in a rundown place like Chesterton there'd been a pecking order and his family had been at the bottom.

But okay, she'd never sold him out to the press, though many others had.

Bond Street tube station lights flickered directly outside, but she made no effort to get out of the car. Tapping his fingers on the leather seat, he waited for her to leave; he had no intention of spending time again with Sasha. Some things were just best left alone—memories, for a start, trampled hearts. Their lost past. 'And?'

'And…' Her mouth tightened into a thin line as anxiety flitted across her eyes. 'The school I work at? It's Chesterton High.'

Un-frickin-believable.

He'd put all this behind him and had no desire to go back there again. For any of them, least of all her.

'So let me get this right. In the precious amount of spare time I have, you want me to drop everything to help you, and help that school too, after all that happened?'

Her eyes widened, her chin tilted higher, daring him to agree to her ridiculous suggestion. 'Yes.'

'Not a chance, sweet thing.'

She gasped. Using the nickname he'd called her throughout their two-year relationship seemed to strike a chord. Her mouth fell open as if she was about to say something, then she closed it.

He leaned across her, careful not to brush against that hair, or those curves, caught the handle of the car and opened the door. 'I'm sorry. This crazy plan of yours won't be happening. You can go now.'

'Wait.' Pausing with one foot on the pavement and the other in the car, she tilted her head to him. 'There is another reason I thought you might want to help us.'

'I can't wait for this. What could possibly be more compelling than what you've suggested so far?'

Her discomfort was palpable, her eyes turbulent with emotion. Now the words tumbled out in a rush as she dragged in a breath. 'It's a mixed ability choir…called No Limits.'

The ache in his chest was swift and sudden, finding all the empty places and filling them. Disarmed by her words, and the way she looked at him with empathy and sadness, he was thrown off kilter. 'You really know how to turn the screw, don't you, Sasha? You think I'd want to help because of my brother?'

'Marshall loved singing and dancing, Nate. And he loved being in the school choir.'

Marshall had loved Sasha, too, almost as much as Nate had. But he'd hated the school. He'd hated the bullies that ruined his life. And Nate's, for a while. But revenge was sweet when it came wrapped in international stardom.

And then…the ache deepened in wave after wave of pain. None of his success would bring Marshall back. 'So now you're using Marshall as collateral? Are there no limits to the lengths to which you'll stoop?'

'I just thought it might make a difference to you.' She'd

never treated Marshall as different, and he knew she'd have been as devastated as he was when Marshall died. At least, he assumed she knew of his death even though he'd tried to keep it quiet. But the furore afterwards as he'd lost control had been splashed over the newspapers.

'But this?'

'You wanted me to be honest, so hear me out. The kids in the choir are just like him. Excited, hopeful...special. They want to go to the national competition and be part of something that's normal. And they've got a good chance of placing too. They just need a break.'

'And me as a draw card.'

This was a game-changer. But he didn't know if he could walk into a room full of kids like Marshall and not make a fool of himself by losing it. He'd ploughed thousands of dollars into research, donated anonymously to charities, but he was scared about coming face to face with a kid like his brother.

'I never pegged you as a coward, Nate.'

'I'm not a coward.' Irritation tripped down his spine mixing with the other emotions she'd dredged up in him. 'I just don't need to go back there. I have nothing to prove.'

The laugh gushing from her throat was filled with passion. 'Oh, yeah? The Nathan Munro I knew always had something to prove. You've spent the last ten years showing the world how good you can be despite your upbringing. But right now the only thing you're proving is how much you've changed. And not for the better.'

Retrieving a card from her purse, she regained her composure. Which was a shame, because something about her all fired up connected with something deep in him. 'If, by any kind of miracle, you change your mind here's my contact details. And the school—well, you know where that is. Please just think about.'

He didn't need to. He wasn't doing it.

Crumpling the card into his fist, he frowned. 'Sasha, I could find that school with my eyes closed. I just don't want to.'

'That's okay. I understand. It was worth a try, though, eh?' She pressed her lips together and shrugged. 'Good to see you after all this time.'

'Yeah, sure.' Was it? He didn't know. But one thing he was sure of: he didn't want to see that school or her again. He just didn't trust her or the weird and immediate effect she had on him.

Then she dashed out of the door and into the tube station. Leaving him with a distinct unease, accompanied by a determination not to let Sasha Sweet get to him.

But as he looked at the tatty bit of cardboard with her name on it, he got the feeling that was going to be very hard to do.

CHAPTER THREE

'WHAT IS IT with men?' Sasha slumped into the deep cushions on her lumpy old sofa and shook her head. 'I'll never understand them.'

'What you really mean is, what is it with Nate Munro?' Cassie came through from the kitchenette, bearing mugs of thick creamy hot chocolate topped with marshmallows, and snuggled in next to her. Mainly because in Sasha's cramped flat there was just no space for another piece of furniture.

'Aaaargh. He's so annoying.' And so was her body's reaction to him.

'I can't believe you rode in his limo, you lucky thing. I bet it was amazing.'

'It wasn't like I had a choice. It was tantamount to kidnapping. And I wasn't looking at the interior décor.' Technically she'd been tagged as a desperate groupie and bundled in like a piece of merchandise. But she doubted that would make it seem less glamorous in Cassie's eyes.

Inhaling the chocolate aroma, Sasha tried to instill calm. Nothing was ever so bad that chocolate couldn't help. Except…she breathed in again…nothing changed. Her pulse still jittered, her head pounded, and every time she closed her eyes she could see his lazy smile. Only instead of feeling angry with him she felt flustered and breathless and strangely confused. First time ever the chocolate magic hadn't worked.

Cassie nudged her. 'You can hardly blame him, sis, you knew he'd never come through. He's too famous, too busy. Too darned hot to care about a school he was expelled from or an ex from years back.'

Hot for sure. Yes, yes, Sasha knew that, and she hated to admit it. Since the second she'd laid eyes on him again she'd been fighting to keep her hormones under control. And failing.

It had always been the same with him; he had a way of making her whole body light up with a touch. After he'd gone she'd thrown herself into forgetting him, and that had worked just fine. Until now.

'And you can stop with the sighing too, Cassie. He might be beautiful, but he's not kind if he can turn my lovely choir down like that. He's selfish and brooding and...' She stopped right there. Thoughts straying in his direction were not good for her mental health.

'And you really are hooked on finding someone kind, aren't you? You're a lost cause.' Cassie giggled. 'Top of my list comes abs, eyes...ass. Rich helps. Sense of humour, definitely—'

Sasha sighed, grateful for Cassie's never-ending sense of optimism and fun. Grateful too, that, with Suzy's help, Sasha had shielded their adorable little sister from the fall-out of their father's death. At least one of the three sisters had survived intact.

'I just can't see me falling for anyone who doesn't treat me as an equal. I want to feel safe, and cherished. I don't want to live on an edge or spend my life worrying whether he loves me or not. I want boring. Old tatty slippers and cardigans. Holding hands for our sixtieth wedding anniversary like Granny and Gramps.'

After her father had died all ideas of being safe either emotionally or financially were ripped apart, leaving the whole family bereft. She didn't want to invite more hurt into her life and the few less-than-successful experiences she'd had with men had proved her right. Loving someone could be unpredictable, based on lies that hurt like hell.

So when her Prince Charming arrived, he'd be driving a Volvo and wearing sensible brogues.

Immediately, her thoughts strayed to slim long legs and big biker boots, tiled toilet floors and flashy limousines.

She shuddered. Way too dangerous.

'I know…' Cassie sat up and squished her left leg underneath her bottom, eyes firing with excitement. 'Do you want me to get Nate arrested? Then we can *convince* him to do it. Pat's a great policeman—I'm sure he'd find something on him.'

Sasha eyed Cassie in the way only a big sister could—a look that said *I love you, now shut up* at the same time. 'Will you stop with that? Ever since you started dating Pat the Plod you've been offering for him to arrest someone.'

'I know. I can't help it—the thought of him being all masculine and strong—ooh.' Cassie clasped her mug to her chest and sighed. 'Divine.'

'Just as I thought, it has more to do with the idea of handcuffs than an inflated sense of civic duty.' Sasha laughed and shook her head. 'But if the papers are to be believed Nate's been arrested way too many times already.'

'I'm sure they make half of that stuff up.'

'I dare say.' But the one time it had mattered—the first time—she'd let him go.

No—she'd turned her back on him like the rest. And with due cause. The man had attacked someone and she'd had enough violence in her life to put up with it from a boyfriend too. Seeing Nathan's aggressive reaction had sparked a deeply buried memory that she couldn't bear to relive. So she'd walked away.

'It's probably a good thing, anyway. I just have to work out a Plan B for the choir. Leave it with me…' She thought for a moment and came up with…precisely nothing. 'Okay, arresting him suddenly seems very attractive. Especially if I get to read him his rights…'

Tinny music jolted her attention.

Her mobile.

Knots tightened in her stomach as she relived the moment it slithered across the toilet tiles; the wretched thing had got her into too much trouble already tonight. She checked the number. No one she knew.

Cassie leaned over her shoulder and eyeballed the display. 'Answer it.'

'No. It's way past midnight. Who'd ring at this time? It'll be a crank.'

'Answer the darned thing. Or…I will.' Cassie grabbed for it. Sasha jumped off the sofa and stared at the unfamiliar number.

No way was she taking a chance on her flirtatious little sister nudging in on the act. If it was Nate Munro she needed to be professional and responsible, remember that this was about the choir, and not about herself, or her drumming heart rate. Probably a wrong number anyway. 'Hello?'

'Hey, sweet thing, is that you?'

'Once was funny, now it's just irritating. Stop calling me that.' Hearing the pet name she'd loved hit her hard in the gut. After ten years of honing her career into shape she was so far from being a sweet thing it was laughable. So, occasionally she allowed the pupils to think they'd got the better of her just so they'd see her as human and approachable. But she was always in control. Always.

But there was her body reacting all by itself again. The drumming developed into full-on bongos in her chest, her hands grew sticky and her peripheral vision fuzzied.

But her head was in full control. 'I thought you were on a date? What's the problem—couldn't she keep up with your ego, or the delightful twins' bimbo competition?'

A deep rumble permeated down the phone. 'Date? Oh, yes. That. It was great.'

'Didn't last long. Don't tell me, you peaked too soon.'

'Sweet thing, believe me, I haven't even started.' His voice lowered to a growl that sounded a lot like sex, and he knew damned well he was winding her up. 'You know, you show way more spirit over the phone than in person. Easy when you can't see me, eh? But don't forget I know how easy it is to make you blush.'

Too right. On cue heat swept across her cheeks and down her neck as if proving his point. Maybe her cocky attitude would ruin their chances, but somehow she didn't think so. She guessed he had his fair share of yes-people in his life. But Nate wouldn't like that. He liked down-to-earth honesty and playfulness rather than false praise. At least he used to. 'And you called because?' She crossed her fingers and prayed.

'I've been thinking.'

'Gosh, well done.'

'See? Spirit. I'd forgotten that.' His laugh was gentle and surprising. 'About your project. You want to give me more details? Dates, times…'

Hope rose as the drumming beat faster in off-beat demi-semi quavers. That hurt. 'So you'll do it? You'll do the concert?'

In answer to Sasha's thumbs-up sign and broad grin, Cassie gyrated across the floor, wiggling her skinny backside in an attempt to mimic Nate's very sexy stage performance.

Sasha held her breath and tried to control the relieved laughter. 'Thank you. Thank you so much—you don't know how much this means to the choir—'

'Hold on, Sasha, I'm not making any promises. I need to check my schedule. Text your address to this number and I'll send a car for you tomorrow at seven p.m. You can come to my hotel and we'll talk more.'

'Not that it doesn't sound fancy, and I'm very grateful, but I've been making my own way around London for years.' She didn't need any more reasons to be beholden to him. 'Just tell me where you're staying. I'll get there.'

'No.' He clearly didn't trust her with that kind of information. Not surprising really after she'd turned her back on him. At the time she'd called it self-preservation but, in hindsight, he'd probably seen it as betrayal. 'My car will be there at seven. Be ready.'

'But…'

'Sasha, this works better for me. I don't want anyone getting wind of this yet, okay? And the press have a way of finding things out.'

'And being nice interferes with your bad-boy image?'

'Really? You think I care what the press think? It's way too late for that. I don't want to get the kids' hopes up and then not be able to follow through. And it's my private cellphone, so don't ever give this number to anyone.'

Normally she didn't take kindly to being bossed around, but the guy had just given her an opening. The choir would be thrilled, their financial problems solved, if she could pull it off. And keep her jumping heart out of it. 'Okay. Seven p.m. tomorrow, then.'

'Oh, and one last thing, Sasha. This is just for Marshall, okay?'

'Mr Munro will see you now.' The bear appeared in the reception of the Grand Riverview Hotel, complete with earpiece and grimace. 'This way.'

'Nice to see a familiar face,' Sasha breathed as she struggled to keep up along the elegant corridor.

Velvet-embossed wallpaper in golden hues served as a backdrop to nineteen-twenties-style furniture. Petite bronze statuettes of dancers flanked the walls. *The price of one of those would pay for the whole choir to fly to Manchester, first class.* She was so out of her league, and then some. But, fingers clutching her briefcase, she determined to meet Nathan face to face as a music professional.

'We get a lot of familiar faces here, sweetheart, for a day or two.' Giving her just enough time to process the ramifications of that statement, the bear opened the door.

You're nothing special, his feigned smile said as he looked her up and down. Standing aside to let her in, he bowed lightly, muttering, 'Don't get too comfortable.'

Like that would happen. Especially with Mr Warm and Fuzzy here.

She blinked once, twice, not knowing what was more impressive: the expansive suite with panoramic views across London, or the fact that Nate was in it, looking extremely comfortable, standing by the bar. Looking extremely gorgeous too. Relaxed and confident. In control of everything: his staff, his surroundings, his emotions.

He'd grown in a way she hadn't. At least she didn't see herself like that—uber confident and all grown-up—even though she tried to be. He'd probably honed it from absorbing the adoration of thousands of fans, from years of live performances where self-belief was mandatory.

But regardless of the man he was now she knew his essence, where he'd come from, what he was truly like—the good, the bad and the downright ugly.

And yet, despite knowing what he was capable of, he was still strangely compelling to be with. Walking leisurely towards her, he smiled. Slim black jeans hung from slender hips, a black faded T-shirt hugged his toned frame.

She didn't have to guess what was under that T because she'd seen it over the years in the music press, smoky black and white images of Nate in various stages of undress, on CD covers that bordered on X-rated. She knew all about the sun-kissed carved abs, the thin line of dark hair… Her mouth dried.

She jerked her head upwards. Big mistake.

The moment she met his caramel-coated gaze her courage faltered. Why did he have to be so beautiful?

Was it appropriate to walk over and kiss him on the cheek? Shake hands? But he saved her the worry by stepping into her space and placing a warm cheek against hers. His lips grazed her skin sending ripples of heat through her veins.

'Sasha. Thanks for coming.'

'Thank you…too.' *Excellent. Excellent start. Not.*

And then the room seemed to press in as his familiar scent washed over her. This was the kind of place he was used to now. So far from the tiny council-flat bedroom he'd shared with Marshall, littered with guitars and sheet music, posters on the wall of his favourite damaged rock heroes. And a photograph of her by his bed.

Her throat filled. So many things she'd pushed to the back of her mind, or had simply forgotten. The honest sweetness of their first date. Their innocent journey to first love.

And now this. Such abject luxury, no wonder he'd offered to write her a cheque without missing a heartbeat. But could high living change a man? Could it tame him?

She'd read about his wild parties in Ibiza, the spats with paparazzi, riding his motorbike through a hotel reception. She guessed that really he was still the same man underneath the wealth.

Leading her to a couch that would never fit into the whole of her flat, even if she knocked the walls down, he held a glass of beer and offered her a flute of champagne. 'Drink?'

'Thanks. Nice place.' She raised her eyebrows and gestured to the door. 'Shame about the company you keep, though. Do you pay him to be rude?'

'Dario?' Nate's smile spread slowly across his lips, reached his eyes, which softened with genuine warmth. 'Only to my friends.'

She laughed. 'God help your enemies, then. I dread to think what you do to them.'

His gaze hardened from toffee to troubled. The hand holding his glass fisted and she thought for a second it might smash.

Brilliant. Bring up the past, why don't you?

He'd never explained why he'd launched the attack that had landed Craig in Intensive Care and she doubted he would now. And even more, it was still none of her business.

The silence that followed was mortifying. She watched as he regained control, softened the tight jawline, turned his back on her and walked to the window. 'You'd better tell me what you need me to do.'

Renewing her purpose, she deposited her flute on the glass coffee table and fished her folders from her well-loved leather messenger bag. She met his authority with her own. 'I have spreadsheets here with a projected timetable, financial forecast, health and safety plan-'

'Huh? Health and safety? I thought it was just a school gig.' It was more a grunt than a laugh, but as she glanced at his face she saw he'd relaxed a little. Ice broken. 'Or are you planning to do something very dangerous to me?'

Planning, no? Thinking, possibly. Fantasising, definitely. Just being in the same air as him was dangerous enough.

As he sat next to her on the couch his leg brushed against hers. Pursing her lips together, she clamped down on the fizz of electricity shooting through her.

This was unreal. The room was alive with vibrations of their moods. So many things remained unsaid, unresolved;

everything was amplified and tangible, mirrored in her erratic heartbeat and the sheen of sweat forming on her brow.

At his proximity she shifted slightly but was thwarted by the thick deep cushions that hemmed her in. His face was too close. He was too close. And just thinking that, breathing him in, sent whispers of something she hadn't felt in a very long time. A low-down tingling, parts of her body aching for his touch.

Well, heck, she couldn't be attracted to him, not in a real sense. From a distance, sure—who wouldn't be turned on by the idea of him? By his sex-god rock-star image? But those kinds of feelings were wishful thinking and daydreams. Not hard reality. Not gut-churning, tachycardia-inducing, libido-stirring reality.

Crazy feelings whirled in her chest, chaotic. Vivid. Hot. Very, very hot. 'It's…er…regulatory…you know.'

He grinned. 'What is? Doing dangerous things to rock stars? I like the sound of that—what do you have in mind?'

Well, she certainly wouldn't be telling him that. 'Obviously the school board needs a safety plan, the choir needs an action plan…'

'Aha…'

'But basically I just turn up to the school hall on the arranged night, do my stuff then leave? It's hardly rocket science. I'll do an unplugged set, so we won't need my band. And if the kids could learn a couple of my songs then we could all sing together in an encore. That's how it usually goes.'

Nate shoved his hands in his pockets and inhaled, inadvertently breathing in the smell of…yeah, sunshine. Stupid as it sounded. Like a lame lyric destined for the trash, but it was true—there was something fresh and new and bright about her.

'Sure, we've been working on a few of your hits already.

They love your stuff.' Her nose wrinkled as she gave him a brief smile. 'Maybe you could stay for a little while after and do some autographs…at least for the choir members.'

'I'm not planning on hanging round and having a big happy reunion with anyone. I don't see the point in nostalgia, do you?'

She blinked, a slight catch in her throat as she spoke, 'No. No, not at all. The past is best left alone. Agreed?'

'Couldn't have said it better myself.' Repetition made reality. *The past is best left alone.* Including ex-girlfriends who had started to haunt his dreams.

In truth he should have got Dario to sort this, as usual; Nate was far too busy to deal with schedules. So call it self-indulgent or just plain dumb, but the thought of seeing her before he went back to LA appealed. More than he wanted to admit.

She was his connection to his past, the experiences that had shaped him, given him the verve to fight hard for what he wanted.

A vibe hovered between them. He'd had lots of vibes before with lots of women. But this was bigger, stronger than ever. He ignored it. Tried to ignore it.

But he couldn't help looking at her, mesmerised by how the simple halter-neck dress with the daisy pattern and flared skirt, the same blue as her eyes, accentuated her fine collarbones. How her hair looked pull-down ready, and how his hand itched to reach out and let the curls flow over her shoulders.

She was gorgeous. Not Cara gorgeous, but then he'd spent a lot of time trying to work out which parts of her were real and which were fake. Certainly, her outspoken ministrations of everlasting love had been false. Everlasting. Pah. In Hollywood everlasting meant five minutes. But then, Sasha had promised him a lifetime too, and look where that had ended.

Man, this was wild. He forced out a breath. He'd forgotten all about her, consigned her to bad history and pushed her to the dark recesses of his brain. Now here she was invading every thought, his space, the flame of red hair looking pretty darned perfect against the cream couch.

But self-indulgence had been too costly in the past and he'd do well to remember that. Sasha might have held his heart once, but she'd damned near thrashed it too. Taking her to bed would be mighty fine, but he'd never trust her with anything more. Never again.

Staring at the papers in her hand, she shrugged. 'We're planning on doing the concert in two weeks' time. Saturday. The twenty-eighth. Spring Bank Holiday weekend.'

'Two weeks? You don't mess about.'

'I told you we were running out of time.'

And there went his month's holiday in Italy. 'I'll get Dario to handle the details, make sure I'm in town.'

'That would be great. Brilliant.' But she didn't look pleased.

'So, what's the problem now?' Crazy, but without thinking he touched her cheek. She curled into his touch briefly, before shifting out of reach, the papers hovering in her hand in mid-air. Her gaze dropped to her lap, but he didn't miss the flash of fire in her eyes and that stoked something in him too. 'You don't seriously want me to be interested in the details?'

'Why wouldn't you be? It's your show. And it makes things run smoothly if we're all on the same page.'

He looked at the papers in neat pink plastic folders all with little stickies on them. 'Which page exactly? You have so many.'

'There's nothing wrong with planning, Nate.'

'Sure. But that's what I pay someone else to do. I see you're still a walking-talking stationery cupboard. You haven't got a smartphone app for all this?'

'I prefer hard copy. It's easier if you can see it all laid out.'

'It's easier if I don't see it at all.' Planning in minutiae had always been Sasha's way of coping after her father's death—of ensuring the ordered life and stability she'd wanted. He used to think her organisational OCD was quirky and endearing, the way she'd carry her diary around religiously and check things, plan. If it hadn't been for her management skills he wouldn't have secured the gigs and the subsequent recording contract.

Their whole future had been mapped out at one point, down to the number of kids they were going to have, and when. He'd had a lucky break there, he'd always thought, when it was over.

Whereas Cassie—she'd always been happy-go-lucky, life's too short sort. Far too scatty for his liking. And serious Suzy, the eldest, had just put her head down and worked hard to protect them all. Three girls hit in different ways by one tragedy.

Then it occurred to him that the gents'-toilet fiasco would have pretty much killed Sasha. Her plans gone awry, then finding herself in his car. All out of her control. She liked to play safe.

And he didn't.

She looked so enthusiastic about her files he decided to indulge her. What did a few more minutes matter? 'Okay, sweet thing, hit me with it. And if I nod off, then, literally, hit me with it.'

An eyebrow peaked. 'Aww, your poor addled rock-star brain can't handle a few simple facts and figures?'

'Hey, I can handle anything you throw at me. Numbers, forecasts, projections. Do your worst.' He stretched his arms out and clicked his fingers. 'Bring it on.'

'You know your problem? You're all talk.'

'What, and no action? That's a dangerous gauntlet you're

throwing at me. You'd want to be very careful.' He held her gaze, wondering what she'd do if he just leaned in and covered that mouth with his. Would she drop the brisk schoolteacher act? Would she kiss him back?

The vibe tugged and tightened.

'Just an observation.' She swallowed. 'And, according to Cassie, careful is my middle name. Now listen.' Laughing nervously, she kicked off her shoes, shuffled up against the arm of the couch and faced him, fingertips running over the lines of ink. Making a good pretence that the heat in the room hadn't just hit scorching point. 'We have to cover the cost of train fares, hotels, my supply-teacher salary for a couple of days…I've broken it down into individual child cost, just for ease, so each one has a personal target to aim for…'

All he could see was page after page of graphs and squiggly lines. Her voice rose and fell in her schoolteacher voice as, head dipped, she focused on every darned detail.

But it gave him a chance to watch her, the tight swallow at her throat as she spoke, the tap of her toes. His gaze tiptoed up her legs, to the folds in her skirt, the tight cinch of her waist. He remembered how his hands had fitted around that waist ten years ago. Looked as if that couldn't happen now—but he liked her filled out a little.

His foolish heart tripped as his eyes travelled up the swell of her breast to her neck, the curve of her lips. And he realised she was frowning.

'Nathan? I said, are we done?'

Before he could stop himself he reached out and tilted her chin so he could see her eyes again. The heat there lit a fire in his gut and he was hit with a sudden need to know if her lips tasted just the way he remembered. 'Hell, Sasha, I don't know. Are we?'

CHAPTER FOUR

So this is where you leave.

Sasha stared up into those honeyed eyes, hazy now with only one thing. One unmistakable thing: desire. A shiver of excitement, and fear, tripped down her spine as heat pooled low in her abdomen. An energy buzzed around them, dancing and jumping with every second he held his fingers against her skin. Suddenly, leaving wasn't as easy as it sounded.

He wasn't supposed to want her. And she sure as heck wasn't supposed to want him back. This was a working relationship. Strictly platonic. Strictly professional.

Strictly temporary.

Edging away from his hands, she fixed a smile she hoped was distinctly non-sensual. Even though she sure as heck felt the most sensual she'd felt in aeons. 'I think that's all I needed to tell you. Questions?'

'None. As always, you're very thorough. Very…impressive.' Judging where his eyes were scrutinising now, she got the feeling Nathan wasn't talking about the reams of paper in her hands or the hours she'd spent on the spreadsheets.

And if he just leaned in a few more inches…

If she leaned forward…

Oh, hell. Seriously? She wanted to kiss him? She fought for a breath.

Maybe it was the champagne lulling her into a false

sense of...*in*security? Because there was nothing secure about the way her heart hammered or her legs weakened. Or the way he was looking at her with possession written all over his beautiful face.

She tore her eyes from his gaze, but they flatly refused to leave his face. Instead, she drank in the thick dark lashes, sculpted cheekbones and strong stubbled jaw. Everything about him screamed confidence, strength, sex appeal.

But more than that, he'd agreed to help her, at a huge personal cost. He'd given her time to go through the details when she knew he probably didn't give a damn, indulging her for no one's benefit but her own.

That just about blew off the assumptions that he was a selfish sex-crazed raiser. Who knew there was a softer side too? Strident. Complicated, not one dimensional like his media persona.

For goodness' sake, where did he get off being kind? And where did that leave her?

Captivated? Hot. Yes, too hot. And aching to feel the press of his mouth on hers.

When she spoke her voice was shaky. 'Why did you invite me over when we could have talked all this through on the phone?'

'Direct as ever. I wanted to see you.' The spark in his eyes swirled with confusion now.

'And what Nate Munro wants, Nate Munro gets, right?'

'Usually.' He shrugged. 'I just had a...feeling about you. Your last entrance made quite an impression. I wondered what you could possibly do for an encore, but I wasn't expecting spreadsheets. Women usually employ other techniques to get me to do things with them.' He laughed. 'You're definitely one of a kind.'

That was new—no one ever had feelings about her. She tried hard to be unobtrusive and not draw attention to herself. Fighting the heat whooshing through her now, making her unsteady and unsure, she swallowed deeply through a dry throat. 'A feeling?'

'Yes, I don't know. A hunch.' But he clearly didn't want to elaborate. For a man famous for heavy, heart-on-your-sleeve rock ballads that wooed the world's women, he kept way too much wrapped up inside when it mattered. 'Why did you agree to come if we could have just talked it through on the phone?'

'Cassie made me. Suzy, of course, would have a fit if she knew I was here.' And no way was she going to admit the guy had been burning a hole in her brain for twenty-four hours.

'Suzy. Suzy.' He shook his head, his mouth kicking up into a rueful half-smile. 'So forthright and ardent and so... righteous. How many times did she warn you off me?'

'Too many to count.' It had been a battle of wills in the end: the more Suzy told her no, the more Sasha had said yes. To Nate. 'But I never took any notice of her.'

'Until the end. Seems she was right after all.'

That he was wrong for her? That he was bad through and through? That he'd break Sasha's heart? 'Yes, I guess she was.'

Her big sister had been right about all of that. But Sasha had ignored the warnings. Just as she was ignoring the alarms blaring in her ears now.

Go. Walk away. She'd got what she wanted from him. Hadn't she? 'So. Is that it? I should go now.'

'Unless...' His hand was on her arm now.

'I don't...I can't...' Can't think.

'Hush, Sasha. I don't want anything you don't want to give.' He'd said that line before too. And she'd ached to give him everything, but every single time she'd stopped short. Unable to truly let go. With him, or anyone else since.

His voice was thick and gruff as the pad of his thumb stroked along her arm, and it felt as if he were stroking her insides too. Her breathing matched his as his fingers wound up the back of her neck, her nerve endings on full alert, rooting her to the spot. 'I'd forgotten just how beautiful you are. How intensely you feel things. Ten years, but you haven't changed so much.'

'You want to bet? If you think I'm still that little lost girl I used to be then you're very mistaken. I've worked hard to be who I am now. I've changed more than you could imagine.'

'Yes.' He smiled as he unhooked a strand of her hair that had caught in her dress strap, then he glanced down her body. 'I guess you have.'

Oh, God. She didn't want him touching her in some sort of rose-coloured grasp at something they'd had, too long ago. Rewinding wouldn't achieve anything but heartache, and moving forward meant grasping her self-respect and waiting for Mr Right, not grabbing a quickie on a couch— however nice—with Mr Very Wrong.

Typical, the first time in years her hormones were demanding usage, and it just had to happen with Mr So-Far-From-Safe not even one of her health and safety policies could help her.

Her hand reached to his hard wall of chest to push him away. But the feel of his T-shirt beneath her palm, and the heat of his skin beneath that, made her fingers curl into the fabric.

His face closed in, his eyes telling her what he wanted, his so familiar spicy scent weaving round her in a sensual web. Breathing became laboured as she waited for the moment she felt his lips against hers. Waiting to see if he still kissed the same way after all this time.

His head inclined towards her but he paused, his face swimming with a mixture of emotions, the most profound of which was confusion. Giving her just enough time for her doubts to jump in and fill the gap.

Wiggle away from the sex god, Sasha.

She knew who she was now, what she wanted, and it definitely wasn't inviting trouble back into her life.

Finding strength from who knew where, she pushed him gently away, then swung her feet to the floor and slipped on her shoes. 'I don't think *this* is a good idea, Nathan. It might be the way you crazy rock stars roll, but it's not how I do things.' Or was this how he wanted to be paid for his help?

Yikes.

'What? Have you invented a whole new way of *doing things* in Chesterton? In LA-LA land we usually start with a kiss and then see how things pan out…'

'Nothing's going to pan out. Is it just a game to you? Something for old times' sake? Play the silly ex-girlfriend and see how far you can get. What happened to leaving the past alone?'

'I was just getting caught up in the moment.' His smile was genuine and warm and reflected in his eyes. Which made her feel even worse. He stood calmly and offered her his hand. 'And so were you.'

Good point. 'But I can't just live in a moment, Nate. My life's not a wild ride like yours. I have responsibilities, I have to work, to pay the mortgage, I have to be a good role model to my students. Moments don't count, the big picture does.'

Her sister Cassie would kiss and walk away without a second's thought. No, Cassie would stay the night and not have a qualm. Cassie would relish the chance of grasping a little vicarious fame, enjoy the buzz of being with a celebrity.

But Sasha wasn't Cassie. She couldn't do the one-kiss thing, and definitely not the one-night thing. She was a forever girl, plain and simple, so there was no way she'd let herself get carried away with him. Especially not to then watch him leave again.

Shaking his touch away as quickly as she could, she smoothed down her dress and her nerves. 'I'll see you at the gig in two weeks. Thanks for taking the time to see me. And for helping in this project.'

'No, seriously, the pleasure was all mine.' But his eyes had darkened and he looked as bewildered as she felt. Standing up, he reached for the hotel phone. 'I'll call the car.'

'You'll do no such thing. I can find my way home from Mayfair.' The further she got away from him, the better. And quickly. Spending time in his car with his people wouldn't help her a jot. And she didn't need to owe him any more. The one lesson she'd learned from her father's suicide—never owe anyone anything.

Nate captured her gaze and shook his head in an *I'll-never-understand-you* kind of gesture, but eventually capitulated to her firm stance. 'Then at least let me walk you to the tube.'

'No. I'm just fine. Thank you. I can manage the tube—' And then she remembered their phone conversation, his chat with Dario the bear in the gent's.

Her hand covered her mouth in horror. She'd been about to commit the most heinous sin in her own book: kissing a man who was already committed to someone else. Her brain had clearly fried with lust. 'And what about your girlfriend?'

'Girlfriend? I haven't got—'

'The other night, after the gig, didn't you have a date? And then…eugh, the tramp twins in the limo? What kind of person are you, Nathan?'

'Misunderstood?' His hands curled into tight fists as bewilderment turned to bitterness. 'Story of my life.'

'I've pegged you as a lot of things over the years, reading reports of you drinking yourself into oblivion, partying for days on end, and hooking up with the most…' she tried to think of a word that didn't sound as condemning or derogatory as her thoughts '…quirky of girlfriends. But I never thought of you as someone who uses women. Not until now.'

Grabbing her handbag, she dashed to the door and down the stairs as quickly as she could.

Only when she'd reached the tube station did she realise that, along with her pride, she'd left her messenger bag and files on his couch. *Goddamn.* The man was turning her brain to a soggy hot mess.

But there was no way she was going back to fetch them, not tonight. Not when she'd had to rip her body away from him. Not when she had only one thing on her mind where Nate Munro was concerned. And it certainly didn't include a whole lot of paper.

Insane.

Yep. Insane in every aspect. Nate stood outside the grimy red brick walls of his old high school and felt the familiar tightening in his gut. How he'd allowed himself to be talked into this he didn't know. And by a woman who hadn't changed much at all no matter how much she protested to the contrary. She still shot first and asked questions…never.

Don't ask, but jump to conclusions. Check.

Don't give him a chance to explain. Check.

That was Sasha all over.

Just being here in this rundown dead-end school was bad enough, never mind spending more time with her.

He found her in the old school hall. Nothing had changed here either—the whole scenario was as if he'd rewound ten years to his adolescent nightmares. If this was the punishment for being the bad boy of rock, he was definitely going to work on his game from now on.

The place still smelt of sweaty socks and cheap lemon

air freshener. Still had scuffs in the dirty cream paintwork, and old velvet curtains that didn't quite fit the stage. Where she was standing. In front of a gaggle of kids who, as it happened, made quite a good noise.

'Sorry to interrupt…' He waited for her to turn round. Watched the silent gasp, the irritated raise of her eyebrows, the flush of her cheeks. The hesitant smile as she saw her bag in his hand.

Sunshine streamed through an upper window, casting bright light across the stage in a perfect arc, catching dust motes dancing almost in rhythm with the song.

Even from this distance he could see the different hues in her hair, not just red, but gold and blonde too, drifting down her back, shimmering with every move.

Goddamn she was sexy. And so different from the women he usually dated. First off, she'd said no to him. *Again.* That never happened.

She wasn't lured by his fame or his wealth; in fact far from that, she didn't want a dime of it for herself. Which was refreshing and curious. And the fact she'd left without taking advantage of what he'd had to offer pushed intriguing to the top of the list of adjectives he already had for her.

She wore another fifties' summery dress today, short capped sleeves, tight V neck and full skirt in a soft green that accentuated her waist and fell in feminine folds to her knees. Demure enough to be suitable for her job, it was cut from some kind of thin fabric that made you want to touch it. Touch her.

Holding her finger towards him to signal him to wait, she led the choir through a medley of three recent number one hits, none of them his, while they performed a quirky dance routine at the same time. A mix of above-average talent and ability, they had enough charisma to pull at the heartstrings of any benevolent audience, but probably not enough to win any prizes. Yet.

Sasha was good with them too. Praising and cajoling when the more timid ones forgot the words, or were reluctant to walk to the front of the stage. Singing along with them in her soft lyrical voice that swung him back to a time he'd be better off forgetting. Swaying her hips as she conducted. Her head tipping back with a gentle laugh as one of them played the fool, then bringing them back to focus again and finishing the song.

Dragging his eyes from her backside, he watched the choir fine-tune the dance moves. One kid in particular caught his eye. So similar to Marshall it made his heart constrict into a tight fist. With his eager wide eyes, too big tongue and dazzling smile he was, as far as Nate was concerned, the star of the show. Just as Marshall had been.

And suddenly the urge to escape across the hardwood floor threatened to overwhelm him. It was too much to relive all at once. Chesterton High. Marshall. Sasha. Too many dark memories he'd worked hard at pushing to the farthest corner of his mind in a blur of hard alcohol and commitment-free sex. Good sex, too. Fast, hot, hard. Sex that had taught him how to be a man, how to please a woman.

Not the kind of sex Sasha would want, all fluff and fairy tales and diarised on her planner. Every Wednesday and Saturday, missionary position only.

He dumped her bag on a chair and turned to leave, but at that moment the choir stopped singing and he heard her voice. 'Guys, I have a visitor I need to talk to. Go through your steps again, from the top. George, you count them in. I won't be long.'

Good, neither would he. 'Security here sucks. I walked straight in and no one batted an eyelid.'

'Nate, it's a school. Public property, really. People come and go all day. Besides, it's four o'clock and almost everyone's gone home. You hardly look like a potential threat.

Hmm…much.' She looked at the baseball cap pulled down over his face and the dark sunglasses disguising his features. Then her gaze stole a quick glance down his black leather jacket and dark jeans.

Her eyes fired with something akin to want. After ten years in this job he knew when a woman wanted him. After two years of loving her he knew when Sasha wanted him too.

Which was all kinds of a turn-on.

'You're risking a mobbing, though. I don't think the kids have worked out they're sharing the same air as Nate Munro, but once they do you'll be swamped.'

'I can handle it.' He nodded to the hall door where Dario stood watch. 'And I have back-up.'

'Oh, Tweedle Dum. How nice.' She waved her fingers over to his manager-cum-minder, who, true to form, did not move a muscle. 'Are you two joined at the hip? That must make your love life very interesting.'

'Aww, he's very discreet. And he's not the jealous type.'

Her eyebrows peaked. 'Really? Could have fooled me.'

'Well, maybe just a little bit, but he has my best interests at heart.'

'He has a heart? Funny.' Stacking chairs along the side wall, she shrugged. 'And clearly I'm not on his list of Nate interests.'

'He thinks this whole project is too distracting.' That was the polite way of describing Dario's reaction. At her frown he smiled and went to help dismantle the rest of the rows of plastic seats. He just couldn't help but wind her up, watch the pink tinge her cheeks. 'And, for the record, my sex life can be very interesting. As interesting as you like, Sasha.'

'Whoa. Down boy. Er…girlfriend?'

'Will you ever listen? There is no girlfriend.' And that was all she needed to know. Private time needed to remain so. There was sex, which he did, and there was dating, which he didn't. 'Is your opinion so low of me that you think I'd do something as crass as run with two women at the same time?'

'Wasn't there a leery story once about you and blonde triplets? Really, and I always thought three was a crowd.'

He smiled at the memory. That had been fun, even though the journalist had exaggerated the details beyond any semblance of truth. But recently he'd lost his appetite for hard and fast with adoring strangers.

'Don't believe everything you read. I might be bad but I do have some morals. Like helping hapless choir teachers when I could be doing something infinitely more relaxing. Here, I brought this.'

He offered her the bag containing way too much paper. No matter how much he'd wanted to scroll through it to find clues about her life he'd managed to keep his eyes away. Her business was her business.

And *her* private life? Yep, damn right he wanted to know more about that. Far more than was good for him.

As she took the bag her line of vision tracked back to the kids on stage. She shifted position, inadvertently stepping a little closer, flowers and vanilla and something… something that made his heart beat a little faster enveloping him. 'What do you think?'

'I think…' She really did not need to know what thoughts were running round his head. 'I'll see you at the concert.' Dario was right: she was distracting. Flirting was all well and good, but with his body reacting so strongly to her the best thing he could do was get out. Fast.

'Oh. Don't you like the choir? I realise we could do with some help.'

Yes, they could. But it was not going to come from him. 'Well, yes, but I have to go.'

'Could you at least tell me your first impressions? Some

pointers?' Her shoulders twitched backwards and the beginning of a pout hovered over her lips.

He huffed out a breath. Seemed she wasn't going to let him off lightly. She held him there with her teacher stare that simultaneously scared the pants off him and turned him on.

'Okay. I like the mash-up, it's a clever mix. But you need to focus more on the harmony in the second verse of "Sunshine Smile", it gets lost, and that whole riff needs simplifying...' He paused to watch her bemused reaction.

'Oh...really? Are you sure?'

'You did ask. If it doesn't suit, then don't change a thing. But you'll be sorry you didn't.' He fought the urge to bury his face in that vibrant hair and tried to refocus on the choir. Not easy. 'While you're at it you should drop the tenors just for that verse, see if it sounds less...busy. And the alto needs to be stronger in "Ways of a Saint"...have you thought about a more abrupt ending instead of the way it finishes on the original?'

'Whoa...slow down.' She held her palms up, scrabbled round for a pen and paper and started jotting down bullet points. 'Isn't that a bit radical?'

'No. You've got to give them something that surprises them. Trust me. This is my job, I live and breathe this kind of stuff.' He hadn't even started, but pointing out all their failings would take time he didn't have. And he didn't much like the idea of hanging around this hall, with all its ghosts and memories, for the next millennia.

'Do you want to walk the kids through your ideas? I'm sure it'd be better coming from you.'

'What? Me? Teach? Them? No, thanks. Like I said, I've got to go.' Always the outsider, he'd never felt as if he'd belonged in this place so there were no warm fuzzies or sentimental reasons keeping him here. None at all. Nothing to compel him to help any more than he already had.

'What? Mr Fabulous and oh-so wild, Mr Off His Head Crazy…scared of a bunch of mixed-ability kids?' She laughed. 'That's hysterical.'

He couldn't see a funny side. 'I'm just busy. Not scared.'

'Prove it, hot-shot music man. Prove you're not scared.' The paper fluttered to the floor as she stared him down, her eyes a mix of serious intent and a playful tease that tugged at long-buried heartstrings.

Prove it. Her mouth formed the words but no sound accompanied them. For a moment he thought she might stick out her tongue as well.

'Don't be immature.'

Then her voice came, soft and appealing. 'Imagine how fantastic it would have been if you'd had a mentor all those years ago. If someone had helped you, even for a few minutes. It might have made such a difference. What have you got to lose?'

She was right. Guidance was scant back then. No one was interested in a loud-mouthed kid with an over-inflated sense of musical skill and entitlement. But…if someone had helped…

He shook his head, shocked he was even considering this…but even if he didn't make a difference to their performance, getting involved could surely make some amends to the damage he'd wreaked when he was young and stupid. When he'd thought he knew what was best, and that the only way to solve problems involved a whole lot of aggression riding on a surge of testosterone.

These kids needed help.

Looking at their hopeful faces, he suddenly didn't want to be the one to poop on their parade. And if that meant he spent more time with Sasha, then so be it. He could keep a lid on his libido.

'Okay. I can spare a few minutes. Bring that boy…' he

pointed to the Marshall lookalike, saw the big open grin
and the thick palms, the intense need to please '…and…'

And just like that his past came crowding back in on
him along with a host of emotions he didn't want. His voice
caught as a dull ache gripped his chest. 'Yes…more to the
front, he's got great rhythm and clearly loves it. You need
enthusiasm like that to carry such a happy song.'

Sasha glanced at the boy and then back at Nate. And
clearly he hadn't been hiding his feelings too well, because
tears filled her eyes and she pressed a palm to her chest.
'Oh, Nate. I'm so sorry.'

That was all he needed, her pity.

Back off. Because, in truth, Sasha was the only person
in the world who'd understand the pain of losing Marshall.
That was a part of his life he never shared and he wasn't re-
visiting any of it again in a hurry. Not when she was within
reach-out-and-hold distance.

'Yeah, me too.' Forcing his voice through the Rock of
Gibraltar that had lodged in his throat, he focused back on
the kids. The ones that mattered now, the ones he could
help. 'Right, let's get this act whipped into shape, shall we?'

CHAPTER FIVE

'MISS SWEET, IS that...is that Nate Munro?'

Readjusting back to the choir took monumental effort. Sasha had been too busy watching the colour in Nate's cheeks bleed away at the memory of Marshall. And she realised at that moment how difficult it must have been for him to come back here. How much she was in his debt that he'd even stepped foot in this hall.

Nate had protected his brother, had fought for him to attend mainstream school at a time when Down's syndrome kids were often regarded as unteachable. And he'd taught them all to embrace differences. So losing his beloved Marshall so young must have been devastating.

She of all people knew how hard it was to lose someone you poured your love into. How difficult to restart your life. How much you clung to a safety raft, the familiar, the known. Because the unknown was too terrible to contemplate. And how you avoided reaching for those painful memories at all cost.

And yet here he was. Making her challenge her assumptions of the kind of man he was.

But now the barriers were up again.

She caught his eye, unsure of how to answer George's question. Of course the kids would click they were in the company of someone important. Just one look at him and his star quality shone through. The dark edgy clothing, his diffident stance that was accentuated with every confident footstep. The whisky-deep voice.

Whispering across the hall, she tried to coax him forward. 'Well? What do you want me to say? I wouldn't try lying—they're not daft.'

'Busted.' Removing his baseball cap, glasses and hoodie, he walked to the edge of the stage and looked up into their wide-eyed faces, smiled at the collective sharp intake of breath. 'Hi. Yes, pleased to meet you all. I'm Nate.'

Her own intake of breath was as instinctive as the choir's. But for a whole different reason. She hoped. Sure, they were blown away by his elevated celebrity status, the face that peered out from magazine racks on the high street. But she just couldn't get used to—or tire of—the way his body moved so fluidly, the way his jeans hugged his toned thighs and appeared not to want to let go.

The taut breadth of his chest, black collared shirt open enough—no, never enough—for her to glimpse the gift of his body underneath. That Californian sunshine sure had kissed his body. And, for a split second, Sasha wondered just how far down that tan went.

'Ahem…it's *Mr* Munro to you lot.' She grinned, finding her breath again and trying to talk over the squeals of excitement. 'We have manners, remember, No Limits choir. Mr Munro has agreed to help us with our fundraising concert, but we have to keep his visit here quiet. He's a busy man and he doesn't need the hassle of a zillion screeching fans every time he comes here—we can save that for concert night. And we have to show him we can be professional too, and listen. And do what we are told. Give me two more minutes while I chat to our guest.'

'Scary teacher voice,' Nathan muttered under his breath and leaned closer, the fresh heat in his eyes melting the sadness she'd seen moments before. And sending a flush to her cheeks, direct hit.

'You haven't seen anything yet,' she whispered back to him out of the corner of her mouth. 'They don't call me Miss Sweet and Sour for nothing.'

'Sweet and Sour? Ouch.' One eyebrow raised as he met her wry smile with one of his own. 'That sucks.'

'It's original, I guess, and they obviously think enough of me to make up a nickname. I try not to be too hard on them. It's a tough area and life's difficult enough as it is. I'm more about building them up than shooting them down.'

'I wish we'd had more teachers like you at school. Ones that gave a damn.' The sentence was loaded with memories, but he smiled back at her, the energy in the air smoothing into something less fraught.

She wondered whether she'd imagined the intense heat in his eyes. But as she risked another glance there was still a warm spark there, simmering, that set her pulse jittering. 'Some days I could cheerfully scream. They have a habit of knowing which buttons to push.'

'But you obviously love it regardless, Miss Sweet and Sour.'

'I get a kick out of helping people, realising potential. It's all I ever wanted to do.' Harnessing her energy into something positive instead of dwelling on the negatives of her life.

'I remember. You wanted to be a music teacher just like Mr Taylor. You had a crush on him.'

'I did not.' She laughed, remembering the very bohemian long-haired music teacher who'd opened up a new world to her. Sure, Mr Taylor had inspired her, but the only person she'd had a crush on in her school years was Nathan Munro.

'You followed him around for the whole of fourth form like a lost puppy.' He leaned close to her ear. 'That's when I started to get jealous.'

If she edged just a little closer they'd be touching. Hip to hip.

Trouble was, she didn't want simple touching, not where he was concerned. She wanted what every hot-blooded woman would want faced with him in close proximity. And that frightened her.

To stop making a fool of herself in front of the whole choir and Mr Celebrity here she shook free and busied herself with the long-lost contents of her bag.

'You weren't even going out with me then.'

'No, but you were very definitely on my radar.'

And he'd been on hers. Out of her league, the cool loner who never quite seemed to belong to one gang or other and had dangerous written all over him. Some things hadn't changed. He still had the remarkable ability to set her on edge. And, worse, after ten years of putting him well behind her, she was reacting like a giddy teenager all over again.

She kept her voice steady and attempted to regain some composure. 'Okay, let's get this thing going. And you, Mr Obnoxious, stand right over there. Away.' *From me.* She ushered him to the back of the hall. 'It's better acoustics.'

An hour and a stratospheric improvement in the choir later Dario tapped Nate on the shoulder. 'Time to go to your next appointment, Nate.'

'Oh, yeah? What is it this time?' Thank God he had someone with their eye on the ball, because right now he was way too engrossed to think of what next.

'De Facto Art Space on Portobello.'

'Okay. Five minutes.' Nate sighed inwardly. And he was having such a good time, a surprisingly good time.

Not least the fact the choir had listened and performed far better than he could have imagined, but working with Sasha had proved easy and fun. She was a natural with the kids and brought out the best in them. Her refreshing honesty and openness made him believe there were some genuine people left in the world. Maybe not in his world. But out here, in reality, away from his chaos.

'I'll be outside waiting. Is she coming too?' Dario nodded towards Sasha as she packed her bag and waved the last stragglers off home.

Another insane idea.

She grimaced at them both, eyes wide. '*She*? Who? Me?' She touched her chest. 'Thank you for such a kind and genuine invitation, but I wouldn't want to cramp the Tweedle twins' style. Besides I have an assembly to prepare…then, paint to watch dry.'

But when her lips curved into such a sweet smile and her eyes shone with teasing Nate didn't want this afternoon to end so quickly. He only had a few hours with her all up—maybe one more rehearsal, then the actual show. Then he'd be out of her life, out of this jaunt into a past he'd stuffed at the back of his mind. A few more hours wouldn't hurt. No big deal. His schedule meant he'd be gone soon enough.

And then what?

More sleepless nights wondering, what if? His imagination running wild over what she wore under those demure dresses, how her bare skin would feel against his, how her cute mouth would taste.

Just once.

He rubbed a hand across the back of his neck. What was he doing? Inviting her to ruin his life again? He knew what being with her cost. How much she'd trampled over everything they'd had. Thrown their relationship back in his face. And yet…he couldn't seem to help himself.

It was a shock, that was all. Meeting her again after so long, wanting to learn more about her, to see how much she'd changed. Finding answers to those half-asked questions that had flitted through his brain every now and then. People reconnected all the time these days—social media was awash with reunited friends.

Normal. Natural. Nothing to get hung up about.

'So you'd really rather stay home than come to a party of celebrities drinking carb-free wine and eating organic macro-vegan canapés? I just don't understand you, sweet thing.'

'Wow.' She laughed. 'You A-listers certainly know how to have a good time. Shame I'm so busy.' She curled a lock of hair round her finger and looked up at him through her fringe. 'Did I mention I was going to cook old-fashioned bangers and mash, with lashings of butter, and onion gravy?'

'Temptress.' He stepped forward and his arm brushed against hers. Like a kid on a first date at the movies, breathless and overflowing with testosterone, he felt the shock and static as they touched. And was it his imagination or did she jump too?

'No, not at all.' She shrugged away and flashed a nonchalant grin. 'It's been a long day. I'm just hungry.'

'Me too. Starving.' Just not for food.

But duty pulled at him. 'The artist's a good friend of mine. I promised I'd go. If the trendy food doesn't tempt you, maybe the art will? It's Rocco Baldini.'

'Rocco?' Her eyes grew large. 'Really? Ohmygod, you know him? Some of his work is…well, amazing.'

Excellent. He'd got her on the hook. Now he just had to reel her in. 'I know. I have one of his installations at my house in Malibu. I'll introduce you if you like.'

'Ooh, gosh, no. I wouldn't know what to say.' Strapping her bag over her shoulder, she walked to the door and flicked off the hall lights. The corridor was empty and shadowed. 'Since when were you into art?'

'There's so much about me you don't know.'

'Oh? I thought since you were such a big media star we all knew everything about you. You certainly live your life out on the page, on the stage…'

'Don't be so naive. I collect art and good wine…race motorbikes, own a gym… You want a copy of my resumé?' He took her arm and walked her through the school, fighting the urge to push her up against the lockers as he used to way back when. 'How about you spend a few more hours with me finding out what I'm really like? Put some of your assumptions to the test? No strings.'

'I can't. I told you—'

'Can't? Or won't? Or…scared? Scared that you might be wrong about me?' He drew to a halt outside room B4. Music class. Where he'd first found the courage to ask her out on a date.

This was a stupid place to come and bring back a host of memories. He had to get out. His hand was on her arm and he searched her eyes for some kind of agreement. Something that said he wasn't the only crazy one here.

But all he found was amusement, shock and a frown that said he was on dangerous ground. 'No. I'm not scared.'

'So…prove it.' He made a pretty poor attempt at her teacher scowl.

She shook her head and laughed. 'Oh, God. How did I not see that coming?'

'Two can play at that game, Miss Sweet and Sour. Besides, one good turn deserves another, right? I need a little help here. I hate going to this kind of place alone, where I'll have to waffle on about texture and depth and stuff.'

'Is that because you wouldn't know what it was? Depth?'

'Hey, I can do deep.'

'Sure. Nothing says deep like a quickie with two hot blondes with big bazookas, followed by a date with a whole different woman.'

'I didn't do that.'

'You were going to.'

'Can't blame a guy for trying.' Seriously, she had no idea. 'That was just guy talk. I didn't do it. And I didn't have a date—it was just an excuse to get Dario off my back. Come on. You owe me. Big time.'

For the first time that afternoon her face grew serious, her eyes dark and hollow. She thought for a second, seemed to reconcile his words. 'I guess I do. Okay, you're right. You've been great with the kids and you're doing the concert—'

'So you'll come, save me from a night of pretentious boredom?'

'Just to help you out. Then the debt's repaid?' She looked down at her soft green dress and wedge sandals. 'I'll need to go home and change.'

'No, don't. I like the way you look, this whole vintage gig.'

'This whole *cheap* gig. Ferret around in junk shops often enough and you can find a real bargain. I like it though. It reminds me of an era when people were honest and faithful and…predictable. When life was safe.'

'Ah, yes.' He loved to watch her face as he teased her, see the dawning realisation. 'The nineteen fifties, time of the Cold War, the Iron Curtain, the threat of nuclear bombs… yes, very safe.'

'Okay.' Her whole face lit up as she smiled. 'So maybe I just like the clothes. They're pretty and feminine.'

'And as luck would have it, I happen to have a thing for big skirts.' Although it was more that he wanted to know what was going on under hers.

She rolled her eyes. 'But I don't think it'll work for tonight.'

'It works for me. It makes you stand out from the crowd, your own style. Unique.' Definitely unique. And if he gave her an out to go home she might change her mind again. He wasn't prepared to take that risk. 'You look amazing. Seriously, amazing. You'll give them all a run for their money.'

* * *

But Sasha didn't feel amazing. Not when she stepped out of the car to the flash of a thousand light bulbs. Not when all she could hear was the screech of Nate's name to look right, left, *who's the date? Who are you wearing?*

Who? Idiots. *Clothes,* she wanted to shout back. Can't you see? And they'd all die if they knew she'd bought hers from a Chesterton High Street charity shop.

'Scaato and Paul, Frederike,' Nate called back, in a language she didn't understand.

And she definitely didn't feel amazing when he leaned in and said, 'It's a bit of a maul but we just have to get through this bit.'

She didn't want to just get through. She wanted it to end. Didn't want them to see her, to ask who she was. She didn't want them to know. The last thing she needed was her past dragged through the papers all over again.

Plan A: she would stay long enough to be polite, then leave through the back door. Plan B? She'd come up with something…just as soon as he removed his distracting hand from her back.

He steered her into the sparse concrete-grey space. Once the front door closed behind them her heart rate normalised. Not many guests so far, but enough to keep the ambient noise above a whisper. And no more photographers.

What groups of people there were she recognised from the TV as they air kissed and *mwah-ed* their way round.

'I feel seriously underdressed,' she whispered.

'You look fine. You look—'

Nate brushed a curl back from her face and looked down at her, his dark eyes locked with hers. A ripple of heat engulfed her, sucking air out of her lungs, stalling her breath. Everything around her lost sharp focus, then he abruptly dropped his hand, startled by something—some war inside him that played out in the shadows of his cheeks. There was a flicker of doubt in those heated pupils, a question that he seemed to be pondering.

Like her. What was she doing here?

Flustered by his proximity, she dragged her eyes away from his, and refocused on the surroundings, trying to make the best of it. After all, it wasn't every day she was invited to such a schooshed-up event. 'This place is astonishing. I've never seen anything like it. Although, I guess for you it's nothing unusual. It's part of your job. A way of life.'

He shrugged. 'It *is* my life. Heart and soul.'

'You never think of stopping? Settling down? Family even?'

Oh, Lordy, where did that come from? She hoped her question didn't sound too much more than idle curiosity. Which it wasn't. Seriously. 'I read that you got engaged once.'

Again with the shrug. She got the feeling he'd brought the shutters down just a little the moment he'd felt her prying, or was it just before that? 'In this job if you stop, you die. Or your profile does, which is about the same thing. Truth is, I'm just not the settling kind.'

And she'd known it, so why her stomach contracted, just a little, she couldn't say. 'Do you get proper time off, ever?'

'No.'

Casting her eye around at all the beautiful people, she asked him, 'Do you have real friends?'

'As opposed to what? Imaginary ones? Because I grew out of those years ago. Of course I have friends.' In a swift motion he stepped back and spread his arms out. Laughed. 'I'm just a regular guy.'

A smile tugged at her mouth, just watching him laugh had a relaxing effect on her. 'Believe me, Nathan, there's nothing regular about you. Or this…'

She pulled her shoulders back and wandered through the cavernous room towards the bar refusing to be intimidated by the designer suits and sky-high heels, people who wouldn't know where Chesterton was or how desperately needy the area was. Who had never met a special-needs kid let alone fought for their rights.

And they were the poorer for it.

Unless, of course, she was being overly judgemental.

And spending time with Nate had shown her that she could be. She'd been wrong about him, after all. Was that how she'd become? Placing people in boxes, with labels? Was that what being safe meant? That she couldn't see further than her own experiences?

She rolled her neck from side to side, eased the muscles, and tried to relax.

Nate leaned against the bar with languorous ease, his legs crossed at the ankles, sleeves rolled up. A regular guy at a regular work function. Worth about a trillion dollars. 'You want a drink, Sash? It might help you relax a little.'

'Just a fruit juice, please.' He had a way of making her want to do things she shouldn't, like attend pretentious parties, lean into his palm on the small of her back. Kiss him.

The thought buzzed round her head like an irritating wasp she couldn't waft away.

Kiss him!

Goodness, no.

So she'd be avoiding alcohol, because that would only lead her further into temptation.

'Let me see,' he said, with a mischievous glint in his eye. 'Fruit juice…lychee or durian?'

'What?' *Oh, merry hell. Beam me up.*

'Kidding.' As he laughed his leg brushed against hers causing a riot of tingling throughout her body. She didn't know if he even realised he was doing it. But by God, she wanted him to stop.

And to never stop.

'Okay, so no to the exotic fruit. How about…oranges that

have been pressed through the thighs of nubile virgins?' He handed her a glass of something thick and bright. 'That's very on trend at the moment.'

'No, darling, that was so last year.' She laughed and took the proffered drink. 'I'm glad you can see how strange this all seems to someone like me.'

'I suppose I've got used to it all. It is what it is.' He paused, his brow creased as he surveyed the room. 'I've never really thought about it, until now. I fell headlong into a life of crazy and it's just a part of me now.' He laughed. 'Some people go to any event to get themselves noticed. I'm more selective these days.'

Sasha shuddered. 'I don't understand this need to be seen. I'd hate having to face those cameras every day.' But then, perhaps not everyone had a past they wanted to keep out of the spotlight.

She followed him to the stark back walls, where bright orange oddly molded objects, made from what looked like balls of Plasticine, hung on tight steel chains.

People around them talked about light and structure and the profound meaning of such stark urban symbolism. Or something.

Nathan's eyebrows peaked and a little frown line appeared on his forehead. She fought an urge to trace her finger along it, down his cheek, to that mouth.

He whispered into her ear, his breath warming her skin. 'Do you like the art?'

She shook her head and bit her lip trying not to be thrown by a situation so utterly out of her comfort zone. Or by her body's irritating response to his every touch. 'Would it be rude if I said no?'

'It's worth a bomb.' His head tipped back as he focused longer on the piece. A laugh rose from his chest, full and hearty. 'But it looks like…earwax?'

'Yup. Thank goodness I'm not the only one to think

so.' As she laughed their gazes snagged again. One second. Two. Something snapped between them, electric and intense. Something deep. Something new. For a moment bewilderment flitted across his face.

'Better not tell Rocco what you think—he's coming over. Don't break his heart.'

A tall scruffy-looking man in an ill-fitting mismatched jacket and trousers sauntered over. He gave Nate a thump on the arm. 'Long time no see, mate. How ya dooin?'

'Great. This is my friend, Sasha.'

'Y'all reet?' The guy was called Rocco, but was from deepest Newcastle? She'd never heard him speak, famous as he was for his Silent Night series—living art that involved a bed, a mouth gag and handcuffs. Whacky didn't cut it.

She watched as Nathan engaged Rocco in quiet intense conversation. Where was the hell-raiser now? Talking knowledgeably about earwax installations and art spaces, drinking champagne and laughing. The more she discovered about him, the more she wanted to know. Which was all kinds of irritating.

He stepped forward as he spoke, and immediately a cold chill snaked up her back.

Ah. Clearly her body was just on physical overdrive. Lust. Hot and sharp, and not lasting.

Physical she could deal with. She had total control over her body; she could wrestle it into submission. It was the psychological she had trouble with. The knowledge that love was fragile, that had been reinforced with every going-nowhere relationship she'd had.

But to make things easy on herself she was going to activate Plan A. Just as soon as she could get a word in.

Edging back from the group, she leaned against the bar and took a moment to watch him in action.

Presently, a statuesque blonde glided by in a curve-hugging dress slashed up the sides and held together by transparent plastic panels. She gave Sasha a quick disappointed once-over, then linked her arm into Nate's and curled into his body like a cat eager for a stroke.

A cat on heat. Her manicured hand strayed to Nate's spectacular backside and squeezed possessively. Another of Nathan's conquests, clearly. Sasha presumed the room was full of them.

But even from here he looked surprised, embarrassed, although no one would ever have known it. His gaze hardened and his jaw twitched enough for Sasha to remember how similarly he'd reacted when he'd tried to cover up for his shortcomings as a youth.

'Jasmine. This is Sasha.' He steered the lofty blonde over. 'She's a friend of mine, from school.'

'Going back to your roots? How very retro of you. Clever boy,' the woman purred. 'Hi…er…Sara? Didn't have time to change? Never mind, you look adorable just as you are. Really.'

Then before Sasha had a chance to retort Jasmine turned her back, pressed a kiss on Nathan's cheek and whispered something into his ear.

A colossal lump stuck in Sasha's throat. If these were his friends then she was better off not knowing them. If ever she'd thought she might fit into his life, even for a moment, being hounded by the press outside and then here in this cold, unfriendly space proved she'd been delusional.

But she tilted her chin up and gifted them all the best smile she could muster. Dignifying Jasmine's comments with a response would only aggravate an already tense situation—and she didn't want to embarrass Nate in public. But she sure as heck wouldn't be accompanying him anywhere else.

'Not tonight, Jasmine.' Nate stepped back and fixed an equally plastic smile that did not reach his eyes. The clenched fist at his side was not unnoticed by Sasha.

'Oh? Busy boy? Tomorrow, then. Whenever you're ready, Nate.' *I'll be waiting.* Jasmine didn't say it, but every pore of her eye-lifted-cheek-filled-lip-plumped face screamed, *Take me to bed.* 'Call me.' Then she pressed another kiss on his cheek, leaving a dark red stain.

That kiss said so much. It said, *I know you.* I've had you. I want you again.

It said she was everything Sasha wasn't. Rich, beautiful. Fabulous, with her enhanced face and triple-F chest. It said she knew the ways of Nate's world. How to act, how to be. How to snag her man. And that she could do it, if she wanted. Right now. In fact, she already had.

And then it happened. Shocking and unexpected.

A swirl of frank jealousy that started as a hot blaze on Sasha's cheeks, rushed to her gut, curling her hands round the stem of her glass, and hit her…smack in the chest.

She'd been lured by his heat, by the reluctant kindness hidden underneath that dark-edged womanising mask. By his to-die-for ass. And now she was becoming far too interested in him. And that could never happen. Never. Again.

CHAPTER SIX

CRAZY REALLY, ONE bar, two exes.

One who was all over him like a rash. The other looking as if she'd rather be any place but here.

Nate unwound himself from his ex-fiancée's grip and went over to Miss Nineteen-Fifty-Seven. For all her bravado she hadn't been able to hide the shot of pink to her cheeks with Jasmine's uncharitable line.

Sometimes he hated how shallow everything was. This world that he'd craved, that he loved, that he used just as much as it used him.

But now, because of it, Sasha looked plain miserable sitting at the bar slugging back red wine and nibbling at the deconstructed asparagus crostini. His stomach growling for proper food and his mood seriously dented, Nate yearned for…what? Damned if he knew. But it wasn't this.

'I'm sorry. Jasmine tends to be a little possessive.'

'So I see. I thought I might need a crowbar to prise her off you.' Sasha raised her glass and took another sip. 'She's clearly a very good friend.'

'An old one.'

Friends? Great question, Sasha. He looked around at the mish-mash of celebrities. He knew every one of them—none of them well. He understood how important it was to be seen at events like this, to raise his profile, to sell records, make deals. But he didn't fit in here. He didn't fit the settled life with Jasmine either. He didn't fit in Chesterton. Where on earth did he fit?

He filled his home, hotel rooms, days and nights with employees, groupies, hangers-on, but he always kept a distance, at least emotionally. That was how he liked it. On the outside looking in—that way he could do as he pleased, when he pleased, and had no one to answer to. No one who invested in him or wanted something back.

Sasha grinned. 'She's very…tactile. At school we have a no-contact rule.' Grabbing a tissue, she swiped at the place Jasmine had kissed his cheek. 'That's better—not quite your colour. She'd get a detention with that kind of behaviour.'

'That's Jasmine, breaking all the rules.' He forced out a laugh. But it was far from honest. It was all mixed up with the sudden realisation that, despite how full his timetable was, his life was pretty damned empty.

And then there was that wild disconnected heartbeat Sasha instilled in him…

The things he wanted to do to her—*with* her—as those navy-blue eyes held his gaze, man, things he'd never craved like that before. To get lost in her until he could find himself.

He already knew that was impossible.

'Actually, I've had enough of this place. We should go.'

'So soon? And I was having so much fun.' Relief flooded her face, her voice upbeat, positive energy flowing from her. 'Where to now? What's next in this riveting instalment of your amazing life?'

'Home. I'll drop you off.' He couldn't help stepping closer just to inhale her flowery smell again, willing her optimistic vibe to weave through him.

'Oh. Yes, of course.' She looked taken aback, not affronted exactly, but surprised. 'Looks like it's sausages for one, then, after all.'

As she leaned forward to pick up her bag he caught a glimpse of lace, creamy flesh, breasts that looked just about perfect. Before he had the chance to tear his gaze away her head dipped back up, and she caught him looking, heat hitting her pupils.

Home sounded like a very good idea. Hers. Now. He failed to swallow the question forming on his tongue. 'How about sausages for two? Catch up on old times?' *Make some new ones too*?

As she wiped her hands on the napkin her eyes grew wide. 'You want to come back to my place? For sausages? That's…novel. No one's ever asked me to do that before.'

'No? Then, Sasha, hold onto your hat. I may even cook.' At the thought of being alone with her his groin tightened.

'Really? Don't you have people to do that for you?' Her lips parted just enough, the quick dart of her tongue to moisten lipstick-free lips. Wet. Hot…

'There are some things I have people for. And some things I really much prefer to do myself.'

Where was he going with this? The last few days had been like an ancient dance, pulling together, parting, touching and stepping away. How easy it would be to crank up the tempo and take it to its logical conclusion.

Easy and pretty stupid to have even one kiss with the woman who had pushed him to his limits years ago.

But his mouth and brain had total disconnect. 'Your place would be much more private.'

'I don't want you getting the wrong idea. Sausages and mashed potatoes—that's all that's on offer. Seriously. Nothing more. So don't even think it.' She swung down from the bar stool and fiddled with her dress, flashed a wry smile. When she spoke again her voice was hoarse and warm. 'You'll have to leave Tweedle Dum and your ego at the door. There's just not enough room. It's the size of a shoebox.'

'Excellent, cosy. Even better. Let's go.' The feel of her

soft hand as it fitted into his sent shivers through him. 'Brace yourself for the cameras again. This isn't going to be pretty. Stick with me.'

Opening the door to a cacophony of camera shutters, Nate dipped his head and focused on the pavement ahead, told her to do the same. Business as usual for him, but she looked scared to death.

A wave of irritation rippled through him as, for a moment, he wished he could shield her from the ugly side of fame.

'Nate!' one of the photographers yelled over as if he were his friend. 'Where are you going to now? Trudy's, Opal? Who's your friend?'

'Mind your own business.' Shoving past them down the street, he tried to decide which direction to follow. 'There's no car.' In his hurry to leave he'd completely overlooked that.

She rolled her eyes. 'Tube? Taxi? Bus? Like normal people. Oh, sorry, I forgot, you're not normal.'

'Tube? Do you have any idea…?' No, she didn't. 'We'll walk until we see a black cab. The trick is to keep moving.' The photographers followed, clicking and whirring, shouting and clamouring. 'Welcome to the greatest show on earth. My private life.'

'It's like being in a zoo.' She grimaced as she tripped over a guy who had his lens in her face. Her eyes flickered with fear as she tried to hide her face. 'Ouch, sorry.'

'Don't apologise to them.' He shouldn't have cajoled her into coming here, knowing how much she liked to play safe. His heart twisting at what he was prepared to put her through for his own needs, Nate came to a halt, put his hand on the man's chest. 'Leave us alone, mate. It's a private night out.'

'Nate, it's fine.' Biting down on her lip, she looked even

more alarmed at his reaction than the gross intrusion of privacy. 'Please, leave it. It's not worth it.'

Maybe they weren't, but she was. The camera jutted into her face. His irritation turned hot.

'I mean it, *mate*.' Nate's hands curled instinctively as he wished he hadn't made that vow ten years ago: that he would never hit another human being again. But, God, the feel of his knuckle against that man's jaw would be sweet right now.

His shoulders ratcheted back as he leaned towards them all, tried to rein in his anger. 'I said leave us alone or I'll slap you with a lawsuit so quick you won't have time to put your lens cap on. Get outta here.'

As one the group stopped moving. They didn't retreat, but they didn't take another step forward either. And the clicking and whirring stopped.

'Nathan.' Sasha's face had leeched of colour and her hand shook against his arm. 'Please.'

He drew her a few more feet away from the photographers and lowered his voice. 'Sasha, listen to me, they'll follow us for ever. Don't you understand?'

No? Hell if he did either.

This need to protect her—where had it come from? And why so intense? It made no sense. Ten years ago, maybe, but not now. Why did she bring out that primal instinct in him when he thought he was through with it?

'No, I don't understand, Nathan. Not at all.' Her gaze was hard as it clashed with his. 'Next time you fancy a fight, don't invite me.'

'What is this?'

She scowled. 'You know I hate this…violence. And yet, here you are showing off or something with your fists. It… it scares me.'

'Hell.' The truth hit him square in the gut. He was acting no better than his own useless father, lashing out and

angry. Again. 'I'm sorry. You know I'd never do anything
to hurt you.'

'Yeah—?' Turning away she suddenly careered forward
into the road, her foot buckling under her. He grabbed out,
caught her as she plunged towards the concrete. Next thing
he knew he was holding her, his chest frozen with fear of
what might have happened. Because of his stupid feral
overreaction. 'Are you okay?'

'I stumbled, that's all.' She shook out of his arms. 'For
goodness' sake, I can manage. I'm not some stupid hapless woman.'

'No. I can see that.' He turned her by the shoulder to face
him. 'But I'm just not prepared to share you with them.'

'So you act like an animal instead? All hot-headed, shoot
first? Have you not learnt a thing?'

'Of course I have. I've been living with the choices I
made for the last decade.'

But this was different, he was different. He could contain the rage now. He just couldn't contain the passion that
fed it. Didn't want to. He wanted to feel things, didn't want
to become the empty carcass that the shrink's uppers and
downers had made him following Marshall's death. 'I'm
not allowed to get angry? To feel things? Is that right?'

'Of course you can feel things. But making a fuss will
clearly make it worse.' Under his fingers tension rippled
through her body, but heat hit her eyes. 'You can't get so…
passionate about things like this. You have to control yourself.'

As she did. Sasha had always tried to control every nu-
ance of emotion to the point it had almost driven him crazy.
'I understand I have to tolerate it. There are times I happily walk that line—I even enjoy it. Don't get me wrong, I
love the fame, the money, the whole thing. But not today…
And not with you.'

'Oh.' Blinking once. Twice. Three times, she opened

her mouth to say more, then obviously decided not to. The hand she held to his chest trembled. But bingo, the heat was returning to those eyes. 'Then why didn't you just say so?'

'You were too busy tearing a strip off me. And I was too busy being a jerk.'

Mouth pursed, she shook her head and tutted. 'Finally he says something sensible.'

'Finally she shuts up long enough to let him. Can you walk?'

'I think so.' She nodded as he wrapped an arm round her waist.

'Then let's get out of here.'

Streetlights flickered into life as the sky darkened, mirroring his mood. As they walked thunderous black clouds blocked the last dying rays of the sun. Thick drops began to fall, slowly at first in a kind of staccato waltz, getting faster and thicker. Good old London in the spring.

Zigzagging through the dark west London streets they finally lost the photographers and lost themselves in the process.

She pushed her palms onto his chest. 'Great one. My shoes are ruined. My foot hurts…This has got to be the best—'

'Let's just take a minute to get our bearings.' He dragged her out of the rain into a shop doorway; bedraggled hair dripped onto her shoulders. Her dress stuck to her, delineating her shape, the tight swell of her breasts, the dip of her waist. Black streaks ran down both cheeks. And yes, normally he'd walk past a woman like her—but just seeing her all fired up made his heart race erratically and his body harden.

'Fine. Great. I'm already soaked to the skin, take as long as you—'

But before she could say another word he grabbed her

wrist, gently now, pinned her against the shop door. 'God, you're beautiful.'

'And you're an idiot.'

'Doing this, here, probably. But I can't help it.'

His arms curled round her waist, brought her closer. Her breasts pressed against his chest, her lips parted just enough for him to feel her warm breath on his face. Heat engulfed him, a fierce need that meshed with the anger at those stupid trolls and the ache to kiss her.

No—his anger dissipated as quickly as it had come. And the gaping hole that was left was filled with her.

The heavy bass beat from the club opposite blurred out of focus; his peripheral vision turned to fuzz. All he could see were huge blue eyes staring up at him, telling him what he needed to know. She felt it too, this wild crazy buzz. And she had no idea what to do with it either.

Careless and foolish to want her here in such a public place, but all he could think of was tasting those lips, feeling her righteous anger and uncertainty and downright sweetness in his arms. And sometimes, just sometimes he regretted courting the publicity that had made him such a success. Sometimes he wished he could live a normal life where no one cared who he kissed.

His thumb tracked to her lip but she didn't move, didn't blink, just kept on staring up at him with eyes that swirled with the same messed-up emotions as he had in his gut.

'Sasha.' He tilted his head towards her, saw the flicker of doubt, but he'd already seen the heat and knew she was fighting it too. 'God, I want you and I can't stop.'

'We have to stop.'

'Really? Do we? No one can see us—it's just you and me.'

She nodded. 'But, what next?'

He rested his forehead against hers. 'I don't know. We'll deal with it.' Somehow.

But when her tongue darted out and licked her bottom lip he was gone. Lost. Flailing around in the essence of her, looking for something to grasp onto. But the only thing that could anchor him was her.

Slanting his mouth over hers, he dipped his head and pressed his lips against the corner of her mouth. He felt her stuttered breath, the jolt of electricity that simultaneously rocked their bodies. And drank in the taste of oranges and stark clear honesty.

He knew this was insane and then some, starting something he could never follow through on. Not the way she'd want him to. It was the craziest messed-up thing he'd ever done—and that was pushing it.

But damn it, he wanted to forget what was right or wrong. Especially when it felt so good.

Oh, hell.

Nate's hands cupped her face, his light nibbles on her bottom lip sending a thousand shots of desire skittering through her, to her back, to her legs, and low down where an ache spread keen and unyielding.

Angling his head closer, he pressed his lips full onto her mouth, eliciting a groan from her throat that was deep and feral and hungry.

It wasn't the clumsy kiss of a teenager as she remembered.

It was the kiss of a man, mature, experienced, unlike her. His hands tangled in her hair, ran down her back, cupping her bottom as the kiss deepened. His tongue gently teased against hers, each stroke making her lose another grip on reality. Making her give in to dangerous temptation; just once. Then she would go back to her nice safe life where passion was a distant memory. Something other people did.

Madness, though, to be doing this with the man who had

taught her how love could make you soar, and how much it could hurt, and who had the capacity to do it all over again.

Nate was a man of sharp contrasts and driven by passion, but he wasn't going to stick around. And he certainly wouldn't suit a nice sensible car and slippers.

But by God, he was divine.

Snaking her arms around his neck, she pulled him closer.

Through his jeans she felt his hardness push against her, showing her just how much he wanted her. And that knowledge seemed to suck the air away between them. Her nipples beaded against his chest; heat pooled in her gut.

Resisting him was hard enough in the daylight, but having him wrapped around her, damp and hot and hard in the dark, was testing her to the limits. He wanted her.

And she wanted him right back. Wanted to feel him, taste him, touch him. A desperate ache tugged at her abdomen as she groaned, imagining how he would feel deep inside her.

No.

She caught her breath as waves of panic rolled through her. She fought for air.

'Stop. Stop.' Turning away from him, she breathed in the spicy smells and the dull thick sounds of the suburb, waited until her heart rate slowed. 'I'm sorry, Nathan. I've told you before—this isn't a game.'

He shook his head, desire and confusion lodged in the dark shadows of his face. 'And I wasn't playing you, Sasha. This wasn't what I planned.'

'And what exactly did you plan?'

'You want a list? Really? Bullet points? I don't know! I'm not like you. I don't plan every single move.'

Yes, and Plan A had been lost somewhere in the depths of his mind-numbing kiss. 'Maybe you should. I definitely should. This can't go anywhere. We're too different—our lives are poles apart.'

He seemed to be trying to shake off the bad mood that had descended. 'We could just have some fun?'

'No. I don't do fun.' Not fun in the sense he meant, because that kind of fun wasn't lasting, or sensible. How to admit that, sexually, she wasn't much more experienced than the last time he'd kissed her? He'd laugh in her face. 'And that sounds so hopelessly sad.'

'Yes. It does.' The moment very definitely deflated, he looked out of the shop front as a yellow light illuminated the street. Grabbing her hand, he pulled her to the kerb and waved. 'A cab. Quick. Let's do something fun, then, shake things up. Where should we go? Brighton? Paris? Edinburgh? New York? Anywhere you want.'

Bed? Maybe she could deal with it now. It had been a long time since she'd tried.

To be honest, the geography didn't matter, but the reality did. 'Oh, sure, I'm all into a spontaneous trip when I have school tomorrow. In the real world people work nine to five. You take it, I'm fine—the tube station's bound to be round here somewhere.' She just needed to get away from him before she was bamboozled into something else, something even more dangerous.

Even in this light she could see the frown and the concern. 'Are you mad? Do you know this area?'

'Not really, not in the dark. But I'll be fine—it's only Portobello.'

'Exactly. You are not wandering the streets on your own. Whatever happened to Miss Safe and Sensible?'

Great question—she'd been wondering that herself. 'Seems she's had a day off, but she's back now and she wants to go home.' On her own.

CHAPTER SEVEN

'CERTIFIABLE. OUT OF your mind bonkers. Deranged. Gaga. Loony. No sister of mine. No sir-ee. You left sex-on-a-stick and went home in a cab? If you don't watch out you'll end up a lonely crazy cat lady.' Cassie's incredulous voice crackled through Sasha's mobile phone as she killed time in the hall between school ending and rehearsals beginning.

Seven days, twelve hours and thirty-five minutes later and her sister still wouldn't let the Nate subject drop. 'I need more details. He was good? Great? The best?'

'All of the above. And I don't have a cat.' She tried for the elder-sister voice but ended up sounding cross. Truth was, she always regretted telling Cassie anything about her private life because she only used it as a rod to beat her with. A sad, pathetic rod dented with a history of lies and let-downs. Safe men, she'd discovered, didn't always look after your heart.

And now this. A spectacularly failed attempt at living dangerously.

Page five in the gossip rags. Albeit a grainy photo of her falling over; no one would even recognise it was her. But Nathan's snarly expression had peered out, accompanied by the usual gory story about his unstable rocky lifestyle.

So she should stay well clear. She didn't want to risk being identified and all the stress that would bring to her family. But the man wouldn't leave her head alone.

'It's only a matter of time, Sash. Before you know it you'll find a cute stray kitten and bring it home…and another to keep it company, and another. Then knitting will suddenly seem really fun, making jam, crocheted toilet-roll holders… It's a slippery slope to spinsterdom.'

'I'm twenty-seven—there's plenty of time to find my soul mate. And people don't say spinster any more. Or *on the shelf.* Smart women choose life partners carefully. They don't jump into bed with the first offer.'

'But they do jump into bed with someone at some point. You need to get laid or you'll be spinster central. You'll have spinster parties. Go on spinster holidays.' Sasha held the phone away from her ear as her irritating sibling continued her tirade. Which, unfortunately, was a hard smack of truth she didn't need to hear.

She'd waited a long time for Mr Right, and he seemed strangely reluctant to show up. Just her luck the only man who'd shown any interest was part gigolo, part magician. One word from him and her common sense had disappeared in a puff of smoke.

'…You can be Queen Spinster. All hail Empress Sasha Spinster the—'

'Okay, okay. Enough already. Do we really need to talk about my sex life?'

'You haven't got one. Sash…' The soft edge to her sister's voice made Sasha wince. 'It's been such a long time. It might be different. You should try again. You just need the right man…and why not Nate?'

'Yes, well…' She would not have a conversation about her sexual inadequacy over the telephone. 'Not everyone wants dirty sex up against a doorway. Even if it is with Mr Obnoxious himself.'

'Oh, really? How disappointing.' The deep voice came from behind Sasha, dark and dangerous and loaded with teasing.

It was perilously close to her ear lobe, and that sensitive spot at the back of her neck, which fired on full alert sparking lust hormones to break out from every pore. 'So where *would* you like dirty sex, Sasha? Because I'm happy to oblige, any time. My jet is on standby. Just say the word.'

Oh. My. God. *Do not turn around. Do not turn around.* Her heart drummed as she winced and overheated at the same time. A shiver of need tore through her body at the mere sound of his voice. That kiss marked a line that they'd crossed, and while her body thrummed her head ached to jump right back to safety.

She fumbled for the phone volume control and hissed, 'Cassie, I have to go.'

'Why? Rehearsals don't start for ten more minutes, so we have plenty of time to run through the details again. Okay. Slowly. From the top…Rain. Doorway. Lips. Tongues? Oh…you wanted him. Oh…he was so gorgeous. But you just couldn't—'

'Shut. Up.'

The wide smug grin that hit her in the face as she turned round to face Nate told her he'd heard. Every single belittling word. She closed her eyes, shook her head and rued the day she'd coached Cassie to speak clearly and loudly for her drama practical exam.

And judging by his smile it seemed Nathan agreed with her sister: a little seeing-to wouldn't go amiss. Why pass up on the chance of some fun? Life was too short, and all that gumbo people used to excuse bad behaviour.

But she'd kissed that smiling mouth. And it had been good. Very, very good. So good the intense tingling through her body had driven her wild ever since. So she could see they had a point. 'Someone's here, Cassie. I've got to go.'

'Who? Oh, your voice. It's changed. Soft, hoarse. Come-to-bed…' Her sister laughed. 'It's him. Isn't it? Nate's there…at the school?'

Prising the phone gently from her hand, Nathan smiled. Wearing his usual uniform of black with black and a dash of…black, he looked lip-smackingly devastatingly beautiful.

A fragile invisible thread pulled her towards him, tugging tighter and tighter. It had started to tense the moment her eyes locked with his in the men's room and now felt so taut it would snap at any moment.

Struggling for breath, she handed her phone over.

'Cassie? Nate here.' He held the phone away from his ear as she squealed. 'Your sister has to go now. We have some…unfinished business to attend to.'

Not bloody likely. Sasha winced again. Seven days, twelve hours and twenty minutes ago she'd made the decision to never look at him with sex on her mind again. To not talk to him unless for purely professional purposes. To not breathe in that gorgeous smell that made her legs weak and her head woozy.

Oops. Too late.

That had been one hell of a kiss.

Long and hard. It had stoked a fierce need in him. And Nate wanted to do it again. Now.

What Nate wanted, Nate always got.

But not Sasha. And that was the biggest bounce his ego had taken in a long time, so much so he'd come back for more. Against all better judgement and Dario's protestations. Strange what frank hot-blooded lust could do to a man.

Two hours of immersing himself in choir rehearsals and he still couldn't take his eyes off her, off the wide-legged trousers and floaty top with a plunging flouncy neckline that gave him enough glimpse of her breasts to strain for more. Couldn't forget how she'd felt in his arms, how she'd wanted that kiss as much as he had. He'd seen it brimming in her eyes, felt it in her body's response.

And, okay, she'd been right to end it. Having seen the salacious photos in the paper he knew his most sensible course of action was to leave her alone.

Harsh truth: he couldn't give her what she wanted. He didn't do relationships; flings yes, togetherness, no. He preferred keeping a distance, not making promises; the only connection he enjoyed was physical. And Sasha was definitely the all-or-nothing fairy-tale melding-of-souls kind of woman.

So it was a good thing he wouldn't see her again after the concert.

Wasn't it?

She walked towards him, heels tapping across the parquet floor, her floral scent drifting around him and drawing him closer, firing all his senses on full alert.

'Once again you've come to the rescue and made the performances so much stronger. You know so much about creating a good show, theatrics, stage presence…everything. The kids really react well to your tuition, Nathan. You're a good teacher.'

'Nah. They're good at listening.' But the swell of pride in his chest left little room for oxygen. He'd spent so much of his time working on his performances, his career, his spectacularly colourful downtime, he hadn't had the chance to think how he might be able to help others. Until now, and it felt surprisingly good.

Sasha had packed everything away apart from a thick wad of large posters in her hand, which she showed him, delight emanating from her erect posture and eager eyes. 'Do you like these? I've sent them to the local radio stations and I'm going to put them in the shop windows in the mall.'

'Wow. They're good.' Artfully crafted and bright enough to catch anyone's eye. 'But can you make my name smaller?

Less bold? It's a shame to have it dominating the line-up when the kids have done all the work.'

'You don't like it?' She seemed deflated. 'We thought we'd sell more tickets if we put you centre. You seem to make headlines whatever you do.'

'Not everyone has the same bouncy positivity you have. I did warn you it would be ugly.'

She shook her head and held up a finger. 'Okay. Well, let's put the other night completely behind us. I've forgotten it already. We need to focus forward on getting those kids to the competition. That's what this is about.'

Forget it? He'd come running back for more.

But she was right, this wasn't about him or that kiss, it was about kids like Marshall. 'How many tickets have you sold?'

'None as yet. I have to collect them from the printers now, on my way to the shops.' Glancing at her watch, she said, 'Oops…before they close.'

'You made the posters. You collect the tickets. You do the drop-offs. Is there no one else to help?'

'Are you offering?'

No way.

At his hesitation she laughed, resignedly. 'I thought not. The kids helped with the poster design and they're all taking tickets home to sell door-to-door. But I said I'd do this. And no, there is no one else to help, Nathan. And that's absolutely fine.'

'I could get someone to do it for you.' That would get the job done without getting his hands dirty, and his head even more messed up by being with her longer than was good for him. 'You know, you work too hard.'

'Says Mr My-job-is-my-life. If I do it I know the information has been given correctly. I'm invested in this. I can't risk someone else making a mess of it.'

'It's a poster, for a kids' show. What mess could they

make? They stick it in a window, with tape.' But okay, he got it. She took her job and her responsibilities very seriously. She was dedicated and ambitious. He respected her drive and attention to detail—even if it did get bloody annoying at times. That, and the fact she was an out-of-control control freak, meant she had to do the donkey work. On her own.

He followed her out into the afternoon sunshine, tried hard not to look at the way the light silhouetted her shapely legs through the flimsy trousers.

Suddenly the thought of her walking the littered grimy streets for those needy kids made his heart ache. 'You want some company?'

What the...?

'No, Nathan. Please don't.' She came to an abrupt halt and looked up at him, doubt and uncertainty swimming in her eyes. Shoulders hiked again around her ears.

'Don't what?'

A muscle in her jaw tensed and he suspected she was biting back what she really wanted to say. 'Don't be kind to me.'

That was a label no one had pinned on him before. 'Whoa, Sasha, no. That wasn't my intention. I was more concerned that the publicity machine cranks into action sooner rather than later. There's only a week to go and I refuse to perform to a half-filled house. You dawdling here chewing the fat isn't getting the job done. But it's okay, do it on your own. Take as long as you like. Fine.'

'Great.' Her eyes rolled. 'You give, and then you take away. Typical.'

'Now I'm the bad guy?'

'Nathan, you're always the bad guy.'

Figures. And he was well and truly backed into a corner. 'I won't try to kiss you again, if that's what you're worried about. Although, I am going to think about it. A lot.'

The shoulders relaxed a little and a hint of a smile played over her lips. 'Thinking I don't particularly care about. Acting is definitely a no-no. There are way too many shop fronts out there. We'd never get any of these posters delivered. Just so you know, and in case you're in any way confused about the issue—kissing is not going to happen again.'

'And there was me thinking you'd forgotten all about it.' So the kiss had been eating her. It had eaten away at him too, but now he just ached for more. And she clearly… didn't. 'Okay. No kissing. You have my word.'

'Good. Definitely.' She chewed the corner of her lip and he wanted to smother those lips all over again. Wanted to explore other parts of her body too. Heat zipped through his veins.

Leaning closer, he whispered in her ear, 'Are you trying to convince me? Or yourself?'

'You. I'm already well and truly convinced. So it's good you understand. Good. Brilliant. Fabulous. No kissing.' She glanced towards the street. 'Er…no one's lurking in the shadows. Are you on your own today? Tweedle Dum gone rogue?'

'I gave Dario the afternoon off. Is that so strange?' Yup. Dario had certainly thought so, seeing as they usually spent pretty much every waking moment together.

But since that doorway kiss Nate hadn't been able to focus on anything, certainly not on scheduling another tour or a round of TV interviews to promote his new album. Couldn't stand being cooped up in an office. Didn't want to be outside. Couldn't bear listening to Dario's retorts about getting too serious about a bunch of kids going nowhere.

Driving around had done nothing to salve his unease. Suddenly he'd found himself back here. Fuelled by lust. No plan, as always. As she said. Rushing headlong into danger, and meeting disaster along the way. 'This gig has my name on it—it's got to work or I look lame. I just wanted to see how rehearsals were going. He didn't. So I came solo.'

'Okay…well, you're here now and it's getting late.' She handed him a roll of tape. 'Put your money where your big mouth is and get sticking. But don't expect a heap of excitement. It's only Chesterton, and you know what that's like.' Her voice was breathy, trying to be nonchalant. 'It'll be dull and dreary.'

It was far from that. Other than having to stop every five minutes for Sasha to speak to a friend, a neighbour, a parent of a pupil, a colleague, they managed a lot of laughs and convinced fifteen shopkeepers to display her poster.

'No one's recognised you yet. Great disguise today, by the way.'

'I guess no one expects Nate Munro to be ambling down the high street.' He pulled the hoodie more tightly over his head, and pushed the aviator shades back, blending in with the other guys milling around.

Nothing had changed. Sure, the hardware store was now a one-pound shop, the butchers had closed down, more estate agents, a couple of different burger bars, the feel was still very much rundown and shabby. Just as he remembered.

But the sun glinted off the windows; people smiled as they walked by; it was shabby with hope. And that hadn't been there ten years ago. At least he'd never seen it. But he'd been so engulfed by his own private war that he hadn't been able to see past his fists and his anger.

Maybe if he'd looked outside instead of dwelling on the inner pain he'd have made fewer devastating mistakes and even stayed a little longer. Who knew what his life would have been like then? Would he have married Sasha as she'd planned? Would he have ordinary friends he could trust instead of people trampling over him to get what they wanted?

Would he have saved Marshall?

Would Marshall have even *needed* saving? That, he didn't want to think about.

She stopped outside a quaint-looking Italian restaurant. Painted bright red with chipped wooden shutters, windows dressed with café-style net curtains, it looked as if it had been uprooted from Nate's favourite Italian village and plonked down in south London. 'This place has the best pasta in town. Do you want to come in and wait while I talk to lovely Luigi? He's bound to want to help the choir—he's always such a good supporter of the school.'

'Lovely Luigi?'

The spike of jealousy that erupted from nowhere must have shown on his face, because she smiled and shoved her hands on her waist. 'The owner. He's about a hundred.'

No man from the age of five upwards would be blind to Sasha's sunny sensual appeal. He wasn't going to take any chances. 'Believe me, sweet thing, it doesn't matter what age they are, if they've got it, they'll use it.'

'Oh, I can manage. I usually fight all those hordes of men off with a stick. But I guess today you'll have to do. Be nice.'

'Aren't I always?'

'No.'

Within seconds they were ensconced at a table with a background of soft lilting opera music. Rather, Nate was ensconced, alone, while Sasha's attention was held at the bar by three elderly Italian men. One stared into her eyes and smiled inanely. One poured her a drink of *prosecco*, and Luigi, the elderly patriarch, brought her little tidbits of food to try from the kitchen.

Eventually she meandered over with two glasses of wine and handed him one, her eyes bright. 'That's eight tickets sold. They're all aware of who you are and they've sworn not to tell a soul that you're here. And they would be honoured to bring you some food, if you have the time.'

Not really but he'd make an exception. He kind of liked the comfortable feel of the place, with no one pressing for his attention or fawning over him. Shucking the hoodie over his head he relaxed into relative anonymity. 'I'd be honoured to eat it. I love Italian food.'

'Me too.' She sat opposite him and ran her hands over the dark green plastic tablecloth. 'I've been saving to go on a trip to Italy one day. Luigi has given me lists of all the best things to do and how to discover the places where the locals eat in Florence and Siena. Apparently they're a well-kept secret.'

'You just need to know who to ask. Usually a bit of grappa works as a bribe.'

'You seem to know a lot about it. Have you been to Italy?' She laughed. 'Stupid question, really, you've probably been everywhere and I must seem like a Hicksville country cousin.'

'There's nothing Hicksville about living in South London. It's more like the wild west. I'm sure you'll get to Italy one day, Sasha. Of all the people I know, you are the one who always achieved what she set out to do.' Without any cut-throat, malicious back-stabbing too. She manoeuvred with ease, making sure everyone else was comfortable and safe too, rather than grasping for what she wanted, regardless. 'You just haven't had the breaks I've had. I've been very lucky to travel the world. Even if I did see most of it from a hotel window.'

'Well, Italy's on my bucket list. It would be a perfect start, especially if they have food like this.' She tore off a piece of bread, offered it to him so naturally, as if caring and nurturing ran in her blood. His heart snagged at the tender gesture. Some guy would be lucky to have her as a wife. A family. She completed that picture.

But not for him. He hadn't been joking when he'd said marriage would be the kiss of death to his career. To his privacy. To the steel he'd constructed around his heart.

He found her a smile of thanks, dipped the bread in a dish of thick dark green olive oil and ate it. It was perfect rustic ciabatta, the like of which he'd only ever had in his local village. The place he told no one about, the only sanctuary he had away from the madness.

And yet suddenly the words were spilling from his lips. 'I have a place in Tuscany. Unfortunately I don't get to visit very often. I haven't been for a couple of years, what with the tour, filming...' He neglected to tell her he'd had plans to go next week, but had cancelled them for her concert. There would be other times.

After swallowing her bread, she cleared her delicate throat, took a sip of the light sparkling wine. 'Aren't you more the party-animal type? Isn't Ibiza more your thing?'

'It was.' He shrugged, suppressing a smile at the chaos of party central and his part in its rise in popularity amongst the celebrity set. 'For a while. Until I got kicked out.'

'Really? Why am I not surprised?' Watching the innocent shock in her eyes was pure delight.

He laughed and felt the warm relaxation that only decent food and good company could bring. Something that had been missing from his life for too long. When he got back to Malibu he was definitely sacking the chef. Too much raw organic food made a man go quietly insane.

'I had a few more-than-wild parties, caused some damage. They wanted to ban me but I make them far too much cash. Mind you, they have to spend a lot too. Driving cars into pools takes some paying for.' He leaned back in his chair, stretched his legs under the table. 'I'm getting just a little tired of that.'

Her brows knotted. 'Nate Munro tired of partying? Is the world coming to an end? What will the papers be full of now? Proper news?'

'Hey, I'm just a little bored of the same old scene, on the lookout for something new, the next big thing. I'm not ready for my pipe and slippers yet.'

'Slippers. Ah, yes. Somehow I just can't see you in woolly tartan.' The smile she gave him was gentle and wistful, as if she was enjoying her own private joke. 'So, tell me about the delightful Jasmine.'

He didn't want to talk about himself, and definitely not about Jasmine. He wanted to find out about Sasha, what made her tick now, what she liked to do. Just listening to her sweet soft voice soothed his aching head.

And watching her mouth as she talked almost drove him mad with desire. Each moment he didn't touch her was a study in self-control. But he was running out. Fast.

'My ex? My wannabe wife. Nothing to say really. She subscribes to the take, take, take, mantra. She always wants more. And it's never enough.' Or he wasn't enough. Jasmine had thrown back at him one too many times that he was missing the human connection gene. *You have to give a little, Nate.* Seemed she didn't just mean his credit card. 'We dated, moved in together for a while. Then she left me, fleeced me but I'm still her fall-back guy, should her master plan to hook an even more rich and famous sucker not work out.'

The little frown lining Sasha's forehead dipped. 'And yet you smile and talk to her like she's so important to you.'

'She's Dario's little sister. I have to show respect.'

'Ah.'

'It's complicated.'

'Is there anything about you that isn't?'

'Probably not. Things get incestuous out there. Every-one's connected to somebody. Or wants to be. Or tries to be.' He grinned at her rapid blink. 'A long time ago Dario helped me when I needed someone. Upshot is, I owe him a lot.' And now he'd said way too much about his private life and still knew nothing about hers. But that was her through and through: she gave a little, but never quite enough. Now, why did that have a familiar ring to it? 'What about you?'

'Me? Oh, I don't owe Dario anything.'

He snorted into his wine. 'Be gentle with me, Sasha. That sharp wit could pierce a man's heart. You know what I mean—what about your life?'

'Oh, okay.' She winked. 'Let me think…I have no minder, no significant ex who fleeced me. I have no houses in Italy and the States…'

'No boyfriend? Husband? Secret baby?'

'If I told you about the baby, it wouldn't be secret then, would it?' At his frown she shrugged. 'Okay, there's no baby.'

'And husband?'

'Ah…' Waving her hand nonchalantly she flashed a serene smile. 'Number one was lovely but secretly gay, but we had a lot of fun shopping. Number two…' She sighed and put a hand to her chest. 'Tragic. Number three—'

'Wait! What? Number three?'

'Come on, Nate. Please. I have no babies. No husbands, ex or otherwise. This is Chesterton not California. And this is me, Sasha, schoolteacher, not your average pack-a-whole-lifetime-in-before-you're-twenty-one Hollywood starlet. After you left town I finished school, went to uni. I haven't found Mr Right yet—he's strangely elusive. Or maybe I'm just too picky.'

'Well, that's a relief.'

'Why?'

Yeah. Why? It was none of his business who she'd slept with or what her marriage plans were. But for some reason he wanted to kick her Mr Right into touch. 'You're far too young to settle down.'

She shot him a look of amusement. 'You need to talk to Cassie then. She thinks I'm over the hill and that I need to find a husband quick, before I get too old and no one would want me.'

How could anyone not want her? The V in her top drew his gaze. Tiny pearl buttons ran over the swell of her breasts and he wondered how easy it would be to pop them open. One. By. One. And once undone, what would he find underneath? Lace? Silk?

His brain filled with a sexual haze. His voice was rough as he spoke. 'Well, make sure you don't rush into anything. Take your time.'

'What? Relationship advice, from you? That's a hoot.' She laughed. 'But don't fret, I'm never one to rush into things. I like to take things slow and steady. You probably think my life is deathly boring but I like it.'

Boring? Most definitely not, but he knew her well enough not to push the subject. Sasha had lived through more trauma than most other people hc knew. Her father's suicide had been a bolt out of the blue, which she always flatly refused to talk about. It was only when other friends had mentioned it at school that he'd found out. Even then, the details had been sketchy. That she hadn't trusted him enough to confide had bitten hard. 'Hey, it's your life, live it how you like. I do.'

'And we all know how well that works out. Meanwhile, I stick to my life plan.' Her mouth tipped into a smile that he wanted to taste.

Kissing her would be very bad. And so damned good. But he'd promised. 'But it is such a waste.'

'Of what?'

'All that brain-power spent on graphs and spreadsheets. So...linear and neat and ordered. When you could

be thinking up ways to spend your time more…messily…'
He leaned closer, watched the flush on her cheeks, imagined her breathless and spent in his bed, her legs wrapped round him. 'Messy is good. Messy is better than good. I could show you some time.'

'Er…no thanks. I'm busy…For ever.' She coughed midfluster, tapping her hand against her cheek, the composed act failing. She was anything but. How easy would it be to strip her back to the hot woman he'd had in his arms on the edge of dirty sex? 'Then, once I qualified I came back here, got my job at Chesterton High and bought my small but perfectly formed flat in the new development on Fairlie Street. I've come full circle.'

'In more ways than one.' He smiled at her confusion as his fingertips brushed against hers. A shot of electricity shot through him as skin met skin. 'You. Me. Us.'

She withdrew her hand immediately, leaving a cold breath of air in its wake. 'Oh, no. No, Nate. Please, don't even think that. There can't be any *us*.'

CHAPTER EIGHT

BRILLIANT. NATE'S STOMACH plummeted. *Good shot, Mr Superstar.*

He'd met presidents and royalty, given speeches and interviews, but had never been tongue-tied by a schoolteacher before.

'Don't get the wrong impression.' Now she'd think he was a nut-job with his spectacular slip of the tongue. 'I meant, it's funny us sitting here in a café in Chesterton after all these years...'

'I see.' She didn't look convinced. And neither was he. He was rattled. He didn't do this. Assumptions, jealousy, possession. What was happening to him?

Before he could explain further Luigi interrupted with plates laden with antipasto, delicious bite-sized chunks of artichokes, glistening plump olives, spicy salami, salty prosciutto. And a jug of dark earthy *chianti classico*. More aromas of garlic and herbs spilled from the kitchen, elemental and sensual. Now he'd have to stick around and worm his way out of embarrassment.

'Eat. Eat. Please,' Luigi pleaded as he fussed around them, squeezing his large belly between the tables. 'There is more coming for my new friend, Nate Munro. And bella Sasha.'

Bella Sasha. That was her in a nutshell. Beautiful. Confident in her own space, and modest. She even had the ancient Luigi eating out of her hand.

'There is one thing, though.' She leaned forward, her words hesitant, as if she was trying to work out the right thing to say. 'I'd like to talk to you about Marshall, to say how sorry I was about his death. I heard from one of your mum's neighbours, and then I heard about her death a few weeks later too. I wanted to send something or to write to you, even go to their funerals, but everything was so private and I didn't want to impose. Marshall was such a joy to know. Everyone loved him.'

Not everyone. But Nate didn't want to go into that now. Regardless of how Sasha made him feel, wanting her in his bed was very different from trusting her with the part of his heart he kept sealed off. The image he'd carefully constructed to keep everyone from knowing the real Nate Munro was too ingrained in him now.

But he could give her a little. Any more than that and he didn't know if he'd be able to stop. 'Yeah. It was a difficult time. If only I…'

She frowned. 'What do you mean? What happened?'

Too late. Pain twisted inside him. 'Nothing.'

A fraught silence hovered between them as she waited for him to explain. When he didn't, she sighed. 'It's okay, I get the picture—you hurt too much. You must miss him terribly.'

He could be upfront about this at least. 'I do. It's like an ache that doesn't go away.'

He'd landed a kid in Intensive Care, lost the respect of his school, the love of his girlfriend, and then the life of his beloved brother and mother. All because he'd had a stupid inflated sense of self-belief.

'Hey, but I certainly mourned them in spectacular fashion. That self-destruct button jammed hard and fast, taking every cliché to excess: wine, women. And the songs.

Introspective and pathetic.' Shrugging, he laughed. 'Gotta love that minor key.'

'But heartfelt and eerily haunting. Truthful.'

'It doesn't matter. It won't right all the wrongs—it won't change the decisions I made, the stupid stuff. It won't bring him back.' The stab to his heart was tight and sharp.

'If it's any consolation, I know how you feel, Nate. It's like…like a light has gone out in your soul.'

For a second his mask almost slipped as he looked up and saw the tears swimming in her eyes. Her hand touched his as she fought to control the wobbling lip. His hurt was all mixed up with the loss of her father.

And he fought to breathe through the weight pressing in on his chest. He didn't do this. Open Pandora's box and let his emotions out, not when he had no idea how to shut them off again without a struggle.

He needed to get out before he hit that self-destruct button again, and dragged beautiful, innocent Sasha down with him.

Scraping the chair back, he stood. 'I've got to go.'

The school hall buzzed with thick, palpable excitement. A queue for entry had begun four hours before the doors opened and, judging by the din of chatter out there, the audience were just as excited as the performers.

'George, Tyler, please stay away from the curtain. We don't want the audience to see you before the opening song—it'll ruin the surprise.' Keeping the kids focused was like trying to herd cats. 'Let's pretend this is the actual competition instead of the fundraiser. Be professional and confident but, most of all, enjoy yourselves. Big smiles.'

'Hey, Miss Sweet. Cute outfit.' There it was again. Behind her. That dark voice that made her weak-kneed. The press of his palm on her back. The scent that made her heart do loop-the-loops. She wasn't sure he'd even turn up after his disappearing act the minute she'd probed a little deeper under that thick skin of his. Even if he didn't have a sign round his neck flashing *keep out*, she'd certainly got the message.

'Nate!' She pulled him to the shadows at the side of the stage, ostensibly to prep him for the show, but in reality to grab a few seconds with him, alone. 'Do you ever approach anyone from the front?'

'And spoil the element of surprise?'

'One of these days you're going to give me a heart attack.' One day? No more days. Two more hours and he'd be gone.

And he looked awful. Sure, he was picture-perfect performance ready, and few would notice the dark shadows round his eyes, the clenched jaw, the hollowed-out cheeks. But she did. She knew enough about Nate Munro to read the signs.

'Big night last night?'

'Yep. And the night before...and the one before that... you get the picture. Too many early mornings and late nights.' How easily he slipped back into his life. At least he hadn't said *too many women*. For that she was grateful. He ran a hand through his masterfully scruffed hair. Which she would not touch. Would. Not. 'Don't worry, I'll live, and I won't let you all down. I'm still match fit.'

'Well, I suppose we should be grateful you're here at all, then, even if you do look like crap.'

'Hey, steady with the compliments—you'll give me a big head.'

'Very unlikely. Is it possible for it to get any bigger?'

'I'll never have a big head with you keeping me grounded.' He grinned, but she couldn't help thinking his deterioration had something to do with their last conversation about Marshall. Clearly there was a lot more to the story than he was prepared to share. But it wasn't her place to ask questions and push him into a corner, she'd learnt to her cost—the last time that had happened he'd screamed at her about breaking trust. And then walked out of her life.

He grinned. 'Excited about tonight?'

'Yes. Very much. Thank you for doing this.'

'My pleasure. To be honest, I wasn't convinced at first, but this whole experience has been…interesting.' His mouth twitched and his arm wrapped round her waist, pressing her long black silk dress to her body as he slipped a nonchalant kiss on her cheek.

The fingers of his other hand played with the way-more-than-she-wanted-to-pay professionally styled curls bouncing around her cheeks. 'And just look at you, sweet thing. Amazing. You've done well for yourself—you should be proud.'

'I am.'

Now his hand ran across the dip of her very bare collarbone sending hot shivers of desire arcing through her.

She reached to the zipper on his leather jacket, and looked up into his face wishing she could stop time and stay wrapped in his arms for a few more minutes.

For for ever? The thought shook through her. Once that had been all she'd dreamed of, but now it seemed a ridiculous idea. Things had changed: *she'd* changed. Moved on, wanted very different things. But it was enough to be the sole focus of those caramel eyes for a few more minutes.

She smiled, warily. 'Listen, I'm sorry about the other night.'

'Hey. Hush.' Pressing a finger to her lips, he stopped her. She remembered the way his mouth had fitted so perfectly over hers, how he had tasted. And her gut twisted with an ache for more.

He shook his head. '*I'm* sorry. It was my fault, not yours. I shouldn't have dodged out so fast, I should have stayed.'

Her heart squeezed. When? Ten years ago? Or the other day?

She laughed it off. 'But that's you all over, Nate. Always rushing on to the next thing.' Always running away when things get tough.

'I like to keep busy—it keeps me out of mischief. I could have done with being busy these last few days.' His eyes widened and she wondered what he'd been doing. But she had no claims on him.

'Please, spare me the gory details.'

'It's not what you think. The only…liaison…I had was with my old mate Jack. *Daniels*. We had some serious catching up to do. He's a good friend, but he does make my head hurt after a while.' As her blood pressure steadied he tipped his head towards the stage. 'They look awesome. You're going to knock that audience's socks off.'

The choir had assembled ready to start, resplendent in their black tuxedoes. 'Gosh yes, I'm so proud of them. They've come so far, and worked so hard. Tonight's just a first step on their journey.'

But for her and Nate it was with the end.

'Almost curtain up.' He winked as the front of house dimmed and an expectant hush shivered through the hall. Breathing deeply, he grinned. 'Can you feel that buzz? Man, I love this stuff. Every. Single. Time. It's like a drug. It's what keeps me alive. Break a leg, sweet thing.'

'You too.' She paused, and then words escaped her lips before she had a chance to stop them. 'And then?'

It was almost a whisper, swamped as the music started to play. What she was hoping for she didn't know. A declaration that he felt the same way as she did? Which was unsure and rocky, but turned on. That he wanted to see where these feelings could take them?

She just wanted more time to…to what? To get to know Nathan all over again? No, to understand this new Nate.

The man behind the public image. The one she was already too intrigued by. Mr Wrong.

And not a slipper in sight.

To hell with bloody slippers. A decision crystallised. Every look he gave her told her he wanted her. Even though he would leave. She was okay with that.

She was sick of being scared, allowing her need for control to define her. She would let go. Grasp the passion she'd denied herself for so long. Just once. Give in to dangerous temptation, then she could go back to her nice safe life where passion was a distant memory. Something other people did.

If he asked, she would say yes. She would take him for herself.

The curtain began to open.

He turned to her, his mouth kicked up in a smile that looked a lot like regret. Because, in reality she was way too late. The chances he'd offered her were now just a forgotten living-for-the-moment rock-star whim. He was probably already planning his next conquest.

'And then, Sasha, I'm getting the first plane out of here.'

Once the applause died down Nate took the microphone ready to squeeze the appreciative audience for everything they had. If she wouldn't take a cent from him he'd make sure Sasha got what she needed and more, somehow. It was the least he could do before he headed back home to the States.

'Thanks very much for your support, everyone. Weren't they amazing? There are some buckets going round for your donations—please dig deep. You know it's for a good cause. Let's get this choir to Manchester.'

'Thanks. Wow. That was…bloody brilliant.' Sasha greeted him as he finally left the stage, her smile as bright as the spotlights.

'Language, Miss Sweet. Brilliant? It was epic.' He fist-pumped the air in lieu of picking her up and hugging her. Touching her made him want her even more. He'd almost kissed her backstage, and that would have been a big mistake so close to leaving.

'They were great. They did everything we asked, and more. Man, that was fun.'

'Thank you so much. Just…thank you, thank you. We've made enough money to make Manchester a real trip to remember. It won't matter if we don't win the competition after this—it feels like we've won the jackpot already.' Tiptoeing, she pressed a kiss to his cheek. 'They've excelled under your guidance. You're a natural with kids.'

At the briefest touch of her skin against his heat flared through him; all thought of the choir and the applause faded away. The rush of his usual post-performance heat hit Nate square in the groin, but, instead of being a need for a quick release, this time it was a long intense ache that threatened to overpower him.

The ache belonged to Sasha. Just her. Not the performance. Not the adoration from his fans. Just Sasha. Nothing else matched the adrenaline boost he got just being with her and he didn't want to lose that, not yet.

Her lips parted, just enough for him to see the tip of her tongue, the wet that he wanted to taste. Her breathing quickened and her gaze locked with his. For a nanosecond the air stilled and that invisible connection tightened around them, weaving in more complex patterns, snaring them like a spider's web, until there was nothing, no one in the world but them, caught in a magical sphere from which there was no escape.

The truth flickered in her eyes. She wanted him. And he wanted her. Wanted to kiss that mouth, to explore those curves. To lose himself in her.

But he'd already packed his bags.

'Come with me.' His voice was more growl than groan as he pressed his mouth to her ear. For a second he thought he meant *back to LA*. Anywhere. But he brushed that idea away as too intense, too complex. He couldn't think past now. Here.

Dragging her into the darkest corner he could find, he pressed her against a wall. Ran his fingertips over the curve of her cheek, into her hairline, couldn't take his eyes away from her heated gaze. His thumb ran tiny circles along her jaw until it hit the corner of her mouth, which puckered. But what turned him on most was the sheer need in those eyes.

Before he knew what he was doing he crushed his mouth on hers. This time he didn't want to be gentle, didn't want to savour her taste, he wanted to take her, possess her.

And she responded with equal hunger, a greedy meshing of souls, with a deep thirst for more. Her desire fuelled his as she rocked against him, gentle moans coming from her throat, her hands cupping his backside and pulling him closer until they were body on body, skin on skin.

It was too much, but nowhere near enough.

And all too quickly she pushed away, breathless and hot. 'God, what are we doing?'

Searching her face, he wondered whether she was joking. He couldn't help the smile. 'I think that's pretty obvious.'

'But we can't.'

'We just did.'

'Not here, you noggin. There's…there's too many reasons. There's way too much to do out there. We can't get carried away. Goodness.' She playfully struggled against him, but she was laughing, her head tipped back, and the delicate curve of her throat moved with the musical sound.

He planted a kiss to the racing pulse at her throat, breathed in her scent, and she wrapped her arms around his neck, pressing closer so he could feel the soft shape of her beneath the silky fabric.

'Forget everything else, Sash. Let someone else sort it out. One of the other teachers, the mums. The choir. Somebody. Anybody. But not you.' His hands ran down the back of the soft fabric; on their way they discovered the ridge of a bra strap, the outline of her pants. 'I have plans for you right here.'

'What if the cash gets stolen?'

'You know, you worry too much.'

'Hey, I live in this neighbourhood. I have due cause to worry.' She squirmed as he licked against the nape of her neck, whispering through a stifled giggle, 'Besides, someone might see us.'

'Story of my life.' He sighed and leaned his head against hers. They were hidden enough behind large boxes and electrical equipment, but she had a point.

Sasha always had a good point, but he was always too busy enjoying the moment to think through the consequences of his actions. But, well, he didn't want to let go of *this* moment. 'This thing between us, it isn't going away, is it?'

'No, I guess not.'

'Staying away doesn't help. Being with you makes it worse. D'you think we should do something about it?' When he palmed her breast through the folds of her dress she moaned and pressed harder against him.

'I could be convinced.' She bit her bottom lip and her cheeks pinked. She knew exactly what he was asking, and her blatant answer surprised him. 'But where would we go?'

'I don't know. There's a prowl of photographers out there just waiting to catch me. They'll follow us to my hotel, make a scene.'

Pushing her hands against his chest, she nodded. 'My place, then. They surely won't be interested in me and how I leave this place. My car's out the back. The pink saloon nearest the gym. You want to risk it?'

Good question. Risk what? His privacy? Hers? His heart? 'Do you?'

Stupid to ask her that question—now uncertainty flitted across her face. A sharp intake of breath. A frown. He could see the workings of her mind, the answers she struggled to find. Sasha, who planned everything, who factored danger and risk into every moment. 'I…I don't…know…'

He took one of her hands. 'Sasha, I can't promise you anything, certainly not the stable future you crave. You need to know I am going back to LA.'

So where was he going with this? *Sleep with me. Make love with me. Stay with me, just once.* First time in living memory that he'd had to ask. And he liked her all the more for it.

He hoped she could see that he was being genuine for once in his life, and that this wasn't some kind of play. That it was Sasha he wanted, not just anyone.

Was it? Whether he played her or not, he hoped the end result would be the same. Him. Her. Hot, and sticky.

Her gaze burnt with desire.

He fought the need to have her now against the back wall. But it almost killed him. 'Sasha, I swear to God, if you don't stop looking at me like that I won't be held responsible for the headlines tomorrow. *Teacher and rock star found in flagrante backstage.*'

She ran her finger along his jawline, the passion mingling with anxiety as she struggled with the enticement of living dangerously. Foreign territory for a practical planning kind of girl.

Fiddling with a lock of her hair, she sighed. 'What about your plans? Your flight?'

'It's just an interview. It can wait. I'll reschedule, go tomorrow.' He was losing her.

Kissing her neck seemed to focus her on task—which involved her hand on his back, running up and down his spine. Those lips against his neck. Her breasts pressed tight against him. Her scent stoking the fire burning in his gut. 'What do you say, come on, do something spontaneous, let's have a few more minutes together. I'll make it worth every second, I promise.'

'I don't know…'

'Come on, we're good together—you can't deny that. I'll get Dario to head the press off out the front.'

'So he does have some uses after all. He's starting to grow on me.' Her red curls shivered as she seemed to reconcile some kind of battle going on in her head. She took a long deep breath but didn't come up with the reply he was hedging towards.

'It's an easy answer, woman. Yes or no. No need to make a whole new plan or a quick list of pros and cons. It'll be good, I promise you that.' He spoke into her ear. Slowly. Making sure she understood. 'Very. Very. Good.'

To his relief she nodded. 'Okay, I'll sort out the cash and the mess. Meet you out the back in, what, fifteen minutes?'

'Fifteen? Can't you be any quicker?' Fifteen minutes was enough time for all those doubts to start creeping back. Nuzzling his hardness against her thigh, he nibbled her ear lobe. 'Make it ten?'

Her moan was frank and loud. 'God, if you promise to do that again, I'll be ready in five.'

CHAPTER NINE

SOMEHOW, SASHA COULDN'T remember how, they'd reached her apartment, fallen onto her bed, their kisses hard and hot and turning her brain to mush. Nathan's hands were like magic, sending spasms of ecstasy through her with every touch. She wanted more of his kisses. She wanted him naked. She wanted him now.

She fumbled with his belt, tugged at his zip, the hardness of his erection making her stomach clench in anticipation. And just a little fear. He was so big. So hard.

You can handle this.

He lay against her, eyes dark with frank desire as he unfastened her bra and cupped her breast. 'Hey, slow down, Sasha. We've got all night.' His head tipped and he sucked her nipple into his mouth, sending heat shimmering through to her core. 'You're right, you have changed. You're in a hurry.'

She wanted to tell him, no. That she was still the same scared person underneath, that she didn't know if she would be enough for him, that she didn't know what she was doing, but, God, it felt so good.

He pressed against her, the thick weight of him, the smell of him filling her body with sensations she'd never had before, breathtaking, heart-stalling sensations that made her lose touch with reality. Her hands ran along the waistband of his trousers to the hard-muscled V of his abdomen as she relished his sharp intake of breath, his skin puckering under her fingers; his T-shirt, like her dress, long since cast aside, who knew where. 'Sorry. I just…I just…'

She needed to have him before her courage faltered.

He stopped her shaking hand with his. 'I know. Crazy, eh? But take it steady. I've waited a long time for this and now I want to enjoy you.' His tongue ran tiny circles down her ribcage, across her abdomen, tracing a wet trail towards her pants, his hands making her sigh with pleasure as he stroked the inside of her thigh. 'I want to make you moan.'

She did, long and hard. And again as he ripped her pants aside, opened her legs and slid his fingers over her opening. Fierce heat almost engulfed her. 'Oh, God. Oh, God. Oh—'

As she writhed against his hand a delicious ache deep inside began to swell, flushing her body in heat, a feeling she was losing herself to something beautiful, amazing. She needed more pressure, more heat…Losing herself. Losing…

Stop.

No.

Clear as day, the words rang loudly in her head. *Stop. Stop.*

No!

She clutched the duvet in her fist. Shifted away from his hand.

Why? Why always this? Why couldn't it be different with Nathan? She *wanted* to submit to the pleasure he gave her. She *wanted* to be carried away on a tide of passion. She *wanted* to lose control.

But it was as if she were outside her body looking down on them on the bed, all feelings bolted in a flurry of panic. The surge from his touch cut, like a power outage.

He followed her up the bed, his hands still locked on her buttocks. 'You okay?'

'I…um…'

In the dim light she watched confusion flit across his face. *Yeah, you and me too.* He shifted next to her and stroked a knuckle down her cheek. 'Did I tell you how beautiful you are?'

She nodded, curling into his hand, caught her bottom lip with her teeth. 'Yes.'

'Do you believe me?' He thought she was worried about how she looked? Just like all the other Hollywood women he usually slept with, no doubt. If only it were that simple. 'You're so...real, Sash. Raw. Honest. The most beautiful woman I've ever met.'

Bringing her face to his, he dropped feather kisses along her swollen mouth, to her neck. Her eyes fluttered closed as she tried to relax into his arms again.

But she couldn't. After a moment of trying she put her hands on his shoulders and gave gentle pressure. 'I'm sorry. I'm not ready for this.'

He smiled so tenderly it almost took her breath away. 'What is it? What's wrong?' Then he hit his head with his palm, eyes wide. Was he covering up a *laugh*? 'Tell me you're not still a virgin? Surely...'

'No.' But she might as well be. A rash of heat bloomed in her core and spread out to her skin. How to say this? 'I mean...there have been a couple of times. I never really... well, it didn't do much for me.'

'Seriously, girl. You've been doing it with the wrong men.'

As if she didn't know that already.

But it wasn't really their fault. She'd been too wound up, too worried about whether she could do it, about giving herself up to someone else, each thrust had caused her pain and the more she'd tensed, the worse it had become. Until she'd given up trying.

'It hurts, usually. I can't ever seem to relax properly. And I've never...you know...come.'

His laugh was soft. 'But I think you almost did.'

'That's the point exactly. *Almost.*'

'You just need to go with the flow. Let yourself ride with it. Let go.'

'Easy for you to say. You're so laid-back you're hardly holding on in the first place.' She wanted to hide her face in embarrassment. This was what she was, after twenty-seven years? She'd managed easy relationships with the kids at school and her friends, family—sure. She'd never given any more of herself than she needed, always kept something back. Intimacy scared her but not as much as trusting someone.

And with Nathan? The thought of giving herself over to someone so sexually experienced, and who instilled such fierce emotions in her, was terrifying.

No. Impossible.

And now he would leave and she was a big fat failure.

But instead of leaving he covered her with the duvet and spooned against her, his chest against her back. For a moment she thought he was going to try to sleep, as with two fingers he closed both her eyelids. He spoke in a soft voice as he cuddled against her. 'It's okay. Let's take it really slow. Tell me, what do you want, Sasha? What do you like?'

'I don't know. What do you mean?' She tried to sit up but he held her close.

'Hey, it's just talking. That's all. You can do that.' He chuckled. 'I don't want a checklist. I want you to tell me what turns you on. Close your eyes. Do you like it when I kiss you?'

'Of course.' She closed her eyes again, sank into the pillows and thought about his kisses. They made her feel hot. So hot. Wanted. Sexy. 'Yes.'

'Tell me, then. Say it.'

'I like it when you kiss me.'

'Do you like my tongue in your mouth?'

'Yes.' She swallowed, hard. Her mouth suddenly dry and wet at the same time.

'Tell me more. Do you like it when I kiss your nipples?

'Yes.' God, yes. 'But I'm no good at this.'

'It's not a test. Just say it. I like it when you kiss my nipples.'

'I like it when you kiss…' She hardly recognised her own voice; it was thick and hoarse.

'Kiss what?'

'My nipples.' Her breasts ached and tingled for his hands, his mouth. All air seemed to have been sucked out of her lungs; she focused on breathing. In. Out.

She felt a gentle pressure against her hips as he began to rock against her. Just a little, but it sent skittering electricity through her. She pressed back against him, feeling his erection on her bottom. Wanting to touch it.

But he held her hand, kissed the soft underside of her wrist, leant his head against hers, whispering into her ear, 'What else do you like, Sasha? Did you like it when I touched you?'

'Oh. God. Yes.' Was it the sensation of his breath against her neck, or just thinking about his hands on her that made her shiver with anticipation?

'I know you did. I liked it too.' But he didn't lower his head to her thighs as she thought he might. Hoped he might.

His fingers tiptoed to her outer thigh. Then her inner thigh. Stroking slowly. So slowly she thought she might explode if he didn't touch her. There. Her whole body screamed out for his touch. 'Yes. There. Please, Nate. There.'

'Not yet. Just wait.' He rocked. She rocked back against his thickness. If she shifted her leg…oh. She felt him pressing along the edge of her sex. A fug of desire filled her head.

'What else do you like, Sasha?' Then his thumb found

the spot. Sweet soft pressure that wasn't nearly enough to satisfy her.

'I want…I want you to…' She couldn't think past his thumb circling and pressing, past the wild hunger swirling through her body. Through her head. She was losing herself.

'What do you want?'

Losing…

'What do you want?' His voice was louder now, focusing her on him. 'Sasha. Tell me what you want.'

'I want this.' Fierce need swelled up once again from deep inside, in a huge crescendo that she rode. Wave after wave of delicious peaks, each time bigger, better than the last. But still not enough…'I want this. I want…' Harder. Faster. Deeper. 'Oh, God. Oh, God. I want you.'

Her fingers slipped round his erection and she turned to face him, steering him towards her, her breath coming in short gasps. Nate didn't know if he could hold on long enough to get the condom on. If she could hold on. She was so close to the edge.

'Now, Nathan, please.'

'I don't want to hurt you. Steady, wait.'

'Now. *Please.*'

He quickly sheathed himself and pushed gently into her. Felt the stretch, the hesitation, the shock, but he kept up the pressure with his fingers, stroking and rubbing, until she relaxed. As she bucked against his hand he eased deeper into her heat.

For the first time ever he needed solid self-control. Didn't know if he could dredge it up. He had to get this right. For her. For himself. He had to show her what she'd been missing out on for so long. But watching her finally so close to the edge, unbuttoning that prim uptight exterior, feeling her nails rake against his back, had him alight with a raging fire.

Tight. Hot. Wet.

Slowly at first, until he couldn't hold back any more. He wanted to bury himself so deep inside her, deeper and deeper still.

And she met him stroke for stroke. Her legs inching up his thighs as she gripped and bucked against him. He found her mouth and kissed her greedily, taking every ounce of her that he could. She arched, her head thrown back, her gaze catching his, consuming him.

Until…

Until he thought he might lose himself completely in an arc of blinding pleasure, in the soft sound of her cries, in her sweet tightness as she finally let herself go and took him with her.

Twisting out of the tumble of sheets Sasha jolted upright and looked around her bedroom, then down at her bed.

Oh, double merry hell. It hadn't been a dream at all. A three-times-a-night kind of dream. A Best. Sex. Ever. Dream.

Next to her Nathan slept, his hair messed up, little laughter lines around his eyes. Butt naked, the cotton sheet strategically covering one of his best features, he looked like a model in a magazine shoot.

In her bed!

Her heart stuttered just to look at him. Even though she'd tried hard to prevent it she knew she was losing herself to him, little by little.

She hadn't known it was possible to soar so high, or how amazing sex could be when she finally let herself relax into it. To feel like a real woman. To feel wanted by a man like Nate. She'd grasped at an opportunity instead of planning the pros and cons. And there'd been a whole lot of pros.

But what on earth happened now? She hadn't planned for that either. Hadn't planned for the completeness of having him inside her and the emptiness of knowing he was going to leave. Or the stark fact that it was very unlikely that slipper-man, should he ever bother to rock on up, would be able to make her feel that absolute glow that Nathan had made her feel last night.

Torn between needing him gone so she could clear her head, and wanting to snuggle down next to him, she pulled on a robe and wandered through to the lounge, looking for some middle ground.

Facts were:

1) He lived in LA. She lived here.

2) His life involved chaos and extremes. She liked order.

3) He was a moment-by-moment type of guy. She planned everything to the nth degree.

Until last night, when she'd decided to be someone different.

But he wasn't her kind of man.

Which brought her to undeniable fact number four: he was unpredictable, volatile and untamed. Everything she hated; everything she avoided in a relationship.

And no amount of backward planning would extricate her from the world-shifting uncertainty hammering in her chest.

'Sasha?' His sleep-filled voice made her jump and ramped up the jittery butterflies dancing in her stomach. 'It's only six-thirty—the day hasn't started yet. What's going on?'

Every cell in her body craved his touch, heat surged through her veins, but she busied herself in the kitchenette, not knowing the rules for this kind of thing. But she bet it wasn't making a scene. She found him a smile. 'There you are again with the behind thing.'

'Sasha, this postage-stamp-sized apartment leaves little room for the element of surprise. I could probably have poked my head out of bed and you'd have seen me from here.' He leaned against the kitchen bench, half-zipped jeans slung on his hips—there was no way he could be wearing any underwear with them riding so low.

The thought of him commando, of what was under that denim, had her mouth watering and her body prickling with heat. The hard wall of his chest rippled as he moved. She remembered the feel of it under her fingertips, the slick press of it against her naked body.

The butterflies fluttered against her heart, sending ripples of a strange kind of pain in her chest.

She tucked her confusion away and quieted the darned insects. 'Don't you have a plane to catch, Nate? Somewhere to be?'

'You want to get rid of me already?' Was that a flicker of relief in his eyes? Did he feel as confused as she did? He took the mug of coffee she offered him. 'No problem. I've rearranged my flight for one o'clock this afternoon.'

Probably the first flight out, so he couldn't wait to leave. 'I see, and is everyone okay with that?' Was she okay with that?

He blinked. 'I'm the star, Sasha. I get to decide what happens.'

What the—? Back to business as usual, then. The tender amazing lover had done a bunk, replaced by the egomaniac. 'Er...not with me, you don't. I make my own decisions—at least, I'm used to negotiating, talking...'

'Someone's tetchy this morning. Not enough sleep perhaps?' He gave her a half-smile that told her he was struggling with the realities of spur-of-the-moment sex too. Or maybe it was just a reaction to her mood, which she knew was off. But she needed to protect herself somehow.

In lieu of there being nowhere else for him to sit he joined her on the sofa. 'I mean, I get to organise my timetable. If that doesn't work for you then I can change it. Push it back, bring it forward.'

'Forward might be a good idea. The world goes on regardless.'

He looked at her for a long moment. 'Regardless of what?'

'This. Last night.'

'Look, Sash, I had a great time, the best. Really, the best.' He hesitantly took her hand. 'But I do have to go. I know this is hard.'

'It's fine.' She shook her hand free from his, reluctant to open herself up to even more emotional exposure. The more locked-off she made herself, the better.

'No, it isn't fine at all. I can see it all over your face. You did something amazing—and, Sasha, we were good. So, so good. But...' he smoothed her hair with his palm '...I can't give you anything more. I was always upfront about that.'

Tears pricked at the backs of her eyes but she steadfastly would not let him see them. She'd known this all along and it was only her stupid heart doing a little rebellion.

She added lightness to a voice that was anything but. 'Hey, I'm not the clingy type so don't worry, I won't accost you at art-gallery parties or be rude to other women you're with. You have your life, I have mine and this was just a bit of random fun.'

So why weren't they laughing?

After taking another gulp of coffee he dipped his gaze and seemed lost in thought. Or a struggle. Or something. But when he looked back to her his eyes were softer, his smile almost tender. 'Maybe I could come back again. Some time.'

'Sure. In another ten years?' *Damn*. The words just blurted out. It wasn't as if she'd waited for him to come back; she'd got on with her life despite him leaving. *Hell*.

The sound of a heavy-duty motorbike engine revving and growling down in the street made them both jump.

'Honestly, some people, it's way too early for that.' She turned towards the noise, which set her nerves on edge. Unease shuddered down her spine as she watched Nathan storm to the window, the chill in the room taking a further nosedive.

But the growl didn't stop, accompanied now by a darker, more sinister one from Nathan's throat that sent her heart racing and a sickening drop in her stomach. He peered through a chink in the closed curtains, a shaft of bright early sunshine illuminating his straight back and hands fisting at his sides. 'What the—? Scumbags.'

His voice was too loud and too angry as he dropped the curtain but Nate couldn't contain his anger, not even for Sasha. Not even after the best night of his life. Her smell coated his skin, his hair. The taste of her lingered in his mouth. And his body ached to take her straight back to bed for a rerun. But that wasn't going to happen—she'd made that clear. And she was right.

He didn't do this—staying over. Wanting more.

So he didn't know whether his inflated reaction was caused by the guys outside, or the fact he'd been thrown off kilter by the mixed-up feelings swirling round his chest. Factor in a mess of photographers and his mood was shot. 'They must have followed us last night when I thought we'd given them the slip.'

'Who? What is it? What's happening?' Instead of coming to the window she shunted further into the sofa cushions, eyes wide and spooked.

And that was the moment he determined she couldn't be part of his life long-term. Jasmine, Cara, the plastic sisterhood—they all adored publicity and fed off it like piranhas.

Sasha wasn't like them. She was a regular—no, a stellar—high-school teacher who wanted to stay being just that.

She didn't crave fame for her own end. And he'd dragged her into a chaos of his own making. He should have kept away. Should have gone back to his hotel alone last night, instead of giving in to temptation.

But she'd been so sweet to put her inexperience in his hands, then so incredibly hot, it wasn't something he'd ever regret. Perfect. Bloody perfect. He just needed to get his head round it, but that didn't seem to be happening.

'Cameras, paps…lowlife.' He forced his voice to soften. 'They either followed us, or had a tip-off and spent the night trawling the Internet to find things out about you.'

'Pull the curtains closed, then. I don't want them here. How can we get rid of them?'

'Without making a scene? Very little. But they'll know now what you do as a job. What your credit rating is. What kind of junk…er car you drive.'

'If you're trying to make me feel better, it's not working.' An indignant smile broke through the frown. 'I happen to love that car. I bought it when I was twenty-two, the down-payment was from my first pay packet.'

'Boy, you teachers must have really low wages.'

Perfectly shaped eyebrows peaked. 'Yeah. Ha. Ha. It's reliable—mostly. And it's pink, easy to spot in a car park. Bonus.'

'It's a wreck and clearly way too distinctive to be a get-away car. Let me buy you another one? Whatever you want, it's the least I can do.'

Sitting up, she frowned. 'What? You sleep with me and then want to pay me out with a car? What is this? Guilt money or…worse? I don't want anything from you. That's not what this is about.'

'Hey. Stop right there.' Whatever else happened here he needed to erase that hurt simmering in her eyes. No way did he want that to be the last image he had of her. 'Most people do want something from me. I just can't get used to the fact that you don't.' But he wouldn't put up with that kind of accusation.

He tipped her chin up so he could see her face properly. So she could see his. 'I slept with you because you're beautiful and hot, and I like you. And I'm glad I did.' And of all the women he'd slept with, none had made him feel so stirred up that he didn't know how to leave. Or how to stay.

'Oh. Okay. Me too…I suppose.' She managed a weak smile and looked up at him under thick black eyelashes.

It took a huge amount of effort not to say something stupid or sentimental that would cause more damage in the long run. 'And I want to buy you a car because I can afford to. That's all. That car is so old it could be dangerous.' He flicked his thumb to the window. 'Like these idiots here are dangerous. They can ruin lives.'

'Yes, I know all about that too. Thank you very much.' She shook her head as if closing off that line of thought. She was good at that—bringing down the barriers about her private past or about any kind of emotional pain. 'How can we get rid of them? Police?'

'Unlikely. They've never been much help before. A lot of them think celebs are fair game, as far as I can see.' But Sasha wasn't.

Anger swelled from nowhere and before he could contain it his fist landed on the coffee table with a thump.

Her shoulders twitched and the spooky look on her face darkened. 'Hey. Stop that. Go ruin your own stuff. Leave mine alone.'

And he was making things worse, again, in his bid to protect her. Where did that come from?

Feisty she might be, but there she sat in the tiniest lounge in living history, lush red hair corkscrewing around her shoulders, completely oblivious to the freak show she was now part of. Every part of her life would be scrutinised and picked apart. There was nothing for it but to shelter her from it all.

But how?

He should just take her lead and leave her to it.

But…well, he couldn't let the circling sharks have their feed on her, not when it was his fault they were here in the first place.

Kneeling down at the sofa, he tugged her hand. 'Come to the bedroom and start packing some clothes while I make a few calls. You need to get away for a few days until all this interest has died down. You're not at school on Monday?'

She tugged her hand back. 'No. We have Spring Bank Holiday week…but I need to work, refine the choreography.'

'Excellent. I'll get onto it. You don't need to be here. You can work on routines wherever you are.'

'Please, it's not necessary. I can look after myself.'

The trill of her cellphone distracted her. 'Hello? Yes, this is Sasha…What? No! No. Go away. Go to hell.'

'What was that about?' Just seeing the panic in her eyes made his gut clench.

'It's just some jerk wanting to know how many times we had sex last night. Did I want an exclusive?' She rolled her eyes. 'Who cares about these things?'

'You don't know these people and the lengths they will go to. We need to lay low for a few days or there'll be lots more calls like that. And if they don't get a story they'll delve into your past, or worse, make something up. Print lies.'

Horrified, she held her head in her hands. 'I couldn't bear that. My sisters would cope—Cassie would probably love the attention—but Mum doesn't deserve to have her past trawled through the papers, not all that stuff about my dad. It was bad enough at the time. She's finally managed to put it all behind her.'

His hands were on her shoulders now, closer than he should be, but he just couldn't help himself. 'So you need to pack.'

'Wait…I know. I know. I just need some time. To think. To organise…'

'Sasha, the sooner we get out—'

'I know. I'm just thinking…'

If he'd had more time and less sense he'd have crushed those lips with his mouth, taken her to bed and kissed her back to some kind of better mood. But instead he picked her up, threw her over his shoulder ignoring her protestations and squeals, and carried her into the cupboard she had the audacity to call a bedroom.

Dumping her on the unmade bed that was still warm from their bodies, he stood over her, refusing to take any more nonsense. Someone had to take control here, and it wasn't going to be her. 'Okay. Take ten seconds to think it over, write a list or a spreadsheet or whatever you need to do to get your head round it all. Ten. That's all you have. Then I'm phoning my pilot.'

Still shocked at the fireman's lift, she stared at him as if trying to process the turn of events. Her shoulders slumped forward, her expression turning from confused to blatant flustered.

Man, it was downright dangerous when she flustered. Her pretty nose crinkled, her cheeks blazed and her eyes got a panicky mist that made him want to wrap her up in his arms. 'Nate, I can't just go somewhere on the cuff like this. I just can't.'

'Yes, you can.' Her clothes were so neatly stacked he had no trouble finding what she might need. 'I'll fly you somewhere safe.'

'Fly? I don't need to go that far away. I can manage fine. I'll drive.'

He pointed to the street outside from where excited chatter permeated their privacy. 'Sasha, they'll chase you from one end of this country to another. If we fly out somewhere then we can muddy the flight details a little. Throw them off scent.'

We? We? He was going to go back to LA and send her to a nice private spa in Switzerland or France—on her own.

You. Not *we*. Goddamn.

'Together?'

Shoot. He exhaled good and hard. Spending more time with her was the far side of crazy, but it made a lot of sense. He could lockdown the house, monitor the papers, keep her safe. Rerun last night…

'This is my fault, I should…look after you. Just for a few days…a week at most.' It was a step closer to protecting her than letting her stay somewhere, spooked, on her own. 'And I need to do it right this time.'

'*This time? This time?* I don't understand. You never needed to look after me before.' Her eyes grew wider. 'Hang on…this isn't just about me and the paparazzi, is it?'

He'd hoped that little slip had gone under the radar too. But no. Nothing went under the radar with Sasha. How was she so perceptive? Feigning nonchalance, he shrugged and struggled for words. Was fluster contagious? 'No…look, I don't know. Leave it alone.'

'It's about something else too. Someone else.' She clicked her fingers as she thought, a wave of a frown on her forehead. 'Of course…it's about Marshall. Something about protecting him? Or failing to. Am I right?'

Yeah? Then she'd just worked out something he hadn't even known about himself. Maybe she was right, maybe everything came back to how he'd let his brother down.

But somehow he doubted it—he'd got over that years ago. Hadn't he?

A sharp ache tore through his chest at the thought of Marshall's smiling face. He buried the pain back. No time for that now. Or ever. 'Hurry and pack. We haven't got time to talk about this.'

'Yes, we do.' With a determined twinkle in her eye she sat on the edge of the bed and folded her arms. 'I can wait, just like those guys outside. As long as it takes, Mr Hotshot. So you can either tell me what this is all about, or you can sit here with me for who knows how long? Because I'm not heading off on any jaunt without knowing the real reason you need to save me.'

Oh, she was good. Holding *him* hostage when he was trying to protect her. But he never shared this.

Never.

Sasha watched, stunned, as he stuffed her clothes into a holdall he'd grabbed from under her bed, doing everything he could to avoid eye contact. 'Nathan. Talk.'

He looked up and opened his mouth, apparently shocked into speaking. 'Marshall had a hard time at school. It was my fault. I pushed for him to go there.' He stopped stuffing. 'Sorry? Why do you need to hear this. Now?'

'Because I do. And you need to tell me, or we don't go anywhere. Whatever the cost. It was challenging for him, sure, a lot of special-needs kids find mainstream school hard. But you did what you thought was best for him.'

He laughed, but it was hollow and cold. 'Like I knew? I *believed* he should go to a regular school instead of living with a label. I *believed* only I knew what was the right thing for him. So I forced the school to take him, in the only way I knew how.'

After his father went to prison Nate had been a gangly teenager forced into taking control of a situation he just didn't know how to deal with. But that had never deterred him.

'I was the man of the house, but I didn't know crap about being a man, other than shouting loudly and getting my own way with violence. So I just walked into the school office and insisted they take him, even accusing them of discriminating against him. They didn't like that.'

'I imagine they didn't. But Marshall loved the school, right? It was definitely the best decision for him.' She reached across the duvet and tried to pull him to sit opposite her. But he resisted.

Instead, he stared into a spot just past her shoulder. 'At first he did, but gradually he grew quieter and less willing to join in things. The only place he seemed happy was the choir. Eventually he admitted he was being bullied.'

'Oh, Nate. That's awful. I had no idea.'

Nate smoothed a palm over the back of his neck. 'I thought he'd brush the whole thing off—he'd always known he was different and accepted it. But then one day I found him in tears holding a note from one of his classmates. It said he should never have been born, that he was dirty and no one liked him. Seemed he'd been bullied for a while.'

'That's terrible. You should have told someone—a teacher. The headmaster.'

'I dealt with it. It didn't need making public. I was the big brother—it was my job to sort it out.' He shrugged nonchalantly, his voice steady and detached, as he slipped back behind the public mask he wore. 'At least that was the plan. I was pretty sure no one would listen anyway. I was having a bad day already and this made it a whole lot worse. I saw red. Stormed out and hunted down the culprit, some no-hoper called Craig. He and I had a brief exchange of words and then—'

'Then you hit him,' she interrupted, the events of their last night together now clear. The way he'd turned up at her house, dishevelled, animated. She'd initially thought his rocky emotional state had been to do with an argument they'd had about her refusal to talk to him about her past. How she didn't trust him enough. He'd been so passionate. Ardent.

And that passion had stirred something so deep in her, as it did again now, they'd finally almost made love, so close.

But then the authorities had hammered her door down in search of him. 'Your knuckles, I remember, they were sore and swollen, but you never did give me the full story, clearly.'

'Because you did exactly what everyone else did. You looked at me as if you'd been expecting it all along. That I was no different from my useless violent father.'

Was that how he saw it? Pain settled under her ribcage. 'No. I knew you were different from him. I knew everyone saw a different side from the one I saw.'

'Sasha, the look in your eyes stayed with me for longer than I cared to remember.'

Because the whole sordid scenario had revived the memories of the night her father had died. Police at the door, shouting. Things getting way out of control. She couldn't witness that kind of aggression and violence again, no matter how justified. And not from someone she'd loved. Or at least, believed she did.

But he'd been acting out of pure love, trying to protect his brother. He'd chosen her as the only person he could turn to when he needed comfort. For love? Trust?

So she could see now how her betrayal, along with the way the town turned their backs on him, had forced him to leave and then spend the next few years forging emotional detachment. The drinking, the endless string of women, the wild parties. And, by saving herself, she'd been partly to blame for that. No wonder the man screamed non-commitment—he probably believed everyone he ever loved would let him down. Walk away. Turn away.

Small wonder then, the rage, the hot-headedness, the ill-contained anger that stirred something raw and new in her, that both attracted and troubled her.

She wanted to pull him back down on the bed and make him understand that she'd had other reasons to walk away all those years ago. But with his tensed muscles and the mask of impartiality he'd slipped back on she didn't think he'd allow it. 'If you'd only explained, I'd have listened.'

'No, you wouldn't. You shut down. And I wasn't making a lot of sense. I'd completely lost control. They had to drag me off Craig. I was an animal. Worse. The only reason they didn't press charges was because I had the letter evidence that Craig had been bullying Marshall.'

'But even so, you can't blame yourself for what happened.'

'Can't I? I failed Marshall by putting him in that situation. I might as well have bullied him myself. I did the wrong thing to get him out of it. Craig ended up in Intensive Care and Marshall never really recovered. He died a couple of years later.'

'I'm so, so sorry.'

'Yes. Well, it was a long time ago.' And with that he turned, swung the wardrobe door open with a crash and reached for more of her clothes.

Conversation over. He'd reached his limit; that was clear.

It almost broke her heart to see him so closed-off, particularly when it was partly her fault. But he was the kind of guy who would take responsibility square on his shoulders, and would never back down.

She didn't know a way forward and didn't want to fill the space with the sound of her own voice so she gathered her toiletries from the bathroom, imagining what the next few days with him would be like when there was so much between them.

An intense connection. Sizzling but bruised. Ice and heat.

Either way, if she didn't protect herself, she was going to get burnt.

Five minutes later he zipped the holdall and pulled out his phone. The smile he gave her was muted, as if a whirlwind of emotion had rattled through and he was dealing with the aftermath. He stretched out a hand and when she took it in hers it was warm and large and solid. Just like his heart—if only he'd let himself believe it.

She smiled back at him.

Then before she could register it his lips were on hers, a sublime pressure that reverberated through her body, melting her bones, leaving her craving more. And more. And…

She kissed him back, hard and deep, gripping his shoulders, forgetting the tension and the uncertainty, the hurt of the past. When he pulled her to him she fitted perfectly into his arms and let the fire raging inside her smoulder and burn some more. The heat subsumed her until she was lost in him, in this, and she wasn't sure she even wanted to find a way back.

Eventually he pulled away, his rough edges softened slightly and, in his face, she caught a glimpse of the man who'd made love to her last night. His voice was thick and hoarse. 'Ready?'

For more of that? Hell, yes, even though she hadn't got any kind of plan as to how she'd survive the next few days in one piece. 'So where will we go?'

'Ah, God, I don't know, Sasha. How does Italy sound?'

CHAPTER TEN

'I DON'T SUPPOSE you'd consider putting the guidebook down and actually taking in the amazing Florence scenery?'

Nathan's teasing was fair, Sasha decided. His mood had lightened with every mile they'd travelled away from Chesterton, but flashes of it lingered in his taut stance as he looked at her with a half-bemused frown.

He'd brought her to the one place in the whole world she wanted to visit, had even organised an unprecedented private half-hour to view the most iconic landmark in the city. So he was right—she should be paying attention.

She looked out from the top of the startling black and white marble Duomo across sun-drenched butterscotch buildings topped with terracotta roofs.

The view from the plane had shown her a patchwork of piazzas, the magical river Arno, and lush green Tuscan hills that protected the city. But nothing compared to breathing real Florence air and seeing the architecture close-up.

At every turn there was an ancient cathedral, a church, an ornate building. Florence oozed charm and history, complete with delicious smells that made her stomach grumble: rich garlic, pungent rosemary and dark thick coffee.

She hit him on the shoulder with the book. 'I'm just reading up about the place. This book suggests the top ten things to do in Tuscany. I want to tick them all off. Did you know you can hire segways to ride around the piazzas, or take a horse and carriage to explore the old quarters?'

'No, Sasha, I didn't.'

'Or that legend says Florence is so breathtakingly beautiful it can make you swoon with its utter majesty?'

He stared out over the rooftops, hands deep in his pockets, and breathed out hard. 'No, Sasha, I didn't.'

'Did you—?'

'Here, give me that…' Snatching the book from her hand, he scanned the list, snapped the book closed and shoved it into a nearby litterbin. 'That's enough of that.'

Tension squeezed her stomach as she looked from his hand to the bin. 'But…'

He held her gaze, the tautness of his jaw and the coolness in his eyes putting her on edge.

If this was how it was going to be she didn't want to stay another minute. 'Clearly you don't want to be here, Nate. I'm sorry if you came under duress. You can always leave. For that matter, so can I.'

'I'm sorry. I'm just a little on edge.' He ran a hand over the back of his neck and looked at her with the same kind of confusion she was feeling.

'Yes, well, this is all weird for me too. I didn't exactly plan it.'

He laughed, just. 'No, Sasha. No, you didn't. And I don't want to be constricted by someone else's idea of how to have a good time. I think I can work that out all by myself. That's a rubbish list, for a start.' Warmth returned to his eyes and he began to smile. Slowly at first. Until his features softened along with his stance. 'It's nothing like *my* top ten things to do in Tuscany.'

'That's because your top ten things are probably X-rated.'

His eyes glinted, giving her every indication that while they were here he had definite plans of his own. 'There's nothing wrong with that. This is a kind of holiday after all. And when you're on holiday you're meant to do things you enjoy. Not things people tell you to do.'

A holiday. A break. A fling. *Strictly temporary.* A fantasy that wasn't even hers—she'd just borrowed it until Mr Boring But Safe came driving along in his racing-green family-sized saloon. A fantasy that clearly involved more time in bed if she wanted it.

All she had to do was agree.

It had taken only a matter of days to swerve her from her life plan. And now, here she was with the poster boy for effortless seduction, on the run from the press. She couldn't have made it up. And she sure as heck hadn't put up much of a fight. One whiff of him opening up to her and she'd been putty in those exquisitely toned arms.

But God, the way he made her feel with just one glance from those intense whisky eyes and the mesmerising just-for-her smile he was flashing at her now… Some of her misgivings began to drift away with the gentle Tuscan breeze.

His fingers stole up her back. 'And seeing as you're getting so good at it…'

'That's because I have a very good teacher.' The giggle that came from her throat surprised her, she never giggled. Well, heck, it seemed she did now. She was changing in surprising ways.

'Takes one to know one.' He shrugged. 'But we do have a lot more to cover…'

He'd put himself out for her—the least she could do was enjoy it. She could do this. She could enjoy him and this fantasy while still protecting herself. She could. All she had to do was let go. It would seem very rude not to.

And fit in as much sightseeing as humanly possible. 'But please can we visit the Ponte Vecchio, the Uffizi…?'

'I've arranged a private viewing at the Uffizi at three.

Before that we can take a drive to the bridge. There's an amazing gelato shop just the other side.'

'Okay.' She turned to take the rickety worn steps back down to ground level. 'So, bridge, then ice cream, then Uffizi? What about—?'

'Sasha, your lists are starting to drive me crazy.' He shook his head. 'I need something to distract me. Luckily, I know just the thing…'

He pushed her against the old cool wall, imprinted no doubt with hundreds of years of stolen moments just like this.

The moment his mouth found hers she forgot the buildings and the art and the book in the bin; the only thing she wanted to look at was his face as he kissed her. To commit this moment to memory so she could bring it out when she was old and grey and remember it. Remember him.

The kiss was soft and gentle, not the heated urgent need of desperation and fire. The kind of kiss you sank into and never wanted to be rescued from. If she hadn't been leaning against the wall she'd have fallen, her legs woozy with pleasure and the swell in her heart.

'And after the sightseeing…' She gave him her best seductive smile. 'What will we do then?'

'You want another list? Yes, I suppose you do.' He nuzzled against the dip of her neck, his hand cupping her breast making every cell in her body scream for skin on skin. 'Okay, my house, my list. Let me see…lazy mornings in my four-poster at the castello…long, long nights…You get the picture.'

'Typical man. Sex…and sex.'

'You have a problem with that?'

She twisted to face him, giving him what she knew was a full-watt smile, wishing…wishing what? That he'd said he wanted something more than physical? 'But you can do that anywhere.'

'Is that an offer? You want to start now? Only, I think the priests downstairs might have a problem with that…'

'Oh, yes. Good point. Save it for later.'

He groaned. 'I can't wait.'

'But you have to wait…' Her fingers trailed towards his jeans zipper, and she heard his gasp, the increase in his breathing. 'Just for the record, Nathan, your lists are getting better all the time.'

She swallowed deeply, relishing her new-found sexual power—instilling such desire in a man, making him want more. Making him want *her*. If only she could have the same effect on his brain and find out what was really going on in that superstar fame-filled head of his.

He gave her so much…but never everything…allowing her a glimpse of his inner private self, before slamming the shutters down pretty resolutely. She knew he was damaged but a survivor, tender and funny. Reluctantly kind. Sexy as anything. She knew exactly what he wanted her to know—and no more.

Strip away the rest of that alpha bravado and what else would she find underneath? Did she really want to know?

Three days, and a lot of extra-curricular activity later, Nate sat in a private dining room overlooking his local town's busy piazza. Strains of soft music floated through the shutters as the local community began their evening promenade, smiling, nodding and taking absolutely no notice of Nate and his beautiful dinner guest. For that, he was grateful.

'*Risotto ai funghi, per favore*?' Sasha smiled up at the waiter, nibbling her bottom lip as if worried about her accent.

Nate's stomach clenched. First smile of the day and she'd given it to someone else.

He leaned across the table. 'If I'd known you spoke the

language I'd have let you do the talking instead of my pathetic efforts.'

'I've only just plucked up enough courage to try it out. When in Rome, and all that… I've got one of those language DVDs at home.' She smiled for him, just. 'Goes to show how little you really know about me.'

'I know the best bits very well. But I'm always open to a reminder.'

His gaze travelled down her body, lingered over flawless breasts that he ached to touch again and again.

Her eyes widened, and even though she was pretending to be shocked he caught the spark and fire and heard the crackle of desire in her throat as she spoke. 'Nathan! Please don't look at me like that.'

'Like what?'

'Like you want to eat me.'

'But I do.' Seemed he'd lost his appetite for anything else lately. This time her smile was genuine, as was the full-body blush.

'And what about your *Bistecca alla Fiorentina*?'

'Oh, the food can wait.' He slipped into the seat next to her, unable to wait any longer to feel the brush of her skin against his. Cupping her cheek, he turned her to face him. By God, he'd go to hell for this. 'But this can't.'

He ran his tongue along her bottom lip, felt her brief hesitation, then his heart lifted as she opened her mouth, a tiny growl deep in her throat. He held her face in his hands. 'I want you. Here,' he groaned.

She shifted away from him. 'The food will be here in a minute. We can't keep doing this. We're going to get banned from every eatery in Greve.'

He looked across the candlelit empty room towards the closed door. Knew the waiters would keep their distance unless absolutely necessary. 'We could…if we wanted to. I want to.'

'I can tell. But I'm an upstanding citizen, not a rock star with no morals.'

Something was bugging her and he had no idea what.

Worse—he cared. Cared that she was cranky. And that scared the heck out of him. Mainly, because he didn't *know* what to feel when he was with her, other than warm, strangely contented and more aroused than at any other time in his life.

Caring? He didn't do that. He hadn't done that for a very long time.

He was losing his edge.

'Hey! Steady. I do have a few morals, I'm sure…somewhere…' He patted his pockets as if trying to locate them. 'Just not the ones you want me to have. I do charitable deeds. Isn't that enough?'

She pulled even further back. 'You do charity? Which one? Over-sexed Rock Stars Anonymous? You know, with your money you could do a great deal to help kids like Marshall.'

'I've been thinking about doing more, and I will. I just need to get a few things sorted out. I'll look into it when I get back home.'

Spending time with her and those choir kids had opened him up to other ideas too. Maybe it was timing; the end of a tour that had sucked his energy, the chance to rethink where his life was going, or maybe it was just her. She made him want to clean up his act.

The frown that had been hovering over her forehead all day returned, just when he'd thought he'd erased it.

'So what else do you do in LA? When you're not busy being rich and famous?'

'I'm away touring for nine months, maybe a year, at a time and I'm usually pretty beat up when we're done. I work hard but then I need to let off steam and play hard. Very hard. Sometimes I get to take time out, like this, but usually we go from touring to the studio, a new album, then touring again. It's a bit like being a hamster in a wheel. Same old. Same old. But, as I say, I like to keep busy. It keeps me out of trouble.'

And only a few more days to go in exile and he'd be back on an even keel again. Maybe that was his problem—he was getting too used to the easy life, getting too used to… well, Sasha and her weird lists and her quirky ways, getting used to her soft folds and sweet smiles. He was getting too used to waking up with her every morning and the bright slash of lightness that burned in his chest.

Yeah, getting wasted in a different city every night would do him a power of good. There was nothing like stranger sex to make a guy forget a girl. But the more he thought about it, the less it appealed. Strange. 'Call me empty and shallow, but what you see is pretty much what you get.'

She shook her head. 'No. No, that's not true at all. I know you have this stage persona and then there's this other person. I think I've met him a couple of times. Briefly. Who is he?'

'Oh, you have questions? Go ahead.' He peered into her handbag and pretended to look for something. 'You want me to fill out a questionnaire? A checklist?' At the pursed lips and exaggerated frown he continued, 'No? Really, you are slacking, *list girl*. Let's start with the physical. I have full-working body parts, but then, you know that.'

'Oh…yes, I do. Full working order.' Her hesitant smile sparkled a little and grew as she drummed fingers on the table. 'A checklist. I can't believe I didn't think of that. Let me see, what would I be looking to ask?' Her nose wrinkled as he ran his fingers down her spine. 'Hey, I know, we could do a SWOT analysis.'

'Are you serious?'

'It couldn't hurt.'

He laughed. 'You are serious? Sasha—this isn't a bloody employment interview. Although, I do have a lot of strengths.' No way was he going to get sucked into any kind of self-analysis. He'd paid way too much to shrinks to be told he had commitment issues, he struggled with emotional attachment. Blah. Blah. Like every man he'd ever met.

He certainly struggled with something when Sasha was around. But usually it was the fact she was wearing way too many clothes. Today's dress was vintage black silk cocktail with thin straps that kept falling off her shoulder. Perfect for a sophisticated dinner out, but he wanted to rip the damn thing off her.

Sophisticated was hellishly overrated.

He nibbled across her collarbone, feeling her reluctant squirm, the softening of her muscles.

She giggled. 'Okay. So you're very good at that. Now, stop it…I'm being serious.' Serious with a devilish smile and a promise in her eye. He wanted her naked. Now. But she kept right on talking. 'How about hobbies, dreams, long-term plans…or your business strategies…pension scheme?'

'I think you'll find I'm financially secure.' Thank God something was, because his heart was dancing around like a firecracker. But so typical of Sasha that she'd consider a pension scheme in her tick list of qualities in a man.

'I much preferred talking about the physical, but as you're so insistent…I have fund managers and investors to deal with the fiscal side. I'm the creative one, but there are others, like Dario, the band, producers, stage management, roadies, choreographers, stylists, caterers, marketeers and the rest…It takes a lot of people to make a global brand work. And that's all I am in reality. A product. We have a lot of meetings, with bits of paper and folders and everything. You'd love it. If I gave it all up there'd be a lot of people without jobs.'

'Gosh, I never thought of it like that before—so many people dependent on your success. That's quite a weight to carry around.'

'I have broad shoulders.'

'Indeed.' She sighed, but she tipped her head to one side looking at him, eyes full of questions that he didn't think had much to do with this particular conversation. 'Okay, weaknesses?'

'None.'

'How about tall, blonde, big bazookas?'

'The girls?' He laughed, was she a mind-reader? He really hadn't thought about that kind of game for a while. Not since... He tried to think. Not since losing himself in rose-scented red hair and list-making had become his top two favourite pastimes. 'No. Not interested, at all. Looks like you're my only weakness.' Dangerous, yet compelling. 'And I can't think of any threats.'

He wrapped his arms round her and pulled her close. Then his hand ran along her thigh until she squirmed. But he held her tight, not allowing her to escape no matter how much she wriggled. He stole another quick kiss. 'And I make sure I always grab every opportunity.'

'Yes, yes.' She laughed, her shoulders relaxing and the shadows around her eyes melting a little. Her fingers tiptoed across his pecs. 'So which part of the Nate Munro product is the real you and which is fake?'

Leaning back in the leather seat, he clasped his hands behind his head and grinned. 'Believe me, sweet thing. I'm all real.'

'Idiot.'

He hadn't expected the thwack to his upper arm, but it hardly registered. 'Hey...and you've seen me naked. How much more real do you need me to be?'

'Nathan, half the women in California have seen you naked.'

'Good point. But I've never brought any of them here and I've never spoken to them about Marshall or my previous life—'

That truth jolted him. He was getting in too deep, opening up too many wounds. And she was getting too involved.

He shouldn't give her the impression she was any more special than the rest. He wasn't the guy she needed to fall in love with. He couldn't give her what she deserved, the promises bit, the stable home life bit. And it wasn't that he didn't want to live that kind of life at some point; he just didn't know how.

But somehow he just couldn't stop.

The heavy mahogany door creaked open and a waiter appeared with their food.

Sasha jumped and sidled to the edge of her chair, her cheeks reddening. 'You'd better go back to your seat, Casanova. The show's over and I'm starving.'

'Okay,' Nate whispered across the space, trying to deflect the ache that had settled in his chest, trying to make things light. 'Okay, I have an idea. Let's play a game.'

CHAPTER ELEVEN

SASHA SWALLOWED A mouthful of the most exquisite risotto she'd ever eaten, then leaned in. She liked to play. So long as they played safe. 'What exactly?'

'I name two things and you choose which one you prefer. See if we like the same things and if we're remotely compatible.'

'I already know we're woefully incompatible. If you're talking lists I could write one with all the reasons we shouldn't be doing this.'

'I'm sure you could, and probably already have.'

'Well, maybe. One or two.' She blushed; he'd certainly got the measure of her. But she was curious about his game. That couldn't hurt. Could it? 'Okay, then. Who goes first?'

A mischievous grin settled on his very sexy lips. 'Me. Easy start: which super power would you prefer to have— telepathy or X-ray vision?'

She laughed. 'And I thought this was going to be sensible. Typical male question. To read minds or see through clothes? Let me guess, you'd prefer X-rays, right?'

'Oh, yes. I don't think I want to know what's going on in any woman's head the whole time. But I'm guessing you like that kind of thing?'

She laughed and muttered into her glass of white wine, 'See? Chalk and cheese.'

'Sorry, is that a question? Because that's not how it works. The choices have to be kind of the same but—'

'Don't be stupid.' She stifled another giggle. No matter how hard she tried to be serious and get her sensible point across the man blocked her. Every time. 'I was just saying we're like chalk and cheese. So very different in every way. And please don't give me that awful opposites attract gumbo.'

'Are you sure you don't already have telepathy? Because that is exactly what I was thinking.' He raised his palms towards her. 'No, don't answer that. Telepathy doesn't exist.'

'When I was little I thought my mum and dad had it. They finished each other's sentences, knew what the other was thinking...'

But that wasn't true and she knew it now. Growing up, she'd believed her parents had the best of marriages and that her father had killed himself because he couldn't bear to let the woman he loved down, that he'd been brave and proud and that was why he'd left them.

But now, with more experience of people's hearts and minds, she wasn't so sure. Maybe her parents hadn't been soul mates after all. Maybe they'd just been two ordinary people who'd had arguments and compromised and muddled through. Maybe it wasn't that her father had loved them too much, maybe he just hadn't loved them enough.

Because if he'd truly loved them with all his heart, why had he done what he did? That wasn't brave, that was... hard. So very bloody gut-wrenchingly hard. 'At least that's what I always thought. I'm not convinced at all now though.'

Nathan's hand covered hers and she let his warmth rush through her. 'Hey, things between two people are never what they seem to the outside world, Sasha. There's always an element of pretence, a front.'

'Don't I know it? Seems to me that everyone's hiding something. So it's pretty hard to work out what the truth is.'

'I guess that's why you don't give your heart easily.'

'Trust has to work both ways as far as I'm concerned. And I'm done with trying to second-guess everyone.'

Her father's death, Nathan's story, even hearing it a decade later was mired in complex emotion and, if not deception, then a woeful lack of truth.

But then, she'd been as guilty as everyone else in holding things back. She was too frightened of the fallout.

The main course finished, Nate sat back and studied her. 'Do you want to talk about it? About your mum and dad?'

'No, thanks. You know that's off limits. And ancient history.' She refused to look him in the eye and let him see the shadows she knew were there, or pay attention to the sudden fist of pain in her ribcage. So she quickly changed the subject. Forced a smile that came easily when she looked at him. 'Back to the game. That's far more fun.'

He shrugged, his body freezing, his jaw tightening. 'Another time, then.'

Never. 'Starter or dessert?'

Even though she knew her refusal annoyed him, she couldn't lose even more of herself to him.

He looked as if he was consciously trying to relax, stretching out his fingers. 'I usually prefer a starter, but here they make the best *struffoli* in Italy. So I'd have to go with that.'

'Sounds like it should be a musical term. *Play the piece allegro with struffoli.*'

His mouth creased into a small smile. 'That would be very messy seeing as they're sticky balls of dough, covered in honey. Delicious. We should get some.' Ringing a bell, he caught the waiter's attention and started a little debate between the staff. 'Apparently they're only usually served at Christmas and for celebrations, but they're willing to make an exception. It may take a little time.'

She laughed, rolling her eyes. 'Of course. How marvellous to have everyone at your beck and call. Anything for you. Mr Wonderful.'

'Apart from you. Why don't you make an exception too, Sash?' His voice deepened, more a command than a question. 'Tell me.'

'No. Just no.' It wasn't her way. She'd kept everything shut down for so long, and her family wouldn't thank her for sharing their shame and their heartache. Her mother didn't need to go through that again. And Nathan lived too much in the public eye and too little in private; she didn't want to risk telling him anything if there was a chance it might ever get out again.

And, really, she was too damned scared to relive it all again.

'I'm sorry, but I'm not going to ruin a lovely evening.'

Heart pounding, she angled across the table and changed the subject the only way that worked with Nate Munro. She kissed him.

Long and hard and fast. Greedy, bold and powerful, meshing her lips to his, taking exactly what she needed, and giving him more in return. It certainly shut him up.

She pulled back and rubbed her hands together. 'Okay, back to business. Your turn for the preference game. Hit me with it.'

Surprise flickered across his eyes. 'You know, you're the only woman who's ever turned me down?'

Twice. No, more than that. Refused to share her pathetic life story. Refused to make love with him so many times she'd lost count and held him to a solemn promise that had taken ten years to follow through.

Her smile widened. It had been worth the wait. Every single second. It wasn't something she'd ever regret, even though watching him go would be so very hard. Chesterton was her reality and she wanted to live out a fantasy just a little while longer. 'And it's about time someone did. It's good for you. You shouldn't be able to have everything you want. You need to suffer once in a while, and learn to ask nicely. Oh, and to wait a little, not have everyone jumping around after you. It's what normal people do. It's character forming.'

'I have enough character as it is.'

'Too true. Way too much.' And every inch of it to die for, if not slightly maddening. 'Now, Mr Superstar, next question: if you can't think of one, then let me. Pool or ocean?'

He thought a while and rubbed a hand over his stubbled jaw. 'I have both, so it's a tough choice. Surfing versus boring laps? Saltwater versus disgusting chlorinated. Ocean's winning so far, I have to admit. But right now…Here? Definitely the pool.' His eyes heated; little flecks of gold sparked in the dark caramel. 'And a chance of skinny dipping…'

Another thing to tick off her bucket list. She laughed. 'Maybe…if you're good and ask nicely and wait a little…I could be convinced.'

'Sweet thing, I'll wait as long as you want. So long as it's about ten seconds.' He slid back into the seat beside her, his fingers stealing their way to her thigh, where he pressed his palm down hard, his thumb dangerously and enticingly too close for comfort.

The pressure was electric, sending spasms of need through her every nerve cell. She twisted to face him, her breath coming in tight gasps. She couldn't deny him, couldn't refuse him. Skinny dipping it was. Plus a whole lot of everything else.

Maybe telepathy did exist after all, because right now she knew exactly what was going on in his mind. 'You want to get the *struffoli* to go?'

'Fast or slow?' Nathan whispered into Sasha's ear as he finally found the strength to let go of her. She'd come through on the skinny dipping, and more. So much more. And holding her, inside her, watching her lose control again and again, tipping over the edge, had been the most sensual thing he'd ever done.

She shifted underneath him, breathless and satiated, pulling faux-fur blankets over them as they lay on the sun lounger in the dark.

'Hmmm, tricky.' She sighed, her breath like a gentle kiss on his neck, her curves fitting against him like a hand in a glove. A perfect fit. 'Either. Both. So long as it's with you...' Her hand cupped his cheek as she gazed at him. 'Eyes or mouth?'

Man, he loved this game. It cut through the crap and got down to the heart of things.

He loved the aftermath of great sex too, the fading glow, the deep relaxation it brought, the soft purr of satisfaction that rippled through his muscles.

And with a zillion stars winking at him through the silver slash of the Milky Way, a beautiful woman slick and wet from their midnight swim wrapped in his arms, it was as if he'd been teleported to a wild out-of-this-world film set.

'A man should never have to make a choice like that. Your eyes are amazing, but your mouth...' He groaned into the tumble of red curls, remembering the things her mouth had done to him...He groaned. 'Sasha, your mouth should be X-rated. Your mouth should never be allowed in Chesterton High again. Your mouth—'

But before he could finish she'd filled his mouth with her taste, her tongue. Soft and yielding, her kiss was filled with something that made his heart stutter.

She pulled away, tied her silk robe loosely round her waist, laid her head back on his shoulder and looked up at the sky. 'Heart or brain?'

'Whoa, Sasha. That's the biggest question in the universe. I wish I could say heart. But truly? You've got to go with brain every time.'

'Why?'

'Because otherwise you get sucked in by sentiment, make poor choices. I've been doing that way too long. It's got to be brain.'

She sighed. 'Disappointing then, given that we're lying here, doing this.'

'Believe me, if I'd led with my heart I'd have had you that first night. In the limo.'

'That would have been leading with your groin. There is a difference.'

'Huh? Really?' Yes, he knew that. But looking back it was the same thing. Heart, brain and body, all bowled over when the Sasha tornado hit. She was smart, funny, sexy and not interested in his fame or money. She had a huge heart and brought out the best in people. She was…well, goddamn it…she was perfect.

For the settling kind of guy. But instead of relief he felt a strange sense of regret, the slow thud of his heart as it contracted.

She turned her face up to him and her smile just about undid him. He scrambled around for some kind of distraction before he did or said something stupid. 'Okay, so this brings me nicely onto: romance or…er, horror?'

Seemingly oblivious to the effect she had on him, she bit the corner of her lip and he fell just a little bit deeper under her spell. 'I've had my fair share of one and not enough of the other.'

'Okay, don't say any more, I don't think I want to know about how many men have tried to win your heart. Or how many times you've given them it.'

'I wasn't saying I'd had a lot of romance. I meant I'd had enough of horror.'

'I guess teaching teenagers can do that to you, Miss Sweet.' But she was serious. Her body stiffened and the chill air drifted into the spaces that had been filled with their heat. This was the in-road he'd been waiting for. So he grabbed it. 'Now's a good time, Sasha.'

'No. I'm fine.' She didn't even ask what he was talking about, but she knew.

'Really?'

'Yes. Yes. Absolutely.' The upturn in her lips was a poor attempt at a smile.

'So why the fake smile? I can spot one at fifty paces. Don't forget, sweetheart, I'm usually surrounded by them.' Memories of their break-up night swam back to him. She'd been on the brink of telling him, finally, but then she'd held back. Refused to share the one thing that had driven a wedge between them, the reason she wouldn't ever trust him wholly. 'Ten years you've kept this from me. More. Stop trying to be so tough.'

'I'm not trying to be tough. I just don't want to go there.'

He huffed out a breath, trying not to sound too angry when all he wanted was to be angry. Angry with who he wasn't too sure.

'Really? Over it as in your body reacts instinctively at the mere thought of whatever it was that hurt you? Over it as in you can now willingly, honestly and openly allow yourself to start trusting people?' He paused, took control of his rippling anger, subsuming the feeling of betrayal. 'Do you even want to?'

'Of course. Of course I do.' She inhaled deeply then shuddered out the breath. 'You're a good man, Nate Munro, whatever anyone prints about you. And if I was going to talk to anyone about it, it'd be you…'

And that was a screwed-up sucker punch to his heart. He'd been called a lot of things in his career, but *a good man* was never one of them. But he was clearly not good enough. 'If I'm that damned good why can't you talk to me?'

A pause lengthened between them as the breeze dropped,

leaving nothing but the sound of their breathing cutting through the night.

'The truth is…I'm scared to say it out loud. Because that way it makes it real all over again.' Her lips trembled as she thought. After a second or two she nodded. 'I suppose if you looked hard enough you could find out anyway. It was big news back then. *Mr Business fails spectacularly*.' The laugh in her voice was sarcastic and cold, just like the breeze settling over the night.

Eventually she turned over onto her back and stared up at the sky. 'Okay…Well…you know my dad…committed suicide?'

'Aha.' His heart pounded hard and loud. Nate didn't want to speak, didn't want to stop her from purging herself of whatever it was that had formed the essence of this strong yet vulnerable woman.

But he was scared too. Scared for her, scared that she'd had to endure something that was clearly very ugly. So instead of speaking he held her, his throat raw with the pressure of the unknown, nodding slowly into her hair as she shook. Waiting for the fallout.

He didn't have to wait long. Her voice was so small that he had to strain to hear it.

'I was the one who found him.'

CHAPTER TWELVE

'I WAS TEN years old, craving attention from a daddy who'd changed over the months from being kind and attentive to silent and reclusive.'

How had it got to this? Fast, slow. Black, white. Secrets, lies. Past, present.

Sasha took another breath. It seemed there'd never be enough air to squeeze down her fast-closing throat. Repressed images from that night flickered through her brain like a bad old movie while deep inside a rising panic threatened, but she swallowed it back.

'He was in his study staring blankly out of the window. And I wanted my old happy dad back so I scuttled in and tried to sit on his knee, asking if he could help me get my bike from the back of the garage. But he pushed me away and shouted that he was too busy. That I was selfish and spoilt. He yelled and yelled, getting more and more worked up. Then...he did something he'd never done before...'

Even now after all this time she couldn't believe it. Sure, she'd rationalised his motives, but the actual physical act had been so unlike the father she'd grown up with. 'He hit me. A loud smack across my face that sent me reeling to the floor. Hard and sharp and thick on my cheek.'

She could have sworn the sting flared again as she touched her face. Nate's hand followed and he grasped her fingers in his fist, his touch spurring her on.

'And he just kept staring at me, grey with horror, as if unable to understand what he'd done, saying, *"I'm sorry. I'm sorry. I'm sorry."* Then he rushed out of the room.'

'Some people react badly under pressure.' Nate squeezed her hand. 'I should know.'

'But my upbringing was nothing like yours, Nate. I didn't know violence. My life had been a fairy tale until then, although I'd always thought it was boringly normal. Then he changed. I was scared. Everything seemed to be unwinding out of control.'

'And then…?'

'I heard my sisters laughing and chatting downstairs. My mum working in the kitchen. The slam of the garage door. A car backfiring in the street.'

'Only it wasn't a car?' Nate's voice was quiet and gentle.

She shook her head, inhaled deeply, unsure if she could continue. Tears stung the backs of her eyes, but she refused to let them fall. 'No. It wasn't. But I didn't know that. I'd heard the garage door and I headed there for my bike, thinking he'd gone to get it for me.'

'Oh, God…but he hadn't…'

For some reason her leg had started to jitter, up and down, up and down. She couldn't stop it. It beat a wild, out-of-control rhythm.

And there was Nate's palm resting a light pressure on it to slow it down. For once, the steady to her chaos and, God knew, she needed him right now. Needed this. Needed his arms around her, his chest to lie against, his heart to pump a regular rhythm she could follow.

'A smell hit me; weird, smoky, metallic, pure, but terrifying. And no noise. Nothing at all, not even the sound of his breathing. But there he was. So much blood over everything. And over me eventually, when he wouldn't wake up. And then my mum was behind me, telling me to come back into the house with her.'

'I'm so sorry you had to go through that, Sasha.'

'Me too.' She was suddenly cold through to her bones. So cold.

Nate's eyes closed for a moment. When he opened them they were tormented. 'But why? Why would he do that?'

'He'd put all his money into a pension company that failed. His business partner—his best friend—disappeared with all the cash, leaving Dad to face the creditors. He'd tried to protect us, but there was hate mail, a pending court case, prospective jail time, and massive media coverage, journalists at the door braying for his blood.' She couldn't stop the bitter laugh. 'Well, they got it.'

Nate shifted as he became more animated, his hands raised and his fists clenched. 'But why didn't he face them all? Fight them? Why did it have to be so...?'

'Final? Violent? Cowardly? Afterwards I thought it was cowardly to leave us all. But Daddy had never been a coward. He was strong and honourable and always did the right thing. Whatever made him take his own life must have been a dark force that overwhelmed him.'

She sank further into Nate's arms, taking comfort from his heat. 'But he was a broken man too. Trust came too easily to him and he couldn't believe what had happened. Eventually it must have become too much for him to cope with. I guess, faced with all that, it seemed the only way out.'

And yet getting over his actions had held her and her family prisoner for the rest of their lives, in one way or another.

Over the years she'd worked hard to erase the images from her head, shutting the door on that part of her life. But the scars were there still, she now realised, dressed up in her inability to allow herself to dream or to relax, or, indeed, to trust anyone not to do something so extreme again.

Laughable really. She hated extremes and chaos. Yet

here she was opening her soul to the human embodiment of them.

His fingers stroked down her back. 'But instead of wallowing in it, or taking your anger and grief out on the world, you became a teacher and give so much to everyone. And you never ask for anything in return.'

'The way I see it, school was my constant, the one thing I could rely on to be the same every day. No surprises, just routine where I felt safe and could leave the chaos of home behind. And, to be honest, there were some pretty decent adults who wanted the best for me. If there's one kid at Chesterton High who needs that, then I'm there for them. Plus, channelling energy into something positive is empowering too…A bit like sex.'

She'd never realised how powerful a woman could become when she let her sexual instincts take over. How liberating letting go could be. It had only taken seventeen years for her to understand. Heck, she was a slow learner.

But now she had a good teacher and the things his hands could make her feel…

'Now that I can understand, sweet thing. Sometimes you surprise even me.'

His knuckle ran across her cheek, then his mouth followed, tracing tiny kisses over her lips, her cheeks, the nub of her nose, her eyelids. Back to her mouth where he pressed his lips against hers and she opened to him, safe and warm in his arms.

Here was a man who would face bad times—*had* faced bad times, and would fight back with everything he had. Bare knuckle if need be, but he'd fight.

His life might well be played out in public, but his love was kept so preciously and deeply private.

He tasted sweet and soft and of hope. And at that moment she knew she could truly fall for him. Hard. She could learn to love him too, perhaps, given some time and a chance. Maybe she already did. Because how could she not?

The pain in her chest melted slowly, overwhelmed by something else, something equally weighty, but not as devastating, or as hollow. Eventually he pulled away and offered Sasha his hand to stand. 'I think it's time we went inside and worked a bit more on Sasha-empowerment, don't you?'

'Most definitely. And this time I get to call the shots.'

'Oh, God, I've unleashed a monster.' He laughed. 'We've got all night. And the next…'

Wrapping a blanket around her shoulders, he took her hand, and walked her up the terracotta steps towards his amazing terracotta castello. A bright silver moon illuminated the endless fields of vines casting an ethereal glow, almost magical. Here, she figured, anything was possible. Even talking about something she'd never mentioned to a soul. Or maybe she'd been lucky with finding the right person to listen.

She followed him past the library, the dining room, into the opulent lounge, breathing in the reassuring centuries-old aroma of polished wood mixed with new vine growth, eucalyptus, fresh air.

'Here, have this, it'll make you feel better.' He gave her a glass of something from a crystal decanter. Thick and dark, it burnt her throat but it hit the spot. Almost immediately the horror started to fade, replaced by a warmth deep in her gut.

He took a big gulp, then looked at her, brows furrowed. 'Just one thing. Why didn't you tell me this all those years ago? Why keep something like that bottled up?'

'I was raw and damaged. Would it have made a difference?'

'I don't know. I'd like to think I'd have tried to help you work it out. I guess my efforts would have been clumsy, but I always felt you were holding something back from me. Something that stopped you trusting me. You remember that last day? You were quiet at school, but I knew there was something bothering you. You refused to talk about it, and…'

'Because I wouldn't trust enough to confide in you, you went looking for a fight. And you got one.'

He was right. However much she dressed up her insecurities in organisational perfection and her, quite literally, uptight approach to sex, it all amounted to her holding everyone at arm's length. Even to the point of pushing him to his limits. And losing him in the process.

'And now you know why. We moved to Chesterton to get away from all the attention. My mum was sick from the stress. She refused to talk about it and tried to put on a brave face. We all did. I packaged everything up and pushed it deep inside myself as far as it would go. In a matter of months our happy ordinary life was ripped apart—everything I knew had changed and bowled out of control. Not talking about it made me feel like it couldn't possibly have happened.'

'So you micro-managed everything. If you controlled things, things wouldn't get out of control. Right?' He smiled gently, pinning a rogue curl of hair behind her ear. 'Those lists. The reluctance to just pack up and leave.'

'I guess so. I was only ten and I didn't think like that. It was more like, if I behaved well and made sure I planned everything then nothing bad would happen.' She smiled. 'The OCD just developed.'

'And the trust thing?'

Oh, yes. She took another sip as she thought, bought some time. 'The million-dollar question? Trust comes hard when you see what can happen. I'm working on it. But then sometimes there's this little voice in the back of my head asking: *what if something so bad happens again*? And that sense of threat tarnishes everything. It makes you see the world differently, takes away your ability to get close to anyone.' She noticed the glass shaking in her hand and fought to steady herself. 'You're just waiting for it all to fall apart again. And what if it does?'

It took a long time for his answer to come. He peered down into his drink, as if the crystal held all the answers in the universe. When he finally spoke his voice was the most serious it had ever been, his eyes burning with a fierce passion. 'Then I'll be there for you. I'll catch you, Sasha. I won't even let it happen in the first place.'

He believed it so fervently she almost allowed herself to believe him too.

But she wouldn't get carried away. They only had a few short days left and she was under no illusion what was going to happen at the end. 'Well, don't dare treat me any differently, Nate. One show of pity and I'm gone.'

He brought her to an ornate antique chaise and sat down, pulling her onto his knee. 'God, sweet thing, I don't pity you at all. I've been through some stuff, but it's nothing compared to you. Big respect. As Dario would say, you're one seriously cool chick.'

'Aww, he's got such a way with words.'

'Well, I'm not about to let him loose with any lyrics just yet, but he's right. So, so right.'

And then he held her on his knee, slowly stroking her hair. The mantelpiece clock ticked sonorously on and on as liquor and a solid pair of arms eased her transition from a nightmare past back to the present.

For how long they stayed there she didn't know. But it was enough. Enough to send the ghosts shivering back to where they came from, unable to hurt her any more. Enough to give her time to adjust to the new Sasha she could be now that her secrets had been unlocked.

She straddled his lap and leaned forward to press a kiss

onto his forehead, his cheek, his lips. Ran her hands down his sculpted sun-tanned chest. 'So, we have four more days, Nathan Munro, and I'm really out on a limb here with no schedule and no planner, pushing all my trauma issues to the limit. So you'd better make it worth my while, d'you hear?'

Her bikini bottoms were no barrier to the warmth of his skin and the sudden shock of his physical reaction to her.

Four days. That was all they had left and she was going to make the most of it. Because she wanted him now, and she was through with living scared. She'd deal with the consequences later.

A buzz of renewed desire prickled over her, a reawakening of her innate reaction every time she saw him. 'Kiss me? Take me to bed? Surprise me? Let me surprise you?'

This time when his lips crushed hers they were ardent and heated. Gone was the soft caressing, replaced now by an urgency that deepened with every stroke of his tongue. Something fundamental had changed between them and it showed in the way he tasted, the intense way he gazed at her, a new respect. A deeper connection. Deepening all the time.

'God, Sasha, you've been through hell and missed out on so much loving.' His hands slid the length of her back, stopping briefly to untie the strings on her bikini, then he cupped her bottom, groaning as she rocked against his erection. 'And I'm going to spend the next few days making it up to you.'

CHAPTER THIRTEEN

AND HE'D BEEN as good as his word, Sasha mused as she dragged her eyes away from Nate and watched the London skyline come into view.

A tight knot settled in her chest. The last few days had passed in a blur of long delicious lunches in remote ancient villages, hair-raising scooter rides under bright blue Tuscan skies and endless sunshine, not to mention the journey of sexual discovery he'd taken her on.

To say she'd been liberated was an understatement. Every inch of her had succumbed to the Nate Munro treatment and he'd sensationally shown her how to express her feelings through touch.

Particularly last night. Their last night. Which had passed in a heart-wrenching blur that she had never wanted to end, of alternating laughter and long pauses where they'd simply looked at each other, a world of emotion passing between them. How could they get so lucky to have found each other again? To have shared this incredible time together?

But they'd made no plans past this day. This hour. And her brain was starting to feel like a rudderless boat, going round and round in circles. The reality of their very different lives was evident in this private jet, the crystal champagne flutes and very personal attention.

'Mr Munro, Miss Sweet, please fasten your seat belts

for landing.' The air stewardess flashed a plastic smile at Sasha and a very open and genuine one to Nate. 'Captain Walsh says he's secured you a seat on the two-thirty to LA. It'll be a bit of a squeeze, time-wise, but there'll be a car at Denham waiting to take you to Heathrow.'

Time was going too fast. Sasha's stomach tightened. She tried not to look too possessive as she gripped his hand through the turbulence that heralded their descent through thick grey clouds.

But for the last few moments of their trip she wanted to savour him and she was almost past caring who saw her. 'So it's welcome back to the real world, then, Nate. I think I'm going into culture shock already.'

His brows lifted but his beautiful face became a mask of impartiality. Sasha got the feeling it was because of the air-crew, so protective was he of his emotions, but she couldn't help thinking she was losing him already. 'Reality has to hit some time, baby. We can't hide away for ever.'

Baby? Back to his act now? Rock-star-speak not Nathan-speak. The walls were building brick by brick with every metre the plane descended. While frustration and hope-lessness nibbled away at her insides. 'Can't we? More's the pity.'

He frowned. 'I thought you loved your job?'

'I do, absolutely. I have the competition coming up and I have to work on that for a start. I just wish…oh, never mind.' After so many hours of being open and honest with him she couldn't find the words to express her feelings now. Yes, she wanted her old life back, but she wanted some-thing more now too.

She wanted him. A future with him.

The real him he'd allowed her to see, the Nathan Munro who had wrapped her in his arms and listened to her story, who made her laugh, made her heart soar. Who made her believe she could be so much more. Free. Alive. Wanted.

Even though the 'L' word had been mentioned ever so casually it had never been said in that momentous way she imagined it should be. *I love you.*

No. Neither of them had ever said that, but she could have. Despite all her efforts she had fallen hopelessly in love with him. No slippers, no family saloon, no promises for ever. Not even a plan past tomorrow. Mr Absolutely, Very Definitely, Heart-Stoppingly Wrong In Every Way.

I love you.

The urge to shout it almost drove her mad. Was it so selfish to crave something so utterly precious, yet so undeniably unsafe? But she'd learnt from her father's suicide that even the most secure things could become broken.

Old Sasha might well have sat back and planned how to mend her broken heart, but new Sasha was going to try and work out a way they could both have their dreams, their lives. Somehow.

She'd spent too long looking at the world with fear-filled vision. Lived life in the shadow of her father's death. She didn't want to be scared any more. She didn't want to take what made her safe. She wanted to take what made her happy.

Nathan Munro.

She would tell him she loved him. She would work out a plan for them both.

Her heart thumped loud and hard. She felt as if she were on the edge of a precipice dredging up the nerve to jump—absolute fear and exhilaration mingling in her blood.

Then the plane jerked to a halt. The air stewardess spoke to them again. Nate reached for his bag. Chatted to the pilot.

Before she knew it they'd hit the stairs and were breathing fresh English air, the sound of her voice drowned out by aircraft engine and a cruel northerly wind.

I love you.

As they crossed the tarmac to the terminal building he

gave her a weary smile that almost broke her heart. He took her hand, more in an effort to speed her up, she thought, than in any kind of romantic gesture.

'Right, Sash. So you have to be at school first thing tomorrow morning. And I'm getting the next flight to LA. I have to do that interview and a whole bunch of promo for my new album. Come on, we have to keep moving.'

Damn. Damn. Damn. Why the harsh tone? He was hurting her.

But Nate couldn't help himself. He'd spent the best part of a decade learning how to be someone else, especially in public, and he couldn't shake that off. Not even for her. And he had no way of coming to terms with how he felt. He didn't even *know* how he felt. Apart from that something important was coming to an end and he didn't know how to stop it, and that if he didn't act soon he'd lose her for ever.

He caught her arm as they entered the tiny private airport transit hall; once outside the other end they would both be going home. Not together.

He couldn't fathom the screwed-up twisting in his chest. It hurt. Actually hurt. He loved going back to LA. Going home. Loved it. But now? He couldn't contemplate that big empty space in LA, and Sasha in her shoebox, here.

His throat was raw. Every bloody emotion had bundled up in his ribcage and he had to keep hauling in air just to stay upright.

He wanted to say something to make everything right. But what? He didn't know what right was. He hadn't promised her anything after all. 'Hey, look, Sasha. I'm sorry—'

A bright flash made them turn towards the immigration desk. Further along the corridor he saw a group of photographers he recognised from countless times before. The ones that took the risks, but got the shots.

And then he saw Sasha's eyes darken. 'How did they know we were here? It's a private airfield.'

That sharp ache in his chest? Just got a whole lot worse. He pulled her closer. 'Someone will have told them. And if I find out who…'

'Nate! Sasha! Sasha Sweet!' One of the men stepped forward and clicked. *'Are you taming our bad boy?'*

'Sir, your cab is waiting. Your flight is leaving soon.' An airline representative pressed into his face. 'Sir. Mr Munro. We have to—'

'Where's Security? We're not stepping foot out there,' he rallied back at the staff member.

'I've radioed them, sir. I don't know where they are. They should be here. They're always here. I can only apologise.'

'Too right. This is ridiculous. How did they even get in here?'

'Sasha! Tell us about your father.'

'What?' Sasha glanced angrily from the airline rep to Nate, to the photographers, clearly trying to come to terms with the intrusion. 'Er…no comment.'

'Don't dignify their presence with one word. They're not worth it.' Nate pressed a finger to her lips, determined not to rise to their bait. While his fists balled.

He ignored the tightening in his chest, and kept his voice steady for Sasha. 'Let me sort it out.'

'Why did he screw those people out of their pensions?'

His focus narrowed to that one sorry excuse for a man. 'What did you say, pal?'

'William Sweet. CEO of Sweetly Secure Finances. Screwed a lot of people out of a lot of money.'

He took a step forward. 'Where do you get off with this kind of drivel? Hey?'

Judging by the hack's quick retreat against the wall, he knew he'd crossed a line in gutter journalism.

Something inside Nate snapped.

So yeah, he'd made a promise not to get riled by these guys. Yes, he'd made a silent vow to curb his angry outbursts in front of Sasha. To even let it all wash over him. But that all faded into nothing in the face of her being dragged into this bloody circus.

The blood left Nate's fingers as he squeezed them tight. This was all his fault.

The one thing he'd said he'd do—protect her—and he couldn't. Disappointment didn't cut it.

But rage did.

It started as a deep ache in his gut, rose like bile to his throat, then rushed through him.

Without thinking he vaulted over the desk, grabbed the camera by the lens and tried to pull it away from the man. Nate's hand caught in the strap and suddenly he and the reporter were collapsing to the floor. As they fell he heard running footsteps, loud voices.

Finally. Security.

'Nathan.' But it was Sasha he came face to face with, hands firmly on her hips, as he stood up. Somehow, she seemed taller, stronger, braver. Pure indignation sparked from her eyes, infusing him with immense admiration and sending a shot of fire to his groin.

She flashed him an understanding smile. 'Honey, you know we talked about this.'

God. Sasha's body pulsed with a powerful rush of adrenaline as she stared at the two men. No, as she stared at Nate.

The ripped muscles, the feral reaction, the intense heat in his eyes as he'd leapt the barrier in her defence, fired something primal in her blood. Pure anger whirled with flagrant desire inside her and now she wanted a piece of the action too.

Maybe she was mad. Or just free. Free from doing everything right, from following her rigid rules, from not making waves just in case she got hurt.

Because she was hurting already—at Nathan, for retreating back into his shell when there was a whole lot of things they still needed to say. Hurting that this was the way their week was going to end. In a brawl on the floor. Hurting that someone would dredge up her father's death and use it as a weapon against her.

'It's okay, really. I get that you're pissed off. I understand. It's a blatant intrusion of our privacy, especially here, where it's supposed to be private...But getting angry isn't enough. Getting even is.'

'Too bloody right.' Nate stepped forward, but she stopped him with her hand on his chest.

'No. Wait. I've got this.'

He swiped a hand over his jaw and raised his eyebrows. 'Okay. Go for your life, sweet thing.'

Out of the corner of her eye she saw the reporter shuffling backwards, but she stomped on the camera strap. Stopped him short. Felt the ripple of anger seep through her cells, her bones, her skin, and waited for it to grow enough to harness it.

Years of dealing with stroppy, surly, unruly teenagers had honed her for *this* moment. Years of being too frightened to step out of her box had honed her for *this* moment.

It was time to fight for what she believed in.

'You.' She pinned the reporter with her take-no-crap stare. 'You should be ashamed of yourself.'

The little man nodded.

'Everyone has a right to a little privacy, right? You want people prowling round your house? Stalking your mother? Your sister...'

He shook his head.

'Your daughter? Making their lives hell? Going through

their bins? Telling their secrets? Because everyone has secrets, right? Even you?'

The weasel nodded again. Was that all he could do? He was like a puppet.

'You want me to start searching your history up?'

Now he was starting to look ill.

'I thought not. Because that would be crass, wouldn't it? Low. But I'm not like you. I don't stoop that far.' She stepped closer and lowered her voice, commanding every bit of his worthless attention. 'So take your camera and your lousy morals and your greed and your pathetic desire to destroy other people's lives and stick it…'

But before she could tell him exactly where to stick it he'd scrambled up and fled to the exit. Coward.

'Coward!' She chased him up the corridor and watched, with a great deal of satisfaction, as he disappeared into the car park.

Yes! God, that felt so good.

What a team. Now where was Nathan?

Nathan. Her heart stalled. Tears pricked the backs of her eyes. His flight. For a brief moment she'd forgotten he wasn't going to the same place she was. And there was still so much to say.

She turned to see him standing at the immigration desk flanked by a security guard and the airline rep. She could see by Nate's tense stance that he'd climbed further into that shell. The distance he'd put between them was way more than physical. Despite the passion he'd felt for her, despite everything they'd shared, it just wasn't enough to make him stay.

This was definitely the end. Of that she had no doubt. There was no fairy-tale ending about to happen here.

The after-effects of the adrenaline shot made her start to shake and suddenly she felt bruised and battered as if her heart had been punched right out of her. She walked towards him.

Did she have to fight for him too?

A tight fist of pain lodged in Nate's chest. Part pride, part desolation, all awe.

'Wow…Sasha, you're on fire,' he said gently, to the woman he now knew he absolutely loved with every part of his soul. The one who had made him whole again, who had glued back together those hollow pieces he'd been pretending were his heart for far too long. Loved her. Completely.

Which was why this next conversation was going to shatter it all over again.

She stared up at him, eyes brimming with tears. Her hands trembled as she placed a finger on his mouth. 'Don't say it. Just…don't.'

'Mr Munro.' The airport rep tugged at his sleeve. 'They're starting to board. There's just enough time.'

'Mate, give me a minute. There'll be another flight.' But never another moment like this, a last moment that he wanted to treasure.

I love you.

He understood what that meant now. That subtle soft melding of souls, the sharp crackle of electricity. Laughter. A certain scent. Respect. A bone-melting ache. A lot of paper, too, it would seem, and files and stickies and paperclips and lists. And now, absolute awe.

Yeah, he loved Sasha Sweet with every cell in his body.

She was strong, stronger than he was, and she'd just proved she didn't need protecting. She didn't need him. And, sad truth was, he had nothing else to give her.

She'd hate him for doing this. But he'd spent a good part of his life doing the wrong thing, now it was time to man-up.

And she would survive, after all. She'd survived the

worst kind of nightmare that put his problems deep in the shade, and grown into a beautiful woman.

He didn't know what to do with all this chaos swirling in his head, his body. He was way out of control.

That scared the hell out of him.

He looked deep into those navy eyes that melted his heart Every. Single. Time. 'I have to go. The flight's waiting.'

'That's it? Finished? You're not even going to try to make it work?' Hauling in a deep breath, she pushed her fist into his chest. 'All this…us…and that's it? *I have to go*?'

'Look at it logically. We both have jobs, futures, lives and responsibilities, thousands of miles apart. You hate my world and I don't…can't fit into yours. Opposites don't attract, they just circle each other for a while and inevitably they go in separate directions.'

Her fist grabbed his shirt and she twisted the fabric into a ball. 'So what now? Thanks for the memories? Will I hear about it all in a number-one hit?'

'I don't think so.' He took his life in his hands and ran a finger down her cheek, caught the first tear but didn't show her that he'd noticed. 'You really are wired.'

'One of us has to be.' She blinked. And again. And he just knew she was trying to stop the tears from falling. 'Because I happen to think what we have is pretty special. No—really once-in-a-lifetime special.'

'But it can't be for ever. I never promised you that.' Man, this was the hardest thing he'd ever done. By a long way. Burying his brother and his mother had broken him, but this…this was a whole other depth of loss.

I love you. He ached to say those words, but if he did he would only make things worse. Better for her to believe she was a temporary fixture in his life than permanently etched on his heart. Otherwise she might do something crazy, like convince him to stay. 'If you ever need anything, anything at all, make sure to come find me. Okay?'

'Sure.' She couldn't hide the catch in her throat, the crack in her voice. 'I hear the men's room is the best place to get you these days.'

He took her wrist, drew a small heart with his fingertip on the sensitive skin, something he used to do so long ago he'd forgotten, sending shivers through him and a lump to his throat. 'Okay. Okay. Goodbye, sweet thing.'

'Hey, well, at least this time you actually said goodbye.'

CHAPTER FOURTEEN

Not So Sweet Talkin' Woman!

Lobby group, Celebrities Against Media Intrusion (CAMI), found itself an unlikely new advocate yesterday in the guise of spirited schoolteacher, Sasha Sweet.

The apparently very private Ms Sweet, Head of Music at Chesterton High School, learned firsthand the perils of media fame when she landed at a northwest London private airfield, accompanied by rock star, Nate Munro. The notorious bad boy of rock, whose hits include platinum bestsellers 'Sweet Talkin'' and 'Sex Me Up', and his alleged new paramour, Sasha, were returning to London after a week's break at a secret hideaway.

Their attempt at a cloak and dagger arrival was scuppered when News.com *reporter, Malcolm Price, tried to snap them leaving the airport hand in hand. But Miss Sweet, described by a former pupil as 'shy but strict', very definitely put Mr Price in the naughty corner as she rallied against him with a verbal attack on media intrusion...*

...Ms Sweet, however, is no stranger to scandal. As the daughter of the CEO of maligned pension company...

*...The hilarious outburst, caught on camera by
an airfield employee, shows Ms Sweet jumping to
Munro's defence as he rugby-tackles the reporter to
the floor. She then wags her finger at Mr Price, no
doubt threatening him with a week's detention...and
a hundred lines...*

JUST BRILLIANT. EXCELLENT. So much for girl power.

Sasha lay back in her bed and dropped the paper to the
floor, unable to read the rest of the article again.

Stupid teary swollen eyes.

But she didn't need any kind of clear vision to see what
an epic mistake she'd made. She should never have gone
with him to Italy. Crikey, she shouldn't have sought him
out in the first place, and she certainly shouldn't have acted
in such an outlandish way. Even if it had felt right, and so
good.

Glancing down at the crumpled tabloid, she sighed. But
then, if she hadn't gone she would never have truly known
what love meant, that you could feel safe with the most
dangerous of men. You could finally open yourself up to
trust and it felt amazing. That one man could give you the
gift of self-belief and the courage to let go.

One man. Nathan. *Only ever Nathan.*

Damn him. Did he really have to break her heart into
too many pieces all over again?

Her cellphone rang. *Cassie.*

Oh, hell. Drawing in a deep breath, she answered. 'Hi
Cass.'

'Who are you and what have you done with my sister?'
Her sister's laughter caught Sasha off guard. 'Have you
seen the papers? You made front page, second and fourth.
And the video's gone viral on the Internet. You go, girl!'

'Yes and it's all rubbish. So I said a few things—'

'A few? You were epic. You should see the comments...

sassy, sexy, siren. You've sparked a whole new debate about privacy laws. Famous people are lining up to endorse what you said. You're a legend!'

Sasha cursed. She didn't want to be a legend, she wanted to be left alone to wallow with her broken heart. 'But they raked all that stuff up about Dad again. I feel terrible. Have you spoken to Mum? Suzy? I can't get through to them.'

'Yeah. Suzy is not amused—she's been fighting off reporters at the hospital and it's interfering with her job. If you ask me she spends far too much time there anyway. The distraction will do her good. And Mum? She was surprisingly sanguine about the whole thing. Time heals and all that.'

Sasha hoped to God it did. If only time could move a little more quickly. She could do with a little healing. Okay, a lot of healing. Starting now. 'I was worried it might set her back. I remember what she was like…before. I couldn't bear to have her go through that again.'

'Hey, stop worrying.' Cassie's voice softened. She'd been protected by them all and knew few details about the circumstances of her father's death. 'It was a long time ago, Sash. I think she's truly moved on now. She'll get over this. And so will you.'

Maybe she was right—maybe Sasha was the only one still living with the effects of the past. Not any more. Nate had seen to that. 'Thanks. I'm getting there.'

'But hey, what does Mr Killer-ass think? Are you planning more secret hideaways? Can I come?'

'No.' *Gosh, that hurts.* Sasha blinked away more tears. She was done with crying over him now. 'He's gone back to the States.'

'But you're seeing him again. Right?'

'No.' Okay, so she wasn't quite done with the tears. She scraped back the wet hair stuck to her cheek.

Her sister gasped. 'So what happened? He's gone? Leaving you to face this mess?'

Sasha looked at the flashing answer-phone machine full of messages he'd left as soon as he hit the tarmac in LAX. The ones that said he'd got lawyers on to the newspaper. That he'd do everything he could to stop any more information getting out. The ones that didn't say he was coming back any time soon.

If he couldn't see that what they had was worth fighting for then it was his loss. 'I don't need anyone to help me. I'm fine without him.'

'So he has gone. For good?'

'Yep.'

'Oh, I'm sorry, sis. I'm sorry I suggested it, that I encouraged it. I just wanted you to have some fun.'

'I did. I really did. It was the best time of my life.' She sighed. 'But now I'm definitely saving myself for the slippers man. And I'm prepared to wait a very long time.' For a man who'd never touch her heart the way Nathan had.

Cassie's voice turned just a little too bright. 'So, focus on you. You are beautiful. Your body is curvy in all the right places. You have amazing eyes, a beautiful smile and a generous heart. You are funny and talented and have so much to give the right guy, you just need to get out—what are you laughing at?'

'It's okay, thanks, Cass, but you know me. I already have a plan.'

'And why doesn't that surprise me? Spill.'

'That reporter needed telling—they all do. I'll never forget the way Mum used to hide behind the curtains, the little notes they'd push through the letterbox. The lies. So I've decided I'm going to do an interview with someone reputable and put the world straight about what really happened to Daddy. Tell the truth about the business, his colleague, the suicide.'

Her sister whooped. 'I was wrong about you. You're one feisty chick. Are you sure you want to put yourself on the line like that?'

'You know what? I'm sick of hiding behind it. You never know, it might help someone…someone like me.'

And being angry felt a damned sight better than thinking about how much her heart had shattered.

Her throat almost seized up. 'It's time for us all to have a fresh start. They're always printing lies. Even Nathan gets his share of far-fetched stories. Instead of ignoring them I'm going to turn this whole experience into something positive.'

Once she'd found the strength to actually get out of bed.

Then she was also going to write a whole new bucket list. One that definitely didn't include falling in love.

The sad truth was, with his passion and her planning they could have done something amazing together, improved life for others like her, or people like Marshall. After everything they'd been through they could have been happy—the missing part of each other's hearts. If she'd been enough for him to want to stay. If he'd thought that what they had was worth truly fighting for. Clearly he didn't.

Which was a crying shame.

Because she did.

But even if she could turn back the clock she'd still fall in love with Nathan Munro again, in a heartbeat.

Dario's grin was as wide as his bullish shoulders as he greeted Nate from the glittering stage at the National Music Awards. 'So you just got how many awards?'

'Five.'

'And the night's not over yet…' Dario clapped him between the shoulder blades and took a slug of very expensive French champagne. 'You're at the top of the game, man. Top. Of. The. Game. Best album. Best single. Best male artist…'

Nate put this latest award on the table alongside the others and stared at them all in dismay. What was he doing putting on a show? Smiling and schmoozing.

Why? Because that was what he did. He acted his part and played the game, never showing who he really was or what things really meant to him.

'Yeah. Yeah. So I guess I should be happy. Right?'

'You're not?' At Nate's shrug Dario shook his head. 'You're not.'

'Think I'm getting old, buddy. This kind of gig doesn't give me the same buzz any more. It feels a bit hollow.' Without someone to share it with.

Okay. Without Sasha to share it. He'd messed up again and a zillion awards wouldn't make him feel like a better man, never mind best damned male.

'So what are you saying? What are you going to do?'

'I have no idea. But I'm through with playing the wild bad boy. People get hurt.' Mainly him, and those around him. Sasha.

She'd been the only one to see through the packaging to his core. And she hadn't found him wanting—she'd believed in the best of him. She brought out a side of him he didn't know he had.

'Ah, mate.' Dario grabbed his arm and dragged him out of the auditorium to the accompaniment of shushes and angry whispers. But what the hell? It didn't matter any more. None of this. 'Come with me.'

'What? What are you doing?' Nate shrugged out of Dario's grip, uninterested in playing games or getting laid. 'If this is another of your booty-calls, I'm out. I'm just not interested.'

'I know you're not. You haven't been interested in anything since you got back from London.' He grinned and affected a feminine voice. 'You don't call, you don't text…'

'Yeah. Yeah. I've been…distracted.'

'Well, you need to snap out of it. You're rude in interviews, lacklustre in the studio. You need to pull it together, man. Unless…' His oldest friend took out a smartphone and held the screen up to Nate. 'This is the reason?'

Nate's heart dropped to his boots as there, flickering to life, was a video of Sasha in some TV interview. Sweet, strong, courageous and so perfect it made his heart ache, she talked of her father's death, of the effects that had on her life. Of her family. Her love for her job and the importance of special-needs support. She was eloquent, beautiful.

Not once would she answer questions about their brief *affair*, as the journalist dubbed it. But he saw the pain in her eyes. The same pain he'd seen as he'd walked away. The same pain twisting his heart right now.

He missed her. Missed her smell, her smile, even the lists that drove him crazy.

'Classy lady. And she's got a big following out there now. Quite the lobbyist. She's changing things, Nate. Changing people's opinions about press freedom to walk all over your private life.' Dario's voice cut through. 'Sack me if you want to, but I'm going to say it anyway…I reckon you need to stop acting like an idiot and start getting serious about a few things too. Clean up your act. Stop pushing people away. Start letting people in.'

'What do you mean?'

'I'm not going to get all California psycho-babble on you, Nate. But you need to give people a chance to get to know you. I mean, really get to know you. You've got a chip there on that shoulder and you're hiding behind it.'

'Nah, this is me. I've never been any different. Nate Munro.'

Dario frowned. 'It's been ten years, Nate. I've watched

you drink yourself into oblivion, do everything to excess, push yourself deeper and faster into wine and women. And never once have you made a proper lasting connection. Not once.'

Wow, this was an eye-opener he didn't need. But Dario was right, Nate conceded reluctantly. He did push people away, unable to handle any kind of honest contact or emotion. He'd realised it in the art gallery when he'd looked round and seen strangers' eyes staring out of his so-called friends' faces. Living in some kind of wilderness where he was thinking, acting but not feeling. Not living, not really.

Wild, definitely. Sane? Not so much.

But Sasha challenged that. She fired feelings in him he didn't think were possible. Bright light feelings, strong deep feelings and a sense of belonging to something, to someone, something good. He'd never had that before.

But he hadn't been able to handle it, preferring not to feel anything, as he had for the last God knew how many years. Scared that he'd be consumed by the feelings, the inevitable pain.

And so he'd done what he did best.

Ran away. Came back to a place that now felt nothing like home. And she hadn't even been here but it felt empty without her.

Everything did.

He'd hidden behind excuses fuelled with alcohol and anger instead of facing up to reality. Shunned real intimacy. Pretended that living off the rails was fine, great even. That being damaged was like wearing a badge of honour. The act had become reality.

Facing Dario, he took a breath. 'Okay, I need you to set up a couple of urgent meetings with my lawyers for to-morrow morning, first thing. And then organise flights to London immediately after.'

'You think she's going to take you back after you walked away from her? Twice?'

Nate's gut tightened at the risk he was going to take. 'Hell if I know. But I have to try to convince her. I don't care what you say, I'm not backing down.'

'But London—?'

He leaned into Dario's face. 'Will you listen to me? Yes, London.'

'No, Dumbo.' Dario's finger prodded Nate's chest but he was shaking his head and laughing. 'You listen to me. Not London. Manchester.'

'What?'

'It's that music contest thing tomorrow. She won't be in London. She'll be in Manchester.' He shook his head. 'Thank God someone's kept an eye on things while you moped around the house with a sore head for two weeks.'

'You kept an eye on her?'

Dario shrugged, flashing a wry smile. 'Well, she kind of grew on me. And you were different because of her. In a good way.'

Manchester. He'd forgotten. Dario was right: he'd been too busy staring at the bottom of a liquor bottle to keep up with the days.

'Cheers, mate.' He grabbed his friend's big bear face between his hands and kissed his bald head. 'I owe you.'

'Yeah, yeah, I know. More than you can ever imagine.' Dario drew away, laughing. 'I just hope she's worth it.'

'Oh, she is. But first I have to find her.'

CHAPTER FIFTEEN

'THIRD PLACE GOES to No Limits, Chesterton High School!'

'Oh wow. Just wow.' *Oh My God.* Sasha couldn't hear her own thoughts above the screams and her hammering heart. It was more then she'd dared hope for. 'Quick everyone. Up onto the stage.'

A sea of faces came in and out of focus as she stepped up to accept the award and passed it around to the choir. Just to see their delighted faces made this moment the proudest of her life. They'd come so far and worked so darned hard.

It was just such a shame that Nathan couldn't be here to share it with them. After all, he'd done so much to get them there.

Her heart contracted a little. Too bad. It was his loss to have made such a difference and not even know.

She drew in air and tried to steady herself. Ever since he'd left she'd ricocheted from sheer joy at the memories they'd made to utter despair. And now she had to speak through a throat thick with emotion.

'Just a quick thank you to everyone who has helped in this wonderful achievement. You were very kind and gave of your time generously. We owe you a huge debt. Without a doubt we wouldn't have got here without you.'

She hoped, if Nathan ever saw this on the Internet, if he'd even bother to look, that he would know she meant him, more than anyone else. He'd given them all such a gift of self-belief; if only he could find it within himself.

A movement in the wings distracted her momentarily, but when she turned her head to look she couldn't see anything but blackness and the folds of open curtains.

Strange.

Focus.

'Er...and I wanted to say how proud I am of these wonderful gifted kids—'

Now the tiny hairs all over her body prickled, making her lose track of her speech. Great. She was going to be the laughing stock of the whole competition. *Teacher struck dumb at singing contest.*

But...something...

She glanced again to the side of the stage and saw the silhouette of a man. Proud jawline. The arrogant stance that told the world he didn't give a damn, when she knew he'd cared deeply.

But not deeply enough.

Nathan.

Her heart stalled as he caught her gaze. Every fibre in her body craved his touch; heat pooled in her abdomen then seeped out to her skin. Was he here for the show? The final act? But there'd been nothing on the programme about a special guest.

In which case...did that mean...? What she thought it might mean? That he was here for her? Her chest grew tighter and tighter.

Hello? An audience of three thousand...

Oops. She leaned into the microphone again. 'And... er...so...thank you to the organisers...' Damned dry mouth.

She looked over to him again. Was he meant to be presenting an award? Was he supposed to be up here too?

She raised her eyebrows to him in question. *What am I supposed to do now?*

He held up his palm and shook his head, urging her to continue her speech.

Great, all very well for you to say that now, Mr Hotshot. Now that I'm truly speechless.

The sea of faces started to look bemused. People began to shuffle, stare down at their shoes, whisper. *This was the teacher who made the news? Catatonic.*

Oh, hell.

'Er…and thank you all very much. Goodnight.' Stepping away from the microphone, she whispered to the choir, 'Very well done. Now we just have to go backstage to wait for the other announcements.'

While she either calmed down or got arrested for the murder of an infuriating rock god with an ass to die for.

I was provoked, Your Honour.

Wiping her sweaty palms down her dress, she walked off the stage on extremely shaky legs flanked by fourteen hyper-excited singers, who surged towards Nate giving high fives, squealing, jumping, pulling at his arms.

Above their heads he watched her, his eyes assessing, unsure, cautious.

Good.

It took a few moments to herd them into some kind of order, then he held out his arms to her as if she might walk straight into them.

Not a chance. 'Great timing, Mr Munro. Couldn't you have waited until I'd finished my moment of glory on stage? Now the world is going to think I haven't got a sensible brain cell in my head.'

He flashed her a grin that made him look devilishly handsome. 'No. I think I win that particular award.'

'Well, we knew that already.'

Wariness flickered across his eyes. 'Can we talk?'

'Sure, go right ahead.'

'Somewhere private?' *Please.* His eyes pleaded with her as he gestured towards the choir, whose heads bounced back and forth between Nate and Sasha as if watching a tennis match. 'Fourteen's a crowd?'

'Aren't you used to dealing with large audiences?' She folded her arms, enjoying every moment of his predicament. 'I can't leave them, and I'm sure they'd all love to hear what you have to say.'

'Yes! Yes! Yes!'

For someone so used to working with adoring fans hanging off his every word, he looked strangely sheepish. Pale even.

He coughed, his mouth tightening into a grimace. 'Okay. Well…That was…awesome, No Limits. Congratulations everyone. I've booked a couple of limos for afterwards and we're all going to go for a celebratory ride. Okay?' He pulled them into a tight huddle. 'Now, Miss Sweet and I have something very important to discuss, so go back to your seats and we'll be along shortly.'

'Are you going to kiss her?' It was George, the boy who reminded Nate so much of his brother. Lovely George. Knew all the right questions.

Nate looked right at her. Deep down into her soul, which did a little jig no matter how much she tried to stop it. 'Yes. If she'll let me.'

More whoops.

The folded arms clenched across her chest, she shook her head resolutely. 'No. He. Is. Not.'

'Well, no man kisses a lady, with an audience.'

A collective of shoulders drooped. 'Awww…sir…that's not fair.'

Silence descended as they disappeared back into the theatre.

Nate grew serious. She thought about kicking up more

of a fuss, but, what the heck? She should at least hear him out. Then she'd kick that sorry splendid ass.

'Sash, I came to apologise.'

'And so you should. But here? Now? When I have fourteen teenagers to chaperone?'

'I wasn't thinking straight. I thought—'

She blinked, trying to contain the hope rising in her chest. They'd been here before and it hadn't ended nicely. 'That what Nate Munro wants, Nate Munro always gets, right? I'm surprised you didn't hop up onto the stage there and then. Do a little song or something…just for me. Or make a cringing speech. A flash mob. A huge embarrassing gesture. That would've ensured a few headlines.'

'Some things are just better kept out of the limelight.'

His eyes were warm with flecks of gold. Or it could have been the reflection of the stage lighting. Either way, the effect was mesmerising. *He* was mesmerising, even at his most vulnerable, right now, out of his depth and yet still commanding every scrap of her attention.

A lump squeezed in her throat. 'Oh? What kind of things?'

'I love you,' he said, the words carrying the weight of his emotions, steady and true. 'From the second I saw you in Dario's arms, all feisty and fighting and flustered. I just didn't think it would be enough for us to overcome all these damned obstacles.' He stopped. Took a breath. Continued. 'And I was pretty damn stupid to run away.'

'Again.'

'Yes. Again.

'See, I've been running away for a long time—from myself, mainly. And then you came along again, out of the blue, making me feel things. Things I didn't want to feel. It was too intense. I wasn't ready for it—you were so fresh, so bright and then…so brave. So beautiful. You bowled me over. You bowled me right out of the emotional wasteland I'd been wallowing in and, wham—straight into full Technicolor feelings.' He smiled his just-for-her smile. 'I was scared. Terrified. I didn't want to feel those things. I didn't want to fall in love with you. I wasn't sure I even knew how—but you showed me.'

His arm wound round her waist and he edged her deeper into the folds of the black curtain backstage. Not in some brash Nate rock-star kind of way, but in a gentle Nathan kind of way. His closeness, his smell and heat wrapped around her like a cloak of safety.

'And—?' She should have said more, but the butterflies had hatched again in her stomach and were doing a crazy dance.

'I want to create a future with you, Sash. Somehow. You don't fit into my life and I don't fit into yours, so let's make a new one for ourselves. You and me.'

Her body screamed *yes*. But she held back. 'I can't. I just can't risk falling for you third time lucky. If you left me again I don't think I'd get out whole.'

'I won't leave you. I love you.'

He loved her.

She tried to ignore the emotions that threatened to overwhelm her. Yes, he was right, it was scary. But what was there in life that was really worth having, really worth taking a risk on, that wasn't just a little bit scary? If only she could believe that he actually meant every word.

'Since you left me *for the second time* I've got busy, quit my job. I'm going to live a little before I find Mr Right and settle down with my slippers and the safest car in Europe.'

'Mr Right?' Nate felt his fists clench... No other man would ever get the chance to touch her.

Stop.

Dragging in oxygen, he let his anger go and focused on loving her, even when she didn't want him to.

Stroking his hand over those breathtaking red curls, he told her, 'No one could love you more than I do. Heart and soul. You got me. I know I'm far from perfect, but I have changed. I want to be with you. I don't care about anything else. Answer me this—do you think you can love someone more than you love me?'

The pause gave him hope.

'No…Nathan. I don't. But I don't see how it can work.'

Nate's heart bounded up into his mouth. He'd blown the whole damned thing. He had to convince her that he was ready to fight for her, not with his fists, but with his heart.

'I know you hate my world, so I've taken an indefinite sabbatical. And I've done some stupid pointless things in my past, and I want to make amends, so I've set up a foundation for kids with special needs and I want you to help me run it. You and me.'

She stepped back, placing her palm between them. 'Whoa, not so fast. You've taken a sabbatical?'

'Time off, just to—well—to spend time with you and hopefully run a charity in Marshall's memory. In London.'

She smiled again. 'Gosh, really? That's such a wonderful thing to do. And I'd be honoured to help. But—'

'I do have some commitments I have to keep. The occasional dinner, a couple of small gigs. They won't take me away for long. And I'll be back. Straight away.'

The smile slipped. 'So I won't even be invited to these events?'

'Do you want to be?'

'I'd like to give it a try. It is only fair that if you step into my world, I step into yours.' Her brows lifted. 'I'm sure a girl could get used to designer dresses, fancy shoes and fine champagne, given time.'

'Then you'll be with me every step of the way. By my

side. Whatever you want. Anything.' He took her hand and held it against his chest.

'Anything?' A glimmer of a coy smile flitted back over her lips, a spark of light in her eyes, her hands tiptoeing up his shirt. 'So, I have a new bucket list.'

'Of course you have.' He felt the smile start from his heart and spread upwards. 'Does it include kissing a famous but hapless rock star backstage at the Manchester Globe Theatre?'

'It could.' As she pressed her lips against his he took the chance to tell her how he felt through his kiss. Just in case she missed his point. *I love you*. She stepped back breathless and flustered. 'Check.'

God, she was beautiful. 'Excellent. I could grow to really like lists. How about falling in love with a famous but hapless rock star?'

She nodded, hesitantly at first, then more confidently. 'Yes. Definitely. Very definitely. Head over heels.'

'Even more excellent.' He was on a roll, so he had to strike while the girl was hot. 'And I don't suppose it could also include marrying that same famous but hapless rock star?'

'Hmm. You're not exactly marriage material. You're an impulsive nomad who runs at the first whiff of commitment.' But she didn't let go of his hand. 'Lucky for you that's exactly the kind of guy I'm looking for.'

'So is that a yes? You'll marry me?' He whipped her into his arms, vowing silently never to let her go again.

She wound her hands round his neck. 'Was that what you LA people call a proposal?'

'I guess. Yes. Yes, it was. Marry me?'

'Hmm. I don't know…' But her long slow smile gave him the answer he'd been hoping for. Then her long slow kiss confirmed it. She was his. For ever. When she pulled back she bit her lip and wriggled her hips against his. 'But you'll have to do some serious work to convince me.'

'As long as it takes, sweet thing.' *For ever.* 'That's the bit I'm looking forward to the most.'

* * * * *